Also by Carolyn Brown

LUCKY COWBOYS
Lucky in Love
One Lucky Cowboy
Getting Lucky
Talk Cowboy to Me

HONKY TONK
I Love This Bar
Hell, Yeah
My Give a Damn's Busted
Honky Tonk Christmas

SPIKES & SPURS
Love Drunk Cowboy
Red's Hot Cowboy
Darn Good Cowboy Christmas
One Hot Cowboy Wedding
Mistletoe Cowboy
Just a Cowboy and His Baby
Cowboy Seeks Bride

COWBOYS & BRIDES
Billion Dollar Cowboy
The Cowboy's Christmas Baby
The Cowboy's Mail Order Bride
How to Marry a Cowboy

BURNT BOOT, TEXAS
Cowboy Boots for Christmas
The Trouble with Texas Cowboys
One Texas Cowboy Too Many
A Cowboy Christmas Miracle

What Happens in Texas

A Heap of Texas Trouble

GETTING *Lucky*

CAROLYN
BROWN

Published by Sourcebooks Casablanca, an imprint of Sourcebooks, Inc.
P.O. Box 4410, Naperville, Illinois 60567-4410
(630) 961-3900
Fax: (630) 961-2168
sourcebooks.com

Printed and bound in the United States of America.
OPM 10 9 8 7 6 5 4 3 2 1

This one is for all my fans who love cowboys as much as I do

Chapter 1

Julie Donavan, the new kindergarten teacher, was on her knees consoling a little boy named Chuck on the first day of school when she noticed movement in the doorway. She gasped when she looked up. Her eyes widened and high color filled her cheeks. The most striking cowboy she'd ever laid eyes on had just walked through the door. Well, she had laid eyes on him one time before, but that time they'd been two-point-five sheets to the wind. One less drink that night and they'd have stopped before they got to the motel. Two more and neither would have remembered a damn thing. But the combination had been just right, and now he was there in her kindergarten classroom in Saint Jo, Texas.

Her first thought was, "Damn, he looks even better with hair."

Her second was, "What in the devil is he doing here?"

Her third was, "Oh, shit, what do I do now?"

The man stopped in front of her and looked down. "Hello, we are the Luckadeaus. This is my daughter, Lizzy; she's in your class this year."

And I'm the woman you met in Dallas six years ago, she wanted to shout at him. *Remember me? I'm Red.*

Griffin Luckadeau waited for her to finish with the little boy, his pulse racing and his heart thumping. God Almighty, he'd never been this attracted to a redhead before. That was his brother's choice of women. No one had told him the new kindergarten teacher was knock-down gorgeous, or that she had eyes that could see straight into his soul. Desire shot through his body—or was it plain old lust? Either one was something he hadn't allowed in a very long time and he was determined to get control of it before he spoke again.

Julie's daughter, Annie, came running from across the room, her jet-black pigtails bouncing on her shoulders, the white poliosis streak in her hair parted so that the majority of it was on the left side. She stopped dead in her tracks in front of the other little girl.

They eyed each other for several moments, mirror images of each other, doubles in almost every sense of the word. Jet-black hair with a white streak from the forehead back several inches, crystal-clear blue eyes, a slight dent in their chins.

Finally, Annie grabbed Lizzy's hand and said, "Come sit by me. My momma is the teacher; she won't mind."

Lizzy let go of her father's hand and ran off with Annie, her ponytail waving from side to side, the white streak in her hair slicked straight back.

Neither of their parents could peel their eyes away from the two little girls giggling together. Julie felt the world tilt backward on its axis and the concrete floor of the elementary school tremor as if Texas was having a rare earthquake.

"Who are you?" Griffin whispered. Desire took a back seat to shock. His blue eyes narrowed into slits. Who was the redhead and where had that child come from?

"I'm going to be your child's teacher, but we knew each other a long time ago. You don't remember?"

He shook his head. "I've never met you before in my life, but that little girl could be my Lizzy's sister, with that white forelock."

"It's time for school to start. We'll have to discuss this later. Guess they each just met their double," Julie said. If he wanted to play dumb as a box of rocks, then she could do the same thing.

He spun around and marched out the door without a backward glance.

Julie would have liked nothing better than to follow him, screaming like a fishwife, but she had a classroom of kindergarteners waiting. However, if G. Luckadeau thought he'd gotten off easy, then he'd best think again—and this time with the head on his shoulders instead of the one behind his zipper. That visual sent her staggering backward to hold on to her desk and look out over more than a dozen little children, all looking to her with a bit of fear in their eyes. She had to get her raw nerves under control and teach a class. She had to put aside the multitude of sinful thoughts—the foremost of which was homicide at that point. Not far behind it was anger, and running a close race was the urge to pick up Annie and run as fast and as far as she could.

"Okay, class, it's time for us all to meet each other," Julie said. Her words came out as though she'd just run a mile, but she took two deep breaths and composed herself. "This is Chuck Chester and he's five years old. Can the rest of you stand up beside your desk and tell me what your name is?" She led Chuck to the desk directly in front of hers and settled him in. She always had one child in her classroom like Chuck: backward, dressed poorly, almost malnourished but not enough to call the authorities, unsure of himself. It broke her heart but it happened every year.

Both Annie and Lizzy turned to look at the little boy—Lizzy on his left, Annie on his right. Annie popped up from her seat and said, "I'm Annie Donavan and that is my momma." She pointed at Julie.

"But in the classroom I'll be Miss Julie, won't I?" Julie's naturally lovely smile was strained amid the turmoil in her chest. She tried to control the inner chaos tearing up her nerves like a class-five tornado ripping across Texas, but she was so pissed off it was impossible. She wanted to strangle Mr. Luckadeau until his pretty blue eyes popped out and rolled around on the floor like ping-pong balls. How in the hell had he come to live right there in Saint Jo and, more importantly, why? He had to live close by for his daughter to be enrolled in Julie's classroom. How many more little white-forelocked kids were running around the county, and how many more women had he sweet-talked into sleeping with him?

Lizzy hopped to her feet and said, "I'm Lizzy Luckadeau. My daddy is Griffin Luckadeau and I almost didn't get to come to school, but I cried and cried and Marita said I would be safe."

The principal, Mrs. Amos, stuck her head in the open door. "Could I have a word with you?"

Julie motioned her inside. One hour into the first day and Julie was sure she was already fired. G. Luckadeau had most likely gone straight to the big dog in the office when he saw Annie and insisted that hussy mother of hers be fired on the spot.

Mrs. Amos stopped in front of Julie's desk and

lowered her voice considerably. "I want to make you aware of special arrangements for Lizzy Luckadeau. Her father, Griffin, was going to homeschool her but finally agreed—with lots of talking from me and his housekeeper—that Lizzy needed to come to school. That's why you didn't see her name on the student sheet. He just made up his mind last night. She is not to leave this school with anyone other than Griffin or Marita; I'll point her out to you if she comes to pick up Lizzy. And Lizzy is never to ride the bus home."

"May I ask why?" Julie asked softly.

"Nervous father. That's as much as I can say. Amazing how much Lizzy and your Annie look alike. You sure you've never been in these parts or ever known Griff?"

Her boss knew the secret. Her twinkling eyes said it all. The very thing Julie was running from had circled back around and taken a huge bite out of her ass when she least expected it.

"No, ma'am. Didn't even know Saint Jo existed until I heard about the job," she said.

"Well, they say everyone has a twin. Guess those little girls found theirs early on in life," Mrs. Amos said as she left the room.

By the end of the day, Lizzy, Annie, and Chuck were inseparable.

When the last bell sounded, a thin woman with dyed-blonde hair and four inches of dark-brown roots appeared in the doorway and yelled at Chuck to hurry. He cringed at the sight of her and dropped his glasses in his rush.

"You break those again, boy, and you're gettin' in big trouble. The insurance company said that if you have to get another pair, we'd have to pay for them. So if you break 'em, you won't be able to see. Now get a move on. We've got places we need to go."

Chuck rushed out and they were gone.

Julie wanted to mop up the floor with that woman. She smirked when she realized the woman's hair looked like it had been left out on the clothesline to dry. The look changed when her eyes went back to the little boy. She'd taught long enough to recognize the signs of a child who was mentally as well as physically abused.

She'd barely cooled down from that episode when the light was completely obliterated in the doorway by one Griffin Luckadeau. Would the day never end? From lust to shock to anger and now back to lust. Damn!

He was every bit as fine a cowboy as he had been the first time she'd seen him—that time he'd been a soldier. And still he had a puzzled look in his eyes, as if he'd never seen her before. Well, he'd best think hard and long, because he'd seen every square inch of her and they'd done a hell of a lot more than exchange phone numbers. Annie was proof positive of that.

Lizzy ran to his side, grabbed his hand, and started to chatter about Chuck and Annie being her new friends. Griffin picked her up and hugged her close, then shot one more look over his shoulder at Julie. He'd remember someone that pretty even if it had been a long time ago. He'd racked his brain all day and not one memory had surfaced. Why would she think she'd known him?

Julie hoped he choked to death when Lizzy went running into their house telling *her* mother about the little girl in the classroom that looked just like her. Mr. Griffin Luckadeau was fixing to find out just what it meant to face off with a mad woman. His wife would never believe that he hadn't been unfaithful when she clapped eyes on Annie.

And that made Julie the other woman, a part that she never, ever intended to play after the pain of confronting the other woman in her own husband's life. In her defense, she hadn't known Griffin was married when she'd wound up in bed with him six years ago. He hadn't been wearing a wedding band. She might have had a few drinks too many, but she did remember checking for that particular item, and there hadn't even been a white ring where it should have been.

After all the students were gone, Julie and Annie shut and locked the door and headed home. Julie's hands shook as she put the key in the ignition of her truck. For a long minute she sat in stunned silence, her head on the steering wheel, while she tried to tame a million memories and racing thoughts. It was a useless endeavor; taming her thoughts was like attempting to take the wild out of a Texas longhorn. Some things simply weren't possible.

"Momma, why does Lizzy look just like me? And Chuck didn't like that stuff they put on his plate in the lunchroom today so I gave him half my sandwich," Annie said.

"You aren't the only little girl in the world with a white streak in her hair. We just haven't seen any of the others. And why didn't Chuck eat his lunch?"

Annie exhaled in impatience. "Because he don't like fish sticks. He said they make him puke. I gave him half of my sandwich."

"What did Lizzy bring?"

"She had ham and cheese with mustard, just like me.

And potato chips and a cookie and chocolate milk," Annie said.

Julie started the engine and headed north toward their new home. "Let's go home, baby. We've got lots of things to do."

Surprisingly enough, the sun still hung in the sky and the world had not come to an abrupt end. It had been a day of miracles. She'd kept her cool when Griffin Luckadeau had waltzed into her classroom. Mrs. Amos hadn't fired her. And Julie hadn't tried to mop up Saint Jo's main street with Chuck Chester's mother. All in all, not as bad as it could have been.

"Lizzy gave Chuck half her cookie," Annie said.

"Well, I suppose Chuck ate well today," Julie said.

"Yes, he did. I like him and Lizzy. They are my bestest friends," Annie pronounced.

Children were wonderful. They had no preconceived notions of who to like or not like. Money or the lack thereof didn't affect them at all. From the looks of Lizzy, she came from a comfortable family. Chuck, according to Mrs. Amos when they'd discussed Julie's students the day before, lived in a trailer south of Saint Jo and his father had been arrested multiple times on drug charges.

A person had to pass a test to get a driver's license. They had to prove they were credit-worthy to buy a house. But any drug-dealing son of a bitch could be a father.

Or any handsome soldier on his way to Iraq. Julie's jaw clamped shut. A woman couldn't even berate an SOB without her conscience putting in her two bits.

By the time Julie stopped at the local grocery store and picked up supplies, she had convinced herself that Griffin Luckadeau really had been three sheets to the wind and didn't remember the night he'd spent with her in the hotel room.

That was her blessing for holding her temper all day. He flat-out didn't remember. Thank God! She sure wouldn't ever bring it up to him. That was a solid fact.

She turned right less than a mile outside of town into a gravel driveway and parked on the north side of her new property. Five acres, a two-bedroom house with an orchard and garden space. That's what the real estate agent had said that day when she'd taken Julie out to look at the property. What she hadn't said in advance was that all the paint had peeled off the house and the wood was as gray as fog, that the driveway was full of potholes big enough to bury an army tank, or that the roof needed new shingles.

Julie had driven up to interview for the job back in the summer and been hired on the spot. When she went to the only Realtor in town to ask about an apartment to rent, the lady had taken her to this place on the outskirts of town to look at purchasing rather than renting. Her argument was that the payment would be far less than an apartment and she'd have lots more room.

Julie had taken a look at the place and fallen in love with it at first sight, despite its worn appearance. She couldn't believe the low asking price until the Realtor explained that the estate was to go as it sat, and cleaning it out wasn't going to be an easy job. The money from the sale was going to the Methodist Church in Saint Jo, where Edna Lassiter, the former owner, had attended. Julie had written a check for the total price and gone home to Jefferson, Texas, to pack.

"Momma, are we going to sit here all day or get out?" Annie asked.

"I'm sorry. I was thinking," Julie said.

"Me too. I was thinking about Lizzy. When do you think her birthday is?" Annie asked.

"The papers they sent to me say that it's two days before yours. So she was five in May, just like you," Julie said. "You big enough to help me unload groceries?"

"Yes, I am," Annie said seriously.

Julie picked up the bags holding milk and soda pop. Since she'd bought the house "as is," she had been surprised the day before when she and Annie had arrived to find the cabinets stocked with staples and the freezer full. She'd known the furniture would be there and all the closets would be full, but she hadn't thought about food.

Her mind went back to the fact that there were only two days between Lizzy's and Annie's birthdays. Griffin had to have had sex with his wife just before he left for Iraq. One thing for sure, Julie really had been his good luck charm, because he had returned home all in one big, sexy package. Just exactly what kind of man was he, anyway? Having sex with his wife, going off to war, and having sex with a stranger on the way?

He's probably wondering the same thing about you. Are you a schoolteacher by day and a sleazy, two-bit hooker on weekends who doesn't even ask a man if he's got a wife at home before she falls into bed with him?

But he didn't have a wedding ring, she argued with her conscience.

She shook off the voice inside her head and set the groceries on the porch, found the key in her purse, and opened the front door. The living room was small, with a kitchen through an archway straight ahead. An orange floral sofa sat on the north wall under a window covered with lace curtains. Tables on either end were covered with crocheted doilies, on which sat orange ceramic lamps. An old, black, dial telephone was on the end table nearest the kitchen, a covered crystal dish full of hard butterscotch candy on the other. Fairly current copies of *Ladies' Home Journal*, *Southern Living*, and *Better Homes and Gardens* were neatly arranged on the coffee table, which did not match the end tables. The walls were painted a soft yellow and decorated with watercolor paintings, all signed *E. Lassiter* in the corner. A leather recliner on the west wall faced a floor model television set from the '80s—but it still worked and that was all that mattered to Julie. It had all reminded her of Mayberry when she'd looked at it the first time. Now she felt more as though it had segued into *The Twilight Zone*.

Mother and daughter carried their bags to the kitchen, the only modern room in the house. It was as if Aunt Bea from Mayberry had put together the house and Martha Stewart had designed the kitchen—new wood cabinets, stainless-steel stove with a double-door refrigerator to match, dishwasher, trash compacter, heavy-duty mixer and blender.

The wood table and four chairs looked as out of place as a kitten at a dogfight, though. The white paint was chipped and the chairs were mismatched, so Martha Stewart must have lost the fight for something made of glass and brass.

Julie put the food away and sighed. The house had looked like a blessing when she first saw the place. She wouldn't have to move furniture or think about things like towels and bed linens. She could paint the outside of the house herself, and it was so small, the roof shouldn't cost too much to repair She loved to garden, and it was still producing. And they'd be away from everyone. People who kept looking at Annie, their eyes betraying their thoughts: What had happened? Julie was such a good girl. Did everything right and married well. When had she had the affair that'd made her husband divorce her? And where was Annie's father, anyway? It had to have been his genes that gave her that white streak in the front of her coal-black hair. Must be a low-down, good-for-nothing, worthless bastard not to even come around to see his daughter.

Julie had wanted a baby so badly, had tried every fertility drug known to doctors, and was thinking about adoption when suddenly, after that weekend in Cancún, she was pregnant. It seemed as though God was telling her that she belonged with Derrick after all and working out their problems had been the right answer. It didn't take long for her to figure out it was Lucifer, not God, meddling in her life.

Julie put thoughts of the past away and faced the present. She had boxes to unpack. Closets to clean. Cabinets to rearrange.

"Momma, can I change clothes and go play with the kittens?" Annie asked.

"Sure you can. But stay in the backyard and don't go near the road."

Annie giggled. "Momma, there ain't no road in the backyard. That's in the front yard. Lizzy said she's got some kittens, too. Did you know that?"

Julie hugged Annie. "Okay, I stand corrected. Go play with the kittens. Take that quilt from the back of the recliner in the living room and spread it out to sit on. And no, I did not know that Lizzy had kittens at her house."

"Not house, Momma. Ranch. Lizzy lives on a big ranch, and Chuck has goats in his yard. Can we get a goat, Momma?"

Julie shivered. "No, ma'am, we are not having goats. They'd eat up my garden. Your mother cat and those kittens are enough livestock for us."

Annie took off down the hall toward her bedroom like a shot. In minutes, she'd changed from her white sundress into denim shorts and a faded T-shirt. She ran through the kitchen, the small utility room barely big enough for a washer and dryer, and out the back door into the yard, where five kittens met her meowing and begging to be petted.

Julie headed down the hallway, which had a doorway on the left to one bedroom, one on the right to the second, and a bathroom at the very end. Annie's bedroom had an old full-size iron bedstead painted pink with white daisies on the headboard, a six-drawer, oak dresser, and a matching chest of drawers that would probably bring more at an antique auction than Julie had paid for the house. A pale-blue chenille bedspread with a basket of pink flowers covered the bed, which had been made up with ironed sheets and pillowcases.

"Enjoy the wrinkle-free linens, my child," Julie mumbled. "Because this lady doesn't iron sheets or pillowcases, even if Miss Edna did."

Julie's bedroom had a four-poster oak bed with a matching ten-drawer dresser and five-drawer chest, one nightstand, and a modern lamp that looked as out of place as a pig at a Sunday afternoon social. An off-white chenille spread covered the bed. The pillowcases were embroidered with peacocks and matched the doilies on every piece of furniture in the room.

"Straight out of the Sears & Roebuck catalog in 1958. Why did it all look so charming to me two weeks ago?" she mumbled as she changed into a pair of cut-off jeans and an orange tank top with bleach stains on the front. She pulled her thick, naturally curly, red hair up into a high ponytail and wiped sweat from her face. She'd had central air in her previous apartment, so she'd have to get used to adjusting window units in each room. She tucked the lace curtains back, looked out the window at Annie, still playing with five balls of fur, and turned on the noisy air conditioner. Her goal was to clean out the closet in her bedroom that afternoon and not think about the striking cowboy named Griffin who she'd thought of for years as a soldier named G. Luckadeau.

Griffin and Lizzy ordered ice cream cones at the Dairy Queen, but he could scarcely eat his. He dreaded taking Lizzy home. Marita would have a thousand questions the first time Lizzy started in about the little girl with the white streak just like hers. He didn't mind answering questions if he had answers, but there were none. One minute he was living in his own little chunk of Montague County, minding his own business, and then this morning, it all fell apart. He damn sure couldn't pull answers out of his ass to satisfy Marita.

Who was that schoolteacher, anyway? And how'd she get a Luckadeau child? He knew how the child was made. But short of his mother having another son she never told anyone about, he didn't know anything else.

Griffin's mother had inherited her white streak from her father, and that was where Griffin's came from. His sister, Melinda, got the Luckadeau blond hair and her two sons were trademark Luckadeaus. Griffin had the poliosis streak in his hair, and Lizzy had inherited the gene from him. If it ran true, she'd give it to her sons but not her daughters.

It was a rare birthmark, and when Lizzy was born with it, he'd had her tested just to be sure. The doctor had run tests on everything from Marfan syndrome to Waardenburg syndrome, but it was simply a genetic trait where her forelock had no pigment—just like her father's.

Griffin might have dismissed seeing the same birthmark on the other little girl if she hadn't had the Luckadeau blue eyes to go with it, as well as the cheekbones and that little dimple in her chin. There was no doubt that child was as much a Luckadeau as Lizzy. Hell, she looked like her twin: Lizzy was barely taller and the other girl a few pounds heavier, but then that's the way it was with twins most of the time.

He stared out the Dairy Queen window.

"Daddy, Annie is my friend. She and Chuck are my bestest friends. We played together all day. Annie has kittens and Chuck has some goats. Can we get a goat?" Lizzy asked.

"I don't know, honey. What are Annie's and Chuck's last names?"

"You know, Daddy. Annie is Miss Julie's girl. Her name is Donavan, and Chuck is Chuck Chester."

Graham swallowed hard. He hadn't wanted to let Lizzy go to school that year and he'd been right. The son of the biggest meth producer in Montague County had become her best friend the first day, and then there was the mystery behind her new teacher, whom Mrs. Amos had told him was a single mother and a fine teacher. Mrs. Amos must be getting old and losing her touch. Used to be she had eyes in the back of her head and was the meanest teacher in school when Griffin was a child.

"Did you see Lizzy's hair, Daddy? She's got a lucky streak in her hair and blue eyes and nobody better call us a skunk and if they did we could both beat them up and—" She finally stopped for air.

"What you have is not common, but you aren't the only girl in the world with it. That little girl has one, too. We'll have no more talk about beating people up. No one has called you a skunk since that party at Slade's house."

"But they will because that's what I look like. Can we make it go away, Daddy? I don't want to be different. Me and Annie could put stuff on our hair and make it go away," she said.

"No, we cannot make it go away, Lizzy. It's what makes you special. Remember what Jane told you that day at Slade's ranch? She said only little girls with lucky streaks can find the pot of gold."

"Then me and Annie will be special together. Can we fix Chuck's hair to match ours so he will be special?" Lizzy asked.

"Is Chuck that little red-haired boy who has freckles and wears glasses?" Griffin remembered the child Julie had been consoling when he walked into the room. "Are you sure his name is Chester? His hair looked like your new teacher's hair. Maybe that's her son."

Lizzy scooped up the last of her ice cream sundae. "No, Daddy. He is Chuck Chester. His Momma came to the school before you got there. She's not nice. She yelled at Chuck and made him cry. Miss Julie only has Annie."

Griffin pushed his white forelock back with his fingertips. "Maybe his Momma was having a tough day. Let's get on home and see if Nana Rita is making cookies. I bet she is and you can help her. And we've got feed in the back of our truck, so we have to unload that. We've got lots of jobs to do."

"Okay." She drew the word out with a sigh. "I like school. I wish I could live there or that Annie could come live with me."

He didn't respond to such an absurd proclamation. He helped Lizzy into the back seat of his club cab truck and drove north out of Saint Jo.

"Daddy, look. Hurry, right there where the old witch used to live—there is Annie and Miss Julie getting out of their truck. Can I go play with her today, Daddy? That old witch woman isn't still in the house, is she?" Lizzy bounced around in the back seat, only the seat belt keeping her from barreling out of the truck and running toward the ramshackle house that Edna Lassiter had lived in for more than fifty years.

So the woman had actually *bought* property in Saint Jo. Folks didn't buy property unless they were planning on sticking around because it could be years before they were able to unload it.

Griffin gritted his teeth, slapped the steering wheel, and swore under his breath, then immediately looked in the rearview mirror to see if Lizzy had heard him. She was too busy looking at the house to hear anything. Of all the kids in the classroom, why did she have to befriend those two?

The Lucky Clover Ranch property started a mile out of Saint Jo and covered most of the ground on the east side of the road from there to Capps Corner. Griffin also owned a fair-sized chunk of land on up toward Illinois Bend, a small community on the border of the Red River. It had a church and a few scattered houses. Capps Corner was only slightly bigger. Saint Jo had less than a thousand people, and Alvera Clancy said that was counting the dogs and depending on several girls to get pregnant and keep up the population. Why would any single mother come to Saint Jo?

He made a right-hand turn down the paved lane and through a brick-and-wood arch with a swinging sign at the top. The ranch brand, a four-leaf clover, was burned into the wood on either side of the words *Welcome to the Lucky Clover Ranch*. It was the truth: everyone was welcome at the ranch.

Everyone except Edna Lassiter, who had kept a hundred-year-old feud alive with the Luckadeau family. She had gone to the courthouse once a year to file a restraining order on anyone with the last name of Luckadeau or anyone who might be kin to those "heathens," as she called the whole family. As if he or any of his family preceding him would have any business on that ramshackle property of hers. There was an old rumor that the feud went back further than her generation—something about a Lassiter being jilted by a Luckadeau a hundred years before.

Edna had been a recluse except for Sunday morning services, so not many people even knew she existed. However, there was that day that she'd called Lizzy "the spawn of the devil" when Lizzy had bumped into her cane in the church parking lot. Lizzy had no trouble speaking her mind, but she whispered the word *spawn* anytime she used it and had been terrified of the elderly, gray-haired woman after that.

Griffin wondered why in the world a schoolteacher would buy that property. The house was probably haunted, and if the inside looked like the outside, no one would want to live there.

Lizzy opened the truck door and bailed out, taking off in a dead run toward the two-story ranch house with a porch around three sides on both the bottom and upper floors. Painted white, it sat in a grove of pecan trees and had a white picket fence all around the yard. Lizzy left the gate hanging with a yell for her father to close it and went tearing into the house hollering for Nana Rita.

"Right here, child. What is the matter?" A thin Mexican lady emerged from the kitchen, wiping her hands on the tail of her apron. Her black hair was pulled up into a bun on top of her head. Her jeans bagged slightly on her slim frame, and a red T-shirt peeked out from under her bibbed apron made of red gingham checks.

"There's another me. She's in my class Nana Rita, and her name is Annie. She's got a streak in her hair just like mine and blue eyes just like mine and even a dent in her chin. Her momma is my teacher, Miss Julie, and she's got curly, red hair but she don't have a lucky streak. Is Annie my sister? Why didn't Daddy tell me I have a sister just like me?"

"Because you don't," Griffin said from the doorway.

Marita tucked her chin and raised an eyebrow. The questions were on the way and he still didn't have an answer for any of them.

"She *might* be my twin sister. We're just alike," Lizzy argued.

"I was there in the delivery room when your mother gave birth to you. Believe me, you were the only baby born to us," Griffin said.

"But I want her to be my twin sister. Can you go buy her so she can be?" Lizzy asked.

"No, he cannot buy a little girl. Now you come in this kitchen and help me make cookies. You can tell me more about this little girl while we cook. And you"—Marita pursed her lips at Griffin—"can tell me about the new teacher later."

Griffin nodded. At least he wouldn't have to go into the whole thing that day. Maybe by the time he did have to discuss it, he'd have more information. He'd heard that everyone had a double somewhere in the world. Evidently, Lizzy had found hers on the first day of school. Probably by the time they were in school a week, they'd be fighting and wouldn't be friends anymore. Or maybe the teacher and her daughter would be gone when he took Lizzy to school the next day.

Julie opened the closet doors to the slightly sweet smell of baby powder and an old woman's cologne. Starting at one end, she took down dresses and pantsuits—some of which had to be thirty years old, judging from the material and style—and folded them neatly into big, black garbage bags to take to the nearest Goodwill store.

When she picked up a pink floral double-knit dress, she sat down on the floor and leaned back against the wall. Her aunt Flossie had a dress just like that and had worn it to the hospital to see her when Annie was born. She'd taken one look at the baby and quickly came to the same conclusion Derrick had.

"That baby is beautiful, but she does not belong to your husband. You've been sinning, Julie Donavan, and it has come back to bite you on the ass," Aunt Flossie had whispered. Julie had been as surprised to hear that word come out of Aunt Flossie's mouth as she'd been when they'd laid the new baby in her arms the first time. Aunt Flossie didn't even use the word *pregnant* in mixed company and said it behind her hand when she absolutely had to use it among female friends. Most of the time the lady was "in the family way."

That damned pink dress brought on a flood of memories Julie thought she'd buried and faced for the last time several years ago. She'd moved from Jefferson, Texas, to Saint Jo to get away from the gossip, and here it was, following her around like a puppy in the form of a blasted pink double-knit dress with a zipper down the front. Along with one fine-looking cowboy who didn't even remember who she was. Had Aunt Flossie still been alive, she would have blushed at the string of scalding words that flowed from her niece's mouth right then.

It had all started when Julie discovered her husband Derrick had been sleeping with the female engineer in the oil company his family owned. Julie and Derrick had been married six years, and she had tried every fertility drug and concept on the market to have a baby. When she confronted him about the affair, he'd declared with bravado that it was her obsession with pregnancy that had driven him to the other woman. It was all Julie's fault because sex had become nothing but a means to a baby, not a spontaneous spark of fun like it had been in the beginning. Pompous son of a bitch that he was, he'd laid a guilt trip on her.

"Yeah right," Julie said aloud. "He unzipped his pants. I damn sure didn't do it for him, grab his tally-whacker, and lead him to the cute little engineer."

She had filed for divorce even though a little tiny bit of her had always wondered if he was right and it had been her fault. Before the divorce was final, she, her sister, and a few friends had gone to Dallas for a weekend of shopping and fun. They met some college buddies who'd driven in from San Antonio, rented motel rooms, and shopped all day Saturday. That night they hit a singles' bar and Julie met had Griffin. Only that night they weren't Julie and Griffin—they were Lucky and Red, and they were both drunk by the time they staggered into her room.

He had been sitting at a table with a dozen other freshly recruited military men, all looking very handsome in BDUs and shined boots, and with shaved heads. She had stumbled over his boots when she was returning from the bathroom and he caught her before she fell. She'd looked up into the bluest eyes she'd ever seen.

"Well, they don't call me Lucky for nothing," he said with a smile.

"I'm so sorry. I was clumsy and not looking where I was going," she had apologized.

"Don't be. I saw you come in. I'm a sucker for red hair. Care to dance?"

And so it began. An evening with too many drinks,

too much laughter, and two people hailing a cab back to her motel room. She wouldn't even have known his name if she hadn't noticed it stenciled above the pocket of his shirt: G. Luckadeau. What the hell kind of name was Luckadeau anyway? French? Cajun?

"So what does the G stand for?" she'd asked.

"I'm off to Iraq tomorrow morning, bright and early. Just call me Lucky because that's what I am. You're my red-haired good luck charm who's going to make sure I come back in one piece. I'm calling you Red."

But what had been funny that night was awkward the next morning.

When he had left, it was with a backward glance that said he liked what he saw, and if he wasn't going to Iraq, he might call her again.

"Goodbye, Lucky. Come home in one piece," she'd said from the bed.

"I promise I will. How can I not? I just slept with the most beautiful redhead in the whole state of Texas."

"That line is so damn corny it's funny. Besides, darlin', we didn't sleep," she said before she pulled the covers over her face and fell asleep.

"Goodbye, Red," he'd said with a grin.

The grin hadn't changed in six years, but the look in his eyes sure had. At school that morning, Julie had recognized nothing but shock. His hair had grown out and she had seen for absolute sure what gene pool Annie had dipped her head in to get her white streak, but six years had been good to Griffin Luckadeau. He was just as handsome as he'd been back then.

Julie had been rudely awakened by her sister pounding on the door at fifteen minutes until eleven, rushing her around so they could make the checkout time.

The next week, Derrick called. Honey dripped from his words. He missed her. He was sorry. They shouldn't throw away a six-year marriage because of his mistake. He was willing to take full blame and it would never happen again. Please give him another chance.

Guilt had caused her to set aside the divorce. To celebrate, Derrick had taken a week off work and they'd flown to Cancún.

"There's a sucker born every second," Julie said aloud as she kept packing Edna's clothes.

Her thoughts went back to six weeks after she and Derrick had gone to Cancún. She had found out she was pregnant, and although he was reserved about the news, she was ecstatic. The day Julie gave birth to Annie, he'd taken one look at his daughter and ordered a DNA test.

"I'm willing to wait for the proof, Julie, and if the child is mine, I will admit I'm wrong, but she's not. I see now why you were so agreeable to take me back. I won't be home until the DNA test results come in. That will give you time to move out. I'll be filing for divorce on grounds of adultery as soon as I know for sure."

Julie had nodded numbly. One look at the baby they'd pulled from her and she'd immediately known who the father was: G. Luckadeau. She'd even bet dollars to doughnuts that had his head not been shaven slick as a baby's butt, he would have had a white streak in his dark hair. Her new baby daughter had one in the front of all that beautiful black hair, along with a dimple in her chin and big, round eyes that Julie had no doubt would be crystal-clear blue in a few weeks.

A DNA test was just a formality. The baby did not belong to Derrick Wayne Williams, III. When Julie filled out the birth certificate, she left the father's space blank and named her daughter Annie Grace Donavan, because one thing Julie would insist on was getting her maiden name back. Annie was not a Williams, and Julie wanted nothing from Derrick, not his property or his name.

She'd never blamed Derrick. Maybe he'd really been trying to make the marriage work and had felt betrayed. Julie certainly had felt that way when she'd discovered the affair with his engineer.

She'd taken her baby home from the hospital, moved into the garage apartment her parents rented out for extra cash, and paid her mother to keep Annie while she taught school. Five years later, her Aunt Flossie died and left Julie her entire estate. It wasn't millions, but it was enough to buy the Lassiter property.

She folded the pink dress and packed it into the garbage sack, hoping the memories would stay in the sack and not haunt her anymore. Evidently Lucky had left a pregnant wife behind when he went to Iraq, because Lizzy and Annie were born only two days apart. They were almost the same height, the same size, and could easily pass for twins.

Julie felt sorry for his wife. She'd been the wife; she didn't ever want to be the other woman.

That must be why he'd pretended not to remember her earlier that day. He sure didn't want to go home and explain that he'd just run into a drunken one-night stand and the little girl it had produced.

"Momma, can I bring the kittens inside?" Annie whispered.

Julie jumped. "You scared me," she said.

"It's hot out there and there's a spider on the back porch and I know the kittens are afraid of it. Can I bring them in the house?"

She nodded. "We'll have to make a litter pan in case they need to go when they are visiting you in the house. I'll find an old pan and put some gravel from the driveway in it. You go bring them into your room and I'll turn on the air conditioner in there. And I'll take care of that spider on my way to the driveway."

"You are the best momma in the whole world." Annie beamed. "But you know what? I wish Lizzy was my sister, then I'd have a real person to play with instead of the kittens, and we could play with them together. I bet she'd like yellow kittens, Momma, I just know it."

"I've been thinking some about that little girl, Annie. Some folks say that everybody has a double. Do you know what that means?"

Annie shook her head.

"It means somewhere in the world there is a little girl who looks so much like you that it was like you were looking in the mirror if you looked at her. I think Lizzy is your double."

Annie hung her head. "Can she be my sister if I wish real, real hard?"

"I don't think so. Now you go get your baby kittens and I'll get them a potty box."

"And some milk in a bowl for snack time?" Annie pushed.

Julie smiled. "Yes, but just a tiny bit. Their momma is still feeding them and her milk is better than the kind we buy in a jug. It's special just for them."

A while later, Julie hauled the garbage bag out to the storage shed and brought in a box marked "Julie's Stuff" on the side. She organized as she unpacked. Shirts. Slacks. Jeans. Dress clothes. Looking at her closet, she felt peace. She'd made the right decision when she bought the place. She was home.

Griffin Luckadeau could just stay out of her way and she'd do her best to grant him the same favor.

Chapter 2

The Saint Jo Methodist Church was located on Boggess Street, which was also Highway 677 from Saint Jo up to Illinois Bend. It was an old, redbrick, two-story church with two entrances at the front, a peaked roof over part of it, and a corner that looked as if kids had been playing with Lego blocks, built a square piece three stories high, and glued it to one side.

It was considerably smaller than the church Julie and Annie had attended with her parents in Jefferson, but she wanted a small place with no history where she and Annie could put down roots.

Annie was dressed in a powder-blue dress with white lace trim around the neck and hemline. Her long, black hair with the white streak had been pulled back into a ponytail with a blue ribbon around the base. Julie had chosen a floral, tiered skirt, predominantly mint green with splashes of bright pink and yellow, and a yellow tank top with lace trim around the neck. She wore white sandals and had spent extra time that morning taming her red curls with mousse and lots of patience.

She held Annie's hand and they walked through the doors in time for the first hymn. They stopped at a pew about halfway up the aisle that had enough space at the end for them to sit comfortably. An older lady scooted over to give them a little more room and then stared at Annie as if she were seeing a ghost.

The music director gave out the hymn. Julie picked up a songbook from the back of the pew in front of her and held it so Annie could see. She couldn't read yet, but she did try on the hymns she'd heard most often.

Then announcements were made: two babies were born that week. A grin tickled the corners of Julie's mouth—people had sex in Saint Jo in spite of the name of the town, which suggested that only the pure and holy lived there. Mrs. Smith had died, and the funeral lunch would be in the fellowship hall on Tuesday. Anyone interested in bringing food should contact Mamie Pickett over at Miss Molly's Shoppe. A potluck dinner was planned on Friday for the senior citizens Sunday school class.

Julie recognized the name Mamie Pickett. She was the Realtor Julie had dealt with when she bought the Lassiter place. She was still thinking about Mamie when the preacher began his sermon. She had barely settled into listening mode when Annie tugged on her arm. She looked down to see her daughter with the biggest smile on her face and her small finger pointing straight ahead.

Julie whispered behind her hand into her daughter's ears. "Annie, don't point at the preacher. It's rude and it will make him nervous."

"Look." Annie squirmed and kept pointing.

Julie finally looked where she was pointing. Griffin Luckadeau sat right there, not three feet from her in the next pew. God must carry a grudge for a long time. She'd expected bad things to happen after Derrick had divorced her, but life had gone on the same as always. Now, when she thought she'd been forgiven, she was being punished.

Lizzy had turned around on her knees in the pew

right in front of them and was smiling at Annie. When her father touched her arm and said something to her, she flipped around, but all through the sermon, she and Annie both wiggled at the same speed—which was a little faster than if they'd had ants in their pants but not quite enough to rub the velvet off the pew cushions.

Julie checked her watch every thirty seconds. The thirty-minute sermon lasted three days past eternity, and she didn't have the foggiest notion of what the preacher had said. He could have been advocating burning in hell for one-night stands or asking for donations to build a new barn for an elder member of the church for all she knew when he finished his sermon. Julie couldn't keep her mind or thoughts from straying to the Luckadeau man sitting in front of her. She studied the shape of his head and resisted the urge to brush a lock of hair from his shirt collar. She got angry all over again for her decision to move to Saint Jo without at least checking the phone book for the Luckadeau name.

Finally the preacher asked Griffin Luckadeau to give the benediction as he tiptoed down the aisle to the door to greet people as they left.

Julie fidgeted while he prayed. Evidently, he had come home from Iraq and gotten saved, sanctified, and dehorned, because the man she'd slept with hadn't appeared to be so big on prayers. There was no getting around it, under it, or through it—she'd have to see Griffin six days a week whether she liked it or not. Or she'd have to find a different church, and explaining to her Methodist minister father why she'd changed her faith would be more difficult than biting the bullet and staying where she was.

Annie waved at Lizzy the minute the prayer ended. Lizzy's smile covered half her face, her blue eyes danced, and the dimple in her chin deepened. She tugged on her father's arm, but he was in conversation with a man to his left.

Julie grabbed Annie's hand, moved toward the front door, and every few seconds glanced over her shoulder to see if he was looking her way. She shook the preacher's hand and told him she'd enjoyed the sermon and was out the door long before Griffin ever finished his conversation.

"Momma, I want to go to Sunday school next week so I can play with Lizzy, and maybe I can sit with her next week and ain't that wonderful?" Annie prattled on without coming up for air. "Can we please sit with her and her daddy next Sunday? I can't wait to see her in school and tell her we can sit together in church, and maybe we'll be together in Sunday school." Annie bounced in the pickup seat.

Julie put her off with a wave of her hand and let her keep right on chattering about Lizzy.

Griffin kept talking, blocking Lizzy's way into the aisle with his tall, strong body and his back to Julie. Finally, he stopped talking and looked down at Lizzy, who was fidgeting.

"Daddy, she was right here behind me in the church, and when I go to school, I'm going to tell her to come to Sunday school next week and we can sit together in church." Lizzy talked nonstop all the way to the church doors.

"What are you talking about?" Griffin asked. The hair on his neck stood up and itched. His pulse picked up speed just thinking about the new teacher. Why in the devil had she shown up at his church?

"I'm talkin' about Annie! She was behind us. I turned around in the seat and she looked at me and she smiled and hurry, Daddy, she's getting in that blue truck with her momma and maybe we can take them home with us for dinner today." Lizzy talked fast and furious, gesturing toward the truck the whole time.

Griffin looked up in time to see the schoolteacher helping her daughter into an older model Ford truck. The sun bounced off the white streak in Annie's hair. Julie looked beautiful in her Sunday dress and sandals, with the sun throwing highlights in her hair. He had a strange notion that involved running his hands through her hair, maybe even tilting that pert, little chin back for a kiss. He shook his head violently to erase the image. He didn't know that woman and couldn't even figure out what game she had up her sleeve. Kissing her was out of the question. Besides, his girlfriend, Rachel, would go up in flames.

The preacher called out to him, "Griffin, I didn't know you had relatives in the area. That child has to be a Luckadeau. I didn't know they were your relatives until they were already gone. I'd have visited a little longer."

"Don't worry about it," Griffin said. It was a lot easier said than done. It had been on his mind for a whole week.

"Relatives? Does that mean kinfolks like Jane and Slade and Milli and Katy Scarlett? Does that mean Annie is my kinfolk?" Lizzy asked on the way to the truck.

"I'm not sure what it means, but we're going home. Nana Rita will have dinner ready, and she made banana pudding this morning." Griffin tried to steer the conversation away from the mystery surrounding the new schoolteacher.

It didn't work. Lizzy talked nonstop all the way to the ranch about nothing else but Annie Donavan.

Julie made grilled cheese sandwiches and tomato soup for lunch. She'd set a quart of frozen peaches out to thaw that morning before they'd gone to church and had looked forward to them right up until the time she'd realized Griffin was sitting in front of her. Seeing him there had just flat killed her appetite.

It seemed strange to think of him with a name. He'd always been G. Luckadeau when she had let him into her memories.

Annie rattled on and on while she ate all her soup and sandwich, asked for more, and polished off the last half of her mother's. Julie managed a few bites, but she might as well have been eating a sawdust sandwich. The peaches didn't even look good to her. They'd barely finished lunch and were thinking about cleaning out Annie's closet when the knock came to the front door.

Julie jumped. She was not prepared for the showdown, but if Griffin wanted a fight, then she wasn't running from it, either. She would tell him exactly what she thought and without a single stutter.

She took a deep breath and swung the door open to find Mamie Pickett standing there with an apple pie in her hands.

"Welcome to our neck of the woods in Montague County!" She smiled brightly. "Did I come at a bad time? You look like you saw a ghost."

"No, not at all. Please come in. Thank you for the pie. Bring it into the kitchen and drag up a chair. I'll make us a glass of tea and we'll share the pie," Julie said.

Mamie followed Julie into the kitchen, set the pie on the table, and smiled at Annie. "Well, hello. You would be Annie? I'm Mamie Pickett, the lady who sold your mother this place. Think we could be friends?"

Annie nodded. "But my best friend is Lizzy and then Chuck. Are they your friends?"

"That would be Lizzy Luckadeau and Chuck Chester?" Mamie asked.

"Yes, those are my friends. I'm glad we came here because this is where Lizzy and Chuck live. Momma, can I go play with the kittens and can I take a quilt? I think they are ready for me to tell them a story."

"Yes, you can, but you know the rules. Stay in the backyard and—"

Annie rolled her big blue eyes and intoned, "Don't go in the front yard where there's no fence."

"That's right," Julie said.

She slammed the old wooden screen door when she took off into the backyard.

"I thought I'd like that door when I bought this place. It reminds me of one in a parsonage where we lived when I was just a little girl. I loved the way the slam sounded. It's not as nostalgic as I thought it would be," Julie admitted.

"I hear you and understand. There was one on the house where I grew up, too. Maybe that's why I was always told not to slam the door," Mamie said.

Julie poured tea into two recycled jelly glasses filled with ice and set one before her first guest. Mamie had light-brown, shoulder-length, straight hair she wore feathered around her square face, thin lips, and deep-set green eyes. She wore pink seersucker capris and a T-shirt and sandals.

"I wanted to welcome you to our part of Texas, but I also came for a couple of other reasons, Julie. I own and operate my late grandmother's shop on the town square. Miss Molly's Shoppe—but most folks just call it Molly's. I do the realty business right out of the shop. In a town this size, you've got to diversify. Anyway, my grandmother died years ago, but she and Edna were friends of a sort. They grew up together up in Illinois Bend, and Edna made jellies and jams and pie filling, about anything that could go in a jar for us to sell. Did pretty good with it most years."

She stopped to sip the tea. "There's a cellar under this house. Did I forget to mention that when we talked about it? Don't tell anyone. I'm supposed to do the complete disclosure thing and I forgot. I've only been doing this about a year. Anyway, I'll show you how to get down there."

Mamie went into the living room and set aside one of the end tables. The carpet had been cut to fit a place about three feet wide and a little longer. "This picks up and the door leads to the cellar where Edna kept the stock that she sold to me. I brought along the price list from last year. Last time I was here, there was still some stock left and I'm running low. Would you sell me what's left?"

Julie nodded. "Sure. Did she use particular recipes for her stuff?"

"I'm sure she did and they're probably somewhere in the kitchen. Would you be interested in keeping up the business? I'll buy all I can sell, and that's a lot. You want to lead the way, or you want me to go first?"

Julie took the first step into the dark cellar. Mamie followed and flipped a switch at the bottom of the narrow staircase. The walls and floor were concrete, which kept the cellar cool without being musty. There had to be vents somewhere. Julie found them up near the top of the shelves, which lined every possible inch and were filled with jams, jellies, canned fruit, pie filling, picante sauce, and other home-canned delicacies. There were so many names on the fancy little labels that Julie couldn't possibly remember them all.

Mamie picked up an empty box and began to fill it. "I'll take some pepper jelly. You'd be surprised how well it sells to tourists. I've been out of picante sauce for two weeks, so I'd best have half a dozen jars of that."

"Where did she get the labels?" Julie asked.

"I have no idea, but I bet there's paperwork somewhere around here. You got a computer? With just a little work, I bet you could make them yourself and you could change the label to fit whatever you want to call your business."

"I'll have to think about it," Julie said, but she was already thinking about making squash relish from the abundant crop of yellow squash in the garden.

They carried two boxes to the kitchen and set them on the table—twenty-four quart jars of merchandise. Mamie wrote her a check for a hundred and eighty dollars. "I sell this stuff for $14.95 a jar and can't keep it on the shelves. I pay seven-fifty a jar for it. If you want to go up on your prices should you decide to keep the business going, that's fine. I'll just adjust my prices when you do yours."

"I'll think about it for sure. I love gardening and canning. I cleaned out her closets yesterday. Know anyone who'd be interested in having her clothing?" Julie asked.

"There's a Goodwill store over in Wichita Falls. I'm going over there tomorrow for a meeting. Want me to take them for you?"

Julie refilled their glasses. "That would be great."

"Cute kid out there. She looks just like Lizzy Luckadeau."

"She's so excited about having someone else around with that streak in her hair that it's all I hear about," Julie said. She didn't want to discuss the fact that her daughter belonged to Griffin. She hadn't even had time to process the information much less put any part of it into words.

Mamie finished the last bite of her second piece of pie and began, "Now, before I dig into the other reason I came out here, let me give you some background. Back during the Civil War, some folks came out here and settled at Illinois Bend. Called it Wardville at first but then, when the post office was granted, they named it Illinois Bend because a lot of them came from that state. It had about three hundred people back then. That would be back when my great-something-grandmother was born. She and Edna's grandmother knew each other, and the next generation were friends, and then Molly and Edna were born right before the flu epidemic of 1918. They would have been about two or three years old then. They talked about losing relatives during that time."

"Why did she never marry?" Julie asked.

"It was the Lassiter curse. Her aunt got left at the altar by a man and died an old maid, and then the exact same thing happened to Edna. She never talked about her experience, but Granny Molly knew about it. She said she was to stand up with Edna, and the night before the wedding, the man took off without even telling her why. He joined the army during World War II and when he came home, he didn't try to explain. The feud actually started back when her aunt was left high and dry at the altar. The strange thing was that Edna fell in love with one of that man's relatives, like it happened back in the Hatfield and McCoy days. Then he pulled the same stunt and Edna just holed up on her five acres and died an old maid."

"That's sad," Julie said.

"Not really. She was a spunky old girl. Said her piece and didn't let anyone get ahead of her, even if she was a hermit of sorts."

"Wow! Since I bought her property does that make me a Hatfield or a McCoy?"

"Hmmm." Mamie eyed her closely. "I think you look more like a McCoy with that red hair. Got to be Irish or Scottish blood in there somewhere. I bet you've got a hellacious temper, too," Mamie teased.

"You a prophet or a fortune-teller?" Julie asked.

Mamie giggled. "Now, on to the other reason why I stopped by today. We've got this big fight going on in the city. We have a Fourth of July shindig and no one is against that; it's solid tradition. But I'm heading up a committee to do an event for the holidays. Maybe a parade on the Saturday after Thanksgiving to kick off the season. A drawing on Saturdays with tickets you get when you shop in town. Something to bring some winter trade back to Saint Jo. I think it's a wonderful idea. Old folks like Clarice Utley don't want any part of the thing. Come to the town meeting with me next Thursday night. I'd love to have some young folks to help me out. Especially a teacher. Y'all are always so good at speaking to a group. But right now I'm running late, so I'd best be going. You think about the canning business, and don't let that McCoy temper get the best of you."

Julie walked her to the door. "Wouldn't think of letting the McCoy temper have full rein. I'm going to spend the afternoon searching for those recipes and deciding if I want to make jelly."

"See you later. I live just up the road a ways, and my shop is open six days a week most of the time. Tomorrow morning I'll open late because I have to go to Wichita Falls. Where's those clothes?" Mamie said.

"In the shed. I'll haul them around to the front. Stop by anytime. I'd love the company," Julie said.

They quickly threw the sacks into Mamie's car and she waved as she drove away.

Lizzy rode her pony right up to the fence line and looked at the little girl on the quilt playing with a whole litter of yellow kittens. She slung her leg over the side, slid off the Shetland pony, and tethered it to a mesquite tree. She wasn't supposed to ride past the fence, and she'd get in big trouble if her father found out that she'd not only gone through the gate but had ridden more than a mile down the road to Annie's house.

But the idea of knowing where Annie lived drew

her to the house like ants to the syrup bottle in the pantry. She had to make sure her new friend was aware of the witch who used to live in her house and tell her to be careful. That mean old lady might make her a spawn, too.

Annie looked up to see the little girl sitting on the ground staring through the chain-link fence at her. "Lizzy! How did you get here?"

"I rode my horse. I'm not supposed to ride him outside of our ranch, but I saw where you lived and I wanted to talk to you."

"Come around the end of the fence and play with me. I'll show you my kittens," Annie said.

Lizzy shook her head. "I can't come in your yard, but we can talk. Daddy says we're like doubles. He says that there's somebody out there who looks just like somebody else and we are like that."

"My momma said the same thing. Do you believe it?"

"I guess so. Did anyone ever call you a skunk?" Lizzy asked.

Annie blushed. "A little boy did one time in the grocery store."

"He was a mean little boy just like those little girls were mean that called me one. Hey, I got black-and-white kittens. Want to trade? I'll give you a black-and-white one for a yellow one," Lizzy said.

Annie nodded. "You got a black-and-white one on your horse?"

"No, I didn't bring it today. But I'll take one of yours and bring mine back to you another day."

"Okay. Come around to the front yard and there's a gate. You can pick out whichever one you want, but don't want this one because I really want to keep him because he's my favorite," Annie said.

Lizzy shook her head again. "I can't come in your yard. A witch lives there in that house. My Nana Rita said so. I'm afraid of the witch. She called me a spawn."

Annie left the kittens and went to the fence. She looped her small fingers in the holes and looked right into Lizzy's eyes. "Are you trying to scare me? You can't be my friend if you do, and anyway, what's a spawn?"

Lizzy walked up to the fence, laced her fingers over Annie's, and whispered, "I'm tellin' you the truth and I don't know what a spawn is but the devil makes them 'cause she said I was a devil's spawn. I saw her at church lots of times, and I rode my pony up to the trees and watched her but I didn't tell Daddy. She had gray hair and a long nose. She looked at me real mean and never did talk to my daddy and her name was Edna Lassyturn. She died but her ghost still lives here because she was so mean."

"My momma don't know she bought a witch's house. I'll have to tell her."

Lizzy nodded very seriously. "Nana Rita said nothing could kill something that mean."

"Who is Nana Rita?" Annie asked.

"She's kind of like my grandma, only I have one of those, too. She lives in… I can't remember, but it's a long way to her house. She's Daddy's momma and I call her Granny, but Nana Rita lives in a house on the ranch and she comes every day to cook and keep me."

"I had one of those. She lived in the house beside ours, and I went there every day. I called her Grammy. I miss her but I'm glad my momma bought this place because I found you for my friend and we both got a white streak in our hair," Annie said.

Lizzy touched her white forelock. "It's my lucky streak."

Annie touched her hair. "Is mine lucky, too?"

"We'll ask Jane. She's Slade's wife now. She's my friend and I like her a lot. She'll tell us if yours is a lucky streak. You think you can put a yellow kitten through the fence so I don't have to come in there?"

"Yes, I can. There's a hole. I found it yesterday when the momma cat got under the fence. I can give it to you back there. Which one do you want?" Annie whispered so the ghost of that Lassyturn woman couldn't hear.

Lizzy pointed toward the back side of the yard. "Can you bring them all back there and we'll look at them?"

Annie picked up five squirming kittens and carried them to the place where Lizzy stopped. They sat down, one on each side of the fence, passing kittens back and forth and giggling like only five-year-old little girls can.

After half an hour, Lizzy had made her choice and mounted up, waved goodbye to Annie, and rode back toward the ranch house. Lizzy was happy until she looked up and saw the car in the driveway. *She* was there. Lizzy determined she'd stay in the barn until *she* was gone. Sometimes her daddy was so stupid. Nana Rita even said he was when it came to *her*.

She stayed out in the barn with the momma cat, who accepted the yellow one right in with her three black-and-white babies without so much as a slap or a meow. Lizzy played with all of them until her stomach started growling and she had to go inside.

"Where have you been?" Griffin asked. "We were ready to come looking for you."

"I was playing with my kittens," Lizzy said.

"Well, get washed up for supper. Rachel is staying with us. Isn't that nice?"

Lizzy dragged her heavy heart back to the bathroom without answering. She could think of nothing worse than Rachel staying for dinner. She lathered up her hands and stood on her tiptoes so she could see in the mirror. Looking back at her was Annie, or so she pretended.

"She's mean when Daddy isn't looking. You are my friend. What would you do?" Lizzy giggled at what came to her mind, which she was sure came from Annie in the mirror.

The three of them sat down at the big table in the dining room for supper.

"So what did you do today?" Rachel asked.

Lizzy shrugged.

"You rode your pony, didn't you?" Griffin asked.

Lizzy nodded.

"Cat got your tongue?" Rachel asked.

Lizzy shrugged.

The phone rang and Griffin excused himself to answer it, stepping out of the dining room into the foyer. His voice was low and his tone serious.

"What's the matter with you?" Rachel asked Lizzy.

"Nothing," she answered.

"You can talk to me. I intend to live here before very long, and you're going to be my stepdaughter. You'll have to talk to me then, so you might as well start now." Rachel's tone was syrupy sweet.

Lizzy decided to give her a chance. "Do you like cats?"

"No, I hate them and you aren't going to bring any of those horrible barn cats in this house when I move in here. That will be understood from the first day." The tone was suddenly snappy and sour.

"You aren't very pretty when you do that with your eyes and make your mouth all puckered up," Lizzy said.

"You are a horrible little girl," Rachel said.

"Hey, you two, go ahead and eat. I'll be back in fifteen minutes. There's a cow down and I've got to help Carl pull the calf," Griffin yelled from the other room.

Lizzy jumped up from the table. "I'll go with you, Daddy."

"No, you stay here and talk to Rachel."

Lizzy kept walking. "But I want to go with you."

He frowned. "I said you will stay here with Rachel."

She sat back down and hunched her thin shoulders, dropping her chin to her chest in a pout.

Rachel waited until she heard the door shut before she turned to Lizzy.

"Little girl, you better understand something right now. I *will* marry your father. Now straighten up your back and eat your carrots."

"I don't like carrots." Lizzy glared at Rachel. If *she* moved to the Lucky Clover, then Lizzy was going to ride her pony to Annie's house and live there. Even that Lassyturn witch wasn't as mean as Rachel.

"Eat them anyway or else."

"I told you I don't like carrots. Daddy never puts them on my plate and he won't make me eat them," Lizzy said.

"Do you like a spanking? I can turn you over my knee so fast that it'll make you dizzy. I said eat those carrots."

Rachel's eyes narrowed into slits. She was almost as tall as Griffin at five feet eleven inches. Her black hair came straight from a bottle and her eyes were dark brown. No little girl was about to refuse to do something she told her to do.

Lizzy shook her head.

Rachel jerked her up by the arm, bent her over her lap, and swatted her twice. She plopped her back down on the chair hard enough to make a thud.

So that's what a spanking feels like, Lizzy thought, but she didn't cry. She'd heard about spankings but she'd never had one. She'd asked Nana Rita about them, but Nana Rita said spankings were for really bad things. Little girls who just did something a little bad had to stay in their rooms all afternoon, or sometimes they didn't get to ride their ponies or play with their kittens. Lizzy couldn't wait to tell Annie all about it tomorrow at school.

"I still hate carrots," she said.

"It doesn't matter. If I tell you to eat them, then you will eat them," Rachel said.

"I'm going to my room and I'm not eating them carrots. You can tell my daddy that you whipped me."

Rachel pointed her finger at Lizzy. "I'm not telling him anything and neither are you or you'll get twice as many swats next time. I'm coming back next Saturday to spend the whole day because Marita and Carl need to be away from the ranch. You'll learn to mind me, little girl."

Lizzy raced up to her bedroom and slammed the door.

Julie had trouble getting to sleep that night. She'd found Edna's recipes written neatly in a notebook, along with last year's price of sugar, spices, and jars that she bought at the Walmart store in Gainesville. It wouldn't be so difficult to keep the business going, and it would give her a little extra income.

She finally drifted off at midnight and woke to hear Annie screaming. Fear glued her to the bed for a moment before the adrenaline rush set in. She ran to the bedroom to find Annie as white as a sheet, sitting straight up in bed, her eyes opened so wide they were frightening.

"What is the matter, baby?" Julie tried to soothe her.

"It's a witch. Her name is Edna and she won't die. She's a mean old woman and she hates me because I look like Lizzy. She said she was going to put me in a dark place and never let me out, and she said I was a spawn like Lizzy."

"It was just a dream," Julie said. "You must have overheard Mamie talking today. Edna is dead. She died and is buried at the cemetery here in Saint Jo. She can't put you in a dark place because she's not here."

"Promise?" Annie asked.

"I promise."

"Will you sleep with me?"

"Only tonight."

"Lizzy would sleep with me but she's afraid to come in our house because of that mean, old witch," Annie said.

It must have been a hell of a nightmare, Julie thought as she crawled into the bed and cradled her daughter in her arms.

Chapter 3

Not a leaf was stirring, and the dirt kicked up by Griffin's tractor settled back to the earth quickly. August was even hotter than June and July, and they'd broken heat records during those months. It had been weeks since they'd had rain, and there was none in the next week's forecast. The temperatures had been over the hundred-degree mark for days on end.

Over to his right he could see Paul, one of his hired hands, driving the John Deere to the barbed-wire fence. He made a turn and started another round. Griffin did the same thing in the pasture on the other side of the fence.

Thank goodness for air-conditioned cabs on his tractors or he'd have been spitting dust for a week. While he plowed, his thoughts went to Rachel, who was back at the ranch house, keeping Lizzy. Griffin was thinking about taking their relationship up to the next notch. Lizzy was getting to the age when she needed a mother. The past five years had passed like a blur. Before long, she'd need a woman to talk to about things like sex and boys.

Griffin's brows knit into a solid black line. His little girl and boys? He was frowning when his cell phone rang. He groped in the pocket of his bibbed overalls for the phone. It rang three times before he fished it out of his pocket. "I know it's dinnertime. I'm on my way."

"Dinner is on the bar. I put it out there twenty minutes ago, just like the instructions Marita left me said to do. Several of the hired hands have already been in and eaten. I'm just calling to remind you and Lizzy to come on home to eat," Rachel said.

Every hair on Griffin's neck stood straight up. "Lizzy isn't with me. Isn't she there with you?"

"Haven't seen her all morning. I figured she'd begged to go with you and you let her. You know you spoil her too much, Griff."

"When did you see her last?" Griffin asked.

"I haven't seen her. When I got here you were leaving and said to let her sleep since you two watched a late movie together. At ten I decided she'd slept long enough so I went to wake her and she wasn't there. I checked the barn about fifteen minutes ago to see if she was playing with those miserable cats. But since she wasn't there, I figured she was with you on the tractor," Rachel said.

Griffin stopped the tractor and jogged to his truck parked at the side of the field. His pulse raced and he felt as though a band of steel had tightened around his heart. For some silly reason, Lizzy didn't like Rachel. He'd asked her about it the night before when they were watching a movie and she'd only shrugged.

The ranch was safe, and everyone knew Lizzy. No one could steal her right out of her bedroom, could they? She'd been told that she could not ride her pony except when Griff told her it was okay, and even then, she was never to leave the property.

"Dian?" he said aloud, then discarded the idea. Lizzy's mother had agreed on a settlement and left Lizzy in his care when she was two months old. Surely after five years, she hadn't gotten a maternal itch and come back to steal Lizzy.

The band got tighter and tighter.

He figured that Lizzy was hiding from Rachel and would come out from behind a playhouse made of hay bales when he called her name. He hit the back porch at a run and swung open the door.

Rachel met him, shaking her finger at him. "You give that kid too much freedom, Griffin. She's allowed to run all over the place and ride that pony of hers wherever she wants on the ranch. It's not my fault she's gone. She's spoiled rotten and needs a good solid whipping for scaring us like this."

"No one is whipping my daughter. She'll be punished if she's done something wrong, but there might be an explanation," Griffin said icily.

He went to the bottom of the stairs and called up, "Lizzy! Come down here right now. It's dinnertime."

Silence answered him.

He called her name a dozen times as he went up the steps and checked every bedroom, under the beds, in the back corners of the closets, and even the attic. No Lizzy. By the time he checked the basement, fear had his heart in a vise grip. He hurried out the back door, jumped the fence, and went to the barn.

She'd be in there with her momma cat and the kittens. She had to be. It was the last place she could be unless she'd ridden her pony to one of the far corners of the ranch and gotten hurt. She knew her boundaries and had been told to always put the spare cell phone in her pocket before she left the house.

He grabbed his phone and dialed the number. It rang four times before someone picked up. He let out a whoosh of air.

"Lizzy, where are you?" he demanded before she even said hello.

"This is Rachel. I heard the phone ringing and was about to say hello when you started talking."

He ended the call without another word and began to call Lizzy's name, searching all over the barn—but no Lizzy. He checked the pasture for her pony and found it missing, along with her saddle out of the tack room. Visions of her lying in a pool of blood after a fall raced through his head. He was climbing back down the ladder when kittens gathered around his ankles, meowing and demanding attention. He stepped carefully to keep from stomping a tail or hurting one of them and was already out the door with the phone in his hand to call the Saint Jo police when something stopped him.

There was a yellow kitten in with the black-and-white ones. The old black barn cat that Lizzy called Fluffy always produced black-and-white kittens. Three to five in a litter a couple of times a year. He'd just been out to the barn the day before with Lizzy and they'd played with black-and-white kittens. He turned around abruptly and went back into the barn. Three little kittens with a black mother. He remembered it well because he and Lizzy had watched an old rerun of *The Three Stooges* a few days before and she'd named them Larry, Moe, and Curly. Larry had a black smudge on his nose. Moe had a white streak on his head, and Curly had a white tip on his tail. Now there was one yellow and two black-and-white. Where was Curly?

"Here, kitty, kitty," he called. No more kittens came running.

His phone rang and he snapped it up. "Yes."

"I don't like the way you hung up on me, Griffin. It hurt my feelings and you owe me an apology," Rachel said.

"I'm sorry. I'm worried about Lizzy."

"Well, so am I, but she'll turn up. Come have some dinner and then we'll both go hunt for the little runaway—"

He hung up again and called Marita's cell phone number.

"Hello," she answered.

"Lizzy is missing," he said bluntly. "And there's a yellow cat in our barn with the black-and-white ones."

"Did you call the police? Was it Dian? Did she steal her? Have you gone looking for her? Did she ride her pony?"

"I don't know what's going on. Her pony and saddle are gone, so she's out riding somewhere. The only thing I can find that's weird is that yellow kitten."

"Edna had a yellow cat. She had a notice up in the grocery store for free yellow kittens the week before she died. Didn't you tell me that that schoolteacher bought her place?"

"But it's almost a mile from our property line to the Lassiter place and Lizzy knows better than to ride her pony on the road."

"She knows better, but Annie is all she talks about. Check that house and when I get home we'll comb the rest of the ranch. I'll call the police if you haven't located her in an hour. Dian could be mixed up in this."

"I'm on my way to the Lassiter place. I'll call if I find her."

He didn't go through the house but around it and left a trail of dust behind him as he took off in the truck. He drove to the end of the lane and headed south toward town.

Surely Lizzy hadn't disobeyed him and ridden down the country road that far. Just this past month he'd let her ride the pony out of the yard, and that was with the promise that she'd always have the cell phone in her pocket.

It was a hot Saturday at the end of August.

Not warm.

Not merely hot but stinking hot.

Julie had been outside with a hoe weeding Edna's garden most of the morning. In spite of the heat, the garden was still producing. The squash had golden blossoms the size of saucers, which meant in a few days there would be a crop to make squash relish for Mamie. New cucumbers were two inches long. Just right for bread and butter pickles.

Dust settled into the sweat pouring off her face and neck and found its way into her bra. She wiped the sweat from her brow with the tail of her T-shirt, which had only a few dry patches left. She'd always loved getting her hands dirty, even as a child, so she'd fallen right into taking care of the garden. She loved the feel of the damp earth under her bare feet as she chopped the weeds and turned over the ground around the plants. When she finished, she planned to stretch the garden hose from the back of the house and water the whole area. Then she was having a long bath and reading a good romance novel the rest of the afternoon.

Annie kept making trips inside the house and back out to the garden. She'd talk to Julie for a few minutes, then remember that her dolls needed her and she'd be off to the house again. Julie had figured Annie would be whining all day since it was Saturday and she couldn't see her little friends, but she'd played happily in and out of the house all morning.

The sun was high in the sky and Julie's stomach was beginning to grumble when she finished the job and started toward the back door. That's when she heard tires squealing and a vehicle coming to an abrupt stop on the road in front of her house. She rounded the house in a dead run carrying the hoe with her. Thoughts of Annie disobeying her and running out into the road flooded her mind as she rushed. She shut her eyes and prayed that when she opened them she wouldn't see Annie lying in front of a truck or a car.

She shook her hoe at the truck even before the door opened. Thank God Annie wasn't the reason the driver had come to such an abrupt stop. Julie checked the road, hoping the reckless idiot hadn't hit the momma cat. "What in the hell are you doing driving like that and scaring the bejesus out of me?" she hollered at the truck.

Griffin hopped out of the truck and yelled as he walked toward the yard. "I'm looking for Lizzy. She's been missing all day and we just realized it. I thought she was in the house and everyone else thought she was with me."

Then he really looked at Julie. She was a mess. Red hair escaping that half-assed twist of curls swept up on her head with a crazy-looking plastic clamp. Feet that looked as if they'd never worn shoes or been washed. A stained T-shirt and cut-off jean shorts that could have been rescued from a trash can behind a beer joint. Not a drop of makeup and nothing to make her desirable.

So why in the hell was he thinking about throwing her over his shoulder with her cute little bubble butt pointed up, her red hair swinging behind him at waist level, and her dirty feet kicking the hell out of him? He could even hear her giggling as he swept her away to the loft in his barn and made wild, passionate love to her until they were both so tired they could do nothing but sleep in each other's dirty, sweaty arms.

Julie swiped a hand across her face, smearing dirt and grime. At least he was as dirty as she was, but even then, he was damn sexy. What in the hell was wrong with her? Thinking a man in bibbed overalls and a sleeveless shirt was sexy. She swallowed twice and took two steps closer to him. His blue eyes registered pure worry, and in that moment, she saw him as a father instead of a sexy soldier-slash-cowboy-slash-rancher. Still, her Irish temper got the best of her.

"Well, I haven't seen her since she left school yesterday. Maybe you can't remember where she is like you can't remember when you were Lucky and I was Red and there were no questions? Seems to me you've got selective memory problems these days. Maybe when you came home, you forgot about what you'd done the night before you left," she said.

"Lady, are you crazy? What are you talkin' about? I've never left Saint Jo." He threw up his hands in dismay. "There's a yellow kitten in my barn, one of my black-and-white kittens is missing, and my daughter, Lizzy, is gone. Is she here?"

His heart skipped a beat and his hands went clammy. Why on earth did his body respond to her the way it did? He'd had one crazy wife already and had been fortunate enough to get rid of her with money. He didn't trust women, didn't like red-haired women, and the one standing before him was up to something. So why did he keep having ideas that were so farfetched?

She propped her hands on her hips. "You must have been drunker than I thought that night. You grew your hair back and got six years older but you can't stand there and tell me you don't remember me at all. I was your lucky charm so you'd come home, remember? And I don't know where your daughter is."

Griffin set his jaw and spoke through clenched teeth. "Are you sure you don't have a black kitten and my daughter? I don't care if you are crazy as hell. I just want my daughter. Did she come over here?"

A little dark-haired girl stepped out onto the porch.

Griffin squinted against the hot sun. "Lizzy?"

Annie folded her arms across her chest and tilted her chin down to look at him as mean as she could. Her mother did that when she'd been bad, and it always worked on her. "I'm Annie and you can't have Lizzy. She's mine now. That mean woman hit her."

Before anyone could say another word, Rachel's Mustang came to a screeching halt right behind Griffin's pickup. She bailed out of the car and started into the yard.

Annie puffed out her chest. "I'm Annie, and you are mean and you can't have Lizzy."

"Rachel, there's a restraining order. Luckadeaus can't go on that property," Griffin said.

Rachel kept walking. "I'm not a Luckadeau yet and I can go anywhere I damn well please. Young lady, don't you tell me you aren't Lizzy Luckadeau. I'd know you anywhere and you are in big trouble." Her long strides ate up the ground until she was within a foot of Julie.

"You take another step, lady, and I'll whip your sorry

ass myself. This is my place and you aren't touching my daughter or talking to her like that," Julie said just before Rachel stepped onto her porch.

Rachel stopped and glared at Julie. "What gives you that right? This isn't your property. It belongs to that old witch, Edna."

"She died and I bought it. It is my property and you are not welcome. Annie, what are you talking about? Who hit Lizzy?" Julie asked.

Annie pointed her finger. "Is that her daddy's girlfriend?"

"Yes, I am. You know that, Lizzy. What kind of game are you playing?"

"I'm not Lizzy. I'm Annie. Momma, tell her I'm Annie."

"This is my daughter. Go away and leave us alone," Julie said.

Annie narrowed her eyes at Rachel. "You tried to make Lizzy eat carrots and she don't like carrots. I like carrots and she likes peas. I don't like peas, but my momma don't hit me two times on my bottom when I don't eat peas. That woman hit Lizzy, Momma."

Julie glared at Rachel, her mouth set in a firm line. "You hit a child? One that didn't even belong to you? What kind of woman are you?"

Rachel puffed out her chest and looked down at Julie. "She'll be my child before long and it's none of your business."

Griffin watched from the corner of the yard. Everything was moving like slow motion in an old television movie. Rachel had spanked Lizzy because she wouldn't eat her carrots. Rachel was screaming at Julie, and Julie was protecting a child that wasn't even hers like a momma cougar. It was all surreal.

"Could you two stop your fighting long enough to tell me if Lizzy is safe?" he yelled.

"Where is Lizzy?" Julie finally asked Annie.

"She rode her pony to the fence and we put it behind the shed. She is hiding in my bedroom. I took her some crackers for breakfast and we've been playing all day, but we're hungry. Can we make a sandwich now?" Annie answered innocently.

"Will you please tell her to come out here?" Julie asked.

"Please, Annie." Griffin exhaled loudly. At least his daughter was safe.

Rachel frowned. "That *is* Lizzy. She's playing some kind of crazy game with you. Are you stupid, woman?"

"Lady, I'm not known for patience, especially when it comes to child abuse, so you'd do well to hush and let me get to the bottom of this," Julie said hotly.

In spite of the hundred-plus-degree weather, Rachel wrapped her arms around her body as if to stave off a chill. That sawed-off, filthy woman looked as if she was about to wield that hoe like a lance in her direction.

Lizzy stepped out of the doorway and reached for Annie's hand. "Hi, Daddy. I don't like her and she hit me."

Rachel stared blankly at the two little girls. "There's two of them? Griffin, you've got some explaining to do." She turned on him.

"Lizzy, why did you run away?" Griffin asked.

Lizzy's chin quivered. "Because she was going to keep me today, and I don't like carrots, and she said I had to eat them. She said I was spoiled and I don't like her and she already spanked me one time and I don't want her to whip me again because I don't like carrots."

"Griffin Luckadeau, that woman isn't even Lizzy's mother, and you allow her to whip her?" Julie joined the girls on the porch.

"If I keep her, then I'll discipline her," Rachel said.

"Settle down, both of you. To hell with it. Call the damn cops. Let them put me in jail. I'm coming onto your property," Griffin said as he plowed across the yard.

Julie turned her attention away from Rachel and toward Griffin instead. "I never said you couldn't come on my property. I don't have a restraining order on anyone. But that woman better get off my land. I won't need a restraining order if she doesn't because I'll take care of it myself."

That gave Rachel enough time to hurry to the safety of her car.

Griffin gathered Lizzy into his arms. "I'm so sorry, sweetheart. I'm so sorry."

His phone rang in the middle of the hugging. "Hello?"

"Did you find her? Is she all right?" Marita asked.

"She's right here at Edna's old place and she's fine. I'm bringing her home now," he said.

"I'm not going home," Lizzy said with a mean look toward Rachel. "Not 'til Nana Rita gets there. She won't let *her* be mean to me."

Rachel rolled down the window but kept her finger on the button. "Griffin, you've got to take that kid in hand. She's playing you. I only swatted her twice and she deserved it."

"We'll talk later," he said.

Lizzy's eyes grew wide. "Don't make me stay with her no more."

"Rachel won't be coming back to the ranch. Now let's go home," Griffin reassured her.

"Not ever. You promise?" Lizzy asked.

Griffin headed toward the truck. "I promise."

Annie set up a sobbing howl. "But she's my friend. You can't take her away."

Lizzy began to cry right along with her. "Daddy, Annie is my friend. Can she come home with me?"

Griffin looked at Julie. Her curly, red hair was wet with sweat, her bare feet filthy, her cut-off jeans bleach-stained, and her T-shirt had holes in it. Honest to God, he'd never seen the woman before Lizzy's first day of school, and he would definitely remember her if he had. A man would have to be stone blind, stupid, or both to forget someone like Julie Donavan.

"If I leave now, it's over," Rachel yelled.

"I am a father. You've known that since day one." Griffin raised his voice above the din of the girls' crying so that she could hear him.

Rachel rolled up the window and sped away, leaving nothing but a puff of road dust in her wake.

"You really don't remember me?" Julie asked from the porch.

"Sure I remember you. You're Lizzy's teacher and you were at church last Sunday. I don't know what you're talking about 'growing my hair' back. It's been like this since I was a kid."

She sat down on the porch. "Did you get amnesia in Iraq?"

He was busy putting Lizzy in the passenger seat and

shutting the door. When she said *Iraq*, he jerked his head around and frowned. "*I* never went to Iraq."

Julie's green eyes locked with his blue ones and the distance across the yard disappeared. "Then the uniform was a hoax to pick up women?"

Griffin stopped. "Six years ago, my identical twin brother went to Iraq. He was killed two days after he got there. Are you mistaking me for Graham?"

"Holy shit. Two of you?" Julie whispered. Now it made sense. No wonder Griffin hadn't recognized her.

"Yes, ma'am. Graham always was attracted to redheads. You thought I was Graham, and you've come back here to lay claim to your kid's share of the Lucky Clover, haven't you? Well, honey, you've got a surprise in store. It ain't happenin'," he said with enough chill in his voice to drop the temperature forty degrees.

"Mr. Luckadeau, until this moment, I had no idea that there were two of you, and had I known, I damn sure wouldn't have taken a job in Saint Jo. You leave me and my child alone. I don't want a damn thing you've got," Julie declared.

Tears dripped down Annie's face. "Don't be mad at Lizzy's daddy. Lizzy is my friend. We traded kittens so we can be friends. I want her to come and play with me."

Lizzy leaned out the truck window and pointed toward the porch. "I want Annie to be my friend. You can't take her away from me."

Griffin threw up his hands. "Good God, what are we going to do?"

"Right now, *you* are going to take Lizzy home, and *I'm* going to take Annie inside to eat lunch. We'll sort this out another day. I've had about all I can stand for this one."

"She can come back and play, can't she, Momma?" Annie sobbed.

"Lizzy is welcome in this house anytime she wants to come," Julie said.

Annie stopped crying and waved at Lizzy, who had settled back down in the truck.

Griffin drove away and Julie sat down on the porch with a heavy thud. She propped her elbows on her knees. Lizzy was welcome at her house, but she'd be damned to hell for all eternity if she ever gave Annie permission to go to Lizzy's house. She didn't give a damn if Griffin or—what was his brother's name?—Graham were as rich as Midas or if they lived in a tent on the banks of the Red River.

Graham. That was Annie's biological father, and he'd been killed a few days after that motel night. Julie didn't believe in fate. She'd made her own way in life, accepted the consequences for her own mistakes, gathered laurels for her victories. But if it wasn't fate meddling in her life, then how in the hell had she gotten pregnant from a rebellious one-night stand and wound up six years later living next door to the man's twin brother? That was too much to chalk up to coincidence.

"Why?" she muttered.

"Because I wanted a black-and-white kitten and Lizzy wanted a yellow one," Annie answered.

Lizzy ran into the house and straight into Nana Rita's arms. "I ran away but it's all better now acause Daddy said that Rachel won't be coming back to the ranch. She won't spank me no more. Annie's momma said she was going to whip her ass."

Marita looked up at Griffin for an explanation.

He rolled his eyes. "Those are naughty words," he said to Lizzy.

Lizzy went right on talking. "We traded kittens and Annie has got a black-and-white one now. And I played in her room today with her Barbie dolls. I'm hungry. Can I have a sandwich?"

"Griffin?" Marita raised a black eyebrow.

"It's a mess. One big, hellacious mess. This lady—"

Lizzy piped up. "She's not a lady. She's my teacher and I'm going to grow up and be just like her and I don't like Rachel and Daddy said she's not going to spank me no more."

"Lizzy, that is enough." Griffin's tone left no room for argument. "As I was saying, the lady who bought the old Lassiter place is Lizzy's new friend's mother and her teacher."

Lizzy followed Marita to the kitchen and crawled up on a chair on the other side of the island. "Rachel screamed at Annie acause she thought she was me and Rachel is mad at Daddy now."

"I imagine she is." Marita smiled.

"There's a bigger problem over there," Griffin said. "Can you make a couple of sandwiches for me? I missed dinner because I was trying to find this runaway kid. Lizzy, don't you ever, ever do that again. And no matter where you go on this ranch, you take that phone with you. Your punishment for running away is that you can't ride your pony for a month and you can't leave the yard for a whole week. Is that understood?

And I don't want to hear dirty words coming out of your pretty mouth again."

She nodded seriously. "Then Annie will have to come play with me since I can't go play with her. Did you get her phone number so I can call her up and tell her that?"

"I did not," he said. His world was listing to one side and he wondered if it'd ever be right again.

"Her mother's name is Julie Donavan. Just call the 'perator on the phone and ask her for the number," Lizzy said.

"I think you've had enough excitement for one day. *We* certainly have," Marita said.

"I expect you want to talk to me without little corn's big ears?" Griffin said.

Marita nodded. "Bring your sandwich to the backyard and I'll clean up this mess your woman left behind after we talk. Next time I'll take Lizzy with me. It's less trouble than having a heart attack or cleaning up after a messy cook," she fussed.

"I want to go, too," Lizzy said.

"You eat your sandwich right here at the bar, young lady, and then you're going to put on your bathing suit and play in your little pool where I can see you all the time," Marita said.

When they got to the backyard, Griffin was glad to sit and let the adrenaline settle down. He bit off a chunk of sandwich and chewed slowly. Too much had happened too fast. His nerves were frayed worse than the hemline of that Donavan woman's shorts. She had been a sight—wielding that hoe like a weapon and screaming like a momma mountain lion protecting her young.

Marita sat in a lawn chair beside him. "Talk."

"Our new neighbor appears to be someone Graham

met and slept with just before he went to Iraq. That's why her little girl looks so much like Lizzy. They really could be twins but—oh my God, I just realized they are cousins. Lizzy is a little taller. Annie's face is a bit rounder. She's Graham's daughter. DNA couldn't prove it any better."

"Maybe she was just as shocked as you were when she found out she was living in the same area as a Luckadeau. Ever think about giving her the benefit of the doubt?"

"Hell no! She's like all women. Out for what they can get. Look what Dian did," he said.

"You been burned, son, but that's unfair. We're not all like that," Marita huffed.

"Sorry, I didn't mean you," Griffin apologized.

"Apology accepted. What makes you think she's like all women anyway?"

"Look at that place. No one who had any dignity would buy it or live there. Besides, she was filthy," Griffin said.

"What had she been doing?"

"Hell, I don't know what she was doing. She came around the house with a hoe in her hand like she was going to kill me with the damned thing. Then she started yelling and Rachel showed up and they were both yelling and Annie was refusing to get Lizzy, and then Lizzy came out and there was another big fight. It was worse than a three-ring circus on *Jerry Springer*. I thought Rachel and Julie were going to duke it out right there in the yard," he said. No way was he about to admit that he'd been attracted to the schoolteacher even when she was a sweaty mess.

Marita laughed so hard her face hurt. "I would love to have seen that."

"It wasn't pretty," Griffin said, a smile finally tickling the corners of his mouth.

"Who gives a hoot? It would have been a beautiful sight to me because it got rid of Rachel. How big is this redhead?"

"Little ole bitty thing. She might weigh a hundred and twenty soaking wet, and she was sweating like a boar hog. I was glad I was upwind from her. She looked like she would have smelled horrible," Griffin said.

"She must have a dose of Irish in her with a temper like that, plowing into a big old horse of a woman when she's that little. It would have been a hoot to see Rachel get her ass whooped by a little woman. And she was carrying a hoe? Must be a working woman, huh? I bet she'd been weeding the garden in the backyard. What set her off and made her so mad?"

Griffin rubbed his aching forehead with the palm of his hand. "After me, it was the idea that Rachel had whipped Lizzy."

Marita pointed her finger at Griffin. "Let me tell you, if that woman ever lays a hand on Lizzy again, Julie Donavan won't have to touch her. I'll take care of her myself. Now why is it that you've formed an opinion without giving her a chance?"

"Because in order for her to have Graham's daughter, she had to have been with him at least once. He left here for Dallas one day and left the next day for Iraq. She must have been a one-night stand."

Marita started back into the house. "She's raising her daughter and has a respectable job. Sounds like she'd fight a circle saw for her child or yours. Your wife left her child and hasn't been back to see her since, don't even care enough to call on her birthday or send a Christmas present. Who's the bad person here and who's the good mother? You best be rethinkin' your judgment, son."

Griffin threw up his hands in defeat. "This has been a helluva day. I'm going to the field to sort it all out."

"Might be a good idea," Marita threw over her shoulder.

Chapter 4

A BREEZE BLEW ACROSS THE PORCH AS JULIE AND ANNIE waited for Mamie. Like most five-year-old kids, Annie couldn't be still with the excitement of going to her first rodeo. Finally, they heard a car, and Annie ran to the edge of the yard to look up the road.

"It's her! I know it's her and now we can go," Annie said.

Mamie came to a stop without turning into the driveway and waved at Annie.

"Buckle up, cowgirls. We're on our way to the big Chisholm Trail Rodeo," she called.

Julie fastened Annie's belt in the back seat before she opened the door on the passenger side of the car.

"Why do they call it all that, and do men really ride on the backs of bulls?" Annie asked.

"The Chisholm Trail came through here from San Antonio, ran through Fort Worth, and went right up 81, through Oklahoma. That's why they call it the Chisholm Trail Rodeo. Anyway, the trail had feeder trails and the folks who came through Saint Jo back then stopped and watered herds and men at the square. It's all part of the local history," Mamie explained. "Which reminds me. That deal about the winter festival that we had to postpone has been rescheduled for Sunday afternoon. It's the only time Clarice and Everett can work it into their schedules. I'm sure they're hoping that no one will take time out on Sunday, and they'll vote the idea down."

"I'll be there," Julie said. "Might as well dive right in and get in the middle of the town's arguments. Nothing like being on the wrong side to get me fired next year."

"You ain't gettin' fired, girl. Mrs. Amos runs the school and she told me you're doin' a fine job."

"The school board might have something to say about that," Julie said.

"Maybe so, but not a one of them wants to see Mrs. Amos turn in her resignation. If she likes you, darlin', you won't be gettin' a pink slip."

"How'd she get so much pull?" Julie asked.

"She squatted in a field one day and they built the school around her. I can't remember when Mrs. Amos wasn't at the school. She taught for years. Was mine and Griffin's third-grade teacher. Teachers come and go. So do superintendents. But not Mrs. Amos. She's been there since my parents were in school."

"Might be nothing could keep me here," she said.

"Want to talk about it?"

"Not with the back seat driver listenin' in," Julie said.

Mamie had proven to be a good friend the past weeks. She had made a special trip to see Annie with the news that Lizzy had been grounded to her yard for a week and couldn't ride her pony for a whole month—and never back down to Annie's house. Annie had been fine with it until Friday when school let out, and then the pouting began. She missed Lizzy and Chuck, and why couldn't they just call their parents and see if they could come for a play day at her house?

The Saturday night rodeo was a nice diversion to help her get through the weekend.

Julie hadn't been too sure about what to wear to the shindig. When she thought about a rodeo, she pictured women in jeans and shirts with pearl snaps and boots. She had the jeans. A tank top with sequins scattered on the neckline had to work for the shirt. The only boots she had were the rubber ones she slipped over her high-heeled shoes when it rained. She had put on her sandals. Two out of three wasn't bad.

Annie was going to see the horses and the bulls, and she would have worn a Cinderella gown if Julie had let her. Julie talked her into a pair of jeans, a T-shirt with Ariel on it, and sandals.

Mamie wore jeans, boots, and a pearl-snap sleeveless shirt. Three out of three. Did that mean she would go home with the cowboy that night? Julie didn't care if she did.

"Anyone I know going to be here?" she asked Mamie cautiously.

"Just everyone in the whole area who likes rodeos," she said.

Julie bit her lip to keep back a groan. That meant Griffin for sure. He was a rancher, and they did like cows and bullshit, didn't they?

Annie spotted Lizzy before she was even out of the car and began to tug on Julie's hand. Julie looked up and saw Lizzy dragging an older lady across the parking lot toward them. Both little girls stopped a foot from each other, smiles on their faces and their eyes all aglitter. They reached out at the same time and laced their fingers together. From that point, there was no separating them.

The lady held out her hand. "I'm Marita. I've been keeping house at the Lucky Clover since before the twins were born. I take care of Lizzy. You must be Annie's mother. Her name comes up about every five seconds at the ranch."

Her handshake was firm.

"I'm Julie Donavan. It's the same at my house. Lizzy and Chuck are my daughter's new best friends."

"Nana Rita, Miss Julie is the teacher that Daddy told you about. I want to grow up to be just like her," Lizzy said in awe. "Can we sit together, please, Nana Rita, please, please, please?"

"We will all sit together if that's all right with Miss Julie and Miss Mamie." Marita looked at Annie. The child was the image of her father, Graham. His face had always been a bit more round than Griffin's and he'd been just a shade shorter. Wait until Deborah Luckadeau found out there was a remnant of her son still on the earth. She'd be ecstatic.

"Of course it's all right. Is Griff riding tonight?" Mamie asked.

They found seats near the top of the bleachers at the far end for the three adults. The two little girls sat right in front of them.

"If there's the smell of a bull ride within fifty miles, Griffin will be there. He's already drawn his number and got the meanest, blackest bull I've ever seen. Horns out to here"—Marita measured as far as her hands would reach—"and evil in his eyes."

"Where's Carl?" Mamie asked.

"Right down there with him. Egging him on. Making sure he has his lucky clover charm pinned to his hat," Marita said.

"My daddy can stay on a bull eight seconds. That's a long time," Lizzy bragged to Annie.

"Is eight seconds a long, long time?" Annie asked.

Julie wished she could find a big, black cave, drag Annie in it with her, and pull a rock over the entrance. She'd have found an excuse not to go to the rodeo if she'd known Griffin was riding. She eyed Mamie from the corner of her eye. Was she friend or foe? A lamb or a wolf dressed in lamb's clothing?

The announcer gave the name of the first rider and the bull, and a chute opened. Julie had seen bull riding on television when she passed through the living room and her father was channel surfing. She wasn't totally ignorant when it came to the sport, but nothing prepared her for the excitement. The smell, the dust, the clowns, the cheering all around her, Annie's eyes and Lizzy's shouts—they all combined to make her heart pump faster than it had since the fight with Griffin and Rachel. Julie looked around but she couldn't spot the hussy.

"And now, riding old Lucifer himself, the black bull straight from the back forty acres of hell, is Griffin Luckadeau, owner and operator of the Lucky Clover Ranch. Griffin is our three-year winner in the bull-riding contest. Let 'er rip, boys."

Lucifer came out of the chute with his head down and his back feet off the ground. The rider and the bull were one as the animal bucked and Griffin expertly rode the motion. One second seemed like eternity to Julie as she watched Griffin's hat go sailing out into the dust. The next second, she noticed that his white streak flopped back and forth as the bull tried to disengage him from his back. By the third second, Julie had stopped breathing.

The fourth, she didn't even hear the girls jumping up and down and screaming for him to stay with it. Fifth, sixth and seventh, she couldn't even blink.

It was as if her life flashed before her in those eight seconds. She didn't want Griffin to die—but was she attracted to him because he looked so much like his brother that it was unreal, or was it for himself? She wanted him to win the contest because he was a good father and a hell of a bull rider. One part of her wanted to run away from the whole state of Texas, maybe get lost in the backwoods of Montana. The other half was glued to the seat until the ride was finished, all the while thinking about that old song that said something about not calling him a cowboy until you'd seen him ride. *Whew!* If Griffin was as good in bed as he was on that bull, then… She made herself stop at that point and watch the last second of the ride.

"And that's it, ladies and gentlemen. Griffin Luckadeau has stayed with it eight seconds. How many of you up there in the stands think he superglued his sorry old cowboy hind end to that bull? We'll see how many points he's accumulated. The scores are coming in. Looks like Luckadeau has a score of eighty-five points. That'll be a hard score to beat, but it can be done. Next up is…"

Julie managed to suck enough air into her lungs to keep herself from fainting. "Men! They're beyond stupid. His brain must have been damaged at birth."

Mamie nudged her arm. "But when that bull was twistin', spinnin', and swervin', your old heart stopped for a while, didn't it?"

"Crazy damned world, ain't it? We know they're

stupid, but it excites us when we watch something like that," Marita said. "No wonder so many women chase after the rodeo like—" She stopped dead when she noticed both little girls looking up at her and taking in every single word.

"Did Daddy win?" Lizzy asked.

"He's got the most points right now. We'll have to see if anyone makes more," Marita answered.

"That bull had big old horns. Does the one me and you ride have horns that big, and where did you get them boots?" Annie asked Lizzy. "I want a pair just like them."

"Me and you don't get to ride bulls. Daddy said I could ride the sheep but I didn't want to. Tim and Richie, that's my cousins, they ride the mutton," Lizzy said.

"What's a mutton and does it have horns?" Annie asked.

"It's a sheep and no, it don't have horns, and you didn't live on a ranch, did you?" Lizzy asked.

"I grew up at Grammy's house. Momma, is Grammy's house a ranch?" Annie turned around.

"No, it's in town. We don't know much about ranches or rodeos," Julie answered. Her eyes were glued to the cowboy with the white streak in his hair coming up the bleachers straight toward them. Was she never to have a peaceful moment again? Everywhere she went, there he was, his scowl reminding her that he trusted a Texas rattler more than he ever would her.

"Well, where did you get them boots?" Annie asked again.

Lizzy held her foot up and yelled when Griffin was halfway up the stands. "Daddy, Annie needs some boots like me. Where did we buy these boots?"

"At the western wear store in Nocona," Griffin said.

Good Lord, what was that woman doing at the rodeo and why was she sitting with Marita and Lizzy? Had the whole world gone mad? He slapped his leg with his dusty cowboy hat, more out of anger than to knock the arena dust from it. Tonight, she looked like a rodeo woman in her tight-fitting jeans and her hair all fixed. All she needed was a pair of boots and she'd fit right into the scene. He didn't want to find her attractive—it would make her job of fleecing him too easy—but his eyes wouldn't look away from her sitting there with the two little girls. Life sure had gotten complicated in the past few weeks.

Mamie scooted away from Julie, making a space between them. "We'll make room for you to sit. You did good out there. Bet nobody can beat that score."

Griffin had two choices: sit down or refuse to sit beside the woman. For the latter, Marita would have his head on a paper plate for being rude, so that actually left no choice at all.

His arm brushed against Julie's when he sat down and his stomach knotted up worse than when the chute opened for the bull ride. "Hello," he said stiffly.

Julie pulled her arm tighter to her side. She had to stop letting her mind wander to forbidden places because his touch was so damn hot. "Hello, Mr. Luckadeau. Just to set things straight, I called the courthouse and there's no restraining order now. Lizzy can come over anytime she wants."

"Thank you."

"You are welcome."

"Now, see there, that didn't kill either of you," Mamie said.

Julie shot her a dirty look. Mamie had known all

along that Griffin was riding and had probably told Marita to wait for them. She knew the story of what had happened when Lizzy ran away, so why had she put her new friend in such a pickle?

Griffin sat erect, his back straight and his arms folded across his chest. Julie looked a damn sight better than she had the last time he saw her. She'd tamed that kinky red hair. Her waist was small, her hips rounded, and she filled out the top of that knit shirt really well. He'd never been attracted to small women or red-haired ones before. That was Graham's type, not his. But she smelled really good, and when his arm touched hers, the heat that radiated between them was hotter than the weather by far. He flat out couldn't understand why he'd lost control of his own body. Why did he ache for something that wasn't possible? And why the hell couldn't she stay on her five acres and stop showing up at every function he attended? There was no way she was in Saint Jo because of the small-town charm. She had a reason.

Julie watched the next three bull riders, but her heart didn't beat as wildly as it had when Griffin sat on top of nearly two tons of mean bull. Though she kept her eyes straight ahead, she was more interested in keeping at least an inch of space between any of her body parts and Griffin's. If he touched her again, she was afraid she'd either swoon like a heroine in a romance book or else go up in white-hot flames. He smelled like aftershave, mint gum, and sweat—the combination a bit too heady for her—and when his arm touched hers, it created a warm, gushy feeling down deep in her gut.

She determined that she wouldn't lose control again, especially with a man who looked at her like she was beneath him. She'd finish out the year at the school and then move on. That would be the goal that kept her from giving in to the desire to drag him off to the nearest motel room and see if he really was a cowboy in every sense of the word.

"Y'all stayin' around for the dance?" Mamie asked Marita.

"Honey, that's why I come to this thing. Carl and I love to dance. We'll be here until the last song is sung or there's no more leather on the soles of our boots. You?"

"Oh, yes, ma'am. We surely will," Mamie said.

Julie wilted. She'd had no idea there was a dance after the rodeo or she would have brought her own vehicle. Now she had to stay or it would inconvenience Mamie.

"Yippee!" Lizzy yelled. "Annie, we get to stay for the dance. You know how to two-step? I do and I'll teach you."

They put their heads together, whispering back and forth. Blood was thicker than water, Julie thought as she tried to catch what they were saying, but it was impossible above the din of the crowd. That, plus another bull came out of the chute, all four feet off the ground.

Griffin moaned.

"What's your problem?" She flipped around and stared at him. By damn, he had no right to get mad because she was staying for a dance.

"Four feet off the dirt. That's extra points. If he stays on eight seconds, he could beat my time."

"Poor baby," she said.

"Don't you take that tone with me," he said.

"And so the peace ends," Mamie said.

He pointed his finger at Mamie. "You stay out of this, Mamie Pickett."

Mamie slapped his hand away.

"The little girls are behaving better than you two. Am I going to have to put you in a corner?" Marita teased.

Julie almost blushed but got it under control.

Griffin grunted and went back to watching the ride.

When it was all said and done and the points tallied up, he lost his three-year title to a nineteen-year-old boy from Muenster and gave it up with a wave of his hat from the stands. The kid beat him by one point and that was only because the bull had had all four feet straight up. It didn't keep Griffin from feeling old at twenty-eight.

Lizzy reached back and patted him on the leg. "It's all right, Daddy. You done good."

Annie patted him on the other one. "Yep, you done good."

He looked at Julie.

"Hey, cowboy, I don't know anything about bulls or riding them. If that boy beat you by only one point, I'd say you're doing good for your age," she said.

"Ouch!"

"Well, how old are you?" she asked.

"Twenty-eight, last birthday," he said.

She blushed. She'd had no idea six years ago that Graham had been that much younger than she was. Good grief, he had been just a year past the legal age to buy beer. And here she was entertaining notions of jumping Griffin Luckadeau's bones. Well, that just ended that idiotic idea. He was six years younger than she was—not jailbait, but too damn young.

"Just a baby," she muttered.

"And how old are you?" he asked.

"You don't ask a woman that," Marita said.

"Forty?" he asked.

"Ouch!" she said.

"Do you need a Band-Aid, Momma?" Annie asked.

"No, I'm fine," Julie said.

When the rodeo ended, the band set up and the dance began. Marita left Lizzy in Griffin's care and went to find Carl to dance with her. Mamie told Julie she'd meet her at the car when the last song ended and disappeared into the crowd.

"I want to dance, Daddy, and you can dance the first one with me and Annie both," Lizzy said.

"It's a deal. You going to sit up here and watch, or dance?" he asked Julie.

"Oh, honey, I'm not into spectator sports except bull riding. I'm a participator. I'm dancing. It'll be my favorite part of the night," Julie said. Griffin Luckadeau wasn't about to get one step ahead of her, not even if she had to lie. Forty, indeed!

"All four of us on the first dance! Come on, Annie." Lizzy grabbed her hand and they ran down the bleachers like little mountain goats headed for a watering hole.

The band geared up with Gretchen Wilson's "Redneck Woman."

"Seems fitting," Julie said, as they walked up to the girls on the arena floor.

Annie and Lizzy each grabbed one of her hands and one of Griffin's and began to wiggle and dance, moving as though they had no bones in their little bodies and giggling all the while. Julie stood to one side and moved with the beat of the music but spent more time laughing at the girls than she did actually dancing.

When the song ended and the band went right into an oldie, "I Can't Stop Loving You," Lizzy dragged Annie off to see her two cousins, Tim and Richie.

"We got to show them your lucky streak," she said.

"But Jane didn't see it yet and she didn't say it was lucky," Annie said.

"Jane?" Julie looked at Griffin.

"That would be my cousin's new wife. She and Lizzy hit it off from the beginning. Want to dance?"

She took a step forward and put her arm on his shoulder. He tucked her hand inside his and drew her closer. He was so tall that she could lay her head on his chest and listen to his heartbeat. She shut her eyes and tried to let the music soothe her nerves, but it was a useless endeavor. Griffin threw off an aura that surrounded her with wanton desire, and even though she hadn't danced in years, she wanted something more. Griffin Luckadeau could dance even better than he could ride a bull. His hand on her back would leave a burn mark, but waltzing around the arena was worth it.

The singer talked about living her life in dreams of yesterday. Griffin was guilty of doing that, at least until he'd met Julie. Now he wasn't so sure where his dreams were. She had to have a hidden agenda for moving to Saint Jo. Anything else was too much coincidence, and he did not believe in fate. He'd just have to enjoy the dances and then be very, very careful.

"Where are the girls? Are they all right?" she asked, but didn't look up at him for fear he'd see the color in her cheeks and know it had nothing to do with the warm summer Texas wind.

"Lizzy knows her boundaries, and believe me, she's

finding out what happens when she goes past them. Besides, I can see them over there talking to my cousin's kids."

His voice was soft and low, almost sexy. His breath kissed that soft spot on her neck, and it took all her willpower not to think about sex—or the lack of it. She wouldn't!

She forced herself to think about the children. Lizzy's cousins were also Annie's. Annie had been hers alone from day one and Julie wasn't ready to share.

A woman tapped Julie on the shoulder. "Hey, can I cut in?"

Julie stepped back and into the arms of a tall, blond cowboy with Luckadeau eyes at the same time a petite brunette started dancing with Griffin.

"Hello, I'm Slade Luckadeau from over in Ringgold. I'm Griffin's cousin. That'd be my wife, Jane, dancing with Griff. Don't remember seeing you around here."

"Just moved to Saint Jo. I'm a schoolteacher there."

Annie tugged on her mother's jean leg. "Momma, I got to go to the bathroom."

"Hi, Miss Lizzy," Slade said.

"I'm Annie. I got to pee real bad, Momma."

"Excuse me," Julie said and walked away with Annie, leaving Slade with his blue eyes bugged out.

The song ended, and Slade pulled Griffin and Jane to the side. "Look over there, Jane. See that redhead with Lizzy?"

"Sure. Who is she?" Jane asked.

"That would be Julie Donavan, Lizzy's new teacher," Griffin said.

"That ain't Lizzy," Slade said.

"Of course it is," Jane said.

At that very moment, Lizzy tugged on Jane's hand. "Jane! You got to meet Annie. She's got a streak in her hair like mine and we need for you to tell us if hers is a lucky streak too and she lives in Saint Jo and her momma is my teacher and her name is Julie." She took a deep breath and ran off to play with Tim and Richie again.

Jane cocked her head to one side. "Griff?"

Jane was a small woman, like Julie, and had to look up at him, but that didn't prevent her from demanding answers. For a split second, Griffin imagined Julie in a reverse situation and realized she'd be doing the same thing Jane was.

"It's a complicated story," he said with a sigh.

"Then you'd better start talking," Slade said.

Griffin tried to condense it into one sentence but it took three to cover the whole story. Strange, when he thought about it at home, it took him in never-ending circles that had a lot more detail and description. "Apparently Graham had a one-night stand, and as you can see, it produced a child. The woman bought the Lassiter property and you can't tell me it's a coincidence that she showed up here. She probably found out who we were and is here to try to get half the ranch for that child."

Slade clapped him on the shoulder. "You be careful, Griffin. Remember that schoolteacher who had her eye on Beau's ranch? She was all sugar and spice, but when push came to shove, she just wanted his property. Julie is probably thinkin' she'll wind up with her daughter's half of that ranch."

"That's exactly what I said. Marita got all up in my face about it. Said I should give her a chance. I just can't do it. It was Graham who liked red hair, not me. It was Graham who was the wild child, and I do not think for a minute that her showing up in Saint Jo is fate or a coincidence," Griffin said.

Jane watched Julie walk back across the grass with a careful eye. The woman looked harmless and the little girl was a Luckadeau for sure, but the Luckadeau men weren't always smart when it came to women. Slade had sure enough had his stupid moment with a woman before Jane married him. Then there was the schoolteacher that had almost ruined Beau Luckadeau's life. She and Milli would have to keep a close eye on the new woman. She had to have a reason for moving to Saint Jo, and Milli and Jane were just the women to find it out.

"Don't you go pretendin' to be the good boy and Graham the wild one." Slade punched Griffin on the shoulder. "Want me to give dates and times about when you weren't a good boy? Don't forget we're the same age."

Jane smiled at Julie. "I'm Jane Luckadeau. This is my husband, Slade. He's one of a gazillion of Griff's cousins. We live over in Ringgold."

Her words were pleasant, but her tone was something else, and only another woman could understand. Julie nodded. "I'm pleased to meet you. So there are more Luckadeau men than just Griffin and Graham? I had no idea there was but one Luckadeau in the world until I moved to Saint Jo. Excuse me while I go find Mamie," she said.

The music started up again, and Slade and Jane danced off to the other side of the arena. Griffin reached out and touched Julie's arm before she'd taken two steps.

Heat flowed through her and sparks lit up the night like it was the Fourth of July rather than September.

"Might as well dance with me," he said.

"Mercy dance for the old woman?" Julie asked.

"Mercy dance for the bull ridin' loser?" he shot right back.

She melted into his arms and they two-stepped around the arena. With her head against his chest for the second time that night, she finally admitted how easy it would be to give in to her emotions. Griffin was a fine-looking cowboy, and dancing with him was next door to heaven. Her thoughts went around and around like a merry-go-round and she got dizzy just trying to make sense of them.

"So tell me how you met my brother," Griffin said.

Something about his tone brought her out of the clouds and down to earth with a thud. How dare he take that high-and-mighty judgmental tone with her? All the heat she'd been feeling from his proximity boiled into fury.

"I was in the process of a divorce, and I really don't owe you an explanation. I don't give a damn what you think of me. I'm a decent person."

"So you were married and you still slept with Graham?" Griffin asked.

"I was getting divorced."

"Why'd your husband divorce you?"

"He didn't. I was divorcing him."

"Why?" Griffin asked.

"You're just full of questions, aren't you, cowboy? Where's your wife?"

"Hey, now, that's personal."

"And your questions aren't?" Julie asked.

"Touché, honey."

She looked up to find his blue eyes trained on her face. "So the bull rider knows a big word. Don't call me *honey*. If it's an endearment, you don't have the right. If it's sarcasm, I damn sure don't want to be hearin' it. I'm not a hooker or a whore. I slept with your brother one time. It might have been wrong, but it brought me the biggest joy of my life. If I hadn't, I wouldn't have Annie, and she is my world, so I do not regret my decision to go to bed with Graham."

Griffin nodded. "Okay. My wife left when Lizzy was tiny. For ten thousand dollars, she signed all rights over to me and she's never come back. Her name was Dian. She was nineteen when Lizzy was born and hated the whole wife-slash-mother scene. I paid her to relinquish her rights to Lizzy. The court called it a final settlement, but in all honesty, she sold the baby to me."

Julie laid her head back on his chest. "My husband, Derrick, was cheating. I caught him and filed for divorce. I had a one-time, one-night fling with a soldier that I let pick me up at a bar. The next week, my husband begged for a second chance and I gave it to him. For nine months, I thought that my baby belonged to him, never even gave it a second thought. When Annie was born, it was very evident she didn't belong to my husband. *He* divorced *me* that time."

"I bet it *was* pretty damn evident," Griffin chuckled.

Julie changed the subject. She didn't want to remember Graham. She wanted to forget him—but how could she when his duplicate held her in his arms in a slow country dance? "Where did you get that white streak? Slade is so blond."

"All the other Luckadeaus are blond and blue-eyed. Graham and I got the Luckadeau blue eyes from our father. Momma has the poliosis streak. Her father had it and his mother and on back. It must run, at least in our family, from mother to son to daughter to son. My sister, who is one of the few female cousins in the clan, is blonde. Luckadeaus mostly throw male children, so there are lots of boys."

"And you are the only black-haired one?"

"Me and Graham, yes, ma'am. But Graham is gone now, so that just leaves me."

"And Lizzy and Annie," she whispered.

"I'm going to be up front and honest, lady. I don't believe in fate one damn bit. So if you are here to run DNA and claim part of the ranch for your daughter, it won't work."

Julie stopped dancing, dropped her arms, and took a step back. "Mr. Luckadeau, I don't want a teaspoon of your dirt. You can bet your sweet ass that I'm not interested in you or anything you've got. Let Lizzy be Annie's friend. They never have to know they are kin. I'd just as soon they didn't. I've given Annie that old fable about everyone having a double somewhere in the world and she believes me. I don't want her to know that Lizzy is her cousin. She's too young to understand."

"They'll find out soon enough. Everyone already thinks they look like twins," Griffin said.

Life was not one bit fair. The one woman he'd found attractive and desirable since his wife had left him would have to be the very one who'd been to bed with his late brother. He didn't give a damn about the differences in their ages. What ate at him was playing second fiddle, again, to his brother—Graham, the flamboyant Luckadeau who drew women to him like flies on honey. Griffin, the quiet, reserved brother. Graham, with the devil-may-care attitude. Griffin, the responsible one who was always there to get him out of trouble.

That plus the fact that she had a hidden agenda made them as compatible as a rattlesnake and a field mouse. He had no doubt she was the snake, waiting until he poked his head out of the tree stump to strike. He'd have to be very careful with his heart and his ranch.

"May I cut in?" A tall, blond cowboy tapped Griffin on the shoulder.

Julie found herself in the arms of yet another Luckadeau. She could spot them now, and they were everywhere. Blond, tall, sexy, broad-chested, with big biceps, nice smiles, and a dent in their chins. Just like Griffin, only Griffin had dark hair with a sexy white streak instead of a head full of blond hair. She wondered if there was a single ugly duckling sitting in the family tree.

"I'm Beau, Griffin's cousin. Live up by Ardmore, Oklahoma, on the Bar M Ranch. My wife is Milli. Daughter is Katy Scarlett. She'd be that little blonde out there dancing with Lizzy. You that other little dark-haired girl's momma?"

"I am that. Her name is Annie."

"When did you and Griffin know each other?"

"Didn't until a week ago. I'm a schoolteacher here in Saint Jo."

"You got to be kiddin'," Beau said.

"About being a teacher or not ever knowing Griffin?"

"Griffin."

The song ended and a short, dark-haired, dark-eyed

Mexican beauty grabbed Beau's arm. "I'm Milli, Beau's wife. So, you are a schoolteacher?"

"That's right. It's nice meeting you. If you'll excuse me, I'm going to go buy a beer. Dancing works up a thirst, doesn't it?" She disappeared before Milli could say anything more. One Luckadeau woman was enough for one night and two was way too many.

Julie passed the refreshment stand and went to the bathroom, where she put the lid down and sat. Luckadeaus must reproduce like rabbits. Everywhere she turned there was another one. She leaned her head against the cool metal wall. Did she believe in fate? It had to be either that, or the worst damn luck in the whole state of Texas. She remembered her sister coming to Jefferson to visit back in the middle of the summer.

Sally had been all excited about a job five hours away from Jefferson. "Hey, Sis, I met a lady at a party this past weekend in Dallas. She was a friend of a friend of a friend, et cetera. Said there's a last-minute kindergarten job opening in Saint Jo. You've been sayin' you want a fresh start before Annie starts to school. You ought to drive over there and look into it. I'll watch Annie for you."

Julie tried to remember if she'd even shown Mamie a picture of Annie before Mamie told her about the property. Yes, she had. She remembered taking it from her wallet. Mamie had known from day one! That's why she wanted her to buy that property. She'd figured Annie was Griffin's child.

Julie stood up. "I don't believe in fate. I don't. I don't."

Milli and Jane were just coming in the door when Julie swung open the wooden stall door.

"Hello again," Julie said.

They both nodded, and she quickly washed her hands and started out the door.

"Wait a minute. I want to talk to you," Milli said. "Griffin says you had this fling with Graham before he went to Iraq. Griffin is a good man, and we won't have you hurting him."

"Darlin', you got nothing to worry about. I don't want anything to do with any Luckadeau. Him. You. None of the family. I didn't even know there was but one of them. So don't be getting up in my face about Griffin. Trust me, he's safe and there is nothing to talk about."

"I don't trust you at all. We all love Griff and I personally wouldn't trust a schoolteacher as far as I could throw her. He's been hurt once. Just stay away from him," Milli said.

"What got up your ass about schoolteachers?" Julie smarted off.

"I have my reasons. You just stay away from Griff," Milli told her.

Julie nodded. "Like I said, you've got absolutely nothing to worry about, lady. Now if you'll go out there and tell *him* to stay away from *me*, I'd appreciate it. I'm not interested in anything he's got and I'm damn sure not out to jerk his world out from under his sweet ass, so don't waste a single second thinkin' about me or Annie."

She marched out of the ladies' room, searching for Mamie. She didn't care if she had to hitchhike back to Saint Jo, she wasn't spending another minute under the hateful stares of the female Luckadeau population. Luckily, she was saved from walking. Mamie had spilled beer all over the front of her blouse and was heading home to change. Annie threw a pouting fit but Julie held her ground.

Late that night, Julie sat with her legs drawn up to her chin, watching the moon from her bedroom window.

"I wouldn't trust me either if I were Griffin," she whispered.

She vowed she'd avoid places where he might be from that time on. She had to be in church with him, but she could sit across the sanctuary in another pew rather than right behind him. She had to see him when he brought Lizzy to school. Other than that, she'd be careful.

Rodeos were the first place she'd avoid.

Mamie had said they were going to a regatta next Saturday. Right there in the middle of northern Texas, there was the Nocona Sailboat Regatta at Lake Nocona, and Mamie wouldn't take no for an answer when she said they were going.

At least she didn't have to worry about Griffin being there. A bull rider damn sure didn't sail.

Chapter 5

The committee meeting of the tourism group met on Sunday afternoon on the lawn in the center of the town square in front of Molly's. At two thirty that hot September afternoon, Mamie stepped up into the gazebo and called the meeting to order.

"We are here to discuss putting plans in motion for a holiday theme somewhat like the one we have on the Fourth of July. We need to make our decisions now so I can contact the vendors who are eager to come back with their fall merchandise," she said.

Julie stood on the fringe of the crowd of maybe forty people. Some had brought their lawn chairs, but she and Annie stood to one side of the gazebo. She was there to support Mamie, although after her stunt concerning the rodeo, she'd had second thoughts about it. Mamie had admitted on the way home that she had indeed known that Griffin would be at the rodeo, but in her opinion, Julie needed to see more of him, not less. And that she'd wondered about Annie when she'd seen her picture. Her opinion was that Julie should be Griffin's friend since he was Annie's biological uncle, and they should work together for the girls' sake. Julie had set her straight when she told her that Annie was a Donavan and would never fit into that Luckadeau bunch.

Mamie had told her to look at Annie's hair. She was

a Luckadeau no matter what name was on her birth certificate.

"This is an open forum. Does anyone have anything to say?" Mamie asked.

Julie had plenty to say now that she'd slept on the idea, but it had nothing to do with a hoorah for the winter holidays. Most of it had to do with the sleepless night she'd had and the grumpy mood she'd awakened in that morning. Griffin had haunted her dreams. It was definitely him and not his brother. Griffin had hair in her dreams. Graham never did. The few times she dreamed about Graham, he'd been leaving the hotel room, closing the door behind him. When she dreamed about Griffin, she awoke in a sweat, aching for a man's arms around her.

"I've got two bits to put into the pot." Clarice left her chair and marched up to the gazebo.

Julie looked at the older woman and guessed by the way she was walking and the tilt of her chin that she must be the head honcho of Saint Jo. Maybe of all Montague County. Hopefully, she'd be for the idea and not against it.

Mamie stepped aside and let her have the soapbox.

Clarice took control instantly with a dirty look toward Mamie. "I'm against this silly notion. We've had the Fourth of July festival for as long as I can remember, and that's a long time. It brings in people and money but it also brings in riffraff and bad things. I'd be for canceling it in a heartbeat. I damn sure won't vote for any such tomfoolery around the holidays. We've already got more dope in Montague County than we need, and that's the kind that comes to these things. Y'all are crazy as hell if you think it'll bring money into the town. We'll lose things out of our stores and our homes with all that foreign trash coming in here. We'll lose money because the jail will be full of shoplifters and drunks, not to mention drug dealers. It'd be a perfect place for them to snatch away the kids or to sell them dope. No, I vote that this damn crazy idea be abolished." She clapped her hands together in a dramatic gesture and snapped her mouth shut.

"Well, that's negative," Julie muttered.

Clarice squinted at her. "What did you say? You got something to say about me, you just march up here and deliver it. Don't be mumblin' under your breath."

Julie stepped right up into the gazebo with Clarice. The woman wasn't nearly so intimidating when she was standing beside her. She had dyed hair the color of a black stovepipe, wore a long-sleeved black polyester pantsuit in the middle of the summer, and her nails had recently been done in a bright-red enamel to match toenails peeking out from her black sandals. At least all of her nails but the thumbs—they were shiny gold.

"Now what did you say?" Clarice glared at her.

Julie already had a chip on her shoulder labeled *Luckadeau*. She didn't give a royal damn if the one on the other shoulder bore Clarice's name. The woman had no right to look at Mamie like that or to talk down to Julie, either.

"I am the new kindergarten teacher in Saint Jo. I came to this place because it's small and a nice place to raise my daughter, Annie. But anyone can see that the town is about to dry up and blow away. Without some planning, it's going to be listed on the ghost town registry for the state of Texas. It needs money put back into it. Shops need to be reopened around this square, empty buildings filled up again. It can still be a small town and have small-town charm, but it doesn't have to be a trashy small town. Let's get behind Mamie and support this idea. Folks might see what I did if they come around for a parade or a festival. They'll see potential for growth and could come back and invest in opening a store or putting in a café."

"I disagree," a masculine voice said from the back.

Julie would recognize that voice anywhere. She looked out over the tops of people's heads and saw Griffin holding Lizzy's hand. Annie was tugging against Mamie's hand, trying to get to her friend.

Couldn't she go anywhere that Griffin didn't show up? Next thing she knew, he'd be sitting at the end of her garden when she went out to hoe the weeds. If he was, he'd better get ready for the business end of the hoe to be applied to his hard head. Her crazy heart threw in an extra beat, but then her temper set it to beating right on time. How dare he show up at their meeting and disagree with Mamie?

"Then by all means, step right up here and tell us why," Julie said.

He made his way to the gazebo, filling the small space left with his large frame. He looked out over the crowd for a second before he began. Although no one else knew, he was trying to control his thumping heart. One look at the woman and all he wanted to do was take her home to his bed. He hadn't been so intrigued by a woman in his whole life. Not even his ex-wife. Was in every waking thought and haunted his dreams at night, too.

Finally, he spoke. "Saint Jo won't ever be a ghost

town. Don't let this new citified schoolteacher tell you anything like that. She came from a bigger town, and if she don't like the way we do things, she can go back to it. Our little town can only support one festival a year. We have to hire extra help to pick up trash and we have to bring in the Porta-Potties for that day. It'll just be an extra expense to have another festival," Griffin said.

Julie propped her hands on her hips and debated with him. "Jefferson was about to dry up and blow away, somewhat like this town. But the merchants rallied around and now it's one of the best little bed-and-breakfast and tourist towns over near the Louisiana border."

"You like it so well, then go back there and help them keep it that way." Griffin looked down at her. That was his biggest mistake of the day. He should have kept his eyes on any old rancher in the crowd and never looked at her. One look into those daring, green eyes had him ready to pay for the whole festival himself if she wanted it. But he'd taken his stand and no woman was going to lead Griffin Luckadeau around by the nose ever again.

Julie shot him her meanest look. He was making it personal and trying to knock her out of the saddle every time she put a foot in the stirrup. She inhaled deeply. The policeman standing back there with a toothpick in his mouth would take her to jail if she picked up the nearest empty lawn chair and bent the aluminum frame over Griffin's head, but that's what she wanted to do.

"I've stated my opinion. I rest my case. I'm supporting Mamie. Those naysayers who think it's a bad idea should go on home. The rest of you stay and we'll put our ideas for the festival together. It won't hurt to try it one year. If it puts everyone in the red, then cancel it next year," she said.

"I'd be willin' to give it my vote for one time," Everett Mason said from the front row.

"Everett, you old fool. You came here to side with me," Clarice said.

"And I do. I think it's tomfoolery, but let these foolish young'uns try it their way. When it's over and they're having to dig in their pockets to pay for this crazy idea, they'll be running back to us with their tails between their legs," he said.

Clarice glared first at Julie, then at Mamie, who was keeping an eye on Lizzy and Annie. "You'd think Griff's word would be more important than these two. Mamie just wants to get people in her store. This schoolteacher ain't got the sense the good Lord give a pissant. Griff was born and raised here. He knows how things has been done and how we need to keep them the same."

Julie had had no intention of getting into the middle of a city argument. How in the hell had she gotten so entangled in it that she'd already made the big-shot woman in town angry?

"Do we vote or what?" Clarice asked.

"No, we don't vote," a lady said from the middle of the crowd. "Clarice, this ain't London and you ain't the queen of England. You might have had the title of queen of Montague County, Texas, back when we was young and full of piss and vinegar, but we're old. It's time to let these young folks have a go at the business."

Clarice's face was a picture of rage. "You shut up, Alvera."

Alvera made her way to the gazebo from the outer fringes of the group.

Julie didn't know whether to run for her life or stay

and take a chance of getting scratched when the claws came out, because a catfight was definitely on its way. Either way, she could have kissed the woman making her way toward the gazebo. Their bantering had made her forget about Griffin. Alvera wore jeans that were an inch too short and too baggy in the hind end. Her T-shirt was faded and her gray hair cut in a short style that required very little upkeep. She was almost six feet tall and her face was a study in angles and wrinkles. Clarice had to be on mind-altering drugs to stand there and argue with a force like that.

Alvera bumped Clarice with a bony butt when she reached the gazebo. "It's my turn. This is an open forum with no agenda, so I get my say-so just like you do."

Clarice set her mouth in a firm line. Her jaw muscles gritted with suppressed anger, but she stepped aside and gave her spot to Alvera.

"No one cares about your opinion," she whispered.

"And everyone gives a shit about yours?" Alvera whispered back.

She raised her voice so everyone could hear. "I'm glad to see the young folks and the new ones comin' in here have an interest in our community. They've got some good ideas and they're the ones who're goin' to be seein' to it that Saint Jo doesn't rot and fall down around everyone's ears before too many years. Give 'em some rein. Support 'em. We need to stand behind these kids as they try to fill our boots. How in the hell are they going to succeed if we knock 'em down every time they come up with an idea? And that's my opinion."

"You are an old idiot," Clarice said out the side of her mouth.

"And you are an old idiot with dyed hair," Alvera shot back as she left the gazebo.

"Mamie?" Griffin said from the other side of the gazebo where he'd retreated when Alvera started up the two steps into the gazebo. He was grateful for the few feet of space and the few minutes of time away from Julie. Just being in close proximity to her was making him sweat.

"There's no vote to it. Either the city agrees and the police force says they'll back us, or we don't do it," she said.

"Let's all think on it for a week. The next real meeting of the city council is a week from Tuesday. We'll all attend and have a show of hands then," Griffin suggested.

It was a good idea, but the fact that Griffin came up with it instead of Julie sure didn't settle well.

Mamie spoke up. "I agree. Be thinkin' about the issue, and if you are for it, bring your ideas to the meeting. If you aren't, bring your reasons why."

Clarice folded her arms over her chest. "Seems like a bunch of hogwash to me. Me and Everett and the rest of the folks was runnin' this place before y'all kids was dry behind the ears. We know what's best. You'd do well to listen to us."

"She makes as much sense as a bull calf fartin' in the wind," Alvera piped up from her lawn chair.

"Alvera, you'd argue with a stop sign," Clarice yelled.

Alvera smiled. "I would if I thought I was right and the damn thing was wrong."

Griffin spoke up. "Okay, let's all stew on it a week."

"Thank God some kids has sense," Clarice said.

"That's the first thing you've said all evening that has any truth to it." Alvera wasn't finished arguing.

"Refreshments are ready in my store," Mamie yelled.

Several people made their way across the lawn and into her place. By the time Julie and Annie arrived, the store was packed. Everyone had a cup of punch and a cookie or else they were waiting in line to get one. Julie held Annie's hand tightly and got in line behind Griffin and Lizzy.

"Why are you for such a thing?" Griffin asked. Frankly, he'd gone to the town meeting undecided whether he'd want another festival or not. It was Julie being for it that had caused him to speak up against it. Maybe if they were on opposite sides, he'd see her for the conniving witch she had to be.

"Why are you against it?" she shot right back. Frankly, she didn't give a damn whether Saint Jo had one festival, two festivals, or not a blessed one. But Mamie thought it was a good idea and Mamie was her friend, so she would support her. Well, there was the fact that Griffin was against it, too. Maybe if they were on opposite sides, she'd see him for the egotistical, domineering Texan he was and stop fantasizing about him being a wonderful man.

He leaned against a display case. "Because Clarice is right. It's going to bring in the riffraff. Are you even remotely aware of the drug problems around here? Didn't you do a bit of homework before you moved to this area? Don't tell me you had the preconceived notion that Saint Jo was Mayberry."

"Every town has its problems. I didn't move here with my head in the sand, but there's also no reason why Saint Jo couldn't grow," she said.

He shook his head and moved over to talk to Everett, a round man in bibbed overalls and a faded blue shirt.

Mamie made her way through the crowd of people and whispered to Julie, "You'd never guess Alvera and Everett are wealthy ranchers, would you?"

"I figured Clarice owned the town. Thank God for Alvera and Everett. At least they're not as negative as Clarice," Julie whispered.

Evidently all that black hair dye had not harmed Clarice's hearing one bit. She raised her head and shot Julie a look across the room meant to turn her into nothing more than a slightly greasy spot on Mamie's floor. Without blinking, she pushed a couple of men aside and came to stand nose to nose with Julie. "Miss Donavan, I do not like you. I shall talk to Catherine Amos this week, and you will not be back to teach in Saint Jo next year, so your opinion matters less than a frog's ass in my town. Don't get too comfortable and don't be thinkin' to take any of Griff's money just because his brother went to bed with you and you have a Luckadeau child. I've heard all about you, and your kind is the riffraff we don't need in Saint Jo."

Alvera spoke up from near the refreshment table. "Clarice, that's enough of your mudslinging. You want to taste a little mud, I can give you a mouthful. Eat your cookie and think about something that won't raise your blood pressure."

Julie wanted to hide under a table or else hurry up and get the hell out of Dodge—or Saint Jo, as the case was. As red as her face was after that comment from Clarice, she wasn't totally sure she wouldn't set the place on fire. That hateful woman had just outed her and Annie both with her smart mouth. What everyone had wondered about was now out there in living Technicolor on the big screen—Graham Luckadeau had an illegitimate daughter.

"What have I gotten myself into?" Julie whispered.

People stole sideways glances at her and then at Annie and Lizzy sitting side by side on a bench beside the cash register.

So much for keeping Annie's parentage a secret. She might as well stand up on the display case and give them intimate details of that night she'd spent with Graham Luckadeau.

Alvera made her way through the crowd to Julie's side. "Don't listen to that old bag. She thinks she runs the whole damn county and that governors and presidents are in her pocket. Hell, honey, they wouldn't know her from an old Dallas bag lady. She's all hat and no cattle."

"Thank you," Julie said.

"So, that's Graham's daughter, is it? Nice that she's back around her family. You're a fine asset to our community. And don't worry about Catherine. She's my sister. You ain't goin' nowhere."

Chapter 6

A HOT WIND BLEW THE TREE LEAVES, THE HEAT almost cooking Julie's fair skin. They waited on the porch, Julie making a list with her pencil and paper, and Annie spinning around the yard like a ballerina. Julie had applied a liberal dose of sunblock on all her bare skin and then went to work on Annie before tucking the tube into her tote bag. According to Mamie, who'd been to these regattas before, she needed a quilt to toss out on the grass around the lake, sunblock, extra clothing for Annie, and an appetite. Mamie was bringing a cooler full of beer, soda pop, water, and sandwich makings for lunch.

Annie's ponytail flopped with every jump. "I love living here, Momma. It's so much fun."

"Even when you have to help me make squash relish?" Julie asked.

"I don't like the way the squash leaves scratch me when we get them out of the garden, but I like cooking with you. When can I have a pony?" Annie said.

"For now you'll have to be satisfied with your kittens," she said, glad that she didn't have room for a pony. Annie had an adventurous streak even wider than Lizzy's. If she had a pony, she'd be racing off to the Lucky Clover every chance she got, and Julie adamantly did not want her daughter at that ranch.

Julie was doing well with her new canning business. Most of what was in the cellar had sold, and Julie couldn't replenish it because Mamie kept buying everything she had time to put in jars. The new items up for grabs were bread and butter pickles made from Edna's recipe and squash relish and dilled green beans made from Julie's grandmother's recipes. While she waited for Mamie, she made a list of what she'd need the next few days from the grocery store. One recipe took six yellow squash, two onions, and two hot peppers. The garden produced much more than that, so she'd probably do several batches. There was enough salt, celery seed, and mustard seed left in the pantry to last five years. But she was low on sugar and vinegar, so she added those to the list.

"I might as well get forty or fifty pounds of sugar because I'll use it before the garden plays completely out," she mused aloud.

"Sugar? You want sugar?" Annie swirled over and gave her a kiss on the cheek.

"Thank you." Julie beamed and then checked the recipe for the dilled green beans. *Cut green beans to fit fairly tightly in the jars. Add one quarter of a teaspoon of crushed red pepper, one half teaspoon each of mustard seed and dill seed, and a very small clove of garlic to the jar with the beans. Heat five cups of vinegar, five cups of water, and half a cup of salt to the boiling point and pour over the beans. Adjust jar lids. Process in boiling water five minutes. Remove and cool.*

"Vinegar and lots of it. Might as well buy several gallons if I'm going to get through a whole week," she said.

"What are you talking about?" Mamie yelled from the car when she parked.

"Cooking. She wanted sugar, so I gave her some but

I don't have any vinegar," Annie said. "Are we ready? Tell me more about the boats and their pretty sails. I'm hungry. Can we buy hot dogs and cotton candy when we get there?"

"Terrible twos. Questioning fives," Mamie giggled.

"You got that right. Try a classroom of fifteen of those asking never-ending questions," Julie said. "I was going over the squash and bean recipes so I could make a run over to Gainesville after church tomorrow for supplies."

"Make up everything you can lay your hands on by Friday. California is coming through and he said he'd take everything I have in the store. So I can sell everything you've got this week."

"Who is California?" Julie asked.

"This damn good-lookin' man in his forties who visits his mother in Muenster once a year. When he does, he buys my whole stock. I asked him once what he does with it and he says he uses it for gifts if he doesn't eat it. He owns this big company in San Francisco. Want to meet him? I've flirted with him for five years but it doesn't do a bit of good."

"Ever think maybe his train runs a different track?" Julie asked.

"That's it. Praise the Lord, I'm not just fat and ugly," Mamie said.

"If you say that about my friend, we're going to have a big old catfight. Nobody talks about you like that, not even you. Give me a minute to put all this inside and lock the door," Julie said.

"I'm glad you moved here. You are good for me. How do you think the city meeting will go next Tuesday?" Mamie asked.

"We'll win them over on a one-year basis. But we'd better work our hind ends off or that's all we'll ever get and then they'll gloat in their victory. You want to usher the old out and the new in, you'd better get ready to work for the responsibility. Now let's get this hyperactive child of mine to the regatta before she blows a gasket," Julie said.

"Tell me about it again," Annie said from the back seat of the car.

"More than twenty years ago, two sailors moved to the lake area, one on the west side and one on the east. They both had sailboats and liked to sail on the lake and, as luck would have it, they started racing. Then, about fifteen years ago, they invited some of their sailboat friends to the lake and they all had a race. That began the Nocona Sailboat Regatta. It gets bigger every year, and this year ought to be really good because there's a good wind picked up. I heard that the race was going to have thirty boats this year from as far away as Waxahaxie."

"Is that still in Texas or is it on the moon?" Annie asked.

Mamie laughed. "It's still in Texas. The boats are gathering right now at the Storey Boathouse in the middle of the lake. At ten minutes to eleven, the horn will sound four blows. At five minutes 'til eleven, it will sound three blows; one minute 'til, two blows, and then at eleven o'clock it will blow one time and the race will begin."

"Hurry, I want to hear the horn blowing. I've never been to a rematta," Annie said.

"Regatta," Julie and Mamie said at the same time.

"That's what I said," Annie told them.

"What time is the whole thing over?" Julie asked.

"At three thirty, the small boat race starts. At four, the revenge race and multi-hulls start. After that, we'll dash back home, take showers, and get cleaned up for the dinner served up by the Nocona Rural Volunteer Fire Department. Awards and music after that, then the auction."

"All day! Yippeee," Annie said.

"Auction?"

Mamie nosed her car into a parking place. "The regatta has an auction. Donated articles, but pretty nice most of the time. The money goes to the Nocona Rural Fire Department."

"Why Nocona? Why not Saint Jo?"

"It's like this: Capps Corner is thirteen miles to Nocona and about nine to Saint Jo. We support both volunteer fire companies. If a wildfire starts, you'll see why. When pastures start burning, we need all the help we can get out here in the middle of nowhere."

"I see," Julie said.

"I donated a dozen jars of your squash relish to the auction. I'm dying to see how much it sells for and who buys it."

"But California could have bought that," Julie said.

"California can't put out a fire if it's licking at my door."

"In more ways than one," Julie said.

Mamie busted out laughing. "You are a naughty girl, my friend."

"Sometimes."

Annie was bouncing like a rubber ball on concrete. "Let's go. I see the pretty colors. They look like my bathtub boats. I'm going to yell and scream for the one with the red, white, and blue sails."

They were barely stopped when Lizzy came running from Marita's quilt. She was yelling, "Annie! Annie!" before Annie had her seat belt unfastened.

"They're here?" Julie asked.

"Of course. Everyone in the whole area is here. Griffin is a member of the volunteer fire department, and besides, the Luckadeaus always come to the regatta. Come on. Let's get the quilt spread out before the race begins," Mamie said.

Marita waved her over. "Hey, Julie, come put your quilt next to ours. Those girls are going to want to spend their time together anyway."

Mamie and Julie carried their cooler and quilt to the edge of the water and spread it out right next to Marita's. Annie and Lizzy pointed at the sailboats and tried to decide on which one they were going to root for. Annie had fallen in love with the red, white, and blue one, but Lizzy liked the turquoise and yellow, and they wanted to cheer for the same one.

Finally they decided that whoever could throw a rock the longest distance in the lake would pick their favorite boat. Each chose a rock with great care. Lizzy threw hers first. Annie tossed hers second. It wasn't even a contest. Annie's rock went the longest distance, so they'd be yelling for the red, white, and blue sails.

Julie sat down and listened to Marita and Mamie talk about the people they would see and those who weren't there yet. Few names meant anything to her, so she let her mind drift. So the Luckadeaus had their fingers in every pie in the whole county? She could have sworn that a bull rider wouldn't be a candidate for sailboat racing. Her pulse quickened at the idea of Griffin in sailor's garb with his hands around the ropes, but she set it to rights before it got plumb out of hand.

Then Marita said something about Milli and Beau.

"Will they be here?" Julie asked, hoping her voice didn't give away her aggravation at having her day spoiled by an interfering Luckadeau wife.

"No, Milli has gone to visit her parents in Hereford, out in the Panhandle. She has her own little airplane and takes the kids with her once a month to spend a night with her folks. Beau is knee deep in hay and wheat," Marita said. "You'd love Milli, you ever got to know her. She's a hoot. Let me tell you, anything Beau can do, she can do just as well."

Julie didn't answer. She'd never get to know the woman. "How about Jane and Slade?"

Marita shook her head.

"Griffin is the auctioneer tonight, isn't he?" Mamie asked.

"Yes he is and he's going to say words so fast I can't hear them all—wait 'til you hear it, Annie. He talks so fast it sounds funny," Lizzy answered.

Julie almost groaned out loud.

Mamie explained. "The Luckadeaus have always been involved in the town events. Griffin went to auctioneer school when he was still in high school, so he helps out with things like this. Graham was the sailor. Had a boat with a four-leaf clover on the sail. He won the race when he was sixteen. Damn, that boy could sail like he could...well, let's just say he could do a little better than California."

"Mamie!" Julie whispered.

"We were kids. He was pretty. I was..." She stopped.

"I'm going to hush now. Some things don't bear remembering, at least not out loud. Suffice it to say that nothing really happened. Not that I wasn't willing, but he had a girlfriend, and what goes on in a boathouse stays in a boathouse, kind of like Las Vegas."

Or Dallas, Julie thought.

Four blasts let everyone know the race was getting serious. Lizzy counted the honks on her fingers and told Annie what was happening. Annie held up her fingers on the next series and told Lizzy there were three this time. When the boats really set off, both girls began to hop up and down and yell for the red, white, and blue sailboat.

"Hi. Y'all got an extra beer? I'm spittin' dust." Alvera Clancy settled onto their quilt without an invitation.

Mamie popped open a longneck and handed it to her. She downed a fourth of the beer without coming up for air and burped loudly. Both girls giggled and sucked hard on their juice packs and waited, but no burp was forthcoming.

"How are you today?" Alvera looked right at Julie.

"I'm fine. It's a lovely weekend for a regatta, isn't it?"

Alvera smiled. "Yep, it is that. You got your ducks in a row for the big fight on Tuesday? That Clarice has been callin' ever'body in the area to come to the meetin'. God Almighty, but that woman likes to meddle. I told my brother when he married her he was going to be sorry. Ever heard that old sayin', 'Marry in haste, repent at leisure'? Well, that's what he did. He repented long as he could stand it and then he had a heart attack and died. I wanted to put something like that on his tombstone but Clarice had this sticky sweet thing about how he's 'Missed by those who loved him.' She thinks a gold fingernail makes her opinion worth more than anyone else's. You two get your ideas together and present them. I'll be there in case she gets too out of hand."

"She's your sister-in-law?" Julie was amazed.

"You oughta feel sorry for me. I've had to put up with her all her life. Went to school with her when she was a blonde-haired, snotty-nosed kid. Then my brother married her when they wasn't old enough to know no better. The old bitch will be a burr under your saddle until she's dead. Just don't back down from what you want to do. She's goin' to fight you ever' step of the way on ever' decision, but hell, honey, it'll make you strong. Time she's in the grave...hopefully it will be sooner rather than later...you'll have enough steel in your bones to run things proper."

If Julie had kept the grin inside, she would have burst.

Mamie laughed aloud. "Yes, ma'am, we'll do our damnedest to stay in the saddle the full eight seconds at the meetin'."

"I'm countin' on you. Got to go speak to Everett now. Thanks for the beer. Would you look at that? Clarice has arrived in all her pasted-on glory. God dang, she looks like hell," Alvera said as she stood up.

Julie looked around, and sure enough, there was Clarice, getting out of a brand-new Cadillac. She wore turquoise spandex, capri-length pants, a flowing, thin shirt printed with flags of every color of the rainbow, and a bright-red camisole. Her sandals, with kitten heels that sank into the moist grass every time she stepped, were the same color as the pants.

She looked Julie right in the eye, tilted her chin up, and went in the opposite direction.

"Guess she's here to do some politickin'," Mamie said.

"I love this town," Julie said with a giggle. She didn't even realize she'd said the words aloud until Mamie grinned.

"Oh, darlin', you just wait until you get to know all of them and the way their lives entangle. It's a hoot," Mamie said.

Julie felt Griffin's gaze even before she could see him making long strides up the edge of the water and watching the boats. Her nerves frayed out at just the sight of him in those tight jeans and boots. She let her eyes linger another moment—glad for her sunglasses so he couldn't see how he affected her—before she looked back out at the lake.

Griffin noticed her when he heard his daughter squealing and looked around to see the two little girls with white streaks shining. He hadn't thought about her being there but Lizzy would be glad to see Annie. He'd take that child without a second's hesitation if he could, especially if he could adopt her without having to deal with Julie. He wondered if she'd be willing to agree to a *settlement*? He answered his own question with two words: "Hell no!" in a low voice. After the way she'd protected Annie and Lizzy both that day on her porch, he had no doubts that she'd kill anyone who tried to take her child.

He claimed a corner of Marita's quilt. "Hello, ladies."

"Where'd you come from?" Mamie asked.

He opened the cooler. "Had to get the chores done before I could leave. Lizzy was in hot water so Marita brought her early. Want a beer?"

Mamie took the offered longneck.

"You?" he asked Julie.

She reached and he passed. Their fingertips brushed and sparks flew around them like fireworks on New Year's Eve. By continuous refusal to acknowledge the sensations, she hoped they'd simply die out. She'd made a colossal mistake with a Luckadeau one time before and it was not happening again. Hormones shifted into high gear even when women had sex on a regular basis, but when a lady had been celibate as long as she had? Well, it stood to reason the hormones would shoot right on into overdrive.

An old oak tree that had lived out its usefulness would put out a bumper crop of acorns the year before it died. A woman who was on the brink of menopause, especially in the Donavan family when the ladies went through it in their late thirties, would have sexual cravings because her body wanted one more baby. Look around at all the tag-along kids in the world born when a woman was past forty and thought she'd finished having her family.

Thirty had loomed right around the corner when Annie was born, and Julie had tried every fertility drug known to the medical profession. Derrick had refused to be checked, saying that his swimmers were strong. Turned out he was wrong. Annie was proof of that. Now Julie was thirty-four and her biological clock was about to run out of time, so it was setting up a howl for sex. Forget about making love; her body didn't care a flip about love. It was trying to procreate, and by damn, she wasn't letting it have its way even if her decision would cause the governor of the great state of Texas to go blind or Clarice Utley to be nice for a whole day.

Yeah right! her conscience argued. *If Griffin*

Luckadeau gave you a push, you'd fall backward and take him down with you. Wake up, lady. It's move or be miserable. You can't live in Saint Jo and have a moment's peace in your heart.

Griffin stole glances at Julie, who was looking especially pretty today. She seemed more pensive than usual and much less prone to get her hackles up. He studied her from behind mirrored sunglasses and liked what he saw. No wonder his brother had been attracted to her. Mercy, but she was a fine-looking woman. But she'd slept with Graham and that threw up a block so big Griffin could never climb over it.

"Want another beer?" Griffin asked.

Until he spoke, Julie hadn't realized she'd finished off the whole beer. She held up the empty bottle and stared at it for several moments before she shook her head.

"Where were your thoughts? Looked like you were seeing right through that bottle and into eternity," Griffin said.

"My thoughts aren't up for discussion. Why don't you sail?" Julie asked.

"That was Graham's thing. Every time I get on any kind of boat, even a canoe, I get sick. I can't imagine going on a cruise. I'd spend all my time in the bathroom huggin' the toilet and upchucking."

"And yet you can sit on a bull for eight seconds? That doesn't make sense," she said.

"Graham tried bull riding one time. Got so nervous he almost had a heart attack," Griffin said seriously. "It's the twin thing. We looked exactly alike but we had very different tastes. In all things."

She looked at him from the corner of her eye but

couldn't decide if he was delivering a grand slam against her character again or if he was merely stating fact.

He went on, "Graham had this overpowering personality that overshadowed everyone in his presence, including me. The maddest I ever got at him was the day he came home from Wichita Falls and told me he'd joined the Air Force. He was shipping out for boot camp in a week. We about came to blows."

"Why?" Julie asked.

"Because I didn't want him to go. I'd never been away from him for more than a week, and that was for my honeymoon. I was selfish on several sides. He was my brother. I didn't want him over there where he might get killed. I didn't want to run the ranch by myself. My mother's family left their ranch in South Texas to her, and she and Daddy went to take care of it, leaving me and Graham to run this one. I didn't want to do it all by myself and I wanted him to be here with me to share the good times as well as the not-so-good," Griffin said.

"And besides all that, you didn't want him to go have all the fun, did you?" Mamie teased.

"Look what all that fun got him," Griffin said.

Mamie scooted across the quilt and put her arm around him. "I'm sorry, Griff. I didn't mean to be ugly. I was just teasing."

Julie started to stand up. "I'm going now. I'll find somewhere else to sit after a remark like that. I don't even care if you think I'm being insensitive."

Griff laid a hand on her arm. The feel of her bare skin against his callused fingertips created heat from one end of Griffin to the other. "Don't go. I was the one who was insensitive. I wasn't thinking about you or Annie. I was thinking about his fun taking him to Iraq and getting him killed. This damned regatta always brings back the memories. Let's talk about something else. Are you really staying after the way Clarice talked to you, Julie? Or is this a one-year position at the school?" he asked.

Julie pulled her sunglasses down and gave him a long look. "Yes, I am staying. She can't run me off. This is my first home, and Annie is adjusting well here. I love it."

"You didn't own anything with your husband?" Griffin was on a fishing expedition for information.

"My husband owned. I merely lived there."

"Daddy, take us for a walk, please. We want to go up the lake and see if our boat is ahead," Lizzy said.

"I'll take you. I'm getting stiff from sitting." Marita didn't show any signs of stiffness as she popped up and got each girl by a hand. Suddenly, she stopped and turned back around. "I'm sorry, Julie. I assumed it was all right that I take Annie, but I should have asked."

"It's fine. But she's not been around a lake like this so she won't understand the danger," Julie explained. "Annie, listen to Marita and don't try to run off."

"I've got to go, too," Griffin said. Another five minutes and he'd never leave. He'd sit right there and listen to Julie's soft Southern voice all afternoon.

"What's the hurry? I've got beer in my cooler if we run out in yours," Mamie said.

"Got business to take care of," Griffin said.

"Clarice called you yet?" Mamie asked.

"Oh, yes. I'm hearing from her a couple of times a day. Alvera been on your phone?"

"Not once. She don't have to drag out her soapbox

and polish it up. Right is right and speaks for itself," Mamie said.

"Amen to that, sister," Julie added.

"I'm not talkin' shop with you women today. Suffice it to say we're running this election on different platforms," he said as he left.

"So you got a thing for Griffin?" Julie asked Mamie as soon as he was out of hearing distance.

"Hell no! Griffin is my brother figure. Now if Graham was here, it would be a different story."

"Why? They look exactly the same," Julie said.

"Don't have a damn thing to do with looks. Griffin is the sweetheart. He's the good twin, versus Graham, who was the evil twin. There wasn't a woman in Montague County who wouldn't have fallen over backward and had their clothes off by the time they hit the ground for Graham. Passion oozed out of him, and he was so confident. He'd walk into a room and take his pick for the evening, and we all wished he'd pick us. But Griff was the one we went crying to when we broke up with our boyfriends. He was our big-brother figure."

Julie remembered the way Graham had looked at her as if she were his pick of the evening that night in the bar. From the time she literally fell into his arms until they fell into bed, he'd had eyes only for her. Past that, she remembered little, except one hell of a headache the next morning. He must have been good in bed or she would have remembered that he wasn't. Or maybe he wasn't and she wanted to forget.

"So Graham was the resident bad boy of Montague County?" Julie said.

"I'm not sure he wasn't the resident evil boy of the

whole state just before he took off for the service. Didn't ever understand that. One day he's running a ranch at the age of twenty-two, and the next he's in Iraq. Then we're all at his funeral and weeping because we didn't find a way to go to bed with him. Those who did wept the hardest. I've wondered why—if it was because he lived up to his reputation or because he didn't.

"I've got another confession to make. When I saw Annie's picture, I thought she belonged to Griffin. That's why I pushed Edna's house so hard," Mamie admitted.

"Can't hide it in these parts, even though hiding was the reason I came here," Julie said.

"You'd have to understand Griff and Graham, Julie. It was like Graham got all the sex appeal and Griff got the brains. Graham could work on the ranch, but he hated it. Griff loves it. Graham just wanted out. He wanted to see the world beyond Saint Jo, Texas. I'm not faulting him or Griff. They looked alike but that's where the twin stuff ended."

Julie shrugged. "I never wanted to understand either of them, Mamie. I didn't love Graham. I was mad at my husband, freshly divorced—or as good as—horny as hell, and wanting a good time. I got it and Annie out of the deal. I don't give a damn about Griffin or his ranch, his attitude, or his money. I just want to raise my daughter and be left alone. I wasn't asking if you had a thing for Griffin for you to feel like you had to tell me anything."

"Hey, lady, don't pick a fight with me because Griff left," Mamie said.

Julie stared at her a moment before a grin finally split her delicate face. "You're damn good. You'll bear watching."

"Just a good people reader." Mamie grinned. "I'm not matchmaking, honest. I don't care if you fight with him every day or kiss him every night or both. I'm comfortable with you. It was there from the beginning. We're friends."

"Shall we get those little bracelets that say *BFF* on them?" Julie giggled.

"What?"

"You know, best friends forever," Julie said.

"Thank God. I thought the first letter stood for *bitches* and those two F's..."

Julie put her fingers over Mamie's mouth. "Shhhhh. Annie can hear a bad word from three miles away."

"I've got another confession to make," Mamie said.

"Do we need a curtain between us?"

"Not a 'Father, I have sinned, forgive me' confession. It's more like a 'Father, I've been ornery again' confession," Mamie said.

"Sounds to me like you and Graham were kicked out of the same mold," Julie said.

"Sometimes we were, only he was beautiful and I've always been..."

"Are you talking about my friend again? I told you I wouldn't abide it. Mamie was my first friend and she keeps making me get out in the world when I'd be an old hermit and stay on my five acres making dilled beans if she'd let me. So since she's the one who rescues my psyche, you can't talk about her," Julie teased.

"Confession is good for the soul and the BFF. I made you go to the rodeo because I knew Griffin would be there and I made you come with me today for the same reason. At first I thought Annie had to belong to him and for that to be true, then he would have had to have cheated on his sorry wife. I wanted to put you two together and see what happened."

"Good grief!" Julie whispered.

"Sorry," Mamie said.

"Not you. Everyone in the county must think the same thing when they see those two little girls together. I really did jump from the frying pan straight into the damned fire." There was nothing she could do to hide it or keep it quiet. One look at Lizzy and Annie and the whole county knew they were either half sisters or cousins.

"BFFs explain everything. Talk it to death, actually. Look at Annie and Lizzy. I don't think they've hushed since they got together this morning. So what in the hell are you talking about? Let's talk it to death," Mamie said.

Julie sighed. "If you thought that, then everyone else must think the same. I left Jefferson because... It's a long, long story."

"Give me the old *Reader's Digest* version."

"Okay, married seven years to Derrick and wanted a baby very badly, so I went on fertility drugs. Found out Derrick felt pressured and sex was just an automatic thing when the thermometer was right, so he went off and found a mistress who liked things spontaneous. I guess she was giving it to him in the office closet or traveling with him," Julie said.

"Bastard," Mamie muttered. "Don't look at me like that. Annie and Lizzy didn't hear me."

"So I divorced his cheating ass. Divorce was nearly final when my sister, some friends, and I went on a girls' night out to Dallas. Guess who I literally stumbled over?"

"Graham Luckadeau? Oh my! That's such a surprise." Mamie fluttered her hands around her face like a teenager.

"The next week, Derrick must've got to thinking about the property settlement of the divorce and came begging me to take him back. Standard story. 'I'll never do it again, blah, blah, blah.' I did, and didn't even think about the motel night. Guess who sued me for divorce on grounds of adultery nine months later? Took one look at Annie and walked out of the hospital."

"Sorry bastard," Mamie said.

"Now comes the good part. I moved into my folks' little garage apartment. Momma babysat Annie for me during the day while I worked. Jefferson is bigger than Saint Jo, but imagine the gossip vines," Julie said.

"On fire, were they?"

"You got it. I thought if I moved away before she started school, maybe she'd just be the little girl with the white streak in her hair. Different, but not a child that would be called names at school because her white-trash momma slept with a man while she was married to the richest man in Jefferson County. Poor, poor Derrick. Julie Donavan did him so dirty."

It took Mamie several minutes, but finally she pieced the puzzle together and had the picture laid out before her in Technicolor as bright as the sails on the boats racing laps around the lake. "Damn!"

"Yep," Julie agreed.

"You left so she wouldn't be branded and brought her straight to the part of the world where the iron is hot and the town ready to slap an *L* for Luckadeau on her butt for sure," Mamie said.

"Yep," Julie said again.

"But you got to realize. No one would..."

Griffin threw himself back on the quilt, propping

up on an elbow between them. "No one would what? Hand me a beer, please, Mamie. Listening to Mr. Bailey tell Irish stories makes me thirsty." He'd taken care of business and gotten a breather away from Julie, so he'd come back for another beer. At least that was the excuse he'd given himself. He could always invent more excuses to leave if the area got too warm, and he wasn't thinking about the weather. Looking at her sitting there with Mamie was already having its effects.

She handed him a longneck from her cooler.

"Now, what would no one do? What were you talking about?" he asked again.

Mamie poked him on the shoulder. "Darlin', you're like my little brother, but me and Julie are new BFFs and we keep secrets even from you."

"I'm hurt," he said.

"You know what BFF stands for?" Julie asked.

"Sure I do. Lizzy watches those kid shows on television. It's like, it stands for like, Best Friends, like, Forever."

"I wish those Valley girls would have been strangled at birth," Mamie said.

"Or their mouths taped with duct tape and sent off to a convent that prevented talking," Julie said. "Even my kindergarteners use the word *like* more than any other one in the dictionary. I'm afraid it's, like, here to, like, stay."

Marita arrived at that moment, both thirsty girls in tow. She opened the cooler and brought out two juice packs and a bottle of iced tea. "They'd wear an old woman out."

"Is Chuck going to be here?" Annie asked.

"No, he don't get to come to these things," Lizzy said then squealed. "There he is."

His mother had him by the arm instead of the hand and was dragging him across the grass toward a pickup truck several men were leaning against.

"Chuck, come sit with us," Lizzy yelled.

His mother stopped and pulled down her sunglasses. She slowed her pace and let go of his arm. She wore a tank top that was two sizes too small and cut-off jean shorts. A barb-wire tattoo circled both of her upper arms and vines ran from her ankles to her knees. Julie wished she had the hoe and an opportunity to use it on the woman. For what those tats cost, she could buy decent clothing for her child and feed him nutritious food.

"Could we take care of Chuck for you the rest of the day?" Julie asked. "I'm his teacher and—"

"I know who you are and I know that kid of yours belongs to Griffin Luckadeau. His wife was my good friend, and it looks like she wasn't the only one playin' around. Funny, ain't it, Griffin? Guess what goes around comes around. So you want to take care of the kid the rest of the day? I ain't got no problem with that. You know where we live, so you could bring him home tonight?"

"I do," Mamie said.

"I reckon you do. Well, boy, you're stayin' with these people. They'll bring you home come bedtime. I reckon I'll be there by ten but don't hurry yourselves none."

"Don't be too quick to jump to conclusions," Griffin said stiffly.

"Griffin is not Annie's father. His brother, Graham, was her father," Julie said.

"Well, I'll be damned. Don't the world turn around for the rich folks," she said with a harsh laugh.

Chuck stood there with a grin splitting his face from

one side to the other. His jean shorts were worn and smudges of dirt on his knees and elbows said he probably hadn't had a bath the night before. His shirt had stains on the front, and his glasses needed to be cleaned, but he looked so happy Julie almost cried.

"You mind your teacher," his mother said as she thumped him on the back hard enough to send him sprawling forward, barely catching himself before he tumbled into the lake. Then she joined the men beside the truck.

"You didn't have to do that," Griffin said as he turned to Julie.

"I ain't running from the truth. Tried that. It didn't work, so I'll just be honest," Julie said. Down deep, she wondered if he'd ever believe she was an honest woman or if he'd always see a one-night stand when he looked at her.

Lizzy was already fumbling in the cooler. "Come over here and we'll get you a juice box."

"Are you hungry, son?" Marita asked.

Chuck nodded.

"Then we'll have some crackers while we wait on lunch. I've got a box of cheese crackers that should taste pretty good with that juice."

"Let me have those glasses, Chuck. I'll use some of this bottled water and clean them," Julie said.

Chuck removed his black-rimmed glasses and handed them to her at the same time that she and Griffin reached for the water. Their fingertips brushed and sparks lit up the whole area, but only Julie and Griffin could see or feel them. Were all the Luckadeau men so magnetic, or just the ones with dark hair?

Griffin figured it was time to find some other business

that took him away from Julie. Something about the woman kept drawing him back to her side; something about his common sense kept pulling him away.

Julie was trying to get past the awkward moment when Everett Mason popped his lawn chair open and sat down beside their quilt. He wore rubber flip-flops with his overalls and yellow T-shirt that day. His hair was a thin rim around a shiny, bald head.

"Hi, y'all. Griff, I didn't know you had twins." He winked. "Don't look so stunned. I done heard about the little girl. My wife was tellin' me something about Graham and a baby but he never did marry, did he? I don't listen to these old women much as I should. Now tell me about these girls, and open me up a beer. I'm dry as dust."

"I'll tell you," Lizzy said. "Me and Annie are bestest friends. This is our other friend. His name is Chuck," Lizzy said.

Everett winked at Griffin again. "Funny how kittens don't always look like the momma cat, ain't it?"

Julie didn't know whether to laugh or cry.

It really didn't matter which one she did. The truth was out.

Chapter 7

THE ROOM WHERE THEY HELD THE CITY COUNCIL meeting was packed. Griffin sat behind an eight-foot table with four other men. Each one had a folder in front of him. Mamie, Julie, and Annie had barely squeezed into the crowded room. The first order of business concerning a winter festival was opened.

Clarice pushed her way through the crowd to the little podium set up at the end of the table. She was in her glory with a captive audience. She flipped open a notebook and looked around at the faces for thirty seconds before she began. The head she-coon had come loaded for bear, dressed for the occasion in a black pantsuit and with her hair freshly done. Two diamond rings on each hand and glittering studs in her earlobes, along with gold fingernails on her pinky fingers, let everyone know that she was Saint Jo's rich and famous. Anyone worth their salt would sit up and listen when she spoke.

Julie ignored her and stole sideways glances toward Griffin. He was freshly shaven with a tiny nick on his neck. She had the insane desire to reach out and touch it.

Clarice ranted and raved and reiterated all the reasons why she would not support a festival. Then she called for a vote.

Griffin looked up. He'd tried to keep his eyes downcast so that he wouldn't look at Julie. He'd known the minute she came into the room, and in order to keep his mind on the meeting, he couldn't afford to look at her. "Just a minute. You had your say. It's only fair the other side gets their say now. We want this to be fair, Clarice."

She gave him a go-to-hell look. "I thought you was on my side, Griffin Luckadeau. Your grandmother and I were best friends. You're going against your family because of that schoolteacher's word that that kid belongs to your brother."

Julie inhaled deeply. In Jefferson, there had been an undercurrent of disapproval concerning the possibility that one of their teachers had committed adultery against the most powerful man in the county, but no one had embarrassed her like Clarice. Leave it to the small-town big shot to make her life miserable.

Griffin could feel Julie's anguish. If only he could haul her out of there and protect her from all the gossip, he'd do it. "I'm sayin' that this is a council meeting, not a mud-throwing contest. Folks want to throw stones, they'd best be lookin' to see if they're livin' in glass houses. Ain't that right, Clarice?"

"Don't you sass me, boy. I won't have it."

"Okay, then let's do this proper and by the book. Mamie, I think it's your turn," Griffin said.

Mamie gave a prepared ten-minute speech. She would have liked to have had a place to show a PowerPoint presentation so everyone could see what similar festivals in other towns looked like, what kind of revenue they brought the city, etc., but there wasn't time for all that.

"The floor is open now for anyone else to speak. Five minutes. Anyone?" Griffin was about to put it to the vote when Alvera rushed through the door.

"I'm late," Alvera panted. "Had a cow down and had

to pull a calf, but I'm here, and yes, Griffin, I want to talk. You say I've got five minutes? Hit the watch and tell me when my time is up." She talked as she made her way to the podium. A dark stain dotted her chambray shirt and what was on her boots didn't appear to be mud.

"I'm lookin' at a bunch of you old-timers. Remember back when this square was a boomin' place? Remember when we used to go to town on Saturday night, and if we wasn't early, we had to park a block away? Remember when us kids played on the lawn in the square, and our mothers talked recipes and how to get grass stains out of our clothes, and our fathers talked about cows and crops? The stores all stayed open on Saturday night until eight o'clock, and in the summertime, we could buy a snow cone if we had a nickel. Now them was the good old days. I ain't sayin' this one festival will bring it all back in one year, but these kids that's willin' to put in the work and try to build Saint Jo back up is just tryin' to make it look like it did back then. So before you go shootin' 'em down, think on it and give 'em a chance. Is my time up, Griffin?"

He checked his watch. "You got another minute."

"Good. Then I'll use it to talk to the older folks in the room. That would be Clarice and Everett and y'all that are about our age. We won't be here in fifty years, but these kids will be. Let 'em do their best to make things better and I'll guaran-damn-tee you that they'll leave an example for the next generation after them to do the same. To hell with the Porta-Potties and the police force. I'll write a check myself for the extra money to support Mamie's idea," she said.

"Time's up now," Griffin said.

The issue went to the vote. Three councilmen were for the festival. Two, one of which was Griffin, were against it. The people in the room voted next. It was marginal but still the pro vote outnumbered the con vote.

"Mamie, are you going to spearhead this like you do the Fourth of July?" Griffin asked.

"I'm willing to take it on. Julie says she'll help," she said.

"Then I guess it's your baby. It's going to be a lot of work to get it ready for this season. You sure you don't want to wait until next year to kick it off?"

"I'm sure," Mamie said.

"Okay, then it's on to the next item on the agenda. Those of you who came for the festival controversy can go now or else stay for the rest of the meeting."

The place cleared out quickly, with only a handful of people left behind.

"Did we win, Momma?" Annie asked.

"I think we did, but when you consider the work ahead, maybe we didn't," Mamie answered for Julie.

"No one told me Griffin was a councilman," Julie said.

"What was that woman talkin' about? She said your kid, so that's me isn't it, Momma? What did she mean when she said something about Griffin's brother?"

Julie sighed. "We'll talk about it later. Mamie, you got time for a Dairy Queen sundae before we all go home?"

"Honey, I've always got time for ice cream. My little fat cells threaten to go on strike if I don't have at least a cone of vanilla once a day," Mamie laughed.

Alvera caught them in the parking lot. "That was more fun than I've had since the time me and Clarice got into it over the damn Thanksgiving turkey wishbone.

We decided to play poker for it, and when I won, she threw a bitch fit that lasted a whole year. God, I'm hopin' she don't speak to me for two years over tonight. You kids need a donation, you call me first. I'll be glad to help out."

"Thanks for everything, Alvera," Julie said.

Alvera grabbed both Julie and Mamie in a three-way hug. "Thanks hell. I want a hug. I thought I did a fine job up there bringin' 'em around to our way of thinkin'. Can you think up something else to make her mad? I'll stand with you. 'Tween the three of us, we might make her blood pressure go up so high she'll have to go to one of them spas and stay a year or two."

"Ooooh, she don't want to go to no spawn. That's what that mean woman said about Lizzy. That she was a spawn. Is that a dirty word, Momma?" Annie asked.

Alvera's laughter rang up the streets. "I like that kid. She'll be sure to make some changes in this place when her time comes. I'm goin' home now and see about my new baby calf. Y'all have a nice night. Mine is wonderful just knowin' that Clarice can't even bite her fingernail 'cause it's gold."

"She's a piece of work," Julie said when Alvera was in her truck and on her way home.

"A good piece. See you at the Dairy Queen," she said as they parted ways and went to their own vehicles.

They were still sitting in the booth having Peanut Buster Parfaits when Griffin walked through the doors.

"Griff, come and sit with us," Mamie yelled.

Julie could have strangled her new friend right there in the Dairy Queen with everyone who wanted to watch having a ringside seat.

He ordered an ice cream cone and a cup of coffee and joined them.

"Clarice is gunning for you," he said.

"Which one of us?" Mamie asked.

"Both of you. I wouldn't want her mad at me, I'm here to tell you." He propped one leg over the other and accidentally touched Julie's thigh, setting it on fire.

She chewed the inside of her bottom lip. Maybe she ought to put herself in a position to go to bed with him just so she could get over the attraction. *Hell no!* Fighting fire with fire would just give her twice the opportunity to get burned.

"Clarice is more growl than bite," Mamie said.

"She's ninety percent bluff and ten percent mean. But I wouldn't want to test her, Mamie. That ten percent would make a Texas rattler look like a fishin' worm." He licked his ice cream.

That innocent gesture made Julie's insides go to mush. The whole thing with the Luckadeaus living in Saint Jo wasn't fair, and she fully well intended to take up the matter with God when she got home. He could have at least thrown a wrench in her plans or maybe shown her a Luckadeau before she moved to Saint Jo. It was all His fault. He could have done something about it.

"So you going to be all right with the festival?" Mamie asked.

"Have to be. Still don't think you should have another one. Still think you're going to be sorry as hell, but it's your baby, like I said. Raise it or let it die crib death. I don't give a damn. Just don't ask me to help in any way. I do my duty on the Fourth of July. Julie, could I have a word with you in private?"

Julie's gaze went from the last bite of her sundae to his face. Had she heard him right? Had he really just asked for a private word with her? Was it showdown time? Did she need to load her six-guns and put on her stomping boots?

"What for?" she asked.

"I'd rather discuss it outside, please."

"Of course. Mamie?" Julie asked flatly.

"I'll sit right here while Annie finishes her ice cream," Mamie said.

She walked side by side with him to the door. He opened it and stepped aside, and then she followed him out to the bed of his truck. At least he didn't reach out and cup his hand over her elbow. She didn't think she could stand for him to touch her many more times without it driving her completely loco.

"What's so important?" she asked.

"It's confidential. We got a problem, me and you."

"I told you before I'm not here to collect anything for Annie. She's a Donavan and always will be." Julie's tone was one of exasperation.

"I believe you. I do. At first, I didn't, but I do now. The problem hasn't got anything to do with us but with our girls," he said.

"Please don't say that Lizzy can't come back to play at our house. I know it looks horrid on the outside and I'm meanin' to paint it, but with teaching and canning for Mamie, I haven't had time."

"God bless! I'm not that kind of person. I don't care if the place is painted or not. Lizzy loves Annie and the both of them love Chuck, and he's our problem," Griffin said.

"What did he do?" Julie asked.

"Nothing, far as I know. Are you aware that this whole past month our girls have been taking extra food for him?"

"I don't mind. He's just a little boy and he was so skinny. I think I can see him filling out a little bit. Boys are so hungry at that age, and he doesn't like the lunchroom food, especially on fish stick days," Julie said.

"That's because fish sticks were the only food his momma bought for him. They're easy to make in the microwave and he ate them so much he threw them up." Griffin looked out into the night air.

"How'd you know that? And since you do know it, why are you upset about our girls feeding him?"

Griffin squirmed. "It's confidential, like I said. Lizzy and Annie are best friends. I don't want to hinder that and yet... Oh, hell. I know, and I'm not supposed to know, and what I do is going to affect us."

"Spit it out, Griffin. What in the hell is going on?"

"I'm friends with the men on the police force. Tonight they are going to raid the Chesters' trailer. His father and mother are cooking meth in it as well as in their car and their shed. They're going to jail, probably for a very long time. Chuck will go to foster care."

"Oh no!" Julie exhaled and forgot to suck in more air. Her lungs hurt before she remembered.

"There's three or four people in Saint Jo who run foster care homes. They're all full, but Marita and Carl have been foster care parents before, so they're licensed. What do you think of him living at the ranch?"

"You'd do that?" Julie asked.

He nodded. "I called Marita and she said she didn't want the full-time responsibility of a child, but she wouldn't mind watching him with Lizzy. She'd be the actual foster parent, but I'd be his caretaker, so to speak."

"I think it's wonderful."

Griffin propped an arm on the back of the truck. "Okay, here's the thing. When Lizzy comes to play at your house, which is most Saturday afternoons now, is Chuck going to be welcome to come along, too?"

"Of course he is! They'll be delighted that their other friend can join them. I'd take him in myself but I'm not qualified. I'll keep him and Lizzy anytime. Overnight. Anytime you want time," she said.

"Okay, then I'll make some calls. I just wanted to run this by you before I did. Lizzy hasn't ever been happier."

"Neither has Annie," she said.

"Well, then, good night," he said and paused.

The moment was pregnant with tension and for a moment, his eyes went dreamy and half-closed as if he were about to lean down and kiss her. She got ready for it, but he turned his head and started around the truck.

Damn, damn, damn, she swore silently. She'd been ready for his lips to touch hers and more than ready to give back as good as she got. Why did he stop right then? Folks talked about women being a tease; well, Griffin Luckadeau was one that night.

She slapped her leg as he drove away, inhaled several times to get the raw desire under control, and headed back into the Dairy Queen. Next time, by damn, she'd kiss him.

Chapter 8

The gazebo in the center of Saint Jo's town square was decorated in red and green. Christmas music was broadcast over loudspeakers, and the square was filled with vendors of every kind. People milled about buying food or sitting on the square in their lawn chairs. There was a chill in the morning air, but nothing that a light jacket wouldn't take care of. Deborah and Luke Donavan looked at mirror art, carved wooden items, and so many other things that Deborah could scarcely remember them all.

"Ribbons for her hair," she finally said. "That's what I'll buy today. Ribbons and fancy things for Annie's hair. Red and green ones, so she'll have them for the Christmas play at church."

Luke pulled out his wallet to pay for her purchases. "You've missed them terribly, haven't you?"

"Yes, I have. I wonder when they'll get here." She was as excited as a little child on Christmas morning. Watching Julie take Annie to the car that last day had been almost more than she could endure. If it hadn't been for the trip to the Holy Land to look forward to and plan, she was sure she would have lost her mind.

"Anytime. It's five minutes until ten now, and Julie said they'd meet us in Molly's at ten. You don't think we hurt her feelings by staying in the hotel, do you?"

"She remembers how loud you snore," Deborah said.

"Besides, it was an experience I wouldn't have missed. Who would have thought there'd be such a quaint little hotel right here on this square? There's Annie! Oh, look at her, Luke. She's grown so much." Deborah was almost giddy. She'd never gone three months without seeing her daughter or her granddaughter before. She opened up her arms and started toward Annie.

She grasped her heart. "Oh! Oh! Oh! Do something, Luke. Call the police. Do something."

Luke shoved his wallet back in his pocket and grabbed her. "Deborah, are you all right?"

Deborah was as pale as yesterday's ashes and pointing across the square. "Call the police. That man in the baseball hat just grabbed Annie from behind and put her in his truck with a little red-haired boy. Look, they're driving away now. That man just kidnapped our granddaughter!"

"Grammy! Grammy, over here!" Annie yelled from behind her.

The little dark-haired girl barreled into her grandfather's arms and reached for her grandmother to join them in a three-way hug. Julie stood back for a moment before entering in on the embrace.

"But, but..." Deborah kept saying.

"What's goin' on here? Who was that little girl?" Luke asked.

"That's Lizzy. She and Chuck is my bestest friends ever and Chuck gets to live with Lizzy now so he can come to my house and play with us," Annie said.

"What little girl?" Julie asked.

"Your mother was in a panic. She saw that little girl from behind and saw that white streak. She thought Annie had been kidnapped," Luke said.

"It happens." Julie wasn't ready to have this conversation with her parents, not by a long shot. She'd planned on telling them on a need-to-know basis, not hit them with the whole thing the moment she saw them. "How was the hotel? Did the other guests complain about Dad's snoring?"

Deborah laughed nervously. "Not yet. I really was scared, Julie. My heart almost stopped. Who would have ever thought there was another child with a streak in her hair in a town this small?"

"Strange, ain't it?" Julie said.

"Ain't? And you a schoolteacher?" Luke teased.

"Yes, I am, and I'm also a businesswoman. My five acres has a garden and an orchard. Come over to Molly's and see my wares. Sometime this afternoon we'll drive out to the place so you can see it." Julie looped her arm through her mother's and led the way to the little store painted bright yellow on the east side of the square.

Bells jingled when they walked through the door and Mamie came out from behind the counter with a big smile on her face. In keeping with the holiday spirit, she wore a red-and-white, furry Santa hat with a big jingle bell on the point.

The store was small but organized. Shelves lined three walls and offered gifts and gadgets arranged neatly with Julie's canned goods interspersed between everything. The cash register sat on an antique, glass-front counter that displayed costume jewelry, watches, and other small items.

"You must be Julie's mother. She looks exactly like you except for the red hair," Mamie said.

"And this is my poppa and he's my momma's daddy

and did you see Lizzy this morning? I want my grandpa and grandma to meet her," Annie said.

"Yes, I did and she'll be back real soon," Mamie said.

Julie dreaded telling her parents about Lizzy, but the way Annie kept bringing up her name left little choice. She was even more worried about mentioning Griffin. Explaining Graham would be easier by far. That had been a flash in the pan. Griffin was much, much more complicated. More like a slow-burning ember in a fireplace. Julie tried to push her worries away and make her introductions.

"Momma, this is Mamie. Mamie, this is my mother, Deborah, and my father, Luke."

Hands were shaken. Pleasantries exchanged.

Mamie raised an eyebrow, but Julie pretended she didn't notice. She was more nervous than she'd ever been in her life. Her hands were sweaty and her pulse was racing.

Deborah picked up one item and then another. "I love your store. It's exactly what I want someday when Luke retires. We'll need a little something to keep us from sitting down and going to rot," she said.

"Want to buy it?" Mamie asked.

"Is it for sale?"

"Could be."

Deborah looked at the store with a critical eye, looking from floor to ceiling, thinking about how she would add a few boughs of greenery here and red velvet bows over there. "We might talk about it in a couple of years when Luke retires."

"There's a stairway in the supply room. Goes up to a three-room apartment. We haven't used it in years.

Never in my lifetime, but story has it that my grandmother and grandfather lived up there when they first married and this was Granny Molly's sewing shop," Mamie said.

Julie was glad her mother had gotten away from the shock of seeing another child with a white streak in her hair. She held up a jar of dilled beans.

"Momma, take a look at my new business," she said.

Just then, Griffin pushed open the door and joined the conversation. "Her squash relish brought in a hefty amount at the fireman's auction last week."

Julie had been exceptionally pretty that day in her jeans and light jacket, but then she'd look good in anything—or nothing. He rather liked the nothing idea better than the anything idea and let his eyes undress her.

She felt his gaze and turned to find his eyes all dreamy and sexy like they'd been that night at the Dairy Queen. Right there in front of her parents, instead of a place where she could return the favor. She looked away at the same time she heard her mother gasp.

When Deborah sucked in air, Luke looked up and did the same. Annie wiggled until her grandfather set her down.

Mamie grinned, and for that Julie could have shot her—BFFs didn't grin when the other BFF was in boiling-hot water.

Annie grabbed Lizzy's hand and pulled her toward Deborah and Luke. "Lizzy, come and see my grammy and poppa. You come on too, Chuck."

Both children took a step forward, away from Griffin. Chuck had a new pair of wire-rimmed glasses that fit his face much better than the old black plastic frames had and was wearing starched jeans, a clean T-shirt, and a good, warm coat. Lizzy was in jeans with jewel trim on the pockets and pink sneakers. She carried her coat because, according to her, it wasn't cold enough to wear it.

Tension filled the room as each person tried to process the scenario.

"Did someone toot?" Lizzy asked.

"Lizzy!" Griffin said.

"Well, everyone had a funny look on their face, like this." She sucked air noisily into her nostrils and held her breath. "And I wondered if someone tooted."

Annie cocked her head to one side, the exact same way that Griffin did at that very moment. "I don't smell anything. I think it's that candle Mamie is burning. It smells funny."

Chuck sniffed the air. "Smells good to me. Like gingerbread."

Mamie saved the day when she starting introducing everyone. "Griffin, honey, meet Julie's mom and dad. They drove over from Jefferson for the festival. This is Deborah and Luke Donavan and this is Griffin Luckadeau."

Luke extended his hand. "Pleased to meet you."

Luke was shocked but determined he'd give the man the benefit of the doubt. Griffin's handshake was firm. He was clean and a cowboy. It could be the Lord's strange way of working, bringing his daughter together with the man who'd produced his grandchild.

"And that imp is Lizzy, Griffin's daughter, and the boy is Chuck Chester. He lives with Griffin and Lizzy," Mamie continued.

Luke jerked his hand back. What in the hell was going on? Everything was so complicated.

"I can see where Julie gets her looks, Mrs. Donavan. She's the image of you except for that red hair," Griffin said in a slow drawl. It was evident that Julie's parents had already put two and two together and come up with the magic answer—the wrong one, but he didn't owe anyone an explanation about anything. That was Julie's job.

"Got that from her great-grandmother Donavan, my husband's grandmother," Deborah said nervously. She didn't wring her hands, but she sure wanted to. Griffin Luckadeau had fathered those two little girls, and Julie had a lot of explaining to do, and it wouldn't wait until later.

Luke raised an eyebrow. "Julie?"

Mamie poked her in the ribs and whispered barely loud enough that she could hear, "Time to face the music."

Julie poked back. "Some BFF you are."

"Hey, kids, how about I take you outside to the vendors and let you look around?" Griffin offered. He'd give her that much but nothing more. She could do the explaining. He would have to do the same when his parents found out about Annie.

"Good boy versus evil twin," Mamie whispered again.

"But—" Deborah started.

"Ten minutes, Griffin. Then I'll watch them the rest of the day," Julie said. She was nervous as a worm in hot ashes but not too jittery to notice how striking he looked or how good he smelled after a fresh morning shave.

"Hey, that's a deal I can't refuse. Marita is watching a stand for her daughter, who is up from San Antonio, and the kids were going to have to stay with her a while. I'm sure they'd rather be with Annie. Be back in ten minutes. So much for me not getting involved in all this hoorah, huh? How about a snow cone, kids?"

That set up squeals of joy. They joined hands and tried to get out of the store all at the same time, with Griffin right behind them.

Mamie raised a curtain and motioned them through it. "I've got a pot of coffee and some funnel cakes in the back room. Go on back there and help yourself."

Julie sank into one of four folding chairs set up around a card table. She picked up a healthy portion of funnel cake and put it into her mouth. Manners said she couldn't talk with food in her mouth and she needed a few minutes to collect her thoughts. Did she really have to tell it all right now, or could part of it be sidestepped?

"Okay, confession time," she finally said when she couldn't escape it any longer.

"Let me go first," Luke said in a hoarse voice. "I love you unconditionally and figured you'd gotten tired of trying to get pregnant and went to a sperm bank without telling Derrick. I know what he said about adultery, but I never believed it."

Deborah narrowed her eyes at Julie. "Why would a married man donate to a sperm bank? There's no doubt that man is Annie's biological father. Did you know it when you moved here? And where does that little red-haired boy come into the picture? He looks more like he could belong to you than your own child."

Julie slowly shook her head. "First, I didn't go to a sperm bank. I was divorced, although it wasn't final. Remember the weekend Sally and I went to Dallas, the week before Derrick came begging me to take him back?"

"No, I don't," Luke said.

"Well, I went to Dallas with the girls and I did a stupid thing and slept with a man I only met that night and got pregnant. I didn't know it when I went back with Derrick. I did not commit adultery. We were as good as divorced."

"You slept with a married man?" Deborah asked.

"No, I slept with Griffin's twin brother, Graham. And I had no idea the Luckadeaus were from Saint Jo or I would have treated this place like it had the plague. There's more." She told them that Graham had died in Iraq and about how the townspeople already knew about Graham being Annie's father.

"Out of the frying pan right into the fire," Deborah said.

"How does Griffin feel about this all?" Luke asked.

"We started out on the wrong foot, but we're pretty decent friends now. It won't ever be anything more, so don't worry. We are good with both girls and with Chuck, and the kids are inseparable. Lizzy loves me. She says wants to be just like me."

Luke frowned. "Is that right? I wonder why she'd say that?"

"I'm not much of a role model. I slept with his brother. I moved to Saint Jo to a house that looks like crap right now. I haven't had time to paint, and the first time he came to the place when Lizzy ran away, I screamed at him like a fishwife."

"What a mess," Deborah said.

"You got it," Julie said.

"What do you plan to do now?"

"Live right here. I own five acres. I like what I'm doing. I'm making a small profit on my business. Haven't had to touch Aunt Flossie's money yet except, of course, to buy the place, but the balance is still there. The canning business and my paycheck are supporting me and Annie for food and bills so far, and I'm even saving money."

"But everyone probably thinks that you…" Deborah couldn't force the words from her mouth.

"Are an adulteress? I'm sure some of them do, but I'm not running. We tried that and it didn't work. We'll just sit our ground and take our blows," Julie said.

The bell rang at the front of the store, and Mamie asked the customer if she could help. Her friend's tone had a lilt to it that Julie recognized immediately as Mamie's flirting voice. Maybe California had arrived to buy out the stock.

"I hope so," a masculine voice said. "My mother and father were supposed to meet my sister, Julie Donavan, in this store. Have they been in? Do you know them?"

"Eli!" Julie screeched and shoved back the chair. The curtain waved in her wake as she ran into the store and into his arms. "This is such a wonderful surprise. How did you get here?"

Eli pushed her back and looked at her for a long minute. "By car, little sister. I might be a preacher, but I can't sprout wings like an angel just yet."

Griffin poked his head in the door and turned two dark-haired tornadoes and one red-haired one loose. "They are all yours." He stopped midway in the process of shutting the door and stared at the man holding both of Julie's hands. Jealousy shot through him in a white-hot flash. Had her ex-husband returned to beg for another chance?

"This is my brother, Eli," Julie explained. "Eli, this is Griffin Luckadeau. And this is Lizzy, Annie's new best friend. And this little red-haired fellow is Chuck, who is their friend, too. And they are all three my students in kindergarten."

Griffin exhaled slowly and extended his hand.

Eli was speechless, but he shook hands with the man.

Deborah and Luke chose that minute to fan through the curtain.

"Shocking, isn't it?" Luke said.

"I'm off to take care of business," Griffin said. "Pick them up at what time?" No need for him to stick around, and he did have business. A cup of coffee was calling to him from the Texas Kings Hotel lobby.

"When the day is finished. If they get too tired, I'll beg Mom and Dad for the key to their hotel room and put them down for a nap," Julie said.

Eli cocked his head to one side and then the other as he studied the little girls who were almost twins.

"Uncle Eli, you look funny," Annie said.

Eli regained enough composure to scoop up the child talking, hoping he was truly hugging his niece. "That's because you didn't hug me yet."

"Now hug Lizzy and Chuck," Annie said.

Eli stooped down on one knee and opened his arms. Annie pushed her friends toward him.

"It's all right, he's my uncle and he's a preacher," Annie announced.

Julie felt like a one-legged chicken at a coyote convention and sure didn't want to explain it all a second time in less than half an hour. She looked to Mamie for help, only to find her grinning like she'd just won the lottery.

"He's gorgeous," Mamie mouthed.

"Who?" Julie asked.

Mamie pointed discreetly toward Eli.

"Eli?" Julie checked out her brother. He hadn't changed. Same brown hair, light-brown eyes with a few yellow flecks, round baby face like her father's, heavy beard that had been shaved very recently, under six feet tall and just slightly overweight.

Eli, gorgeous?

Mamie needed to put her contacts in or lay off the funnel cakes. All that sugar was affecting her vision for sure.

Lizzy and Chuck both hugged Eli and then the children ran to look out the front window to make sure they weren't missing a single minute of the festival.

"Julie?" Eli stood up.

"I'd like you to meet my new friend, Mamie, who owns this store," Julie said.

Eli nodded toward Mamie. "Pleasure, ma'am."

"Okay, short version or long?" Julie said.

"I don't care which one, but you'd better start talkin'. My brain is working overtime," he said.

Mamie giggled.

"For that little giggle, you get to tell him. I'm taking the kids for a stroll over to the hotel, where I'll meet you in half an hour," Julie said to Mamie.

Mamie tugged at Eli's arm. "Come on back here and have a seat. I'll tell you how all this came about while you have some funnel cake and coffee."

Eli was glad to sit down. His head was spinning out of control and he couldn't grasp a single thought, much less make sense of it.

"We're going to follow Julie," Luke said. "Come on over to the Kings Hotel when Mamie gets through, and get ready for a shock."

"I've already got the shock. Now I want the story," Eli answered.

Julie's heart had settled down to a slow, steady beat by the time she walked across the square to the hotel. The lobby was reminiscent of a hotel right out of the last century, with an ornate pool table sitting atop an off-white-and-mauve rug that looked as though it had been designed after a patchwork quilt. The hardwood floors were as shiny as a freshly polished mirror. The bar had a brass footrest that had seen lots of cowboy boots. The walls were papered in stripes, and tables for four offered seating space. Comfortable leather chairs and a sofa begged for people to get cozy and have a visit.

It was in one of those chairs that Julie found Griffin. Damn his good-old-boy heart and all that surrounded it if he hadn't just lied to her. Said he had a meeting and rushed off to leave her holding the bag. Lizzy ran over to him and crawled up on his knee. Chuck claimed the other one, and Annie put her hand on his shoulder. Julie sank down into the chair next to him.

"So, you got any more family that's likely to tar and feather me this day?" he asked. In the few minutes he'd been sitting, everything had come clear. Julie moving to Saint Jo had been like the luck of the draw. She hadn't known about the Luckadeaus and she wasn't there to fleece him. Not one of her relatives had known about him or his family. He'd been wrong about that part, but it wasn't enough for him to truly let his feelings have free rein. Not by a long shot.

"Hey, I had to meet yours at the rodeo and they still

haven't come back around. They put a big old *A* on my chest, so don't be giving me a hard time," she said.

"It's not all *you* with my family. It's the fact that you are a schoolteacher. Beau was engaged to one before Milli came back into his life. That schoolteacher was ready to take him to the cleaners. Remember Rachel?" Griffin asked.

"I'd like to answer with a no, but yes, I remember her. She reminds me of Clarice," Julie said.

"She should. She's her granddaughter. Well, Amanda was the schoolteacher, and she'd make Rachel look like a humble little housewife," Griffin said.

"Whew! No wonder they turned up their noses at me. Didn't you tell them we are only friends, and that's using the term loosely?" Julie asked.

The look on his face said he hadn't told them anything but the bare bones of the story. Leave it to a man not to explain the way things really were. They said a few words and expected women to fill in the blanks. Only trouble with that was what they filled in the blanks with.

"You are a rat," she said.

Alvera turned around at the bar where she'd been drinking a beer. "Most men are bona fide rats, darlin'. But don't judge him too harsh, even if he did side with Clarice. At least he had the good sense to get rid of my great-niece. She's over in Nocona, flirtin' around a lawyer. Hell, by next summer, she'll have gold fingernails. This is a wonderful festival. The parade was right nice. Y'all did a bang-up good job, didn't they, Griff?"

"I suppose they did, and I'm big enough to say that I was wrong," Griffin said.

"See there, he's a good boy. Don't throw his family

in the Red River just yet. I'm going over to Ringgold this week to see a bull Nellie is thinkin' about sellin'. I'll put in a word with her and Ellen." Alvera said.

"Who in the...devil...are Nellie and Ellen?" Julie asked.

"Your daddy don't like you to cuss, does he? I caught that 'hell' that was on the tip of your tongue. To answer your question, Nellie is Slade's grandmother. Ellen is her sister. They are wonderful old girls. You'd like them. They're just like Alvera," Griffin said.

"They aren't like Clarice, then, are they?"

Clarice came through the door. "Did I hear my name? Oh, it's you. I'd hoped you'd be gone by now. Griffin, honey, you'd best be callin' Rachel and apologizin' for hurtin' her. She's got a date with a lawyer over in Nocona. Looks like you might be losin' your footin' waitin' around like you are." She ignored Julie and poured on the charm for Griffin.

"Reckon I'm content to lose my footin', Clarice. I hope she's happy with the lawyer," Griffin said.

"You Luckadeau men! Ain't a one of you got a lick of horse sense." Clarice huffed her way to the bar and ordered a piña colada.

"Daddy, I'm hungry," Lizzy said.

"There's a taco stand and a hamburger wagon on the square, plus about anything else you could want. Shall we go find food? It's nice to see you, Clarice. We were wrong about the festival, weren't we?" Griffin said.

"No, we were not! Next thing you know, this schoolteacher will be wantin' to have another one in February. Give 'em an inch and they'll want a mile. Good day, Griffin." Clarice didn't even look back.

Julie wrapped her fingers around Griffin's upper arm

and squeezed. Her touch got his attention and he jerked his head up to look into her mossy-green eyes.

Julie let go of his arm and said, "The kids are mine for the day, so you are not taking them to the vendors for lunch. You said so, and Annie is looking forward to spending the day with Lizzy and Chuck so her grandparents can get to know her friends, so suck it up and go on about your business."

Griffin nodded slowly. "Then I get Annie one day at the ranch. Lizzy's been asking and you always say no. The kids have been coming to your house every weekend and whining when they can't. So?"

Custody rights? Something she never thought she'd have to think about when Derrick flatly denied that Annie was his and divorced her. Annie was hers and hers alone. She hadn't even shed a tear when Derrick made his dramatic exit out of the hospital. But right then, she had to swallow hard to keep from crying at the idea of going without Annie for a whole day.

"Please, Momma. Lizzy has a pony and I want to see it and she has a princess Barbie with dark hair and I want to go and she gets Chuck all the time," Annie pleaded.

"Sunday afternoon after church," Julie said. That would only be half a day to start with. No doubt there would be other times he'd want her all day to repay for the times when the children spent the day at Julie's place.

"I'll settle with that for a beginning," Griffin said.

"Yippee. This is the best time ever. Let's go eat," Lizzy said.

Griffin pulled his wallet from his hip pocket.

Julie grabbed his arm again. What would it be like to have those big, strong arms around her in the bedroom?

She blushed all the way to her toes. There were three children right there, and her parents had just walked past the hotel lobby window. How in the devil did that thought about him holding her in the bedroom sneak its way into her consciousness right then? "Put it away," Julie said hoarsely. "Or else I'll send Annie's dinner with her on Sunday."

"Are you fighting?" Annie asked.

"Of course not," Griffin said.

"Yes, we are, and I'm winning," Julie said.

Her father and mother entered the hotel and joined them in the lounging area. "Winning what?"

"She's a mean redhead. See you later." Griffin was out the door before she could reply. He could dodge those people all day. Being around Julie after he'd figured out she was telling the truth created a whole new blast of feelings he didn't want to face or deal with, especially in front of her relatives.

"Grammy, we get to eat lunch together. Do you want to eat with us?" Annie asked.

"You bet I do, and I found a vendor with some hair ribbons I think would be just lovely in your hair, so we'll go there, too."

"And some for Lizzy?" Annie asked.

"Of course. We'll buy them just alike so you can match, and I bet we can find some cute socks for Chuck," Deborah said.

Julie mouthed a thank-you to her mother.

When they passed by Miss Molly's, Mamie still had Eli cornered behind the counter. He had a plate of funnel cakes on his lap and a cup of coffee in his hand. Julie would have given half of her five acres to know exactly how she'd explained Lizzy and Annie to him, much less Chuck. She would consider giving up her recipes for squash relish and dilled beans to know how Mamie told Eli about Griffin and Graham. One thing for sure, he'd know his little sister did not have wings or a halo when he walked out of that gift store.

"So let me get this straight. That man that just passed by the window is actually Annie's uncle," Eli said. "And my sister didn't know he lived here when she bought that hideous place."

"You got it," Mamie said.

"She sent me pictures over the Net of that run-down house. She didn't live in a mansion, but our parsonages were nice. How can she live like that?" he asked.

Mamie fired up angry. "Did you come here to rescue her out of her miserable life?"

"No, no. I'm sorry. That came out wrong."

"You should be sorry. She's very happy. The place where she lives needs paint, but that's all. The inside is very nice."

"My mistake. Thank you for the explanation," Eli said.

"Come on. I'll show you around town," she said.

"But your store?"

"Is my store and there's a lock on the door. I won't make a lot of money today anyway. People spend their hard-earned cash at the vendors out on the square. California can come find me...well, I guess he just did," Mamie said when a tall, dark-haired, well-tanned man opened the door.

"Miss Mamie, how delightful to see you." He crossed the room and planted a quick kiss on each cheek.

"Same here, darlin'," she said.

"Do you have it all boxed up for me?" he asked.

"I can get it that way in about ten minutes. Look around. See if you want to buy anything else. I wasn't expecting you for a few more days."

"Oh, hello." He eyed Eli up and down. "Is he for sale?"

Eli chuckled nervously.

"Sorry, but that chunk of Texas stays in Texas. And he's a preacher," Mamie said.

California clucked his tongue against the roof of his mouth. "Too damn bad."

Eli actually blushed, which endeared him to Mamie even more. "Come on out from behind there and help me get these jars into the boxes. This man is my best customer today."

They loaded a dozen jars into each box and California carried them out the back door to his van, parked behind the store. When he had stripped the shelves of anything with a checked piece of fabric on the lid, he paid with a credit card. "If you get tired of that Texan, kick him over the border to me. I'll play nice," he said as he signed his name with a flourish.

"Sorry, it ain't happening," Mamie said.

"Some days you just can't win," California sighed and left by the front door.

"What in the...devil...was that?" Eli asked.

"You almost used a dirty word, didn't you?" Mamie responded with another question.

"But I didn't. Answers?"

"He comes in once or twice a year and buys my merchandise. Actually, it's Edna's and Julie's merchandise. And he takes it to California and sells some of it and uses the rest for presents and eats the rest, I suppose."

"He's..."

"I know. Julie figured it out for me."

"I'm beginning to think I don't know my sister."

"Oh, yes you do, darlin'. She's still the same Julie you always knew. She's protected you from the ugly because of your preachin'," Mamie said.

"Julie never protected me from a thing. She was a tattletale. You ever hear of the preacher's son? Every story is true and I've got the T-shirt to prove it," Eli said.

"Someday, darlin', you'll have to tell me those stories," Mamie locked the door and looped her arm through his. Preacher or not, she liked those brown eyes and the way he looked at her.

In the middle of the afternoon, Deborah and Julie took the kids up to the room the Donavans had rented at the Texas Kings Hotel. The renovated hotel only had five rooms upstairs over the saloon and kitchen. Julie had no idea that her parents had rented the Rose Room way back when she first moved to Saint Jo and had made plans even that far back to visit her the Saturday after Thanksgiving. That the town was having its first-ever holiday festival celebration just added to the fun.

Julie washed all three kids' sticky faces and then put them to bed for a nap. Of course, it wasn't called a nap. Not at five years old. It was called a resting period. They could hold hands and talk for ten minutes and then they had to shut their eyes for five minutes without talking.

They were all asleep within thirty seconds from the time they shut their eyes.

"They look like twins at first glance, but I see a difference. Annie is a bit shorter and her face just slightly rounder. Is Lizzy older or younger? And that Chuck. I could take him home myself. He looks so much like you did at that age."

"They are all five and go to kindergarten. Chuck is the youngest by a couple of months. Lizzy was five on May twentieth. Annie, on May twenty-second. Chuck's birthday is July tenth."

They sat side by side on chairs with burgundy velvet upholstery at a small table. "This must have been a shock to your system."

"Only you can imagine how much," Julie said.

"Why didn't you tell me?"

"Because you've looked forward to the Holy Land trip for years. I wouldn't spoil it just so I could talk about my own affairs."

Deborah nodded at the children. "They're good together, especially for only children. I'm glad Annie found Lizzy. That streak has always been a cross for her to bear. Now she won't be alone in it. And Chuck is their brother in spirit, even if he's red-haired. But I think it's a good time now for you to tell me about Griffin."

"Nothing to tell. We are friends. He has Lizzy and Chuck, and I have Annie."

"You can't brush off your feelings forever. Call me when you decide you need to talk about this thing between you," Deborah said.

Eli and Luke sat in the leather chairs in the lobby and worked on their second glass of sweet tea and slices of pecan pie.

"Who'd a thought I'd find something like this when I came to visit you and surprise my sister?" Eli said.

"All secrets surface at some time," Luke said. "Noticed that shop owner cornered you pretty fast. You looked good wandering around the square with her on your arm."

"I didn't have much choice. She grabbed my arm and took control," Eli said a bit too quickly.

"Pretty woman, and your sister's good friend," Luke said. His brown hair had red highlights and his face was round. He wore glasses that made his green eyes look bigger than they really were.

"It's that latter that scares me," Eli said.

"It's time you let go, Son. Teresa was a wonderful wife to you, but she's been gone for ten years now. It's time to get on with your life. It doesn't have to be a proposal. Mamie's eyes said that she liked what she saw. Ask her to have dinner while you're here."

"I'm leaving in the morning," Eli said.

"I know that. Where are you staying tonight?"

"On Julie's couch, if she'll let me. Tomorrow I'm going to preach at the Bowie church. You already know that, but don't tell Julie. I don't want to get my hopes up, much less hers."

"If they ask you to preach there, consider it, Eli. Take a look at the map, Son. It's all of twenty-three miles. A perfect distance. You can see her…"

"You're already matchmaking, Dad. Let it go. I'm not so sure I'm ready even after ten years."

"Son, it's past time to let it go."

"I know, but it's not easy."

"Mamie might make it a lot easier."

"You *are* matchmaking," Eli laughed.

Griffin started into the hotel to get a cold beer at the bar but changed his mind when he saw the Donavan men discussing something very serious in the corner. He went back outside and to Molly's, where he found Mamie having a cup of hot chocolate in the back room.

"I miss my kids," he said, taking the cup of hot chocolate she handed him without asking.

"So Julie will miss Annie. I heard she's giving her up on Sunday afternoon."

"It's like they were all hatched from the same egg, Mamie. Two dark-haired girls and one light-haired boy. I'm not so sure I like it," he said.

"It ain't up to you to like or not like. What's done is done, and the past has caught up to the future."

"Chocolate making you philosophical, is it?"

"Fate, Griffin, whether you believe it or not, is a strong thing," she said.

He tilted up the cup and finished it off. "I'm going home for a nap."

"Enjoy. See you later at dark when we light up the Christmas tree."

After sharing hamburgers at the Dairy Queen, everyone checked out the antique car show. Annie declared that someday she would own a 1958 Studebaker Hawk, only she didn't want it black like the one on display. She wanted a red one. Lizzy opted for a 1965 Mustang convertible in bright yellow. Chuck's eyes glistened when he looked at a shiny red pickup truck with yellow flames painted on the side.

Griffin showed up for the Christmas tree ceremony with folding lawn chairs, a cooler full of soda pop, and a quilt for the kids. Lizzy was glad to see him, but not ecstatic. Chuck was the one who ran to him for a hug. Julie got ready for the same reaction from Annie on Sunday. Good grief, what was she supposed to do with herself for a whole afternoon without her daughter? It was different with Griffin. He had a ranch to run, business to take care of, people to see.

Julie had Annie.

"This is a bit awkward," Luke said when Griffin sat down between him and Julie.

"Little bit," Griffin agreed.

"It's a tangled web," Eli said.

"But I didn't deceive. I just didn't tell," Julie protested. "And don't you go getting all self-righteous on me. Remember I'm the one who tattled on you all your life. A tattletale knows things you might not want aired on the public address system."

"Huh!" Griffin grunted. "I thought she was just mean to me."

Luke explained. "It's the red hair. They say my great-grandmother came from County Cork and married a descendent of Daniel O'Donovan. Eli is actually named for that ancestor. His name is Eli Daniel. It's said that her temper was the talk of County Cork and her brothers paid her husband to marry her so they wouldn't have to share the house with her anymore."

"That's the reason I never liked red-haired women. Their tempers get in the way of their good sense," Griffin said.

Luke threw back his head and guffawed.

Julie slapped her father's shoulder. "It's not funny. Look at that white streak. Doesn't it make him evil?"

Annie pointed at her hair with one hand and Lizzy's with another. "We got white streaks, Momma. Are we evil?"

"No, you are not evil. You are very sweet little girls, but you'll have to be very careful that they don't make you ornery," Julie didn't even hesitate to say.

"What's ornery?" Lizzy whispered to Annie.

"I don't know, but I bet it'll get us put in the corner if we do it, so be very, very careful," Chuck whispered back.

Chapter 9

Annie had trouble getting to sleep. She could barely sit still long enough to eat breakfast. She'd fretted over what Barbie and which of her doll's fancy clothing to take with her to church. After all, a girl couldn't go for a play day without the right Barbie and all her clothing. She'd be going home with Lizzy and Chuck right after services and didn't even want to stop on the way home for her things. Julie had suggested she take a change of clothes and her bathing suit, and that had set Annie off like the Energizer Bunny to find even more stuff to put in the duffel bag. Then Julie suggested that she take a Ken doll for Chuck to play with and she was off again.

The preacher's sermon didn't last nearly long enough. All too soon, Julie was watching Griffin drive off with two girls and a little boy in the back seat of his truck. All of them were strapped in, but she still worried that something might happen on the way home.

The whole afternoon and evening stretched out in front of her like eternity.

She drove home and walked around the entire house and picked at loose, peeling paint, checked the garden space, and contemplated making it a little bigger the next spring. She heard the phone ring and panicked, ran into the house, and grabbed it on the fourth ring, her mind galloping as fast as her heart.

Annie was crying and lonely for her already. Griffin had wrecked the truck on the way home. That damn pony had bitten Annie's finger off. The cat had scratched her eye and she'd be blind for life. Julie should have never, ever let her go over there to that ranch of horrors.

"Hello," she said breathlessly.

"Julie, were you running?" Deborah asked.

"I'm so glad it's you. Y'all made it home?" Julie said.

It was Deborah's turn to worry. "Of course we did, but you're in a panic. What's happened? Is Annie all right?"

"Everything is fine. I just let my imagination run away with my emotions. Annie's gone to Lizzy's for the whole day, remember?"

Deborah laughed. "Well, don't just sit there and fret. Do something."

"What?" Julie asked.

"How long has it been since you went to the beauty shop or shopped without Annie underfoot?"

"I can't remember," Julie said.

"Get dressed and get out for the afternoon. It will do you good."

"But what if she needs me or they call or—"

"Does she have your cell phone number?"

"Oh no! I didn't give it to her. I'm a bad mother," Julie said.

"Call the ranch house and tell Griffin. If anything goes wrong, they'll call you and you can be home in an hour if you go to Gainesville. Buy something pretty for school next week or do some Christmas shopping," Deborah said.

Julie agreed but it wasn't easy. She dressed in jeans and a pink T-shirt. She almost changed her mind when she walked out the front door. She couldn't go that far. What-ifs crawled out of every crevice of her imagination.

"This is ridiculous," she said aloud. She fished in her purse for her cell phone and called the ranch number, branded into her mind because she'd dialed it so many times for Annie to talk to Lizzy and Chuck on the days they didn't see each other at school.

On the fifth ring, she got the voicemail and said, "Marita, this is Julie. I'm running over to Gainesville and want to leave my cell phone number in case of emergency. If you need anything I can pick up for you over that way, just call." She rattled off the number and ended the call.

She backed the truck out of the driveway and drove south. In minutes she'd passed a small cemetery and was on Highway 82, headed east. She couldn't begrudge her daughter the day or the friendship, but she damned sure didn't have to like the loneliness.

Half an hour later, she was in Gainesville at the outlet mall. She spent two hours in Burkes buying five outfits, a nightgown with the Disney princesses on it, and a pair of new sneakers for Annie. Then she found the sleepwear rack and there was a Barbie nightshirt with a purple dot on the tag, which meant it was on sale, so she tossed it in the cart.

She found a pair of skinny jeans and two dresses for herself. All of them had colored dots on the tags, which reduced the prices even more. She made a pass through the Old Navy store and added a few more items to Annie's stash and four pairs of socks on sale for a dollar a pair to hers.

She meandered through the discount bookstore and

bought a mystery for two dollars. Maybe she'd have time to read again over the two-week Christmas break. She checked her phone every ten minutes the first hour. After that, she made herself leave it alone. It was turned on and Marita would call if Annie needed her. She trusted that woman as much as she did her own mother.

At midafternoon she treated herself to an apple dumpling at Cracker Barrel. She couldn't remember the last time she'd eaten alone in a restaurant. Family, friends, Derrick, Annie. In that order. When she was a little girl and up until she was sixteen, her dad had taken the family to dinner once a month at a nice restaurant, where they had to be dressed up, so it was an occasion. Then she had her driver's license, a job at the local Subway, and a schedule that interfered with dinners with her parents.

Looking back, she regretted that. She should have made time for them even if she had been going through an independent streak. In those days, she went with her friends to McDonald's or hung out with them at Dairy Queen. Then high school was over and she was in college. Dinners weren't part of the program in those years. Pizza, ordered in, if someone had a few dollars, and ramen noodles cooked in the microwave if they didn't. Dramatic problems solved over a six-pack of beer.

Then there was college graduation and a wedding the same summer. Derrick was five years older and had been courting her for a year. They'd met at a party, and six weeks later had fallen into bed at the Jefferson Inn in a room that had a Jacuzzi tub. Dinners with Derrick were always dress-up affairs, with cloth napkins and wine in crystal stemware, followed by sex in the Jefferson Inn with a bath afterward in the fancy tub. While she soaked in bubbles and jet sprays, he set up his laptop and conducted business.

Annie's dinners out started with her in a high chair making embarrassing-sized messes at first. At three, she'd look at the menu with Julie and they'd decide together whether she'd have macaroni and cheese and carrots or a hamburger. Never peas. She hated peas.

Right then, Annie would be having snacks with the Luckadeaus—her relatives. That brought Julie up short. Annie was really kin to those people. When she was thirty-four, would her dinner memories include the Lucky Clover Ranch and Lizzy and Chuck? Would she start calling that man who owned the ranch Uncle Griff? When Julie thought of all the Luckadeau relatives that would come out of the woodwork, she shuddered.

As she ate, she wondered briefly what her life would have been like if Annie had been a boy. If Griffin was right and only the girls he and his brother produced would have the white streak, then a son would have had blond hair and blue eyes. Derrick might not have ever known the child wasn't his, but Julie would have. Derrick was one of those men that blended in with the surroundings. When he walked into a room or a bar, the women didn't give him a second glance. Graham's son would have had that Luckadeau magnetic force when he entered a room.

She ate slowly, paid her bill, and went to Walmart, where she meandered through the store to kill time. She bought shampoo, deodorant, and a big jug of bubble bath for Annie. When she checked her watch, it was only four o'clock, so she went to the Dollar Tree and bought six coloring books and a new package of crayons for the kids. Chuck was actually better at coloring than the girls. He took his time and went about it slowly, while they hurried and often went outside the lines.

At six, she started home, stopped in Muenster for an ice cream cone at the Dairy Queen, the official stop sign in Texas, according to their advertisements. As she was leaving, she heard an elderly man ask another if he'd heard about the fires up north. She thought that was strange. Fires were raging out west in California. People were being evacuated by the hundreds in northern California. It had been a dry winter so far all across the United States. She wondered about Mamie's buyer. Had any of her squash relish wound up in the fires?

Griffin got the call right after lunch. He and the kids were playing in the backyard on the swing set when Marita called him about a wildfire that had jumped the Red River north of them and was wiping out everything in its path between there and Capps Corner. He and Carl left orders for the hired hands to plow a firebreak around the entire north side of the ranch and headed north with the Saint Jo fire department to suit up for the fight.

It had started west of the Taovayas Indian Bridge on the Oklahoma side of the Red River, traveled east toward the old Courtney schoolhouse, and jumped the river south of that point. It ate up acres of dry grass, leaving ugly, blackened earth behind as it traveled south like a steamroller over the gentle, rolling hills, prairie, and pastures. People were moving cattle, plowing firebreaks, and doing everything possible to keep it from taking their homes and livelihoods with it.

Griffin had fought fires before, but nothing like the blazes higher than a house moving right toward the firefighters. The flames were alive and dancing as the wind fueled them. They dared mere men to tangle with them and reached out with long, hungry tongues to gobble up anything in their path. By the time Griffin was suited up and holding a hose, he knew it was going to be an all-day affair that could stretch on into the night. The only clouds in the sky were those formed from smoke, so they couldn't even expect relief in the form of rain.

At midafternoon, the Saint Jo women brought sandwiches and cold drinks in the back of a pickup truck and fed everyone who could stop for a five-minute break. Griffin ate with one hand and kept working. At six o'clock, it was approaching the northern edge of the ranch and Griffin prayed the fire break would hold. If it didn't, he'd call Marita and tell her to take the kids to town. Cold chills popped out on him when he thought about losing the ranch house. He'd lived there his whole life, married Dian in the backyard, brought Lizzy home from the hospital to that house, fought with his sister and brother all over the place, and made love to his first girlfriend in the hay barn.

"I won't let it burn," he shouted, but no one could hear him above the noise.

He'd long since tossed the fireman's suit into the back of his truck. Even though it was winter, a hot wind blew from the fire and he couldn't breathe with all that equipment. If he got hurt, he'd bear the burden of it. He fished in his overall pocket for his cell phone and called the house. Marita answered on the first ring.

"Time to evacuate?" she asked.

"Not just yet. Kids all right?" he asked.

"They're in Lizzy's room playing. Don't have a clue that there's danger. Told them the smoke might make them cough and that's the reason they had to come inside. Where's it at?"

"One section line road is separating us from it right now. I can see the firebreaks. Hope they hold. There's a hot spot to the south of our place, too. Tell anyone who's not busy to go plow a firebreak around Julie's house. One flicker and that old house will go up like kindling," he said.

"I'm on it. Be careful," Marita said.

"Always." Griffin hung up and watched the flames waltz over the last hill, toward his property.

The tractors arrived to plow a wide furrow all the way around Julie's property, taking out half the garden and a section of her fence. Then the drivers got away from the heat and flames as fast as they could. One spark in the wrong place and a tractor could become a gas bomb.

Fire trucks from Saint Jo, Muenster, Nocona, Wichita Falls, and Wilson and Terral, Oklahoma, were lined up at the section line road. Weary, bone-tired, hungry firefighters held their breath, hoping the gravel road would hold the fire and it wouldn't jump onto the Lucky Clover Ranch. The blaze that bore down on them lost momentum when the wind died down to nothing more than a gentle breeze. It continued to devour the dirt, but it didn't look nearly as formidable as it had. When it reached the road, it had sated its hunger and stopped.

Griffin went to check on Julie's place. One ember had floated across to her garden but the firemen shot it with a blast of water. Her house was standing, even if her garden was all but demolished and her fence on the ground.

Finally, it was basically over at six thirty. Other firemen would keep watch through the night, especially if the wind picked up. It had been a close call. There was nothing left between the ranch and the river to burn, and everything south of the ranch was charred black.

When he called Marita to tell her it was under control, she said that the buildings at Illinois Bend were saved, two homes up near the lake had been damaged but not lost, and a hay barn was still smoldering. He downed a bottle of water and leaned back against the headrest. He couldn't remember the last time he was that tired, physically and emotionally. Or that angry at Graham, either. He shouldn't have gone off to fight a war. He should have been there with him, protecting the ranch.

He heard a vehicle come to a screeching halt behind him, but he was too tired to even look in the rearview mirror to see who was slamming on their brakes.

"What in the hell did you do to my property? Try to burn it down?" Julie screamed at him as she ate up the distance between them with long strides.

He got out of the truck and stood beside it. "I protected it as best I could. Your yard is a mess, but we saved the house."

"Where's Annie? Is she all right?"

"She's still at the ranch. It's not eight o'clock yet, is it?"

Julie slid down the side of his truck until she was sitting on the baked earth. Her place had been pitiful enough before, but now it was truly a mess. Smoke still hung in the air as if the whole county was a cheap, two-bit bar on the wrong side of town. Half the fence was mangled under plowed ground. Her house was standing and the cats were huddled under the porch swing. But everything else looked as though it had barely survived a nuclear attack.

Across the road to the west, the land still smoked. Small fires kicked up when they found a mesquite tree sapling still left on the buffet table. Two rattlesnakes slithered from her yard into the underbrush to the east. A cottontail hopped to the pasture on the other side of Julie's five acres, and a feral cat carrying a kitten in her mouth followed it.

"I should've stayed home," she mumbled.

Griffin sat down beside her. "You ain't that powerful. You couldn't have stopped that fire no matter how mean you are."

"Why in the hell didn't Marita call me? I left my cell phone number on the answering machine." Julie leaned toward him and he wrapped an arm around her shoulders.

"You ever been in the ranch house?" he asked.

"You know damned well I haven't," she snapped.

"Hey, don't be hateful to me. I didn't start the fire and barely got it put out before it leveled your place. I didn't know if you'd been over there when I was out in the fields on some other day, but if you had been, you'd know."

"Know what?" she asked.

"The answering machine is on the phone in the library. Marita seldom goes in there except to clean."

Julie groaned. "Then if something had happened to Annie, she wouldn't even have known where to find me. I should've stayed home."

It was the last straw. She broke down and wept, burying her face in his shoulder.

Julie crying was almost more than he could bear. Fighting him, arguing with him, tempting him—that, he could endure. But to see her broken tore his heart apart.

"It's all right," he said as he patted her back.

"No, it's not." She moved back, putting distance between them.

"Your house is saved," he said.

"But I was gone," she said stiffly.

Griffin's phone rang. He fished it out of his overalls and put it to his ear, hoping all the while that no one was calling to say that the fire had jumped the road on down the section and the trucks were returning.

Marita was crying. "Griffin, come home right now. I don't care where you are."

"Lizzy?" he asked.

"It's Carl. The boys brought him in from the field where he went to check on the break. The ambulance is on the way. I can hear it. I think he's had a heart attack."

All the color left Julie's face. "What is it?"

"It's Carl. Marita says he's had a heart attack. I've got to get home. Get in. You are coming with me until we see what's going on, all right?"

The truck was already moving by the time she rounded the front end and hopped inside, ignoring her vehicle parked on the side of the road. "Is she sure?"

"No, but the ambulance is on the way." Griffin's face was a map of worry. All places led to his eyes, which were a study in anxiety. What would he do without Marita or Carl? Granted, they were both in their mid-sixties, but he'd never thought of them aging. Carl was his right hand on the ranch; Marita more than that in his house.

When they arrived, they met the paramedics taking

Carl out of the house. Lizzy was crying. Annie was trying to comfort her. Chuck was as white as fresh snow as he watched the men take the stretcher to the ambulance. Marita had a bag in one hand and her purse in the other. She told the men about to shut the ambulance doors to move over, she was going with them. When they started to argue, she slung one leg up and was sitting beside Carl before they could finish the first sentence.

Marita pointed at them as the doors closed. "I'll call. Don't be rushing over there until I do. Run this ranch. You help him, Julie. That's an order, not a request."

Julie stood there speechless and dumbfounded. Everything in her world was supposed to be laid-back and calm in sleepy little Saint Jo, Texas. It had been anything but that, and right then, everything was happening too fast for her to digest.

"Momma, we're scared," Annie said behind her.

"Daddy, you stink," Lizzy said.

One turn and three steps later, Julie had three children gathered up in her arms and was consoling them, saying that Carl would be just fine and Marita would bring him home as soon as possible. Tomorrow everything would be back to normal, but for now they needed to go play in Lizzy's room. There had been a big fire up north, and the smoke was still in the sky.

Lizzy popped her thumb in her mouth. "Come with us?"

"She does that when she's afraid or nervous," Griffin whispered.

"Annie twists her hair," she whispered back.

Chuck fidgeted with his hands. Julie had seen that trait in the classroom, but not since he'd moved in with Griffin.

Julie reached out to them. "Of course I'll come with

you, but you'll have to show me the way. I've never been here before."

Griffin followed them inside. "I'm taking a shower. I've been wading through smoke all day. Afterward, I'll expect my hugs."

"From all of us?" Lizzy said around her thumb.

Griffin felt heat crawling up his neck. "From the kids."

"Come on, Momma, I'll show you where everything is." Annie took her hand and led her inside.

The front door opened into a foyer, which had a massive staircase leading up to six bedrooms, and a doorway to the left that led into a great room with a den and kitchen all in one big area. Whoever had built the house had intended to raise lots of children in it. The downstairs had a formal living room, dining room, and library in addition to the great room. The laundry room was beyond the kitchen, with a full bathroom off of it. Julie was given the grand tour.

The den had thick, plush carpet the color of milk chocolate, making it mud- and kid-friendly. The sofa and two chairs flanking the stone fireplace were microfiber: soft, inviting, and very cleanable. Behind the sofa, a big Barbie doll house had been set up and at least five Barbies were in various stages of dress for a ball of some kind. Ken was wearing camouflage, so evidently he wasn't invited to the ball.

The kitchen was pristine white: painted cabinets, Formica tops, tile flooring, appliances, and sink. Except for the curtains above the sink. They were pale-yellow sheers. Julie could imagine the rising sun coming through that window and casting a warm glow over the whole room. She wasn't intimidated or even impressed, just in awe that there was so much house for one man and a little girl, until Chuck had come to live with them a couple of months before.

Griffin took a fast shower and made grilled cheese sandwiches and frozen french fries heated in the oven on a cookie sheet for supper. Julie did manage to get into the kitchen long enough to make iced tea and open a package of store-bought cookies for dessert.

They ate in the kitchen instead of at the table in the big, formal dining room.

Lizzy barely nibbled at her sandwich. "Is it eight o'clock yet, Daddy?"

"Getting close," he said.

Tears began to stream down her face.

"What's the matter?" Julie asked.

"I don't want it to be eight o'clock. I don't want Annie to go away. I'm afraid she'll burn up and never come back, and I'm scared Nana Rita is going to leave us and please don't let Annie go and make Julie stay with us, too. Please, Daddy."

"But..." Griffin raised an eyebrow at Julie.

She shook her head ever so slightly.

"Julie has to go home. Did you know that she didn't even take her things out of the truck yet? She might have milk in there that is spoiling," Griffin said.

The thumb went back into her mouth. "Then you go get it, Daddy, and put it in our fridge."

"Please," Chuck whispered.

"Children, if you are going to play together, you have to know there is a time when the day has to end. We need to make the rules right now. Okay?" Julie said.

Annie began to sob very loudly. "I'm afraid the fire

will burn me up. Nana Rita said if it got any closer that we'd have to run away to Monster. I'm afraid of monsters, Momma."

"That's Muenster. Not Monster," Julie said.

Lizzy stopped sucking her thumb and turned a faint shade of minty green around her mouth. She jumped up and barely made it to the bathroom before everything she'd eaten that day came up.

Julie was the first one in the bathroom and held her black hair back.

Griffin was close behind. He wet a washcloth and wiped her face.

Annie continued to sob.

Chuck stood to one side and wrung his hands.

"Okay, okay. Griffin, would you please drive down to my house and bring all the bags in my truck to me? Here's the keys. Please park it in the driveway and get it off the road. There's everything we need to spend the night here if the invitation is sincere. Lizzy, do you hurt anywhere? Is your side hurting or—?"

"No. Just my heart hurts," she whispered.

"That's what she says when she's upset," Griffin said.

"Annie, stop crying. We'll stay over and go home tomorrow."

Both girls wiped away the tears and went back to the supper table, where they barely ate anything at all. The whole trauma hadn't hurt Chuck's appetite, but he was unusually quiet. Julie had trouble finishing her sandwich, but she did manage to get two glasses of tea down.

"Will she be all right?" Julie asked when the children had gone back to the den to play again.

"Not tonight. If she gets hungry, she'll get something

bland like yogurt or Cheerios. Tomorrow morning, she'll come up out of bed screaming for sausage and eggs with the appetite of an Angus bull."

"How often does she do that?"

"Maybe once a year. It's always if there's turmoil in her life. I was surprised she didn't have an episode with the Rachel ordeal," Griffin said.

"I should've slapped that woman just to make myself feel better." Julie narrowed her eyes.

"Put the claws away and tell me again what it is you want out of that truck and I'll go get it." Griffin's tone left no doubt he was running on raw nerves.

"Number one, I want all the bags. Number two, if I want to bare my claws and leave them out for a week, I will. I've lived with a man who told me what to do, when to do it, how to dress, and when to speak. It won't happen again."

"Don't compare me to your bastard of an ex. All I'm asking is for you to spend the night in my house, not live with me," Griffin said. One night of knowing she was in the next room was the limit of what he could endure, anyway. He had to shake off a vision of her curled up in one of his guest rooms, her red hair splayed out on the pillow and her lashes fanned out on her cheeks.

"Thank God for that. The answer wouldn't be no, but hell no," Julie said.

"The question would never be asked. I wouldn't live with that smart mouth of yours one hour, much less a lifetime."

"Right back atcha." Julie pointed but she did not smile.

That night, she tossed and turned for an hour, beating

at the pillow, getting up finally to check on the children, and then going back to bed. Griffin was in the next room down the hall, and she couldn't shut her eyes without feeling those strong arms around her when she'd fallen apart. It'd felt so good and right, and yet there was no future in it. All because of one stupid mistake she'd made with his brother. She beat at the pillow some more and finally went to sleep, only to dream about him again.

Chapter 10

Julie awoke with a headache and all three kids in their pajamas sitting on the bed staring intently at her. For a moment, she thought she was seeing double but a blink or two brought her into reality. She was in a spare bedroom at the Lucky Clover, and there really were three children on her bed, and she had to get them all to school that morning. She looked at the clock. Six thirty. At least she hadn't overslept.

"Good morning," she said.

All the kids shook their heads in unison.

"It's not a good morning?" she asked.

"Daddy is sad," Lizzy said.

"He won't tell us why. Can you come downstairs and find out?" Annie asked.

Chuck picked up her hand and pulled. "Griffin is almost cryin', Miss Julie. Come and make him all better."

Julie sat up and pushed the sheet back. She reached for her jeans and jerked them on over her bikini underpants and didn't bother with a bra under the tank top she'd slept in. All the way down the stairs, she prayed that Carl hadn't died during the night. The last phone call Marita made was to tell them to stay home, the doctors were still ordering tests, Carl really didn't feel like visitors, and their daughter was on the way from Austin.

Griffin sat at the kitchen table, a cup of cold coffee in front of him, elbows on the table, face in his hands.

Julie came to a halt inside the room and eased down into a chair beside him. He looked as if he bore the weight of the galaxy on his broad shoulders.

"The girls are worried. Lizzy says you won't talk and that you're sad. You're scaring them, Griffin. Tell me what's going on?"

"You want the bad news first or the good news?" he asked.

"With or without the children? They are right behind you," she said.

"Could you go up to your room, Lizzy, and please take Chuck and Annie with you? Julie and I need to have a big-people talk. I'm just fine but I'm very, very tired," Griffin said.

They sounded like elephants thundering up the stairs.

"Good news. I want that first," Julie said.

"I talked to Marita a little while ago. Carl isn't dead and the kittens are in the barn. I saved every one of them and the momma cat."

"Okay." She drew out the word to have six syllables.

"Carl had heatstroke but the tests revealed heart problems. He needs open-heart surgery and he needs to retire. His youngest daughter lives in Austin and she got there early this morning, but Carl and Marita have talked all night. It's a tough decision. They've lived on this ranch since they were first married. But they're going to Austin when he gets out of the hospital. Their daughter and her husband raise horses, and they've got an extra house on their ranch. Marita was crying, but it needs to be done. I'm big enough to see that and so is she, but it hurts like hell. I'm losing my right arm and my left one, too. I don't know what to do."

"What *are* you going to do?" Julie could barely stand to look at the anguish on his face. If she could help, she would. She'd keep the kids for him. Do anything. Well, anything but live with him. That was out of the question. It would be too much punishment for her raging hormones.

"I was still awake at three o'clock this morning trying to figure it out. Marita and I talked again at midnight and she had a suggestion, but I didn't think you'd go for it, at least not then," he said.

Oh no. Oh no. Not even oh no, but oh hell no!

"But I'm going to put it on the table and you think about it."

"Is that the bad news?" she asked.

He went on without answering her question. It was as if he hadn't even heard it but was off in a different world. "It's the best thing for Lizzy. She's only known Marita her whole life," he rambled, "and there's Chuck. I hope I can pull some strings with the DHS and keep him here."

"Don't you play the sympathy card," she said.

"I'd play any card right now. Think about it. Are you going to come running back from Jefferson to whip someone every time Lizzy tells Annie that the new housekeeper was mean to her?"

"What are you talking about? Back from Jefferson? I'm not leaving. And the answer is yes, I love Lizzy enough to take up for her. No one should be mean to a child. And she can stay with me and Annie every day until you find a replacement for Marita. And I'll go with you to the DHS to talk to them about Chuck. If they've got a problem with you keeping him, maybe I can do the job," Julie offered. She could feel more bad news coming and hoped she was wrong.

"Thank you. I can hire a cook, maybe Paul's wife. I can promote Paul to ranch foreman. He's worked here long enough and knows the business, and she can do the housekeeping."

"You don't know how to vacuum and dust?" she asked.

"You ready for the bad news?" he asked.

"I was hoping that was all of it. So what is it? That you can't cook, either?"

"No, it's a little worse than the fact that I burn grilled cheese sandwiches. At three o'clock this morning when I had barely dozed off, I got another fire call." He paused. Of everything he had to say, this was the worst. He almost wished she'd asked for the good news last. "The north wind had picked up just slightly and some embers…"

She tapped her foot under the table. Did he expect her to step up and offer to take Marita's job? Had the situation been reversed, she'd swallow her pride and ask him for the same thing. Annie was the first and foremost thing in her life, just like Lizzy was in his. Add Chuck into the mixture, and she might have begged, not just insinuated.

He stopped and tried to find words to soften the blow, but there didn't seem to be any way but to spit it out. "Remember I told you I saved the kittens and the momma cat? I put them out in the barn with Lizzy's momma cat and kittens. Surprisingly enough, the two old cats aren't hissing. They each found a corner and settled in with their babies."

"What's a bunch of cats got to do with any of this?" Julie frowned.

"They're your cats. The embers blew across the road—probably onto the porch—and your house went up in flames. There must've been a tiny gas leak under the house. It looked like a bomb had gone off. It's leveled. There's nothing there but the old cellar, and the top of it is caved in. The tool shed even burned when the flames from the gas bomb caught it."

Julie gasped. She'd never fainted in her life but the room began to spin and the floor got closer and closer to her face. Frantically she scooted the chair back and stuck her head between her knees. Taking great gulps of air, she finally got control of the dizziness. It could not get any worse, but his face was still stony. No smiles. No twinkles in his eyes. Nothing but sadness.

"What will I do?" she whispered. Everything she and Annie owned except an old momma cat and her kittens was gone.

He went to her side and leaned over her, patting her on the back, each touch as hot as the fire that had taken her house. He wasn't sure if he should drop on one knee and hold her or just let her process the news in her own way. Griffin was all thumbs.

"I know you've got insurance, but it will take a few weeks to get it settled. Would you even consider staying here until that is done? You can have the room you slept in last night. Annie can have her own room or stay with Lizzy. Chuck is already settled. Whichever you think is best. I can find someone to do the housework, I'm sure, but I'm thinking of the kids. They need someone to be here with them and for them. If you'd fix breakfast and take them to school, the cook and housekeeper would take care of the rest. I wouldn't even ask you to make supper. Elsie can do that before she leaves, like Marita did. It's just that..." He talked as he patted her back.

She stood up and threw herself into his arms. She

needed comfort, and he was like the Rock of Gibraltar for her all of a sudden. She hugged as tight as she could, but it didn't make the hurt go away. After several seconds, she pushed herself back.

He liked it when she needed him. He wished it would continue instead of her going all stiff and proper.

"Everything is gone at my place?" she asked.

"I found the cat and kittens in the ditch. She must've moved them when she felt the danger. That's all that's saved. Your truck looks like it's nothing but a burned-out shell of metal." He couldn't stop talking. If he did, he would hug her even tighter to his chest again.

Nothing saved. Not even her pictures or Annie's Barbie dolls. Thank goodness she'd brought her favorite ones to Lizzy's for the play day. "My pictures of Annie when she was a baby?" she whispered.

"It's all gone." Griffin imagined how he would feel if he'd lost everything pertaining to Lizzy and he sat down. His cell phone rang before he was settled into the kitchen chair. He answered it and listened for a moment, then handed it to Julie. "It's for you."

"Darlin', this is Alvera Clancy. I heard this morning about your house and I'm so sorry. Do you need a place to stay? My home is open to you and your daughter. Just come on over here. Do you need money or clothing? You let me know and I'll take care of whatever you need."

"Thank you, Alvera, but Griffin and I are talking about a deal right now. He managed to save Annie's cat and kittens." Julie tried to make light of the situation, but the last words came on the fringe of a sob.

"Don't you be breakin' down. Houses can be

replaced. Cats and kittens can even be replaced, but be thankful you and that precious child were safe. I mean it. My house and checkbook are open to you. Just stay in Saint Jo. We need you, and Catherine says you're a damn good teacher, so the school needs you too."

"Thank you again, Alvera."

"Besides, just think how Clarice would gloat if you decided to throw in the towel and leave because of a fire. Hell, she might've even set the thing," Alvera laughed.

"I'm not running from anything," Julie said stoically.

"That's the spirit. Get on with your life. This is a big thing, but in ten years, we'll all see why it happened. Goodbye, darlin'," Alvera said.

Julie had a fleeting notion that Alvera could see into the future ten years and already knew why it had happened.

Lizzy and Annie rushed into the kitchen with Chuck right behind them. "We're starving, Daddy. Can we please have some cereal? Are you done with the big-people talk?" Lizzy asked.

Griffin looked up.

Julie dropped down on her knees in front of Annie. "Annie, our house burned down last night, but Griffin saved your cat and kittens, and they're out in the barn with Lizzy's cat and kittens."

Annie's lower lip quivered. "What are we going to do, Momma? Please don't take me back to Jefferson. I don't want to leave Lizzy and Chuck and we…"

Tears flowed down Lizzy's cheeks. "Daddy, what are we going to do?"

He pulled all three kids into his big arms. "Come here. All of you. Lizzy, Marita is going to move away to Austin. Poppa Carl has a bad thing wrong with his heart and they can fix it over in Austin, so they're going to go live with Clarissa."

Lizzy broke into sobs. "Who's going to keep me, Daddy?"

"I'll stay," Julie whispered.

"Name your price," he said.

"You don't charge us room and board, and I won't charge you for breakfast," she said.

He nodded. "Deal."

"Annie, do you want to live here for a little while?" Julie said. Words came out of her mouth, but her heart was still just a chunk of stone.

"Yes. Say yes," Lizzy whispered.

"I do want to, Momma, and I wanted me and Lizzy to really be sisters but I didn't want our house to burn down and I'm sorry," she cried.

Julie rolled back and sat down as she pulled Annie into her lap. "You didn't cause that fire, honey."

"I think that's enough to take in for one day," Griffin said. "Thank you, Julie, and now it's time for you kids to eat breakfast and get ready for school. Miss Julie will take you with her this morning and bring you home this evening. Tomorrow, things won't look so bad, I promise."

Tears dried up. Frowns were replaced with smiles as they found places around the table.

"Okay, it's cereal this morning because we are in a hurry," Julie said as she opened the pantry. Anything to keep her mind and hands busy and off the loss. "Tomorrow morning, we'll have something hot."

"Thank you, again," Griffin said.

He put bowls on the table, along with milk. She found cereal and blueberry muffins and carried it all to the kitchen table. She would call Mamie during her break time and ask her what to do about filing insurance claims. She would focus entirely on school to keep her mind off the house. Would she ever find anything else she and Annie liked as well?

The doorbell rang and Griffin went to answer it. She had just set the orange juice on the table when Mamie rushed in, grabbed her in a hug, and gushed on and on about how sorry she was.

"You and Annie can come and live with me for as long as you want. I've already started the insurance claim for you. I brought papers for you to sign. I'm so, so sorry," she said.

"Thank you for the offer, but we're staying here. Griffin and I made a deal. I'll watch the kids, cook breakfast, and take them back and forth to school in exchange for room and board," Julie explained.

Griffin poured three cups of coffee. "Carl had heatstroke but needs heart surgery."

The telephone rang about the time Julie finished the story. When she answered it, Marita was on the other end.

"Julie?" Marita said.

"Marita?"

"Yes, it's me. I'm on my way to the house to pack some bags. Clarissa is here and I'm riding back to Austin with her. They're taking Carl by helicopter. Surgery is tomorrow morning. It's not good, but they say it can be repaired. The heatstroke was actually a blessing. Did Griffin put you to work like I told him?"

"He gave me a job. My house burned down," Julie said.

"I know and I'm sorry, but I'm glad you are there. Lizzy knows and loves you. It will make my leaving at least bearable. He can hire someone to do the work. She just needs a mother figure."

"It's a pretty big job," Julie said around the lump in her throat.

"You'll do just fine. We're at the house now. I'm going to pack and stop by just long enough to hug the kids. Take care of all of them for me." Her voice caught in a sob. "I've had her since she was two months old. This is the hardest thing I've ever faced other than worrying my head off about Carl."

"I'll take care of her, I promise," Julie said.

"I know you will. Just don't let Griff hire someone who won't when you have to leave."

"I promise on that issue, too," Julie said.

"Had to be Marita," Mamie said when Julie put the phone back on the stand.

"It's tough on her."

"She and Carl raised their kids on this ranch. I can't remember how many children they had because they're older than Graham and Griffin and were already married and gone by the time we were good-sized kids. But Lizzy has been her surrogate grandchild. Bless her heart. Things can sure get messed up in a twenty-four-hour stretch, can't they?" Mamie observed.

"I'm still thinking I may be dreaming all this, and if I am, it's the worst nightmare ever. Bring your coffee upstairs. I've got to get ready for school."

Mamie headed for the door. "No, I've got to open shop this morning. I heard about the fire and that you and Annie were fine and stayed here last night, but I had to see about you. Call me if you need anything."

"Thank you," Julie said past the lump in her throat.

Reality was sinking in and it hurt. After all she'd endured the past six months, she should have been a pillar of steel instead of a whimpering woman who had to lean on Griffin for support.

She picked up her purse in her bedroom, dug around for her cell phone, and called her mother.

"Momma, I've got bad news," she said when she heard her mother's voice.

"Is Annie all right?"

"She's fine."

"And you?"

"I'm fine."

"Okay then, I can take anything else. Give it to me," Deborah said.

She repeated the story a second time and started to cry halfway through it. "I've got to go to work and I can't even think," she said.

"Do you want me to drive over there and bring you and Annie home?" Deborah asked. "You've got enough money to live on without working next semester. Then in the fall, you can find another job."

"No, I don't think so. I just needed to hear your voice."

"Is this wise? You working there?" Deborah asked.

"It's for the kids. Griffin and I are friends. At least I think we are. I could care less about the social aspects of it. My reputation is in worse shambles than it was in Jefferson, so I really don't care."

"It would be easy to transfer any feelings you had toward his brother to him, since they look alike," Deborah said.

"It would be the most difficult thing in the world. Every time I look at him, I think of that night and the mistake I made. His brother and I were an accident. Who knows? If we'd both been sober and responsible, we probably wouldn't have liked each other, either."

"You going to rebuild?" Deborah asked.

"Maybe. I may buy a trailer. That would be faster. Got to go. I see Marita out in the yard. I'm sure I'm needed."

"I'm sure you are," her mother said.

Lizzy couldn't begin to fathom life without Nana Rita there every day, and she barely understood the concept of her leaving. She hung on to Marita for a very long time and then backed away.

"Nana Rita, you will come back and see me and call me and make cookies for me and take me to my Christmas play at church?"

"I'll do what I can. You listen to Julie and be a good girl. You have Annie and Chuck, so you won't be lonely. I'm sure Julie will let you help with cookies for the Christmas party," Marita said hoarsely.

Julie had trouble keeping tears at bay watching the young and old trying to make sense of sudden parting. Annie stood to one side in her pajamas and held Lizzy's hand. Chuck held the other hand and watched the whole business with wide eyes. Of all of them, he would be the one who understood most the sorrow of parting. When Marita and Clarissa walked away, the children unclasped their hands and waved, then hurried up to their room to get ready for school. Tomorrow or the next day or maybe even next week, Lizzy might wake up crying for Nana Rita. Thank goodness that was in the future. Julie didn't think she could stand any more terrible things that day.

She hustled that morning to get them ready and out the door at the right time. She was standing on the porch with all three of them when she realized she didn't have a vehicle to take them to school in. Her truck, along with her home, had burned.

"Hey," Griffin said as he rounded the end of the house holding out a set of keys. "The red truck is yours until you can figure out what you want to do. It's the ranch truck and it's got plenty of room to be hauling kids and whatever else you need."

She took the keys from him and said, "Thank you." But it was almost the straw that broke the camel's back. She fought back tears the whole way to school.

The teachers dropped in and out all day, subdued in their condolences for her loss, and asking if there was anything they could provide or do for her. She'd made friends that she didn't even know about, and they came to her side during a difficult time. That day, she saw a light at the end of the tunnel. She belonged in Saint Jo, Texas.

That evening over the supper table, talk turned to Carl and his chances of survival and what they'd do without him on the Lucky Clover. Griffin told Julie and the kids that he had promoted Paul to foreman and his wife, Elsie, would be cooking and housecleaning for them. Starting tomorrow morning, she'd be there six days a week. She'd arrive after they left for school and leave before they came home, but she would be there on Saturdays.

After the supper cleanup was finished and they'd read their sight words through twice, Julie put the girls in the upstairs bathtub and washed their hair. She dressed them in pajamas and called Chuck in for his bath, which he declared vehemently that he could do all by himself.

So Julie let him. Sunday afternoon, she'd take Annie somewhere and buy clothing for both of them. Thank goodness for Aunt Flossie's money, or she would have had to borrow until the insurance check came. The few pieces she'd purchased in Gainesville and the things she'd brought to Lizzy's for the play day were all that they had. Lizzy had been very generous in saying that Annie could have anything of hers, but Annie needed her own room and her own things.

After the kids were tucked in, Julie fell back in a deep recliner and felt like crying, but there was no way she'd let Griffin see her fall apart again. She was a tough woman, and she'd hang on to that with tenacity because right then, it was all she had.

Griffin took a shower, letting the tepid water beat against his weary muscles. Dinner had been good, and Elsie would work out just fine. Lizzy was already fitting into her new world. He'd also called the local police force, and they were going to talk to the DHS to get the ball rolling for him to keep Chuck. He even offered to adopt him outright if his parents would sign the papers.

He finished bathing and dried his body on a big, white towel before he opened a drawer under the vanity and pulled out a pair of boxers and knit pajama bottoms. A well-worn T-shirt came from a different drawer, and once he was dressed, he plodded into the kitchen, barefoot and with water droplets still clinging to his hair, which he'd combed back haphazardly with his fingertips.

Julie looked up and her resolve to be strong melted. She was a master at bluffing, though, and used her expertise at that moment. "We made it through day one." She managed to get out a few words without drooling.

"Yes, we did. Maybe things will even out," he said.

"I hope so." She managed a smile.

His heart melted. She'd been through so much in such a short time, but he could not let that alter his resolve not to get involved with her. Granted, he no longer thought she'd come to Saint Jo to claim whatever rights Annie had to the Lucky Clover. However, she had been with his brother. How would he ever know if she saw Graham every time she looked at him?

"Lizzy and Chuck are already adjusting better than I ever hoped," he said to fill in the silence surrounding them.

"So is Annie. I was afraid she'd be a mess after losing the house. She and Chuck and Lizzy told their story a dozen times today."

"What are you doing this evening?" he asked.

"Got a hot date. The john said to meet him at the end of the lane and he'll have me home by daylight. Figured I could make a little extra money on my own time. You mind watching Annie?" she said.

His black brows knitted together into one solid line. "What?"

"It's my red-haired humor. Sometimes it surfaces," she teased.

He grinned. "You had me there for a minute. I guess first impressions aren't always the right ones. Thank you for all you did today, Julie. I'm really glad you're here."

"Good night, Griff. I'm going up to bed. I think I could sleep a week and this is only Monday."

"Good night, Julie."

She stopped beside him for a minute and wished she

had the nerve to kiss him good night, but she didn't. Not right then. Not when the wound of losing everything was still raw. It would have to wait until later, if it ever happened.

In the second that she hesitated beside him, he wanted to reach out to her, but Graham's memory flashed through his mind and he couldn't. Maybe someday he'd get past that; he hoped so, because Julie was invading every waking moment of every day and most of his nights.

Chapter 11

Julie settled into the routine as if she'd been born to live on a ranch. After school, she drove the three children home and heated whatever Elsie had left on the stove or in the refrigerator for supper. She graded papers or worked on her lesson plans while the kids played. After baths, she helped the children get ready for bed, and she or Griffin or sometimes both of them read a story to the kids or let them watch an hour of television. She and Griffin had a daily talk about the kids, worried about whether the DHS would let them keep Chuck and how it would affect the girls if they didn't, and then it was off to bed for Julie. Mornings were breakfast, making sure teeth were brushed, hair was combed, backpacks ready with lunches and books. Then it started all over again.

It wasn't so very different from the days when it had been just her and Annie. The biggest change was that now Annie had someone to play with and depended less on Julie for entertainment. And nowadays, there was the inner angst every evening when Griff walked into the kitchen in his pajama bottoms and T-shirt with water droplets still hanging on his jet-black hair and smelling so sexy that all she could think about was hauling him off to bed. It wasn't because he looked like Graham, either. She'd put that issue to rest weeks before. Graham had been a smooth-talking, good-looking soldier. Yes,

Griffin looked somewhat like him, only Griffin was much better-looking—softer, not so brittle.

"I've got to go shopping for a trailer," she groaned when she looked in the mirror in her bedroom that Saturday morning. "I get up thinking about when he's coming home for supper. I'm six years older than he is, and he thinks I'm even older, and he's on my mind every waking minute. I need to be in my own place just to put some distance between us."

"Who are you talking to, Momma?" Annie asked from the doorway.

"That old woman in the mirror," Julie said.

Annie peered around her mother's leg and into the floor-length mirror on the back of the closet door. "Where? I don't see an old woman. I see my momma and me."

"You are a sweetheart. What are you doing already up and dressed?"

"Me and Chuck and Lizzy, we waked up early and Elsie said to let you sleep so we did. She made us some oatmeal with brown sugar in it and we got to play outside," Annie said.

"Well, that was very sweet of Elsie. Is it cold?"

"No. Elsie said we had to wear our jackets and I forgetted mine." Annie took off in a run out of Julie's room and into her own.

Julie saw a blur run past her as she started down the stairs and before she reached the bottom, Lizzy came up in a dead run. "Where are you going so fast?" Julie asked.

"Chuck is going to play Barbies with us out in the yard. Elsie said it's warm enough if we put on our coats and we weren't supposed to wake you up because you looked tired last night when she went home and Chuck needs the Ken doll because he says we're going to play like we're in the jungle and Ken is going to save Barbie from getting eat plumb up by the snakes," Lizzy said, finally coming up for air, sucking in twice before she went on. "We got some leaves and sticks and Chuck is building us a jungle. And oh, yeah, I got to pee-pee." Lizzy crossed her legs and wiggled while she talked.

"Looks like you'd better hurry," Julie said with a smile.

She checked out the kitchen window to see Annie and Chuck busy making their jungle out in the middle of the yard. It was a nice, sunny day, and in the middle of December, they might not have many more. Annie had a Barbie in each hand and carried on a dialogue between them. She shook her head, nodded, smiled, frowned, and at one time shook her finger at one of the misbehaving Barbie dolls. Chuck held a Ken and had a stern look on his face. Evidently Barbie wasn't obeying the commander's orders.

"Now that's a sight I'll have to tell Griffin about later," she murmured.

Lizzy came through the kitchen and stopped dead in the middle of the floor. "Oops, I forgot the Ken doll acause I..." She didn't finish the sentence but ran back up the stairs.

Alzheimer's wasn't always to blame for forgetfulness, Julie mused. She picked up the morning paper and scanned the front page headlines. She was getting milk out of the refrigerator when Lizzy shot through the kitchen like a blaze, out into the backyard, and then back into the house.

"Annie? Annie?" Lizzy shouted over the top of the noisy vacuum cleaner Elsie was pushing around in the den. "Chuck, where is Annie?"

"I don't know. I come inside to see what was takin' you so long. I bet she's hidin' from us. Let's go find her," Chuck yelled back.

Julie heard the conversation, but she didn't pay attention. "Lizzy? Lizzy?" or "Chuck? Chuck?" was commonplace when one child lost the others.

The back door slammed and a flash of lightning with dark hair flew through the kitchen and back up the steps. "Annie? Are you up here?" Lizzy called.

It was followed by a streak of red hair and the thundering steps of a little boy hurrying up the stairs and yelling the same name.

Julie poured cereal into a bowl and added milk. Elsie finished vacuuming and put a big cast-iron skillet on top of the stove and set about browning hamburger in it. The note card Julie found on the bar listed the items Elsie planned for lunch. Mexican lasagna casseroles, corn on the cob, pinto beans, and sliced cucumbers and tomatoes. She'd already made three pans of homemade brownies. Julie would rather have had Mexican lasagna for breakfast. Maybe if there were leftovers, she would have it the next morning.

"Looks good, Elsie," Julie said.

"The men like good, heavy food in the winter. You like livin' here?" Elsie asked.

"I do. I'm trying to make up my mind about whether to rebuild or buy a trailer."

Elsie wiped her hands on a towel and carried a cup of coffee to the table. She was a medium-sized woman with dark hair and brown eyes. Maybe sixty years old, but it was hard to tell. Her eyes sparkled with life and she could have been anywhere from fifty to seventy.

"Think on it. There's no hurry. My sister has cooked for Alvera Clancy for years. She says that Alvera would do anything to keep you in Saint Jo."

"Someday I'm going to grow up and be just like Alvera," Julie said.

"I can see it happening," Elsie said. "She's a nice woman. My sister loves working on her ranch."

Lizzy peeked around the corner. "Julie, where is Annie? I can't find her."

"Is she in the bathroom?" Julie asked.

"No, I checked them both and your room and the den and the front porch and I can't find her and where is she?"

Julie's heart skipped a beat. "Annie? Annie! Where are you? Don't you play hide-and-seek with me, young lady," Julie yelled up the stairs and out the back door. She and Lizzy ran all the way around the house together and Chuck took off to the barn, where the cats were located.

No Annie.

Her pulse thumped in her ears as she picked up the phone in the kitchen and called Griffin. "Annie is gone. I can't find her. She never leaves the yard, Griff. She's not in the house and Chuck checked the barn where the kittens are and she's just vanished." Her tone was frantic.

"I'm five minutes away. Keep hunting. I'm on my way," he said.

By the time Griffin arrived, Lizzy was in hysterics, Julie was hoarse from screaming, and still there was no Annie. Griffin hurriedly made one more check and then called the police to report a missing child; then he wrapped his arms around Julie and hugged her close, promising that they would find her.

The warmth of his embrace gave her the strength she needed to keep from falling completely apart in front of the children.

Annie had been having a conversation between two dolls. They were deciding what they'd tell Chuck and Lizzy when they came back from the house.

Then the lady showed up as if she had floated down from the trees.

She was very tall, with funny hair. It had a pink streak in the same place she and Lizzy had white streaks. Annie looked up at her and wondered if her streak was lucky.

"Lizzy, come on, you are going with me," the lady had said.

"I'm Annie. I'm not Lizzy," she had said.

"Don't you play games with me, little girl. I'm your mother, Dian, and you are going with me."

"No, I'm Annie. Lizzy had to go to the bathroom."

"I know my own child and you are Lizzy, so don't tell me shit like that."

"Julie is my momma and she's in the house and my momma is—"

That's when the lady reached down, jerked Annie up from the quilt, put her hand over her mouth to stifle the screams, and carried her to her car parked beside the house. She took her hand from Annie's face, strapped her into the car seat, and said, "You make a sound and I'll beat you to death."

Annie's blue eyes popped wide open, and she slowly looked around the car, terrified to move her head for fear the woman would hit her. She looked at the woman's reflection in the rearview mirror. It wasn't Rachel driving the car; it was a woman with a pink streak in her hair and a pink diamond glued to her nose and lots of pink earrings on her ear. She had on a short, black, shiny skirt and high heels, like one of Barbie's outfits. But Barbie didn't have a pink shirt like the lady wore or a jean jacket like that, either. Annie didn't mean to cry, because she didn't want the lady to hit her, but the tears had a mind of their own, and before they reached the end of the lane, she was sobbing.

"Shut that shit up, Lizzy, or I swear I'll stop this car and whip you. I'm your mother and you are going to live with me from now on. Your father just thought he was paying me off. He's going to give me a wad of child support and you'll love living in the big city. You've got a set of twin brothers that you don't even know about and you can watch them for me. Funny thing is, your daddy was a twin and you were a single birth. My boys' daddy can't even remember a single twin in his background and his boys are twins. Maybe we'll even dye that streak pink, so you'll look a little more like me," the lady said.

"You are not my mother. My mother is Julie," Annie wailed.

"That's probably your stepmother and your father told you she was your mother, but I'm your real mother. My name is Dian. Didn't he ever talk about me?"

"No, you are not. You are Lizzy's mother. She has a picture of you in a big white dress with Griffin. My mother is Julie," Annie kept protesting.

Dian looked in the rearview mirror to make sure the child really was the one she'd given birth to more than five years before. "You think I wouldn't know my own kid, especially with that white streak in your hair? Shut up that bawlin' or I swear I'll shut you up. Just think, we can be together for Christmas. Santa Claus can bring you a present to my house."

Annie hushed but continued to sniffle. "Take me home and you'll see I'm not Lizzy. She went to the bathroom and Chuck forgotted something. That's why I was there by myself. I'm not Lizzy."

"We're going to the Dairy Queen to get some food. I've driven nonstop from California to get you and I'm starving. We'll eat on the road since I've only got so long to get back. Possession is ninety percent of the law and if Griffin Luckadeau wants you, he's going to give me more than a measly ten grand. I may not be able to touch that ranch, but you belong to me."

Annie finally put together a plan. She folded her arms over her chest and waited.

Dian drove up to the drive-up window and ordered two hamburger meal deals and a kids' meal, both with Dr Peppers and a chocolate malt.

"I don't like Dr Pepper and I want chicken strips, not a hamburger," Annie said.

Dian yelled into the voice box. "I need to change the order."

"Thank you but I'm still not Lizzy," Annie said.

Dian looked into the rearview mirror again. The kid looked exactly like Griffin and Graham. "I can't imagine a kid of mine not liking Dr Pepper."

Annie began to wiggle. "Well, I hate it. I like Coke and Momma usually gets me a juice pack or a carton of milk and I've got to pee."

"You sit still. You're not getting out of this car, do

you hear me?" Dian turned around and stared at the child for a long time while she waited for the car ahead of her to move up.

"If you don't let me go in there and go to the bathroom, I'm going to pee in my pants and get the car seat wet," Annie said.

"Okay, okay. I'll park and we'll both go in and use the bathroom. That way we won't have to stop again until we've got a lot of miles behind us."

She backed up and eased around the car in front of her, parked facing west, and held Annie's hand tightly all the way into the Dairy Queen. "Don't you do anything stupid like scream or I'll make you pay for it all the way to California. I swear, Elizabeth, you won't stop for a bathroom break all day if you scream."

Annie glared at her but didn't answer. Her momma would hit her with the hoe when she found her. She waited until they were inside the Dairy Queen and broke loose from Dian's grip. She ran toward the back of the dining area toward the restrooms. She remembered where they were and which one was for girls because Julie stopped and let the kids have an ice cream on Fridays after school.

Annie knew she had to get in there fast or Lizzy's mother was going to take her way off to California. The only thing Annie knew about California was that he bought all her mother's squash relish on the day Grammy and Poppa Carl came to visit. Why would the crazy lady want to take Annie or Lizzy to California? What did he want with a little girl?

Annie ran faster than Dian could in high heels and beat her to the restroom. In one motion, she shut and locked the bathroom door and sat down in the corner behind it.

Dian turned the doorknob but the brat had locked the door. She tried to shake it loose, muttering under her breath the whole time. That didn't work.

She tried sweet persuasion and finally threats. Annie just rolled up tighter and tighter into a ball of fear.

"What's going on?" Annie heard a strange voice ask.

"My little girl has locked herself in and can't get out," Dian said.

"She's not my mother," Annie screamed.

"She's mad because she wanted ice cream and I told her she had to eat her lunch first," Dian said.

"Call my momma at the Lucky Clover Ranch. I'm not Lizzy," Annie screamed again.

"That's Griffin Luckadeau's place," the voice said.

"Yes, he's my ex-husband. I'm taking Lizzy for a few days. Visitation, you know. She didn't want to go with me. Griffin didn't want her to go, either, so I'm sure he's poisoned her mind against me, but the law is the law. I've paid child support for five years, and he can damn well let me have my visitation rights." Dian improvised the lie as she went along.

"I see. Well, I just started working here but I'll go get the key and get her out for you," the voice said.

Annie tried to roll up into an even smaller ball. If Lizzy and Chuck were there, they'd all three run like the wind and get away. They'd slip past the mean woman and just run until a policeman found them. Annie knew the way to Mamie's store, and she could run very, very fast all the way there. Mamie would tell the woman that she was Annie and not Lizzy. Mamie would call Griffin and her momma and everything would be all right.

She stood up and pressed herself against the wall behind the door. When the knob turned, she took a deep breath and waited. When Dian rushed into the bathroom, Annie sped out from behind the door. The woman in the hallway tried to grab Annie, but she slipped from her grasp, took off across the dining room, and was out the door before either of the women could get their balance.

Dian's high heels had straps around her ankles, making it impossible to kick them off and chase after the child, but with every long stride, she felt she was gaining on her. Air burned in her lungs, a product of too little oxygen and too many cigarettes. She swore if she caught that kid, she was going to thump her bottom.

Annie's little legs churned, kicking up dirt as she traveled west toward the square. She darted through yards, across streets without looking until she reached the east side of the square. Dian was only a half a block behind her when she dashed into Molly's store gasping for Mamie.

"What's wrong, Annie? Where did you come from and why are you running?" Mamie asked.

"Mean woman," Annie got out before she raced behind the curtains and hid in the back room.

Mamie had the phone in her hand and was calling Julie's cell number when Dian burst through the front door.

"Where is she? I saw her run in here, Mamie Pickett, and by damn, you'll give her to me or I'll—" Dian bent over and grasped her knees. Her lungs were blazing and her calf muscles were one solid cramp.

Mamie cocked her head to one side as the phone rang the fifth time. "Dian?"

"Hello," Julie said.

"Where are you?" Mamie asked.

"At the ranch. We've lost Annie and Griffin called the police. Mamie, I'm scared out of my mind."

"That merchandise would be in my possession," Mamie said casually.

"*You've* got Annie. Why?"

"Yes, ma'am, that's the correct price. You can pick it up as soon as you can get here."

Julie raised her voice. "Why are you playing games?"

"An old customer has just come by so I'll have to call you later. Dian, can I get you something to drink?"

"I'm on my way," Julie said.

Mamie set the phone back on the stand. "Now what can I do for you?"

"I saw the little bitch. She ran into this store," Dian said.

"Who?"

"Lizzy. She ran away from me at the Dairy Queen and ran into this store."

"I was in the bathroom and just grabbed the phone as I came out. If she ran in here, she kept right on going out the back way. Why would you have Lizzy?"

"She's mine and I'm taking her back. If Griffin wants her, he can pay me more money or give me child support and I'll keep her. I could use a five-year-old to help me with the twins."

"Twins?" Mamie said.

Dian clutched at her side. "Damn that hurts. Boys, I've got twin boys a year old now. I've got to go find that kid. Out the back door you say?"

"Want to sit down?" Mamie asked.

"No, she's probably hiding along the back of one of

the stores. I'll find her and she's in big trouble when I do. Lizzy! Girl, you'd better come out and show your face." Dian marched through the curtain and across the room. She opened the back door and looked both ways, heard a noise to her left, and started that way, calling out to Lizzy every second step.

"Be still and don't move, Annie," Mamie whispered as she locked the door behind Dian. After that, she hurried to the front door, locked it, and called the police.

In less than ten minutes, Julie, Griffin, Chuck, and Lizzy pounded on the front door. Mamie let them inside and led them to the back room, where Annie raced to her mother and broke down into gulping sobs, which caused Lizzy to send up a wail and Chuck to wipe tears from under his glasses. That's when Dian started beating on the back door and hollering at Mamie to let her in.

By the time the police arrived, it was a zoo. Julie was demanding answers. Griffin was trying to explain. Dian hadn't gotten far until a policeman confronted her, and now she was in cuffs, yelling and kicking the poor man. The other policeman was asking which little girl had been abducted; they looked alike to him. The officer who'd cuffed Dian brought her back in the back door when Mamie unlocked it and the place took on the ambience of a catfight in a barroom just before closing on Saturday night. Dian took one look at Griffin and Julie comforting Annie and went up in flames.

"What in the hell did you tell her that bitch was her mother for? You should've at least told her I was her mother, and you got off too damned easy, Griffin Luckadeau. I'm taking her back. I'm her mother and I can do that and you can give me more money or pay child support. Your choice."

"Jim Bob, I have a copy of the papers she signed and my divorce decree. Do you need them?" Griffin asked the chief of police.

"I might. You pressing kidnapping charges against her, Miss Julie?"

Julie glared at the woman. Damn it, but Griffin had the poorest taste in women of any man she'd ever met. He was sexy as hell, but he sure didn't have a lick of sense when it came to picking out a woman if his taste ran to the likes of Dian.

Julie nodded. "You bet your sweet ass I am. Put her in jail until we sort this out."

"You are my momma?" Lizzy peeked out from behind Griffin. She'd always pictured her mother as the lovely lady in the picture that sat in her room. She wore a white wedding dress and carried pink roses. That woman looked like one of those pictures on the front of scary movies at the movie rental over in Nocona. Those ones that her Daddy said they could not rent.

Dian looked at the child and back at the one in Julie's arms. She opened her mouth and gaped like a fish out of water. "You son of a bitch. No wonder you let me go without a fight. You had another woman pregnant at the same time. How much difference is there in their ages?"

"Two days," Julie said. "Not that it's a bit of your business."

"Annie isn't mine," Griffin said.

Dian wiggled against the restraints. "Don't tell me that. You think I'd believe she's not your child, Griffin

Luckadeau? I'm not blind. How could she not be yours? She's the spitting image of you. You were cheating on me all along. I thought she was Lizzy with that white streak and those blue eyes. Get these damned cuffs off me."

"We going to call this a domestic dispute or take it on to the county?" Jim Bob asked.

"You get these cuffs off and I'll show that bitch a thing or two," Dian yelled loud enough that Chuck clapped his hands over his ears and buried his face in Griffin's leg.

Julie was so mad she could see flashes of red light reflecting off that stupid pink hairdo. Why in the hell had Griffin ever married such a wench in the first place? "First of all, don't call me a bitch, and second, stop accusing me of sleeping with Griffin."

"How'd you get that kid if you wasn't messing around with my husband?" Dian sneered.

"He did have a twin brother, remember?" Julie said. She hated to have this conversation in front of Lizzy and Annie.

Dian sucked air and turned pale gray.

"He wouldn't. He left because… He loved…"

"Would you kids all three come up front with me for a little while so these big people can get this all straightened out? I've got a new shipment of candy, and I could sure use you to sample it for me. I can't decide whether to buy more of the chocolate or the caramel next time around," Mamie said soothingly.

"I can't leave my momma," Annie clung harder.

"Is she really my momma?" Lizzy asked again. "She can't make me go with her, can she?"

Julie handed Annie over into Mamie's arms. "Go

with Mamie and let us visit for just a minute. I'll be right here, and the policeman won't let this woman hurt you. See, she's got her hands behind her back in handcuffs. She's not going to hurt me or Griff."

"And yes, she is your momma, but she is not taking you with her anywhere," Griffin told Lizzy.

"Me, either?" Chuck whispered.

"You, either, son. Go on with Mamie. It's going to be all right, I promise," Griff said.

Mamie carried one and ushered the other two out of the room. "Okay, come on and we'll see about that candy."

Dian turned on Julie the minute they were gone. "You're a lying bitch."

"Lady, that is enough," Jim Bob said sternly.

"Graham wouldn't sleep with her. He was in love with me. That's why he enlisted and went away. He said I was the only woman he could ever love, so I know she's lying. That brat belongs to Griffin."

"Well, darlin', Graham Luckadeau lied to you because I met him in Dallas the night he left Saint Jo," Julie said.

Griffin's jaw worked in anger. "Did you? Did he?"

"Hell no! Graham wouldn't touch me because I belonged to you on paper. I was willing, but all I got was a few kisses and even then he felt guilty."

"Annie belongs to Graham," Griffin said.

"And you can't prove it, can you?"

"DNA," he said.

"Which is the same for identical twins, so now what have you got?" Dian changed her tune and began to bite her lower lip. "I've got to get back to California. My mother is keeping my boys and she said she could only watch them a week. Come on, Griffin, let me have her for one week. I'll bring her back, I promise."

"I'm not filing charges on her, Jim Bob, with the stipulation that she leave Saint Jo right now," Julie said.

Dian snarled at Julie. "This isn't your business. I thought she was Lizzy. This is between me and Griffin."

Julie headed through the curtains into the store. "I'm finished. Take her to jail. You can hold her twenty-four hours on disturbing the peace. I'll be in tomorrow morning to press charges for kidnapping and child endangerment and anything else my lawyer can think of between now and then."

Dian sidled up to Griffin. She could sweet-talk him into anything now that the red-haired bitch from hell was gone. She couldn't imagine Griffin with a redhead. It was Graham who liked red hair; that's why she'd dyed hers dark auburn just before he came home from boot camp. "Okay. Okay. I'll leave. But come on, Griff. She's got two little brothers. Twins. A year old. She needs to know her kin."

"Lizzy has everything she needs. You'd better take Julie's offer and leave town. She's pretty protective of those kids. She will press charges and you will go to jail. Then who's going to take care of your other children? Your husband? Child services?" Griffin asked.

"Wake up, Griffin. She's got one that looks like you and that boy can't be a year younger than her daughter and he looks just like her. Looks like she'll sleep with anything," Dian said, smarting off.

"I'd say none of that is your business," he said. He felt absolutely nothing akin to love or lust, either one.

He'd envisioned her coming back home for the first two or three years, and in the dream she'd been sorry that she'd left him, sorry she'd deserted Lizzy, repentant and ready to be a wife and mother.

In the past two years, she had scarcely crossed his mind. Looking at her that sunny December day, all he could think was that she wasn't worth the time he was losing on the ranch that afternoon.

"I never did love you. I just married you because Graham and I had a big fight when I wanted him to propose to me, so I dated you to get back at him. I married you to get back at Graham," Dian spat out.

"The past is like Las Vegas, Dian. What happened there stays there," he said.

Jim Bob raised a hand. "What's it going to be lady? I ain't got all day to listen to you insult my friend."

"I'm going home. Undo these damned cuffs. I'm leaving."

The policeman unlocked the cuffs and she flounced through the curtain. "Goodbye, Lizzy. You have two little brothers you should get to know. A real family that you'll never have here with her two kids. Here's my phone number. Call me if you ever want to come live with me." She pulled a card from her pocket and handed it to Annie.

Annie handed the card back. "I'm Annie. I told you. I'm not Lizzy. She's over there with my momma, Julie."

"Give your sister the card and don't believe a word they're telling you, kid. Griffin is your daddy." Dian tossed the card on the floor and slammed the door behind her as she left.

Mamie picked it up and handed it to Julie. It was a

Mary Kay Cosmetic's card. *Dian Withers* was written on the baby-pink card below the Mary Kay logo. It had a cell phone number beside her name but no address.

"Is my daddy really Annie's daddy, too?" Lizzy asked.

"That woman is crazy, Lizzy," Annie said. "She thought she was my momma. Now she thinks your daddy is mine. I don't have a daddy. Is she really gone, Momma? She won't come back and put her hand over my mouth again, will she?"

"No, she won't be back again. It's all over. Now let's go home. I bet Elsie is worried and I bet dinner is almost ready." Julie was amazed that her voice sounded normal.

"I don't have a daddy, do I? Is Griffin my daddy? If he is, why didn't you tell me?" Annie popped her hands on her hips just like Julie did when she was upset.

"We'll talk about all of that when we get home," Julie said.

Mamie sighed. "I wouldn't want to be in your shoes today."

Annie giggled and her face softened. "Momma's shoes wouldn't fit you."

"No, they wouldn't," Mamie agreed.

Jim Bob and his deputy poked their heads through the curtains and told Julie they were escorting Dian out the back door, taking her to the Dairy Queen in the squad car, and would follow her all the way to Nocona, where they'd radio ahead for a police car to follow her to the western edge of Montague County.

"Are you ready to go home?" Griffin asked Julie.

"As ready as I'll ever be." She dreaded what lay ahead, but the time had come for Annie to know the truth.

The children whispered in the back seat all the way home.

Griffin was quiet. So many skeletons, so much deception. He'd never known that Graham and Dian had dated. The whole story left him drained and riding a guilt trip. If Griffin hadn't dated and eventually married her, then Graham wouldn't have gone into the service, where he got killed.

When they were all safely inside the house, Julie poured each of the kids a glass of milk and set a platter of cookies in the middle of the kitchen table. Elsie worked around them, getting lunch ready for the hired hands. Griffin melted into the chair at the head of the table and sighed loudly. Julie set a cup of steaming hot coffee in front of him and poured herself one.

She sat down on the other end of the kitchen table and sipped the coffee, not knowing where or how to start the conversation. How much to tell? How much to leave out until Annie was older?

"I can see y'all got things to talk about. I can go somewhere else," Elsie said softly.

"No, you can stay. You already know most of what we're going to tell them, anyway," Julie said.

Elsie nodded and kept working.

"You're going to have a visit with us, aren't you?" Annie said seriously.

"Yes, we are," Julie said.

Annie took a deep breath. "I didn't do anything wrong, Momma. I just didn't know what to do but run and run and run to Mamie's store."

Griffin patted her hand. "Honey, we know you didn't do anything wrong, and you were very brave."

"I would have done just what you did, too, Annie. If I hadn't been in the house, I would have bit her on the leg like a dog," Chuck said.

Lizzy still wore a puzzled look. "Are you sure that was my momma, Daddy? She didn't look like the picture in my room. Will she come and steal me like she did Annie? If she does, I'm going to run to Mamie's store."

"No, she's gone back to California," Griffin said.

"But why would she want to live with California? All he has to eat is squash relish and jelly," Annie said.

"What?" Julie asked.

"You know. California comes to Mamie's store and buys your relish and jelly so why would Lizzy's momma want to live with him and besides, why'd she make a pink streak in her hair?" Annie asked.

Julie laughed.

Griffin grinned.

The innocence of children, they thought at the same time.

"The California that Mamie talks about is a man with a real name, but she doesn't ever remember it. California is also the name of a state way far from here, and that's where Lizzy's momma lives. It's two very different things."

Annie wrinkled her brow. "Okay, I just didn't know. I was scared, Momma. I cried."

"I would have too, Annie," Lizzy said seriously.

"Not me," Chuck said. "I would have fought her and she would have let me go. I'll teach you girls how to fight so it won't happen again."

"Okay, Chuck," Lizzy said. "But I'm not going to bite her on the leg. Did you see all that stuff on her leg? It looked like wire. It might hurt my teeth."

"Ah, it's just tats. My momma had them on her leg. She had a rose. It's just pictures. You can bite them and they won't hurt you."

"Did you bite the rose?" Annie asked.

"Huh-uh. She would have kicked me against the wall. She was pretty mean when she didn't have her medicine," Chuck said.

Annie looked at Julie and changed the subject. "Why'd she say Griffin was my daddy?"

Julie took a deep breath, but Griffin touched her hand to stop her from speaking. The warmth of his fingertips on her palm sent tingles flying up and down her arm.

"Let me, please. Annie, I would just love to be your father, but I'm not. I'm sure Julie would love to be Lizzy's mother, but she's not. When I was born, I had a twin brother and we were wonderful friends, just like you and Lizzy. Then we grew up and my brother, who was named Graham, went to the war over in Iraq. That's way, way far away," Griffin explained.

"Even more than California?" Lizzy asked.

"Even farther than California. My brother got killed over there in Iraq right after he got there."

"He's dead? Like Great-Granny Bessie? He's got a grave and a piece of rock on it and all that stuff and they put him in the hole and put dirt on him?" Annie asked. She'd been to one funeral in her five-year life span and it had had a profound effect on her.

"That's right. That's exactly what they did. But before he died, he was your father," Griffin said.

"So I did have a daddy but I don't now? That's why you said my daddy was dead, right, Momma? But why didn't you tell me about Griffin and Lizzy?"

"That's right. Your daddy is dead and I didn't tell you about Griffin and Lizzy because I really didn't know about them until we moved to Saint Jo. Your daddy, Graham, didn't tell me he had a brother and that his brother lived in Saint Jo."

Annie accepted it all with a single word: "Okay."

"Does that make Annie kin to me?" Lizzy asked.

"That makes Annie your cousin," Griffin said.

"Well, hot damn!" Lizzy squealed.

"Lizzy!" Griffin chided.

"You say it all the time. Come on, let's go play in the backyard again. Now we're cousins—can you believe it, we're kinfolks like Tim and Richie! Wait 'til we go to the party at Granny Nellie's. I'm going to tell them I've got a cousin and if they play with those mean girls that called me a skunk, me and you can whip those girls' asses."

"Lizzy!" Griffin raised his voice.

"Okay, okay. I won't say bad words no more."

Chuck ducked his head. "Can I be their cousin, too?"

Julie gathered him into her arms. "Of course you can. Actually, you can be their brother if you want to. Don't you think you look like me with that red hair? Miz Alvera and that woman today thought you were my son."

He grinned. "I'm your cousin, too, and I'll help you whip anybody's ass who calls either one of you a skunk."

"Chuck!" Griffin shook his head.

"Well, I damn sure will. I'll throw them down on the ground and I'll hit them until they say they are sorry," Chuck said.

"No more bad words, or the bunch of you are going to play in your rooms all day alone," Julie said.

"Yes, ma'am," Chuck said but the grin didn't fade.

"Momma, will you be watchin' out the window when we go out and play? That mean woman won't come back, will she?" Annie asked nervously.

"The police are making sure that woman has gone back to California and I will watch out the window," Julie said.

They ran together, hand in hand, back out to their jungle, and began to play as if nothing had happened. Their world was back to normal; hopefully it would remain that way for the rest of their lives.

Julie and Griffin sighed at the same time.

"That went fairly well," Julie said. "Thank you."

"Yes, it damn sure did, and we've got to stop cussin' if we expect the kids to quit," he said.

Chapter 12

Julie opted not to read the girls the story of *Sleeping Beauty* that night or let them watch *The Little Mermaid*, either. Both had a scary witch, and neither Annie nor Lizzy needed to be reminded of the day's events. So she picked up a book about a kitten and how it loved to play in the backyard with its friends, a squirrel and a mouse. Then one day the kitten's other friends came to play and made fun of him because he should have been eating the squirrel and the mouse, not playing with them. The children's eyes were fluttering when she said "the end," and Griffin carried Chuck over to his bedroom while Julie took Annie to hers.

She made sure the front door was locked and then went across the foyer, dining room, and kitchen and out into the backyard. Everything was still and quiet. It was too cold for the frogs and locusts to be putting on their evening performance. A north wind knocked the bare tree limbs against each other, but it wasn't much of a melody. She pulled her fuzzy robe tight around her chest and dug her toes deeper into her fluffy house shoes. Inside, a warm bed and a good book were waiting, but Julie needed to be out of the box called a house so she could think. She sat down on the porch swing, pulled her legs up under her, and buried her chin in the soft collar of the robe.

Griffin made his retreat to the den after he'd tucked

all three kids in one more time. Strange how he'd begun to think of them as that. The kids. Not Annie and Lizzy or Chuck or even one or the other. But in two weeks, they'd become *the children,* and when Annie went missing, the way his heart and mind went completely wild, it was as if she were really his child.

He heard a noise on the back porch and slipped out to check it, his pulse thumping as he wondered what exactly he would do if he found Dian back on his property with intentions of stealing Lizzy again.

He stood in the shadows for several minutes looking at Julie. She'd handled things well that day, and she was a great mother. But it wasn't those qualities that flushed his system with desire every time he looked at her. She was a damn fine-looking woman and sexy as hell, even in a robe and house shoes. It would be so easy to fall in love with her. That four letter word jerked him back to reality.

"Cold to be sittin' out here," he said from the shadows not five feet from her.

She jumped and set the swing to moving again. "You scared the hell out of me, Griffin."

"Then you should be an angel," he teased.

She pulled her knees up tighter under her chin and shivered when the north wind found its way inside her robe.

"Want to talk about today?" he asked.

"I thought we already had."

"We talked around it for the kids' sake. It's been on my mind all day, Julie. Out there, getting things ready for the winter sale, all I could think about were those words Dian said."

"What sale?"

"We have a little cattle sale coming up. I've been deciding which cows to sell, which ones to keep, that kind of thing, but that's not what I want to talk about," he said.

"I see." She'd heard of cattle sales. That meant the trucks would arrive and load up whichever cattle were being culled, and they'd drive away with them.

"I never knew about Graham and Dian, and now I feel angry and guilty at the same time," he said.

"Why? Graham was a big boy. No one put a gun to his head and made him enlist." She shivered and wished he'd put his arm around her so she could be warm.

"It still makes me mad. He should be here today, helping me and enjoying life."

"If he were here, would he be enjoying life? I don't think he liked ranching, did he?" Julie asked.

Griffin wondered how Julie had figured that out after only meeting Graham the one time. "Honestly? No, he didn't. He loved sailing, and the four years we were in college, he hated coming home on weekends. I could hardly wait until Friday noon. He could hardly wait until Sunday after church when we could go back. He should have been a professor."

"Then what makes you think he'd be enjoying life if he were here?" Julie asked.

Griffin thought about that. She was right, but it damned sure galled him to admit it. Graham never did like the ranch, hated getting his hands dirty, and the day his parents turned the ranch over to them, he'd gone to Wichita Falls and come home so drunk he could barely stagger up the stairs to bed.

"And if Graham had stayed," Julie went on, "what

would have happened between you and Dian? She had a heat for him and he liked women. Would you have given him the ranch and your wife?"

Griffin stared at the stars sparkling through the tree leaves. Somewhere a lonely coyote howled, beginning the winter opera with a raspy solo. She was right, and it was well past time after six years that he admitted his brother would had been miserable on the ranch. Just because Graham was dead didn't mean Griffin had to give him a halo and wings.

"Anyone ever accuse you of being outspoken?" he asked.

"Goes with the red hair and the Irish name. You don't have to answer those questions, Griffin. Just don't make your brother into an angel because he's dead. And don't believe for an instant that your ex was telling the whole truth. She was trying to hurt you today. She probably knows how much you and Graham loved each other. Besides, if he was mourning so much for her, why did he pick me up the very next night?"

"Dian always had a flare for the dramatic, but looking back, it all makes sense, and I think there was a core of the truth in her story. I just wish he would have talked to me. Somewhere along the way we lost communication," Griffin said.

"About the time your folks moved away?" Julie asked.

Griffin nodded. Julie should have been a psychoanalyst or at the very least a grief counselor. He should have had these talks years ago and put it all to rest then. If he had, then maybe he would already have moved on.

"I have a sister and a brother, Eli. You met my brother. My sister, Sally, lives in Louisiana. Teaches down there and loves it. We talk on the phone weekly, but it's not like it was when we taught together in the same school," she said.

"You were a teacher in another school?"

"Well, I damn sure wasn't a waitress or a hooker. What did you think I was when I met Graham? You did! I can tell by your face that you thought I was something low class. Do you always jump to conclusions?"

"Don't yell at me. Why'd you quit your previous school and move here?" he asked.

"My aunt Flossie died and left me some money. I bought the Lassiter place and moved up here to get away from the town where Annie was born," she explained. Might as well tell him all of it, now that she'd started.

He sat down on the opposite end of the swing. "Go on."

"I love kids. Wanted a houseful, but it didn't work out that way. Now I'm too..." She stopped a word short of admitting she was old.

"Old?" he finished for her. "How old are you really? Thirty? That's not old. Janet Jackson is still having kids and she's a lot older than you."

"I'm thirty-four and it took six years to get Annie," she admitted.

"It took one night to get Annie," he said.

"Okay, point taken. Jefferson is bigger than Saint Jo. My father is a preacher there and has been for a long time. Can you imagine the gossip when I brought Annie home with that white streak in her hair and my husband divorced me on grounds of adultery? I couldn't fight that at city hall, so I quietly signed off. He got to keep everything. I got my maiden name and sole custodial rights to Annie. It didn't work. Everyone thought she was a bastard anyway. So I moved to where no one would know us or the circumstances of her birth. Guess what? That didn't work, either."

"Thirty-four isn't old, Julie. It's not old at all. It's been a long day and tomorrow comes early. I'm going to bed. Thanks for listening to me and for the honest opinions," he said gruffly.

"You are welcome," she whispered. Shock of shocks! Griffin appreciated her honest opinion about his brother. Graham, who'd been raised to angel status because he died, who'd always been the outgoing extrovert. She hadn't said anything that wasn't the truth according to what she'd understood.

The longest walk Griffin ever took was from that swing up to his bedroom. He slung himself back onto his bed and stared holes into the ceiling. It might be best if Julie moved out of the ranch house after the holidays. If she weren't right there all the time, maybe, just maybe he could move on with his life now.

She sat on the swing awhile longer. When she stood up, her leg had gone to sleep, so she had to stomp the feeling back into it. She stumbled into the house, locked the door, and went to the kitchen, where she ate a piece of leftover coconut pie before going up to bed. The day had held too much excitement. She hoped the next thirteen days of Christmas vacation were so boring that she was ready to go back to school when they ended.

Monday morning, a new routine started. Breakfast for Griffin, with extra coffee in his thermos for him to drink throughout the morning. Julie had given Elsie the day off without consulting Griffin when Elsie mentioned that she hadn't had time to do a bit of Christmas shopping for her grandchildren.

Julie sautéed several rump roasts with onions, put them in the slow cooker, set the temperature to three hundred, and went about making a triple recipe of yeast bread. She rolled forty potatoes in aluminum foil for the oven. While she was washing romaine lettuce for a salad, Lizzy and Annie wandered into the kitchen.

They wore their flannel pajamas. Their hair was tangled and in their eyes. They sat like zombies at the kitchen table—both of them so much like Griffin Luckadeau, it wasn't even funny.

Griffin stumbled into the kitchen and poured a cup of coffee. "Where's Elsie? Please don't tell me she's sick."

"I gave her the day off. I'm cooking for the hands today," Julie said.

"You did what? This is a piss poor time to give Elsie a day off," Griffin bellowed. The words were scarcely out of his mouth before he realized he wasn't angry about Julie taking responsibility on the ranch, but the way she looked that morning in the kitchen—flour on her nose, bustling around as she cooked. She was beautiful beyond what words could describe, and he liked it entirely too much.

Chuck had just made it to the doorway and stopped in his tracks. He put his hands over his ears. "What did I do wrong?"

"Not one thing, sweetheart. This is a big-people fight. You kids are fine. Sit down and have some orange juice. I'm making pancakes for breakfast," Julie said.

He took his hands away but eyed Griffin seriously. "I didn't do anything wrong?"

"No, you didn't. How would you like to help me in the barn today?" Griffin asked. "If Julie is going to cook, then the girls can help her."

Chuck's face lit up like the star on the Christmas tree.

"We get to help?" Lizzy asked.

"Sure you do," Julie said.

She turned back to Griffin. "I should've talked to you, but it was late and she said she didn't have her shopping done. I can cook for a crowd, believe me. I used to cook for the homeless shelter in the summers when we went on mission trips."

Griffin hung his coat back up and waited for Chuck to have breakfast. "It's all right. I just always get antsy the week of our sale."

Julie poured three small glasses of orange juice and set them on the table.

"You'll get to see where the sale is," Lizzy told Chuck while they ate pancakes as fast as Julie could flip them and put them on a platter.

"What's a sale?" Annie asked.

"That's when the people come and buy the cows," Lizzy said.

"Does a big truck come to take the cows away? I saw a truck like that when Momma and me moved to here. It had cows all shoved up in it," Annie said.

"The sale people bring the trucks. We have to make a party for them," Lizzy said.

"Party?" Julie looked at Griffin.

"Don't worry. Elsie knows what to do and it won't interrupt your schedule at all," he said.

After breakfast, she braided Annie's and Lizzy's hair to keep it out of the food and gave them small jobs to do in the kitchen. Lizzy washed lettuce leaves. Annie brushed butter on the tops of the yeast rolls.

After lunch, the girls helped clean up and then went into the den to play Barbies. Chuck begged to go back to the barn with Griffin.

"I forgotted one of the Barbies. We're having a sale dance." Annie skipped through the kitchen and into the foyer on her way to her bedroom to get whatever they had "forgotted."

"How many Barbies does it take to have a sale dance?" Julie followed her into the den.

"Lizzy says it takes a lot, maybe all of them acause the sale dance is the biggest thing ever," Annie said.

The front door opened, and Julie went to see who had arrived. Annie followed her, still afraid that Dian might reappear and cart her off again. Her left hand held the Barbie; her right one clutched her mother's hand tightly. Two women shoved a couple of suitcases through the door and stopped when they saw Julie and Annie.

Julie recognized Griffin's mother immediately. The tall blonde had to be his sister. The older woman with the white streak in her hair opened her arms. "Lizzy, darlin', come and give Grandma a hug."

Annie's lower lip protruded and quivered. "I'm Annie. I'm not Lizzy."

The tall blonde with Griffin's mother giggled. "You been watching that movie again, have you? Remember when she watched it a couple of years ago and wanted a red wig so she could be Annie? Excuse us for barging in. Are you the new babysitter? I'm Melinda, Griffin's sister, and this is our mother, Laura."

Julie stepped forward and extended her hand. "I'm Julie Donavan."

Griffin's mother was breathtaking. She wore jeans and a short-sleeved denim shirt over a red tank top, and there wasn't an ounce of fat on her. She scarcely looked old enough to be Griffin's mother. And his sister: blonde, blue-eyed, model pretty, and slim with long legs. Julie felt unkempt in her faded tank top, her unruly red hair up in a ponytail, wearing no makeup.

"You look surprised. Didn't Griff tell you we were coming?" Laura asked.

Julie shook her head.

"Isn't that just like a man?" Melinda asked. "Okay, here's the deal. The big sale is Friday. We always come to the Lucky Clover to help Marita get things ready. This year I guess we'll be helping Elsie. It'll take the whole week, trust me—with the cooking for the crew and getting the barn decorated for the dance. It's a big, big job and we won't get in your way, but we might enlist your help."

"I see," Julie said.

Just when she thought she had it all under control, another flying saucer came hurling toward her. Griffin might be hanging from the nearest pecan tree come evening. He'd best talk fast or tonight's would be the last meal he ever had.

Lizzy came out of the den and threw herself into Laura's arms. "Grandma! I knew you'd be coming, I knew it because Daddy said the sale was almost here and you always come and I wanted you to see Annie and can we go to the dance just for a little while this year?"

Melinda's face went pale.

Laura's eyes kept darting from Lizzy to Annie.

"Did you see Annie? We're cousins acause my momma came yesterday and stole her and we had to go find her at Mamie's and my momma had pink hair and I didn't like her too much, Grandma. Is that a sin?" Lizzy kept on.

Laura bent down on one knee and looked long and hard at the child. "I don't think so. I'm pleased to meet you, Annie. I see you and Lizzy and I all have the same streak in our hair. That makes us special, doesn't it?"

"Why don't you girls go on back out to your Barbie sale party? Come on in the kitchen. I'm making dinner today for the hired hands. I gave Elsie the day off. I'll explain what I can. It's a long story and I've got to get on with the dinner preparations. I can work while I tell it for the thousandth time," Julie said.

Laura and Melinda were glad to sit. Their heads were spinning faster than a ride at a carnival. From the looks of those two girls, Griffin had a hell of a lot of explaining to do in addition to whatever Julie told them.

"Annie is my child. Lizzy is two days older than Annie. She does not belong to your son, Griffin, Mrs. Luckadeau," Julie began.

"That would be Laura, please."

"Then Laura it is. Annie is not Griffin's child, even though she and Lizzy look like twins."

Laura didn't know she was holding her breath until she let it out in a whoosh.

"She does, however, belong to Graham," Julie said. "So even though I never thought of her having paternal grandparents, I guess you are her grandmother."

"Damn!" Melinda said. "What are you doing here?"

Tears built up behind Laura's big, brown eyes and ran

like tiny rivers down her cheeks to drip onto the collar of her denim shirt. "There's a bit of Graham left in the world. Who are you and why didn't you bring her around before now?" Laura looked at Julie with accusing eyes.

"And what in the hell are you doing here now?" Melinda asked a second time.

Julie explained from start to finish, ending with the Dian story from the day before yesterday.

"And you honestly didn't move here to claim her birthright?" Melinda asked suspiciously.

"I did not," Julie said. "I moved to the country to get away from everyone and to bring my daughter to a place where no one knew about her. I feel like I've been tossed naked into a rattlesnake den. I think maybe it would be best if Annie and I went to my parents for the rest of the holiday and got out of your way."

"I agree," Melinda said.

"I don't," Laura said. "Don't go. I'd like to get to know my granddaughter."

"Not me." Melinda shook her head emphatically. "She's here for something other than Saint Jo sunshine. I bet everyone in town took one look at Annie and thought she was Griff's kid, didn't they?"

"They did, so I had to tell them that she was Graham's. I'm tired of hiding and sneaking around. I'll leave. Tell Griffin when he comes in that we'll be staying with Miz Alvera when we return. I'll get the rest of our things at that time. Dinner is done except for the rolls. Three-fifty for half an hour. Surely you two can take care of the rest of it." Julie started up the stairs.

"Tell Griffin what?" He came in the back door with Chuck in tow. One look at Julie's face told him that she was upset and he was in trouble. A second look at the two women sitting at the table told him exactly why.

Melinda pointed at Chuck. "That she's leaving. Griffin, what in the hell did you mean letting her squirm her way into the house? Is that her kid, too?"

"No, he's my foster child. Julie is not his biological mother. And Julie is not going anywhere. I planned on calling you tonight, Mother. You are here a day early," Griffin said.

"It's Monday, isn't it? We always come on Monday," Laura said.

"Guess it is…and you've met Annie, and Julie told you the story? I was thinkin' you came on Tuesday, but I'm glad you are here."

Melinda crossed her arms over her chest. "She did and I'm not believing a word of it."

"Frankly, Sister, I don't give a damn what you believe. Julie is staying. Lizzy and Chuck have been promised Christmas with Annie and they will have it," Griffin said.

Julie stopped halfway up the stairs. The whole bunch of Luckadeaus were crazy. They had another think coming if they thought they could tell her what to do. "I'll do what I want. You don't tell me what to do and neither does your family, Griff."

"Mother, do you want to get to know Graham's daughter?" Griffin asked.

"Yes, of course I do."

"It's Annie and Julie or nothing. They don't separate."

Melinda cleared her throat. "Griffin, I thought you had better sense. Especially after Dian."

He glared at his sister. "Melinda, that's enough."

Laura looked up. "Please stay. We apologize. It was just the shock, and after Dian..."

"I need a minute," Julie whispered.

The lump in her throat refused to budge. Hindsight was the only truly perfect vision in the world. If she could go back, she'd certainly do things differently. When she reached her room, she picked up the phone and dialed her mother's number.

"Hello, Julie," Deborah said with a lilt in her voice. "Did you change your mind? Are you coming home for Christmas?"

"Right now I'm not sure what I'm doing. Momma, what would you do if Eli had a child and you just now found out about it and he'd only just had a one-night stand with the woman?" she asked.

"Lizzy's grandmother came to visit, didn't she?" Deborah asked. "And did she accept you or throw a hissy fit?"

"She appeared with no warning, and if Griffin hadn't asked me to stay, I'd be on my way to Jefferson in ten minutes," Julie said.

"Okay, first thing is that I wouldn't blame the child. I'd try real hard not to blame the woman, especially if Eli was dead. Am I doing all right? Do you need to come home?" Deborah asked.

"No, I think I'll stay and put up my dukes. Great-Great-Grandma wouldn't have let a bunch of Cajuns run her out of Ireland, would she?"

Deborah laughed so hard that she got the hiccups. "We named you well. You don't have to prove shit to those people, Julie. Make them prove to you that they are worthy to even look at Annie."

Julie held the phone out and looked at it. "Momma, did you just say *shit*?"

"I did. I might pray about it later, but it'll be a hell of a lot later. You are my child and by damn, they can appreciate you for the wonderful person you are or else they can take their sorry asses on home to whatever rock they slithered out from under," she said.

Julie held the phone out away from her and stared at it for a minute.

"Don't be so stunned. They're messin' with my kid now. How would you feel if Annie called you with the same problem in a few years?"

"I'd kick their sorry asses," Julie said.

"Okay then, now you understand," Deborah said. "Stay and tell 'em all to go to hell on a rusty poker if you have to. I'm going now. I think that's enough bad words for one day. You make them prove their worth before you trust her with them."

"You could come help me. I could make reservations at the hotel. I think the house will be full," she said.

"I don't think so. I'm going to stand back and let you take care of this. Call me if you need me, though. It's always good to be needed."

"Remember what you told me when Annie was born?" Julie asked.

"Of course. The same thing my mother told me. Once a mother, always a mother," Deborah said.

"It's time for me to share or this wouldn't be happening, right?" Julie said.

"I think so," Deborah said.

"Sometimes I wonder why all this had to happen," Julie said.

"Sometimes it's hard to get an Irish lass's attention."

"Damn my red hair and name. Thanks, Momma." Julie managed a weak giggle.

"Anytime. Goodbye and good luck."

Julie went back to the lion's den to face off with the vermin only to find both Laura and Melinda sitting on the floor dressing Barbie dolls with the girls. Griffin and Chuck had gone back to the barn.

Laura looked up. "Can we start all over? I'm Laura Luckadeau, Griffin's mother. And this is his older and very much overprotective sister, Melinda, who speaks her mind before she thinks. We are glad you are here."

"I'm Julie, Annie's mother, and thank you for starting all over," Julie said coolly.

Julie went to the kitchen and continued with her lunch preparations. In between jobs, she stole glances at the women with the little girls. Would the Luckadeau grandparents decide to press for grandparents' rights and take Annie away from her for a weekend a month, maybe a month in the summer? The thought gave her chills.

"Mother, we better get busy and let these girls finish their Barbie ball. We need to call the caterers and check on the guest list," Melinda said.

As they walked into the kitchen, Melinda flipped her blonde hair over her shoulder. "Mother will boss, whine, and beg for the rest of the week to get what she wants, but when the two-day sale starts, she'll be as sweet as honey to the buyers. She's damn good at what she does. Dian hated her for it. Oops! Guess I'm not supposed to bring up her name anymore."

"Don't be catty," Julie said. "I don't give a damn if you loved her and talk about her all the time and to her on the phone every single day. Griffin and I are friends. That's all there is to it. You won't make me jealous talking about Dian, so don't be coy."

"You sure speak your mind," Melinda said.

"Always have and always will. Take it or leave it. I don't care one way or the other," Julie said.

"Dian saw Mother as competition rather than a friend," Melinda said.

"I don't see either of you as anything other than Lizzy's grandmother and aunt," Julie told them.

"And Annie's grandmother?" Laura said.

"We'll see," Julie said.

"Fair enough." Laura got up and went to the pantry. She returned with a notebook and a pen and picked up the cordless phone on the kitchen cabinet.

Julie couldn't wait to get Griffin off in a corner and tell him exactly how upset she was with him for unloading all this in her lap without warning. And especially for doing it without telling his mother about Annie.

Griffin dreaded going back in the house that evening, even though he hadn't seen his family since the beginning of the summer and he always loved company. He'd played a dozen scenarios in his mind during the afternoon while he invented reasons for him and Chuck to stay in the barn.

He'd meant to tell Julie that they always helped with the sale, but he thought he'd had at least one more day. It wasn't easy talking to her when, every time he looked at her, all that was on his mind was making love to her. The desire he'd been fighting for weeks kept him tongue-tied and confused. He couldn't act on the ache to feel her in his arms—not after she'd been with his brother and had a child to prove it. Yet he couldn't make it disappear.

So what? his conscience chided. *She's a strong woman, a good mother, and you're damn sure attracted to her now, no matter what happened in the past. It's like Graham used to always say: The past is like Las Vegas; what happens there stays there.*

He was glad to see the old red truck still sitting in the driveway when he parked his vehicle. So she hadn't let his sister's sharp tongue send her packing. That was good because she hadn't let them run her off, but it was also bad because she would be gunning for bear—and he was the bear.

"She's going to be a handful," he said as he crawled out of the truck and made his way to house.

"What's a hamfull?" Chuck asked.

"You'll understand when you get older," Griffin said and went through the gate Chuck had left open.

"Griffin!" Laura said when he walked into the kitchen.

"You're still in trouble," Melinda singsonged from behind the bar where she filled glasses with ice and set them on the table.

"Shut up and give me a hug," he said.

"Not until you've had a shower and shave," she said.

"Daddy, Daddy, guess what? Grandma is Annie's grandma too acause your brother is her daddy." Lizzy paused and tilted her head sideways. "How'd that happen, Daddy?"

"You'll understand it when you are a big girl. Do you mind sharing Grandma with Annie?"

"No and she's going to share her grandma with me acause I don't have a momma's momma."

"Honey, you do have another grandmother. She lives in California with your mother, Dian, but you just don't get to see her. But that's nice that Annie is going to share her grandma with you, too." Melinda looked at Julie.

Julie stood in the corner of the kitchen, arms folded over her chest, with that look on her face that Griffin had seen twice before now—that day in her yard when Lizzy had run away and, more recently, in the back of Mamie's store when Dian had stolen Annie. He had a feeling that today's look had nothing to do with children and everything to do with him.

"Please excuse Julie and me. We've got some things to talk about in the library," he said.

"I thought this was a platonic relationship," Melinda said.

"What it is happens not to be a bit of your damn business, Melinda," Griffin said.

"Momma, she's got him talking like Graham did. Griffin used to be the good twin." Melinda pouted.

"Suck up your lower lip. I'm a big boy. I can even go to the potty all by myself," he said.

"I'm not so sure," Melinda said.

He ignored her and followed Julie into the library. He would have liked a beer, but he'd be damned if his sister saw him getting a little liquid courage.

Julie paced from one end of the small library to the other. Three walls were covered floor to ceiling with filled bookcases. The fourth wall was glass and faced out into a small courtyard, where a white rock and cactus garden waited for spring. A wingback leather chair sat behind an enormous mahogany desk that took up a sizeable chunk of floor space in the middle of the room. She was at the far end of the library when he opened the door.

She turned and started firing questions at him. "Why didn't you tell me they were coming, and why didn't you tell me what the sale involved, and why didn't you tell them about Annie? And why did you leave once you did tell them and I had to face off with both of them alone?"

He sat down in the chair and double-clicked the icon on the computer to bring up his email messages. She crossed the room, reached over his shoulder, and closed the window.

"What are you doing?" he asked.

"Don't you sit there and play with the computer when I ask you something." She had leaned in so close that a red curl brushed his neck and set off a rush of desire.

Yep, she was a handful when she was angry. Living with her would always be a nightmare, so he should get that idea out of his head right now. But what a ride life would be with her. There'd never be a dull moment and she'd keep him on his toes right up until the time he died.

"I was going to tell you they were coming. I thought I had a couple more days. I'm surprised they got here this early. I didn't want to tell you until the last minute because I didn't want you to take Annie and go home for the two weeks they'll be here. Lizzy would drive me insane without Annie around. Even with her grandmother and Aunt Melinda, it would be a nightmare. So if I didn't tell you until it was too late for you to make other plans, then I wouldn't have to deal with that," he said honestly.

She propped a hip on his desk. "You've had weeks to tell your mother about Annie and me and Graham. I had to do it and it damn sure wasn't easy or fair."

He grinned, the dimple in his chin deepening. She had the sudden urge to kiss those lips right above the damned indentation, but he wasn't getting off the hook with a boyish grin. No, sir, she wasn't finished fighting at all.

"All you had to do was ask me to stay. I'm not so eager to separate them either, you know. They should have been twins. Either mine or yours. It's like they've found their other half," she said.

"Well, the way you act, I sure didn't know that. Hell's bells, most of the time, I don't know what you'll do or say."

"Get used to it, honey. I'll never hold my tongue or my emotions again," she lied. Sitting so close to him sent her blood to the boiling point and it had little to do with anger.

"We finished?" he asked. He hoped not. He was alone with her and he liked that.

"For now. We'll talk about this sale thing later. I thought it was a bunch of men who bought cattle and hauled them out in a truck," she said.

"Basically that's right. But it's an auction and a dance and a party, and half the state, including the governor, will probably be here, so get ready to smile until your face hurts," he said.

"I'm not going to that thing. I'm just the hired help," she said.

"No, you are the mother of Graham Luckadeau's daughter, and yes, ma'am, you will be helping with the plans and attending," he said.

"Annie is Julie Donavan's daughter and don't you forget it."

He reached out and moved toward her at the same time. One hand touched her face, the other cupped her chin. He moved in for a kiss and she tilted her chin slightly. He tasted iced tea with a bit of lemon and chocolate. Not a bad combination.

His tongue traced the outline of her lips and glued her to the floor. She wrapped her arms around him and leaned in.

She tasted tea and that bite of yeast bread he had popped into his mouth while he was talking to his family. Not a bad combination.

Julie pulled him closer, tasting more, deepening the kiss until steam shot out of her ears, the passion was so intense. Was there a lock on the door, and would those witches in the kitchen miss them if they stayed gone half an hour?

Griffin sucked on her lower lip and got the full benefit of the kiss. He wished there was a lock on the door and no children or relatives in the house. Living without her after kissing her would be pure hell, he decided just before they broke away.

"What was that all about?" she asked the moment his lips left hers.

"It was about a damn fine kiss," he said and stood straight. "I'll see you in the kitchen."

When he was out of the library, she touched her lips. They were still on fire and she wanted more. Griffin was right. It was one damn fine kiss. The best damn kiss she'd had in all of her thirty-four years, and she would have liked for it to have been more than a damn fine kiss.

Chapter 13

"You get that straightened out?" Melinda asked Griffin when he waltzed into the kitchen as if nothing had happened.

"I did."

She patted the chair beside hers. "Good. Now let's you and me and Momma sit down to the table and plan this year's party. We've already called in a band to play at the dance, and we use the same caterer every year. Barbecued everything that don't move, along with beans, cole slaw, corn bread, and every kind of cheesecake under the sun."

"Julie, you take that chair. I'll pull up another one," Griffin said as she sauntered in.

Melinda shot him a mean look.

"I'll go play with the children awhile," Julie said, then wished she could take the words back because Griffin's bitchy sister would count that as a feather in her cap for sure.

"I'm askin' you to come join us and put your two cents into the pot," Griffin said.

She walked over and sat down. She touched her lips again and hoped they didn't look as bee-stung as they felt. How in the hell could one kiss turn her insides to a quivering bowl of Jell-O? Derrick's kisses had been nice, even passionate at times, and she'd enjoyed them. Graham's had been hot and fiery and sent her hormones on a roller-coaster ride. But when Griffin's mouth had touched hers, it was as if her soul had come home. Later, when she was alone, she'd think more about it, but right then, she wished that bitchy sister and mother would disappear so she could cart that sexy cowboy to a bedroom and do more than just kiss him until she couldn't catch her breath.

That idea brought her up short. She didn't live in the nineteenth century, when a woman didn't kiss a man until she was married to him and damn sure didn't have sex with him until after the vows were said. She lived in the modern-day world...but by damn, she refused to fall for Griffin Luckadeau. There would be too many obstacles in the course from start to finish—beginning with his sister, who was staring daggers at her—and she didn't have the energy to conquer them.

"Griffin, I understand that you are angry because we didn't open up our arms and be all sugar and sweet to Julie," Melinda said, "but remember we've lived through Dian. Not to mention that schoolteacher that almost led Beau to the altar and bankruptcy at the same time. Or how about that witch Slade dated back before Jane came along? We are willing to get past our prejudice, but this is a family thing. It's our sale, not Julie's."

"No, Sis, it's *my* sale. If I want Julie's help, then I'll have it. And one other thing—she will be attending the party as the mother of Graham's daughter and if you don't like it, maybe you'd better not unpack your suitcases," Griffin said.

A grin tickled the corners of Laura's mouth. Her quiet son had finally stood up to his overbearing sister. "Julie, what do you think about a Christmas theme this year? We usually stay away from Christmas because everyone is already about half sick of it, but I was thinking about those little steer figurines with Santa hats for centerpieces."

"Momma, that sounds so…so…absolutely horrible," Melinda said.

"I love it," Julie said.

"I like it, Mother. Call Mamie and ask her where to buy those things," Griffin said.

Melinda set her jaw and tapped her foot on the tile floor. "It'll look—"

"Like we're a bunch of hicks?" Griffin asked with a sideways look at Julie, and they both erupted into full-fledged laughter.

Laura and Melinda stared from one to the other, questions on their faces.

"Inside joke," Griffin finally said when he got it under control. "Oh yeah, I forgot to tell you, Marita said to tell you both hello and she'll miss seeing you this year. She called every day until Carl got out of the hospital. Now she calls every other day. I think she's trying to wean herself away from Lizzy. It can't be easy for either of them. Annie and Chuck help on this end, and I'm sure Clarissa's kids and grandchildren help on that end, but it's still tough."

"I was so sorry to hear about that. Now, shall we serve barbecue—ribs, chicken, quail, beef, and pork?" Laura asked.

"Sure. We using the same caterers?" Griffin asked.

"Yes, that same one out of Fort Worth. They'll arrive in the middle of the afternoon and put cloths on all the tables and make the old barn look as formal as a hotel lobby," Melinda said.

“Then what’s left for us to plan?” Julie asked.

“Decorations. What we’ll be wearing, as well. It’s formal. Men in western tuxes, ladies in gowns. So there’s some shopping to do. We’ll make several trips to Wichita Falls,” Melinda said.

“Formal? In a barn?” Julie asked.

“Of course. If you don’t have anything to wear, you don’t really have to attend. Does she, Griffin?” Melinda asked.

“I assure you, Julie will look just fine. She could come in a burlap bag with a rope as a belt and still look fine. I’m in charge here, Melinda. Get over yourself,” he said.

“Why are you fighting with me?” Melinda asked. “You never have before.”

“It didn’t matter before. It does now. I mean it. I manage to run this place all year without you. I could put on a party without you, too.”

“I’m not sure I like you like this. It’s as if Graham came back alive and crawled in your body,” she said.

Griffin shrugged.

“Don’t you value what you’ve worked your whole life for?” Melinda asked.

“One word: prenup,” he said.

“That means the land and the farm equipment. What about the capital to run the place, to buy feed, to buy cattle? That part could sift through your fingers and into her pocket real quick,” she challenged.

“Two words: ain’t interested,” Julie said.

“I don’t believe you and I don’t believe you are ranch material, either,” Melinda said.

“What makes you an expert?” Julie asked.

“I happen to own and operate a ranch. Momma is an

only child, so when her father died six years ago, she and Daddy went over around Bellville, Texas, where she was raised, and took over the management of the Circle R Ranch. Her mother, Granny Raley, was also a ranching woman, and before she died, she inherited the Bar L near Conroe from her uncle who didn't have children. I'd have to draw you a genealogy chart to make you understand. Anyway, Grandma hired a manager, and when she died, she left the Bar L to me. I married the manager the next year. We've got two sons, Houston and Austin. They're ten and twelve and off on a camping trip with their father right now. He does that with them while I come help Griffin with the sale party. They'll be here the day of the sale and we'll go home together after we have presents. So I do know about ranching and I *am* a damn expert, which is something you will never be."

"So you're older than Griffin?" Julie asked.

"I am forty," Melinda said in a huff.

Julie chuckled. If Melinda looked that damn good at forty, then she didn't mind Griffin thinking she was that old after all.

"What's so funny?" Melinda asked.

"I'd have thought you were just a year older than Griff at the most. And, honey, I'd have pictured you more in the modeling business than the ranching one with those long legs and your looks," Julie said.

Melinda's whole face softened with the compliment. "Momma had given up ever having another child and then—*kaboom*—twin boys with her white streak when I was twelve. They were my toys. I loved them, but I got to admit, I was partial to Graham. He had this magnetism about him, even as a child. By the time he was a teenager, he could sweet-talk the panty hose off a nun."

Julie blushed.

"No offense meant there," Melinda said.

"I'm not Catholic. I'm a dyed-in-the-wool Methodist, and believe me, we were both drunk enough that neither of us had to do much sweet-talking—and I wasn't wearing panty hose."

Griffin excused himself and went to the living room. Julie's kiss was still warm on his lips and he didn't want to hear about his brother and her in that hotel room.

Melinda went on. "Anyway, it about killed me when he died. Don't get me wrong. I love Griffin. I'd fight a circle saw for him, probably quicker than I would have for Graham. Griffin was always a deeper, more complex person. Graham had this devil-may-care, to-hell-with-tomorrow attitude that said *let's go find some trouble and see if we can get into it*. I guess you already know that, since you went to bed with him when you didn't even know the man."

Julie jerked her head up and blinked twice.

"Melinda, watch your tongue," Laura said.

Julie stared Melinda down. "Yes, I did, and yes, he was magnetic. Be careful about throwing stones, though. Could be one will come through your glass house someday. You don't know me. Take me or leave me. I don't care. But if you're going to stay in this house the rest of the week, may I suggest you learn to curb your tongue? My temper can only take so much. So, truce?"

"Or what will you do?" Melinda asked.

"Honey, I will take you outside and mop up the yard with all that pretty blonde hair. I've stood as many slurs and degrading remarks as I intend to," Julie said.

"Momma?"

"She's right," Laura said. "You are my daughter, but I've told you for years that the toughest lesson you'll ever learn is when to shut your mouth."

"You're takin' the part of a one-night stand over your own daughter," Melinda fumed.

"That's one. You get two more. You'd better pace them or you're going to find out what a one-night stand can do in a catfight," Julie said.

"I'm going up to bed. Good night." Melinda left the room as Griffin came back.

Laura fluffed back her hair with her fingertips, then picked up the notebook Melinda had left. There were a few gray strands at her temples that didn't involve that silver streak flowing back from her forehead. "She's always spoken her mind."

"So have I," Julie said.

"I can see where Graham would have liked you," Laura laughed.

Griffin picked up his coat and went right out the back door. For the first time in his life, he wished he'd been born one child instead of a twin.

That evening, Julie read the kids a book and then went to her room. She could hear Griffin talking to his mother and sister in the hallway. Their voices floated through the door, but she couldn't make out a single word, only the tone. Once or twice, Melinda swore and then she laughed. Julie wondered briefly what could be funny, but not for long.

She picked up the new Sue Grafton book she'd bought at the bookstore when she was at the Gainesville mall. Before the fire, she'd owned the whole set, but she hadn't had time to read anything lately.

Footsteps came up the stairs. Two sets went to rooms across the hall. One set stopped at her door for a moment, then continued on to Griffin's room. She wondered if he was aching for a fight about that kiss. Well if he was, then he should have it, right?

She peeked out into the hallway. She could hear Melinda and Laura moving around behind closed doors. She tiptoed to Griffin's door and raised a hand to knock, then thought better of it. One little noise and at least two doors would open in the hallway, with the possibility of a third, if Annie heard it. Explaining to Annie would be easy compared to Laura and Melinda, if they caught her going into Griffin's room. Melinda's temper would ignite into flames and she'd do a dance right there in the hallway singing about being right about the red-haired, white-trash gold digger.

She turned the knob and eased into the dark room. Griffin was stretched out on the bed, his hands laced behind his head. He figured Lizzy was sneaking into his room to ask for a midnight snack. When he looked across the room and saw Julie lit up from the moonlight flowing through the window, he sat up so fast it made him dizzy.

"Which kid needs me?" he whispered.

"Nothing is the matter with the kids. Something is the matter with us," she said.

"Please tell me that kiss didn't spook you into leaving Saint Jo for the holidays..."

"I'm not leaving. Wild horses couldn't drive me away and let your sister win this silly war she's declared on me," she said.

He threw himself backward with enough force to make the bed bounce. She pulled up a rocking chair to the side of his bed and slid into it, drawing her knees up, propping her forearms on them and her chin on her arms.

"Okay, then what is the problem that you'd invade my bedroom without even knocking?"

She was suddenly tongue-tied. What had seemed like a perfectly good idea five minutes ago was suddenly sophomoric and silly. She wasn't a teenager and Griffin wasn't the first man she'd kissed.

"It was the kiss, wasn't it?" he asked.

She nodded.

"Well, rest assured it was just something that happened. Kind of like a knee-jerk reaction to a situation. It won't happen again."

"Why?" she asked.

"What do you mean?"

"Why won't it happen again? Am I ugly? Do I repel you?"

He sat up again. "You most certainly do not!"

He was careful to keep the sheet over his lower body. Just looking at her in that silly nightshirt with Betty Boop on the front had flushed him with desire that wasn't easy to cover up, even with a sheet.

"Then why?"

"Because you..." he stammered.

"Because I was with your brother?"

"That and the fact that you and I could never have a relationship, Julie. Number one, you are not my type. Number two… I can't think of what number two is, but give me a day or two and I'll have a whole list."

She was on her feet in a flash and put a hand on each of Griffin's cheeks. She leaned forward and kissed him soundly and passionately. When she broke away, she ran her tongue over her lips to get the final taste.

"Number one," she said, "you aren't my type either. Number two, I'd rather be your friend. Number three, you kiss damn good and your brother and I were both so plastered that night I can't even remember what his kisses were like. Good night, Griffin. You're right—it won't happen again. I just wanted to make sure the first kiss I'd had since my divorce really was as good as I thought it was."

"And was it?" he asked hoarsely.

"I don't kiss and tell." She slipped out the door.

Griffin's pillow took several beatings before he pounded it into submission enough that he could go to sleep.

"Good morning, Son. Sit down and have some of Elsie's wonderful pancakes," Laura said, all chipper the next morning.

"Griffin has sausage, eggs, biscuits, and gravy," Elsie said. "It's on the stove except for the eggs. Over easy or scrambled?"

"Over easy this morning," he said.

Laura looked up from the notebook she'd been writing in all morning while she ate. "You are spoiled."

"Why would you say that?" Elsie asked.

"Because Marita never made breakfast. We were all on our own for that meal. Cereal. Toast. Frozen waffles. It was grab and run in the morning. You are spoiling him," Laura said.

Elsie smiled. "I usually come to work at the same time Paul does. The children and Miz Julie are already gone to school. But during the holidays, Griffin asked me to come in early while you all are here to give you a hand with whatever you need. The sale party will take a lot of work. It's only for a few days that he'll get my home-cooked breakfasts. I understand Miz Julie does a fine job of making a good hot breakfast when I'm not here."

"I see. So that's the arrangement? Julie makes breakfast and you give her a place to live until her house is ready. Is that because of Lizzy forming such an attachment to Annie and so Julie can help her make the transition after Marita left?" Laura asked.

"It is, and you might have been told that if you hadn't come in here like a bull in a china shop forming opinions before you got the facts," Griffin said.

Julie came into the kitchen and poured a cup of coffee. She sat down at the table and looked at the pancakes on the platter. The kids would be happy to see them. She didn't have much appetite. She hadn't slept well but took comfort in the fact that Griffin hadn't either. The walls were thin enough that she could hear him tossing and turning just as long as she had.

Griffin took a sidelong look at her. This business of living with a desirable woman was going to ruin him. She was beautiful in a robe and house shoes. She was sexy in jeans and a T-shirt. She was desirable in a Betty Boop nightshirt. And she could arouse every male part of his body with one kiss. What would it be like to truly make love to her?

"What facts?" Melinda said from the doorway. "Is that sausage gravy and biscuits? Give the woman a raise, Griff. Marita never made breakfast."

"Want your eggs over easy or scrambled?" Elsie asked.

Melinda took a mug from the cabinet and poured a cup of coffee. "Scrambled, please. Six will do." Melinda sipped her coffee. "On second thought, don't give her a raise. Be mean to her."

"Why?" Julie asked.

"I want Elsie to quit him so I can hire her, if she makes breakfast. I can't cook," Melinda said.

"You can hush that kind of talk right now," Griffin said, glad to be back on familiar ground that didn't shift with every movement Julie made.

"Then you'd better be real nice to her because I'll be waiting at the front door with a getaway truck anytime she wants to leave your sorry ass and work for me. What kind of benefits package are you offering?" Melinda asked.

Griffin glared at his sister.

"I'll give you insurance and two weeks' paid vacation every summer, plus a bonus at the end of the cattle sale. Ours is in October," Melinda said.

"You are a funny woman. I wouldn't leave Griffin or the children. I love working here," Elsie said.

Elsie slipped Griffin's eggs from the skillet onto a plate and handed it to him. While he split two biscuits and topped them with gravy, she whipped six eggs into a yellow froth and poured them into a separate iron skillet where several tablespoons of butter had melted.

Elsie went on, "I like it even better on weekends when

Miz Julie is here. Griffin is a very fortunate man that she was willing to stay after Marita left. Lizzy would have gone crazy without her. And that little Chuck. He's lived in such bad places that he loves it here. This ranch is big and would hold even more children."

"So you've worked your magic on her?" Melinda turned to Julie.

Julie held up two fingers.

"No fair. That wasn't mean. It was a statement," Melinda whined.

"Be careful," Laura said.

"What's going on?" Griffin asked.

"She said she's going to whip my ass all over the front yard," Melinda said.

"Guess you better learn to bite your tongue. I've seen her in action. She'd take on a forest fire with a cup of water," Griffin said.

"Some brother you are."

"Is that two?" Griffin looked at Julie.

She shook her head. "Fight your own battles. I'll take care of mine."

Melinda's face broke into a wide smile. "I might like you after all."

Julie dropped one finger.

"Why don't you just give me Annie? I always wanted a daughter, and everyone would think she was mine, since she looks like Momma," Melinda said.

"Make your own. You've got a husband and the means to make one, unless you're too cold to hatch an egg," Julie said.

Melinda held up one finger.

Griffin roared.

"But I'm forty."

Laura put in her two cents. "So was Julia Roberts and your cousin, Mary Irene. They didn't let age stop them, so if you want a daughter, stop trying to steal what doesn't belong to you and make a baby of your own."

Melinda looked her mother right in the eye. "I'm glad you said that. This is as good a time as any. I'm pregnant."

"So that's why you are so prickly," Griffin sputtered.

"I'm due in May and I'm going to need extra help on the ranch. You get tired here, then give me a call, Elsie," Melinda said.

"And you can eat six eggs?" Julie asked. "Until I was six months, I couldn't hold down anything."

"With this one I can. With both boys, I was so sick it was awful for the first eight months. I think I figured it out, though. Girls in the Luckadeau family are conceived when both parties are drunk, and girls don't make morning sickness. I got pregnant with this one after Matt and I tied one on at a party. This is a girl. I know it," Melinda said.

Elsie scooped up a plate full of eggs and handed it to Melinda, who proceeded to fill the rest of the plate with sausage and biscuits. "Congratulations. The baby will be a blessing to you and a comfort in your old age."

Melinda flinched.

Julie giggled.

"You got anything to say, Momma?" Griffin said.

"I hope it's twins and they make you pay for your raising," Laura said.

"We're not twins," Lizzy said from the kitchen door.

"We're cousins," Annie said right behind her.

"Me too," Chuck said sleepily.

"That's right," Griffin said. "And now I'm going to work. You women hash out all this."

"I don't want hash. I want pancakes and sausage," Annie said.

"And I want pancakes and eggs," Lizzy piped up.

"And I want gravy," Chuck said.

Julie hugged them all at one time, wondering how on earth she could ever split them up since they'd found each other or what they'd do if DHS took Chuck from them. Maybe Griffin would let her take his two with her for holidays. That might be the ace up her sleeve. *Give me the kids for Christmas Eve and you can have them for Christmas on even years. On odd years we'll switch.*

Laura made a few more notes in the book that she carried everywhere. "Today after dinner we'll go to Wichita Falls. First we're shopping for our dresses and then we'll decide how to decorate the barn. After all, we're the stars, so we should make the place suit our style."

"Do we get fancy dresses?" Lizzy asked.

"Of course you do," Laura said. "You can come and eat on the night of the party and each of you can dance two times. Then you will have to go to bed because little children can't stay up all night. And Chuck can have a new western shirt and boots and maybe even a new fancy belt."

For a split second, Julie thought about arguing. Annie was her child. If she didn't want her to attend a grown-up party, then it was her decision, not Laura's. If she wanted Annie to stay up until the last song was sung, the last two-step danced, and the band went home, then she should say so, not Laura. She opened her mouth but stopped when she saw the way Laura looked at the children. She'd had Lizzy since birth, and now she simply included Annie and Chuck into the mix without even thinking about it.

"Okay, now we've all eaten. It's your turn, Julie. What will you have?" Elsie asked. "I'll make you eggs or whatever you want."

"Just bacon and toast, please. And thank you for coming in early," Julie said.

"You are very welcome," Elsie said.

Laura liked Julie after all. She loved the children, and the way she looked at Griffin was amusing. Only friends, huh? Laura figured that would change real soon, and she wasn't so sure she'd be against the change. The attraction was there and it was plain as day that it was driving them both crazy.

Julie's mind ran circles around itself but she couldn't come up with a single reason why she shouldn't go shopping with the two women from hell. But by damn, she wasn't letting them pick out her outfit. And they'd better get used to the new Griffin. He might have been all sweet and kind and the big brother to everyone before, but that wasn't the Griffin she'd come to know and kiss. That white streak was pure white fire coming out of his head, straight from the hottest parts of hell. Her red hair couldn't match that kind of heat, not in a million eternities. He might have them all thinking he was the good little twin, but he didn't fool her one bit. After those two kisses, she bet he was a true cowboy in bed.

Chapter 14

JULIE APPLIED MAKEUP, PUT MOUSSE IN HER HAIR TO TAME the curls, and was about to slip into her dress when two little girls bounced into her room. Their hair in curlers and wearing nothing but cotton underpants, they landed in the middle of her bed, eyes aglitter and happiness written all over them. She'd planned to get them dressed after she was ready so they wouldn't get crumpled or dirty, but as she'd discovered so many times lately, plans were made to be changed.

"Lizzy, you take the curlers out of Annie's hair, very gently now. And then Annie, you take Lizzy's out. I'll get your dresses and shoes, but remember, after you are dressed, you have to be still like ladies in the living room and not get all rumpled," Julie said.

"We won't, Momma. We'll be good. Lizzy says her cousins are coming and they're my cousins, too," Annie said.

"That's right," Julie sighed.

She wasn't ready for all this Luckadeau stuff. She and Laura and Melinda had called a silent truce, but it had been awkward more than once. She was eager for everyone to go home so she and the children could have a quiet Christmas with Griffin and life could get back to normal.

She put bows in their curled hair; dressed them in velvet dresses, ruffled socks, and shiny black shoes; and put their jewelry on and a dab of her perfume behind their ears. They stood before the cheval mirror in her room and admired themselves: both in identical red velvet dresses. Laura had insisted on buying their outfits with the idea that they could wear them to church after the party. They'd wanted formal organdy dresses like flower girls wear to weddings, but thank goodness, Grandma Laura had the future in mind.

Melinda poked her head in the door and motioned for the girls. "Okay, beautiful ladies, it's time to let Momma get dressed now. You both are lovely and everyone at the party is going to be so jealous that you belong to the ranch."

"Thank you," Julie mouthed. It wasn't until they were out of the room that she realized Melinda had said the word *momma* without thinking without thinking.

Melinda was lovely in a calf-length, buttery, cream-colored silk sheath that was the same color as her blonde hair. She'd found it at a discount store in Wichita Falls called Ross's and declared she would have something skin-tight because in a few more weeks, she'd be showing. Julie had been surprised to find both women loved outlet stores. She'd figured nothing short of Neiman Marcus would do for Melinda.

Laura had found a black palazzo pant outfit with flowing slacks, a tank top, and see-through duster that dropped to her ankles. The duster was decorated all the way down the front with rows of rhinestones and glittered like the streak in her hair.

That left Julie, who at Laura's suggestion went against all rules and tried on a fire-engine-red dress with a halter top cut down to her waist in the back. Thank goodness it had a built-in bra and the halter straps were good and tight. The skirt was straight with a slit up the front left side halfway to her hip. When she had walked out of the dressing room, Laura sucked air.

"Who said you couldn't wear red? That is beautiful on you. What size is it?" Melinda paid her the first and only compliment of the week.

"Four," Julie answered.

"I was born in a six, wasn't I, Momma? It ought to be a sin to be able to eat as much as you and wear a four."

"It is a sin to have your height and eyes," Julie shot right back.

Melinda had blown her a kiss.

Now it was time for Julie to put on the red dress, and she didn't want to wear it. Why hadn't she bought two dresses? One for backup in case she lost her nerve, which she just had.

"Attention. Julie has the jitters," she whispered to her reflection.

"Momma, hurry. It's time for us to make our 'pearance," Annie called from the bottom of the steps.

She was glad for the velvet shawl draped around her naked shoulders and wished she could get away with wearing Griffin's camouflage coat and a pair of ratty old jeans to the party. The dress wouldn't do anything to change her white-trash reputation.

These past few days, she'd caught Griffin looking at her strangely several times. There had been no more kisses, but there had been people around nonstop with the sale preparations. *And besides*, she reminded herself as she walked slowly down the stairs in high-heeled, red satin shoes, *he had his kiss and I had mine and there can be no more*.

"Oh, Momma, you are beautiful," Annie said when Julie reached the foyer.

"I wish you were my momma," Lizzy said.

"Tonight I can be momma to all three of you kids. But let's get something straight, kiddos. You get to eat with the big people and dance two dances and then you will be coming back here to go to bed. Is that understood? No begging," Julie said.

"Yes, ma'am." Lizzy grinned.

"Yes, ma'am," Chuck echoed.

"Okay." Annie pouted.

"Are we ready, then?" Laura asked. "It's time for the Luckadeau women to make their appearance."

"I'm not…" Julie started.

"Tonight you are. You birthed my grandchild. You are one of us. After a week with Melinda, you earned the right."

"Well, don't talk about me like I'm not here," Melinda said.

Griffin was visiting with a buyer from Wyoming who'd bought one of his registered Angus bulls the previous afternoon when the women made their grand entrance all together with the three children in tow.

Alvie Marlin was a regular at the Lucky Clover sale each year and always left behind a wad of cash and took a trailer full of Lucky Clover Angus cows or bulls home with him. He was tall, dark-haired, brown-eyed, well-muscled, and wore his western-cut tux and cowboy boots with ease. He whistled when the Luckadeau women entered the barn.

Griffin couldn't have spit, much less whistled, his mouth was so dry when he saw Julie in the red dress.

"I recognize the little girls. Didn't realize you had twins, though. Thought there was just one of them running around with all those fair-haired boys. And that's your mother with the streak like yours, and your sister, Melinda—who I could still cry over every time I see her. But, Griff, who is the one in red? I think I'm in love."

"That would be Julie. I don't have twins. The other little girl is Julie's daughter, who belongs to my late brother, Graham," Griffin managed to get out.

"I remember your brother vaguely. Sorry to hear the word *late* put beside his name. I intend to dance every single dance that woman will let me have. I'm serious. I haven't been so thunderstruck by a woman since I was a teenager. She's one fine-lookin' lady and I'm a sucker for red hair," Alvie said.

On cue, the lead singer for the band took the microphone and announced that the food was ready to be served. The tables were set and the dance floor ready. "Griffin says if you go home hungry or with leather on the bottom of your boots, that's not his problem," the man announced.

The barn glittered with thousands of twinkling lights strung from one side of the catwalk to the other. Red satin flowed in gentle folds from the lights to the barn floor, where just the day before there had been prize cattle offered for sale. The portable stage and dance floor had been brought out of storage and assembled. The rest of the floor was concrete, but it had been washed and treated until it looked like gray marble.

People sat around tables for six or eight and waiters dressed in white tuxedo shirts and black bow ties took and brought orders to them. An open bar was set up along the west wall. Bartenders dressed in blue shirts with red ties took drink orders for those already seated.

Julie felt as though she were in a sheik's tent somewhere in the Sahara rather than in a Texas barn a week before Christmas. Warm air flowed from specially installed heating units rented just for the party. Laura and her husband, Jimmy, sat at a table with Matt and Melinda, along with their two sons. Melinda had asked if the girls could sit with them and Julie had agreed, even though she'd have rather had all three with her.

Griffin escorted Julie to a table where Milli, Beau, Slade, and Jane sat with Slade's grandmother, Nellie, and her sister, Ellen. Julie felt as if she were a crippled pigeon about to be tossed into a den of hungry wolves.

"Well now, I do believe all the ladies at this table are lovely this evening," Ellen said. She was dressed in her usual flamboyant colors. Hot pink that evening: a dress with a tight-fitting bodice scattered with rhinestones and a flowing satin skirt with a sheer overlay studded with more stones around the hem. Diamond jewelry was on her wrist, in her ears, and hanging around her neck. Her red hair was piled up in a do that had been popular thirty years before.

"Thank you, and you are the prettiest one of the bunch," Julie said.

"Honey, come and sit by me," Ellen said.

"You go sit by Griffin, and be careful what you say to this old broad. She eats up compliments like most women do chocolate," Nellie said.

"Don't pay any attention to her. I'm Ellen, Slade's great-aunt. You'd be Julie. I've heard about you. And next week I'm buying something that shade of red. I've always loved it but got told my whole life that a natural redhead couldn't wear it. Guess you just proved them wrong, darlin'."

"Pleased to meet you," Julie said.

"And I'm Slade's grandmother, Nellie Luckadeau. Ellen, most natural redheads can't wear that color because they have freckles. Your red hair comes out of a bottle from Walmart. Sit down here with us, Julie and Griffin. Alvera came over and gave us the lowdown on you, Julie. If that old buzzard likes you, you must be doin' something right."

Alvera piped up from the other side of the table. "You call me an old buzzard again and I'll put pepper sauce in your Preparation H next time I come to visit. I just call the shots the way I see 'em. Julie's my kind of people. I don't care if you like her or not. I do."

"Thanks, Alvera." Julie smiled.

Slade chuckled. "You older ladies better be nice. If you fight tonight, you're going to go to bed without a snack."

"That's fine. Just don't tell me I have to go to bed without a man with all these pretty things running around in tight-fittin' Wranglers and tux coats. That would be punishment worse than finding an empty bottle of Jack Daniel's," Ellen said.

Julie giggled.

"They're always like this," Jane said. "Makes me sorry I never had a sister."

"Me too," Milli said. "Got brothers but no sisters."

"Curse of the Luckadeaus," Beau said. "Not many girls, so we appreciate beauty."

"Which reminds me," Griffin said. "Melinda announced that she's pregnant, and she's of the opinion that all it takes to make a Luckadeau girl is liquor and lots of it."

"Worked for us, didn't it?" Slade said.

Jane nodded and touched his arm lovingly. "It sure did."

"I can vouch that both parties don't have to be drunk. Just the Luckadeau part," Milli said.

Nellie slapped the table and crystal rattled. "Well, I'll be damned. That's why I didn't get a girl. Lester was a teetotaler."

"Melinda says she and Matt both hit the bottle the night she got pregnant. Seems like the night Lizzy was conceived was right after one of these parties, and I was pretty plastered," Griffin said.

Julie turned a faint shade of mint green. She didn't want to hear about Griffin and Dian having sex even though they had been married and produced Lizzy. Then, she was instantly irritated at herself for caring. The past was the past and she had one, too.

"How about Annie?" Milli asked.

"Neither of us were feeling any pain," Julie admitted.

"Well, there's the proof," Milli said. "Our son was conceived when we were sober. Katy Scarlett, our daughter, when Beau was in mourning for his old girlfriend and six sheets to the wind."

"Six?" Julie asked.

"Honey, three wouldn't begin to describe him that night. He was so drunk he barely knew his name, didn't understand me when I told him mine. The only thing he could do other than pass out was… Well, suffice it to say, instinct has its purposes," Milli said.

Jane nodded. "The Luckadeau men do have that instinct even when they're drunk, don't they? Ellie was conceived when we were both piss drunk."

"Hey, hey, let's not tell all the family secrets," Slade said.

Julie listened to the easy banter around the table and ate slowly. At least the women hadn't run her out of the barn with their sharp remarks. Maybe Alvera had a gun hiding in the folds of her rhinestone-studded denim pant set and had threatened to kill the first one who was mean to her. If that was the case, she'd better have lots of bullets, and the first one should have Melinda's name on it.

Griffin was so close that she could smell his aftershave, and that alone caused her hormones to jump into overdrive. The black Wranglers, polished eel boots, big belt buckle, and western-cut tux jacket over a crisp, white shirt didn't help matters much, either. Then there was the little issue of those crystal-clear, blue eyes and that rakish, white streak flowing back from his forehead. Like Melinda had said about Graham, it all combined to make a nun's panty hose creep down around her ankles. Only Graham Luckadeau was just the shell; Griffin was the whole man.

The barbecued brisket was tender, moist, and cooked to perfection. The stuffed baked potato was fine and the salad wonderful, but she might as well have been eating Cream of Wheat and whole wheat toast. She'd never been so nervous in her whole life, not even the day she walked into court and was accused of adultery.

The band played softly while they ate and then, at a signal from Griffin, they picked up the tempo and the lead singer invited Griffin and Julie on the dance floor.

Griffin stood up and held his hand out to Julie. "That would be our cue to start the dancing."

"Why?" she whispered as he led her to the dance floor.

"Usually Momma and Daddy start it for me. I figured it was time for me to step up to the plate and really take over the sale this year. This is an important time for me, Julie. Don't ruin it."

"Ruin it! You pompous snob. I just wondered why," she said.

He slipped an arm around her waist. "Now you know."

She put her hand in his and laid her other hand on his shoulder. He took a step forward until she melted into his chest and the music began. Dancing with Griffin was almost as good as kissing him. If she hadn't known better, she would have sworn those Fourth of July sparklers were real and not just a figment of her imagination. And if dancing with him was this sweet, she couldn't imagine how it would feel to make love with him.

The singer crooned "You Can't Give Up on Love," into the microphone. The song said that love didn't come easy and it was hard to hold, so you couldn't give up on it. Near the end of the song, the singer took a moment to invite everyone else to join Griffin and Julie on the floor. In a few seconds, the whole place was crowded and someone had tapped Griffin on the shoulder.

"If I could cut in, please?" Alvie asked, sweeping off his big black hat.

"Of course," Griffin said politely. He would rather have pulled a .38 Saturday night special from his waistband and shot the man square between the eyes, but he couldn't be rude to someone who'd just dropped more than a hundred grand in the sale pot.

"Hello, pretty lady, I'm Alvie Marlin from up near Jackson Hole, Wyoming. You certainly do look lovely tonight."

"Thank you. I'm Julie Donavan."

"Mighty pleased to meet you, Julie. You ever been to Wyoming?"

"No, sir, I have not."

"Well, we could remedy that right quick. I'm going home tomorrow morning. You've got an open invitation to my little spread," Alvie said.

"But you don't know me. I could be an awful person," she teased.

"Honey, I can take awful. Hell, I can even take mean. I've lived in the wild country my whole life. I could stand the mean if I could come home to that pretty red hair and what goes with it every night," he flirted.

"You might ought to rethink that," she said.

"Dance another one with me and let me tell you a story," he said when the song ended.

The singer began another one by Alan Jackson, "All American Country Boy." She stayed in his arms and he sashayed her around to the quicker tempo.

"This is my song. Just listen to it. Like old Alan says, my neck is a little red and I do drink a little booze and I don't back up. Not anymore. About twenty years ago, I was green as prairie grass in the springtime, and I came down here to the Lucky Clover sale. Saw Melinda and God Almighty, I thought I'd died and gone to heaven and she was a real angel. I stuttered when I asked her to dance. I relived the way she fit in my arms for twenty years and wished I'd asked her to marry me right then. But I didn't, and two years later when I came back, she was married to Matt. I don't take chances no more," Alvie said.

"You flatter me," Julie said.

"Ain't no flatter to it. When you walked in the door

a while ago, all the dreams I had of Melinda just floated out of my mind. Twenty years' worth. I'm forty years old. I own the biggest spread in Wyoming, and, honey, I'll sign every acre of it over to you if you'll go home with me tomorrow."

"I've got a five-year-old daughter that's the product of a one-night stand with Graham Luckadeau. I'm divorced. I don't even have a home of my own. I live here and help Griffin," Julie said.

"Honey, I don't give a damn if you were a two-bit hooker. I'm in love. You can take your time about falling in love with me. I don't care how long. Just go home with me," Alvie said.

For an insane moment, Julie considered it. Alvie was a fine specimen of a cowboy, with his dark hair combed back from a handsome face. His mouth was full and his eyes brooding. He was so honest it was painful. And Wyoming was a hell of a long way from Texas.

"You'll change your mind when the next woman in a red dress walks through the door. Right now I've got to go kiss my daughter good night." Julie left him standing in the middle of the dance floor with a silly grin on his face.

When Julie found the girls, Melinda was ushering all three kids out toward the house, where a sitter awaited.

"See you met Alvie," Melinda said.

"Yes, I did."

"Poor old Alvie. Fell in love with me when we were twenty. He's so handsome and honest it about takes a woman's breath away," Melinda said.

"You knew?" Julie walked beside her.

"Of course. He's been in love with me ever since. Stutters terrible when he's around me. All but tonight.

While you and Griffin were dancing—which by the way, y'all looked good together—Alvie came up and sat at our table for a minute. Talked as straight as me and you. First time ever he didn't stutter around me."

"Why didn't you fall for him like he did you?"

"I'd already met Matt, and he made *me* stutter."

They settled the kids into bed and an elderly lady from the church had a book ready to read to them. When she said, "Once upon a time," Melinda and Julie headed back toward the party.

Alvie met them at the door and held his hand out to Julie. "May I have this dance?"

"I'll be damned," Melinda whispered. "What are you going to do?"

"Run?" Julie said.

"Be easy. He's a darlin'."

Julie took his hand and let him lead her out onto the dance floor.

"I didn't mean to scare you off. It's just that I let one opportunity slip through my fingers and I vowed I'd never do it again," he said. "You'll be thinking I'm a lunatic. So, Miss Julie, would you mind if I called you once in a while just to let you know the offer is real and still stands?"

"That would be fine, Alvie. I'll look forward to your calls," she said.

One moment she was dancing with Alvie, the next Griffin had taken his place with a tap on the shoulder.

"What is going on?" Griffin scowled.

"Alvie just offered to sign his entire kingdom over to me if I'll go home with him," Julie said.

"He did what?" A surge of jealousy swept through Griffin like wildfire.

"I didn't stutter and neither did he," she said.

"You aren't going." A very long pause. "Are you?"

"Not right now, but I did say he could call me. I promise not to talk on your time, boss man."

"You make me so mad sometimes I could spit tacks," he said.

She looked up and batted her eyelashes at him. "Imagine that."

"What about Lizzy and Chuck?"

"Six-month split. You get them six months. I get them the other six months."

"Do I get Annie on alternate six months?"

"Hell no. Annie has always been mine and will always be mine. Lizzy is Annie's and thus part mine. Annie isn't part yours. We can share Chuck."

His blue eyes narrowed. "How in the hell do you figure that?"

"I can figure any way I want. Alvie is going to give me his kingdom, remember. Besides, Lizzy will whine and fret without Annie."

The song ended and everyone clapped. The singer went right into Kenny Chesney's "You Had Me from Hello." Griffin could well identify with the singer when he said something about her smile capturing him and her being in his future and about it being over from the start. Looking back, he'd been as thunderstruck that first day when he saw Julie in the classroom as Alvie had been with Melinda. The only difference was that Alvie had admitted it from the start and didn't know what to do about it; Griffin had been fighting it for months, and it could be too late to do anything about it.

"What are you thinking about? You look like you really could chew up tacks," she said.

"I'm thinking about the songs. Care to dance another one?"

"Sure. I'm not a wallflower, and I'm sure Alvie will dance if you are too tired," Julie said.

"You wouldn't do something foolish, would you?" he asked.

"I don't rush into anything anymore. Not sex or marriage. Both got me in a hell of a lot of trouble," she said.

"Fair enough," he said.

Right then, if she'd been ready to do something insanely impulsive, he would have dropped down on one knee and proposed in front of a whole barn full of people, his momma, and even God to keep her from going.

Alvie claimed the next dance, to no one's surprise, and yet to Griffin's misery. Griffin stood on the sidelines and wished for the first time in his life that he had the kind of personality that Alvie had cultivated in the past twenty years. One that could sweep in and knock a girl off her feet. One like Graham had had.

"So, pretty lady, I've been watching you all evening, and I think I'm a day late and a dollar short again. I've seen you with Griffin and I see the sparks, and—"

She butted in. "There are no sparks between us. We are just friends. Just because my daughter belongs to his brother doesn't mean she or I belong on this ranch permanently."

Alvie smiled, his brown eyes wishing he could believe what his ears heard. But his eyes *had* seen and his heart *had* felt. It wasn't going to work. Griffin had already laid claim to Julie, even if he wasn't wise enough to know it just yet.

"Tell you what I'm going to do. I'm going to wait for you to call me. I'm a patient man, Miss Julie. Very, very patient." Then his eyes widened and his mouth dropped as he looked toward the doors. "Who is that?"

Julie turned her head slightly to see a figure silhouetted in the doorway of the barn. A woman stood there as if she didn't know where she was. She wore tight jeans and a denim jacket over a red T-shirt, and had flamboyant red hair cut in a style that feathered back from her face and flowed almost to her waist.

What in the hell was Sally doing at the Lucky Clover ranch?

"Excuse me. That would be my sister." Julie thought she left him on the dance floor, but when she reached the door he was right behind her.

"Sally?" Julie said.

Sally grabbed her in a fierce hug and whispered, "My God, Julie, you look beautiful, and who is the hunk behind you? I could just cover him in chocolate and have him for a late-night snack."

"What are you doing here?" Julie asked.

"I quit my job and came to get some courage before I go home and tell Momma. She's going to be furious, but I just couldn't do it another day. I couldn't even finish the year, so I quit after the first semester. I *hate* teaching," Sally said.

Julie kept her arm around Sally's shoulder and ran into a grinning Alvie when she turned around. "We're in the middle of a party. Come, join us. The house is full, but you can share my room and stay as long as you like. This would be one of the buyers at the sale, Alvie Marlin, from up near Jackson Hole, Wyoming. Alvie, please meet my sister, Sally."

"P-p-p-pleased to m-m-meet you, S-s-sally," Alvie stuttered.

Julie suppressed a giggle.

"Maybe you'd like to dance with Sally, Alvie?" Julie said.

He nodded, the grin never leaving his face. He'd seen Julie's beauty when she walked through the barn doors in that red dress, but his heart saw Sally. Alvie was in love for real. Even more than with Melinda. He'd just been thunderstruck with all the force that heaven had to offer.

"I'm not dressed for a party. I'll just wait in the house," Sally said.

"Don't be silly. Have you had supper?"

"I ate hours ago, but you know us Donavans. We're always hungry."

Julie hugged her again and whispered, "Dance with him. He only stutters when he's truly in love. It's only happened once before and that was twenty years ago. And when you get tired of dancing, have something to eat."

"Please stay," Alvie said. It came out slow and deliberate, but his brown eyes begged.

"I'd love to," Sally said. "So, Wyoming. I've always had a hankering to see that part of the world. Tell me about it while we dance, Alvie."

Griffin was at Julie's side the moment Alvie and Sally moved to the dance floor. "Who is that?"

"My sister. Every time she walks into a room, every male's IQ drops fifty points and the stock in Viagra drops at least that much. Her name is Sally, and she'll be staying a few days, if that's all right with you?"

"Sally can stay as long as she likes. Come outside with me for a breath of fresh air. I'm getting claustrophobic with so many people around." Griffin laced his fingers in hers.

Her first desire was to draw them back and make an excuse that she needed to stay in the barn with her sister, but one look in that direction assured her that Alvie wasn't going to let Sally out of his sight the rest of the evening. Probably not even out of his arms.

"Why would the stock in Viagra drop?" Griffin asked. Sally was pretty, and Graham would have moved in on her like flies to maple syrup, but she wasn't as beautiful as Julie.

"Because, darlin', no one needs it when Sally is in the room. Everything works fine on the male gender when she smiles. She's two years younger than me. Interested?"

"Not particularly, but I'm glad she came to visit you. It'll be lonely a few days after the party. Kind of like the days after Christmas."

"Alvie stuttered."

A grin split Griffin's face and the dimple in his chin deepened. "For real?"

"He did. I think he was thunderstruck. Funny thing is, I'm not so sure she wasn't thunderstruck, too," Julie said.

"Well, I'll be damned." Griffin didn't care if Sally moved right into the ranch house and stayed forever, if she kept Alvie away from Julie.

"Is it going well?" Julie asked.

"What? Oh, you mean the party. Very, very well. The ranch made enough money on the sale to tide us over until next year without going to the bank. That's one thing Daddy and Mother preached to me and Graham when they gave us the run of the ranch: don't borrow. I haven't had to yet, and the sale this year is the best I've ever had."

"That's wonderful. You going to miss your family when they leave tomorrow? When do they come back for a visit?"

"Not so often. They've got their own businesses to run, too. Lizzy and I usually fly down for Thanksgiving. Stay two days. Christmas we go for a couple of days. Melinda brings her boys so we're all together then. At Easter they all come here for the weekend. And then it's just random visits, whenever we can plan it on the spur of the moment. This year we didn't go for Thanksgiving and we're not going for Christmas. The thing with Chuck…well, I'm not supposed to take him that far without permission, and besides, I thought he'd be more comfortable in a smaller setting," he said.

"My parents have this little apartment above their garage. Annie and I lived in it her whole life until we moved here. Mother kept her while I taught. Summers were wonderful because I had her to myself. But my folks were always next door if I needed them. I saw my mother every day," Julie said.

"Moving wasn't so easy, was it?" he asked.

"Hardest thing I ever did, but the wisest," she said.

He cocked his head to one side. "Wisest?"

"It was time for me and Annie to make our own lives and give my parents back theirs. Even with all the catastrophes, I can still say it was wise. Annie is happy."

He made lazy circles on the top of her hand with his thumb. "And you?"

The sensation drove her crazy, but she wasn't about to let him know. "The jury is still out. Even if it comes in not guilty of happiness, I'll still have a measure of it every time I look at Annie."

His fist went to her chin. He tilted it up and looked deeply into her eyes before leaning forward. The kiss warmed up the cold air around them to the boiling point.

When they broke away, she leaned into his chest wanting more.

He threw an arm around her shoulder and said, "Take a walk with me."

She let him lead her wherever he would.

Griffin paced his steps to hers. Walking across grass wasn't easy in high heels.

"What was that all about?" she asked.

"We can share a kiss. We don't have to break it down by degrees and figure out each little thing every time I kiss you, do we? Sure takes the fun out of it," he grumbled.

"Fun is something I'm almost as careful with as I am sex, marriage, and happiness," she said.

He led her into the hay barn where the kittens were kept. They came running from all corners when they heard voices, meowing and rubbing around Julie's and Griffin's ankles.

"Looks like we'd better go to the loft. Can you climb in those things?" He looked at her feet.

"I can do anything you can do," she said.

He scrambled up the ladder into the loft and she followed him, proving that a woman could indeed do anything a man could, and accomplish it wearing high heels and a party gown. When she reached the top, she found him sitting on a bale of hay beside the open loft doors, staring out across the land. The moon lit up the scattered trees and cattle. The house was a bulk with yellow lights flowing from windows over to the north. Music drifted from the west on the cold north wind. She drew her shawl tightly around her shoulders and shivered.

As she started to sit down beside him, her heel caught in a loose board. He reached out and grabbed her just before she tumbled out the window. He pulled backward, and the momentum of her weight carried them both to the floor, her on top of him when they landed.

He gasped for air and she rolled off his chest to lie beside him. Both sucked in great amounts of air trying to refill their deflated lungs. If he hadn't grabbed her hand, she could have broken her neck. She put a hand over her racing heart and was glad she was lying flat on her back or she would have fainted.

Griffin rolled to his side and brushed a piece of hay from her hair. "Are you all right? Arms? Legs? Nothing broken?"

"I think so," she whispered. Nothing hurt except her pride. "You?"

"I'm fine."

He ran the back of his hand down her jawline and leaned in for a kiss. She closed her eyes. Like two souls starved for love, they hung on until neither of them could breathe. They broke away, but his lips went to her ear and then that erotic soft spot under her ear that no one had ever found before. One thumb made circles as light as butterfly wings on the tender skin between her eye and hairline while his fingers caressed her forehead. The other arm went around her, touching the bare skin on her back, firing up her hormones until she melted in spite of the cold weather. It felt like the man had six hands and every one of them was touching her. She didn't want him to stop and yet knew he should. She should tell him that was enough, but she didn't want to. She wanted it all, up to and including mind-numbing sex.

No one had ever made her feel so tingly in her life. His kisses moved to her neck. She leaned her head over to give him better access. He unfastened the hook and eye at the back of her halter top and let it fall. He took a long, searing moment to look upon the porcelain skin and then started stringing kisses down her body, removing clothing as he went. His kisses were alternately demanding and steamy and then soft and sweet against her skin, his hands rendering touches as soft as cold silk caressing her. Heat and cold all mixed together to send her senses reeling and her body begging for more.

The only thought that crossed her mind was that everyone had been wrong about Griffin. He wasn't the good twin; he was the evil one. The wolf in sheep's clothing. When he slipped her silk bikini panties down to her ankles and tossed them aside, she was biting back moans and the only thought in her head was that she was more than ready for him to get on with the job.

She pressed her naked body against him, arching her back to get closer and closer. But he didn't hurry. He continued to kiss, caress, and make love to Julie until she was ready to scream. When she shivered, he pulled a blanket from a nail on the wall and covered them both.

"Don't look at me," she said.

"Why?" he whispered.

"The stretch marks never went away."

He kissed each of them. "They're not to be ashamed of. You are so beautiful, Julie," he murmured.

When she begged him to make love to her, he told her that, like her, he wasn't going to rush into anything.

His touch created shivers in the weirdest places. She could have sworn her toenails curled and her hair straightened out when his fingertips played with the palm of her hand. The muscles in her legs quivered when he kissed the bottom of her feet. The nerves under her hair vibrated when he brushed his fingers over her breast.

At that moment, she realized she'd had sex, but she'd never truly made love, and she enjoyed the passion as it took her right to the brink of heaven and back again.

"Please," she begged.

"Please what?" he whispered in her ear and strung another line of kisses from her neck to her waist.

She groaned. She couldn't take any more and he was teasing now. She'd show him what *please* meant, and he'd be begging by the time she was finished. She rolled him over on his back and sat on his waist, pulling the blanket up over her back to keep from freezing. As if that would happen. The heat between them was so intense she thought she'd die of heatstroke before she ever talked him into really hot, plain old animal sex. She pushed him backward and very, very slowly unfastened each button on his shirt, kissing the naked spots as they appeared. When his shirt was in a heap with her underpants and dress, she unbuckled his belt.

"Hurry," he groaned.

"Remember, I don't rush into anything. Sex..." She pulled the belt out of the loops.

"Fun." She unsnapped his jeans.

"Love." She unzipped them ever so slowly.

He reached down to slip out of his jeans and she

slapped his hands away. "My turn, Griffin Luckadeau. You have met your match. Sex, marriage, happiness... don't rush. It's not the destination. It's the journey," she whispered in his ear as she stretched out on top of him.

She strung kisses downward as she slipped the jeans from his hips. It was her turn, and it was too late now for either of them to stop. It was going to play out to the finish.

By the time she removed his boots, he was moaning. When she tossed the last sock toward the pile of rumpled clothing in the corner, he reached out and took her in his arms, rolled her over in the hay, and in one swift stroke, was inside her.

It lasted longer than either of them thought it could when their bodies were screaming for release.

"Damn!" she gasped.

He rolled away, yet kept her snuggled into his arms. "Amen. Want to analyze that?"

"No, I want to do it again," she said.

"Right now? We've been gone from the party a long time."

She put her fingers over his lips to shush him. "Shut up and be still. You've got two minutes to get ready to go again or I'll get you ready."

He drew one of her fingers into his mouth and she gasped.

They made it back to the barn as the band announced the last song. Griffin led her out onto the dance floor and she swayed in tune with his body. The singer finished up the night with a request from Laura, which was "The Dance," an older song by Garth Brooks.

"Fitting," she said.

"All of it? Including the hayloft?" he asked.

"Every bit of it," she said.

"Are you going to say goodbye?"

"I don't rush into goodbyes, either. Like the man says, our lives are better left to chance. Who knows what tomorrow might bring? I'm tired of trying to figure it out."

"Hey, Sis." Sally and Alvie danced by them. "Here." Sally put something in the hand Julie had around Griffin's neck.

"What?" Julie asked.

"Just one little piece of hay in your hair. We'll talk about how it got there and about that shit-eatin' grin on your face later. I'll bring the beers. You keep the light burning."

Chapter 15

SALLY'S WET HAIR WAS WRAPPED IN A TOWEL AND SHE wore a T-shirt and cotton underpants. She eased into the room to find her sister sitting up in bed, her knees drawn up like she always did when she was trying to think her way through a problem.

Sally propped two pillows against the headboard and settled in for a visit. "I found the bathroom because the door was open and had a shower. Then I found your room because the light was showing under the door."

"Why did you quit your job?" Julie asked.

"Do you believe in fate?" Sally asked.

"What's that got to do with quitting your job?"

"Everything. I don't believe in fate. Never did. Thought it was the biggest bunch of hogwash in the world. Then Momma called and told me about this thing you are going through with the Luckadeaus. Still didn't believe in it. Coincidence explained it all. I got to admit it was a hell of a lot of coincidence, but still—fate? No way, Sister." Sally poked Julie in the ribs.

"So now you do or now you don't?" Julie poked back.

"Do you?" Sally asked.

"I didn't, but I might be changing my mind," Julie said.

"Okay, hear me out. When you moved here I thought you were crazy like Aunt Flossie. Figured she saw the trait in you and that's why she left you all that money. I couldn't understand why you'd leave

Jefferson—apartment where the rent was never going up, Momma to take care of Annie, Daddy to fix your car or your garbage disposal. Now I think fate brought you here."

"Okay," Julie said.

"There's more. If you hadn't already been here, I wonder if Eli would have taken that job in Bowie."

"Eli is moving to Bowie?" Julie had no idea he was even considering a move from East Texas.

"In a month. He preached at the church there a few weeks ago. The Sunday after Momma and Daddy came for your festival. So you came to Saint Jo and Eli got the courage to leave Linden. He met a woman from here, too. I'm not supposed to tell you because she's your friend and Momma says it might be meddling. Her name is Mamie and they've been out to dinner three times and he's laughing again."

Julie threw up her hands. "Hold on. Eli and Mamie?" So that's why she hadn't seen much of Mamie the past—how long? She had seen her at the festival and when Dian tried to kidnap Annie. But it had been days since they'd talked, what with the sale and the party and the obnoxious Luckadeaus taking so much of her time.

Sally gave her a minute to digest that and went on, "Yep, Eli and Mamie. It's looking serious from Momma's standpoint. She's the first woman he's even been interested in since Teresa died."

Julie still had trouble believing it. "Mamie?"

"That's what Momma called her. I thought she said Amy at first, but she corrected me and said the lady's name is Mamie. Think I could meet her while I'm here?"

"How long are you staying?"

"How long are you going to let me without telling Momma?"

Julie giggled. "Forever. Come with me. I've got something to show you."

"Other than that handsome hunk that has to be Annie's father? How'd you find him? Is that the reason you moved here?"

Julie grabbed her hand and pulled her toward the door. They tiptoed to the next room and Julie opened the door quietly and led her to the bed. Two little girls with white streaks in their hair were side by side, holding hands even in their sleep.

"Good grief! They look so much alike."

"Yes, they do."

"He had a wife while he was having sex with you, then?"

"No. Annie is not Griffin's child. She's his twin brother's. That one is Lizzy. She belongs to Griffin. Annie belongs to Graham."

"This gets weirder and weirder. I think I hear spooky music playing in my head," Sally said.

By the time they got back to Julie's room, Sally had unwrapped her head and strands of damp, deep-red hair flowed down her back. She settled in again and started, "I only got a glimpse of Annie's real father as you two were leaving the bar that night, but I like the twin with the hair better. I can see where the white streak came from for sure. And I met the grandmother briefly. Alvie introduced me."

"Did he stop stuttering?"

"After a while. He apologized to me for offering to run away with you," Sally giggled.

"And?"

"He's staying in Texas for a week."

"Be careful."

"It's fate," Sally said.

"Talk to me."

"Okay, when summer was over last year, and I went back to school, it felt like there was a brick in my chest. Something big and black, and I couldn't shake it. I went to church. I asked God what I should do. I went to parties. I got drunk. Nothing took it away. Not even chocolate." Sally paused.

"Go on."

"I don't know if I can describe it. It was like my heart was somewhere other than my body and the two couldn't live that way," Sally said.

Julie giggled that time. "Exactly the way I felt when I came to Saint Jo and bought the Lassiter property, which burned down. I suppose Momma told you that."

"Yes, but she's kept secrets from us both. Guess she figured we needed to find them out together instead of through her. One morning last week, I woke up and all I could think was, 'Go home to your sister.' Then I thought about how utterly crazy that sounded. My home was not at your house. You didn't even have a house. You were staying with a rancher in North Texas."

Julie patted her hand. "It can be your home until you get your ducks in a row."

"So I came home to my sister and this is the really, really strange part. I think I could fall for Alvie," Sally said.

Julie clamped her hand over her mouth. "What?"

"I told you it was bizarre. We danced and talked and sat in the corner drinking the same kind of beer and talked some more. Tonight I am a converted believer in fate. He's staying a week at a little hotel in Saint Jo. We're going to explore the area. I didn't even know Saint Jo was big enough to have a hotel."

"Did he tell you that he would sign over his ranch to you?" Julie asked.

"No, he said he would give me his heart, the rest was just material possessions and worthless without a heart." Sally blushed.

"You are turning red! I can't believe it," Julie said.

"He's so handsome, and I've never had anyone treat me like that. And, Julie, the heavy weight is gone. I listened to my heart. I came home to my sister and you fixed it."

"So, I've been brought here to this little town to face all my demons so that you and Eli can find happiness and you can meet Alvie?" Julie said.

"Hey, wasn't that a bit of hay I picked from your hair? And you can't fool me, honey. That was definitely afterglow on your face when you and Griffin came back into the barn," Sally said.

Julie blushed even redder than her sister. "It was not."

"Liar, liar, pants on fire. I smell smoke coming from your under britches," Sally teased. "I'm going to sleep now and dream of that good-looking cowboy who has stolen my heart. You might do the same. Tomorrow morning we'll compare notes and see who had the best dream sex ever," Sally said.

"You are incorrigible," Julie said.

"Yes, I am, but I'm so glad to feel good again I don't even care."

Breakfast was on the bar by the time everyone awoke. Julie had made oven omelets and kept them hot by draping a wet tea towel over the pans and shoving them into a barely warm oven. Biscuits, some already buttered, some plain, waited in baskets. The slow cooker held sausage gravy and the griddle was set up for anyone who wanted pancakes.

"This is a treat," Jimmy said when he and Laura made it to the kitchen.

Laura dipped a chunk of omelet out of the pan. "You've got to write down the recipe for this. My cook would love to have it."

"No recipe to it, but I'll write down the layers. First it's scrambled eggs. A dozen to the nine-by-thirteen-inch pan. Then cooked and drained sausage. After that either a layer of thinly sliced Velveeta cheese or whatever kind of grated cheese is your favorite. Then another layer of eggs. Sometimes I put the picante in it, but most of the time I serve it on the side."

"I've already got Elsie's recipe for homemade picante written down," Melinda said from the doorway.

Griffin, Lizzy, Annie, Chuck, and Sally all filed in next. Melinda's husband, Matt, and their two sons, Houston and Austin, followed them. Talk went to how prosperous the sale had been and how much fun the party was. Laura talked about Milli and Jane and how they had fit right into Slade's and Beau's lifestyles. Jimmy talked about that bull he should have bought but let Alvie outbid him.

"Dad, if you wanted the bull, you should have let me know. I wouldn't have even put him in the sale," Griffin said.

"I don't need him. Didn't even realize what a good

animal he was until Alvie started bidding. That man has a sixth sense about cattle. You ever been up to his ranch?"

Julie and Sally had been serving breakfast and talking about their family, but now Griffin noticed that they had stopped talking and were listening to his dad. He kept one ear tuned to what his father was saying, but his mind drifted to the sisters. He wondered why men were drawn to Sally instead of Julie. Of the two, Julie was by far the more striking, to his way of seeing it. And how could Julie act as if nothing had happened the night before?

Jimmy went on. "It's amazing. Most beautiful place I've ever seen outside of Texas. House faces the mountains. It's made of logs and glass. I was there in May and there was still snow even in some low places. If I ever had a hankering to move anywhere, it would be to Wyoming. I swear it's the last frontier," Jimmy said.

"I should have married him, but alas, I was already in love with this cowboy right here." Melinda patted Matt's leg.

Matt turned a little pink. He had prematurely gray hair, a tanned face with no wrinkles, and gorgeous green eyes. No wonder Melinda had fallen for him the first time she visited the ranch near Conroe.

"So how did it go with you and Alvie?" Melinda asked Julie.

"He offered me his kingdom if I'd run away with him," Julie said. Sally's slight green cast didn't escape her notice.

"And what did you tell him?" Laura asked.

"That I didn't rush into anything these days. It gets me into trouble every single time I do. But my glory only lasted a few minutes. I was pushed aside in a hurry when Sally made it to the party," Julie said.

"I saw him dancing with you," Melinda said. "Did he offer you his kingdom?"

"He stuttered," Julie said.

"We definitely have got to talk. This isn't fair. I'm leaving in ten minutes. The car is packed and I'm just waiting on these bottomless pits to fill their stomachs. I'll call you as soon as I get home," Melinda told Sally.

"You like my sister?" Julie was amazed.

"Of course. We have a lot in common. She's not trying to take my baby brother for a cheap ride to the altar," Melinda said.

Julie held up two fingers.

"I'm glad I'm going home. I've had to grow three new tongues just to keep from biting mine off to keep you off my back. I want this baby girl, and if we fight, I might lose her." She touched her flat stomach.

Julie just shook her head.

"What are you two talking about?" Sally asked.

"We don't like each other," Melinda said.

"Honey, if you say ugly things about my sister, I'll take you on. I might not be big enough to whip you, but I'll give it my best shot," Sally said.

Melinda winked. "I think we all might get along fine and I've *got* to talk to you about Alvie. I'll call when I get home and things quiet down."

"Alvie is picking me up in half an hour. We're going to explore the county today," Sally said.

Melinda brushed back an errant strand of blonde hair. "He's staying in Texas?"

"For a week," Julie answered. Sally and Alvie's romance could take center stage and she'd be more than happy to let it.

"I'm hurt. Alvie is finally over me. Now I have no backup plan if this man gets tired of my bossiness and tosses me out on my ear," Melinda intoned dramatically, one hand over her forehead and one over her heart.

"Come on, Miss Drama Queen. I hope this new baby is a boy. I couldn't take another one of you," Matt said.

Melinda swatted at him. "Bite your tongue. I can still try to win Alvie's favor."

Hugs were given. Promises made. Kids gathered up. Kids left on the porch to wave. And then they were all gone. Griffin went to the sale barn to oversee the crew turning it back into a place to store equipment. He left without so much as a wink of acknowledgment that they'd had the most amazing sex the night before. Lizzy, Annie, and Chuck put a board game on the table.

Alvie arrived right on time in a big, white dual-cab truck and carried Sally off to look at happily-ever-after. And Julie went upstairs to find something to do that would take her mind off Griffin.

She'd thrown herself across the bed with a romance book when Griffin filled the doorway.

"We alone in here?" he asked.

"Right now we are," she answered.

"Want to talk about last night?" He came into the room and leaned on the doorjamb.

"Not particularly. I fell off the wagon. I promise to go back to WSA meetings tonight."

"WSA?"

"Wild Sex Anonymous," she said.

"You call that wild?" He shut the door.

"You don't?"

"Honey, you ain't seen nothing yet, but it's on the way. Don't waste your time going to WSA meetings just yet," he said.

She popped up onto her feet and put her hands on her hips. "I've seen all I intend to see. I'm six years older than you and a hundred years wiser. It was very, very good but it ain't happenin' again."

"You wouldn't know wise if it bit you on the ass. See you at dinner," he threw over his shoulder as he opened the door and walked out. She heard him say something to the kids and then something else to Elsie, who'd just arrived for the day.

He whistled all the way to the barn. So she thought it was very, very good, did she? Well, that little foray into sin the previous night had arrived on the heels of a six-year drought. She'd think wonderful when she saw the real Griffin at his best.

"Very good, my ass," he murmured. "I'd call what we shared damned amazing, woman. And who gives a royal rat's ass about age? It's just numbers on paper."

Sally came through the house in a whirlwind at suppertime but didn't even stop long enough for a glass of tea. She yelled at Julie to bring a beer to the bathroom if she had time and hugged the kids on the way up the steps.

Julie popped the lids off two longneck bottles of icy Coors and carried them up to the bathroom where she found Sally submerged in a foot of frothy bubbles. She put the toilet seat down and propped her feet on the edge of the tub. She handed Sally a beer and watched as she guzzled half of it before coming up for air with a noisy burp.

"I'm in love," she said.

"Love or lust?" Julie asked.

"Both. I had to have a cold bath just to cool off my hormones. Lord, that man is the sexiest thing ever put on this earth. Why did it take fate so long to put us together?"

"You're seriously not thinking about..."

"Yes, ma'am, I seriously am," Sally said.

"It's crazy, girl. It's a road to disaster."

"What if it's not? What if it's one of those roads less traveled and I turned the other way because of fear?"

"You afraid? Girl, you'd attack a rattlesnake with nothing but a Sugarland CD and a piece of chocolate candy."

"There's different ways to catch a rattlesnake. Good music and good chocolate will tame most wild critters," Sally retorted. "How's Griffin behaving today?"

"Don't turn this around. This is about you. How on earth would you tell Momma if you decided to go to Wyoming after only knowing a man a week?"

"I wouldn't. You would," Sally said.

"Not no, honey. But hell no. You decide that and you're on the hot griddle. I already had my turn when Annie was born with a white streak in her hair."

"It didn't kill you, did it? I don't expect it will kill me to sit in the fire. We're going to Dallas tonight for supper at the Dixie Stampede. Don't wait up for me, but if there's a light under the door I'll slip in and we can compare notes. If you don't want me in there, hang your bra on the doorknob," Sally said.

"Good God, Sally, we aren't in college. We're adults. I'm thirty-four years old. Griffin is twenty-eight. I'm too damned old for him. Alvie is forty. He's a little old for you, isn't he?"

"Fine wine gets better with age. I don't give a damn if Alvie is sixty. I'm in love and lust, and I'm so glad I quit my job. I've never felt so alive in all my thirty-two years."

"Wyoming is lonely. You like action and the city," Julie said.

"Downtown New York could be lonely, Sister. It's all in how you look at it. No place is lonely if you are happy there, and there's different kinds of action, isn't there? " Sally asked.

Julie threw a washcloth at her sister. "Who died and made you a sage?"

"I don't know, but I'm damn sure glad they did."

"You sure do cuss a lot for a preacher's daughter," Julie laughed.

"Preachers' kids are the worst of the lot. You might tell your friend Mamie that when she comes around all moony-eyed over Eli. He was always the good one of us three, but that ain't sayin' much, is it?"

"How'd he get to be so good and us so bad?" Julie mused.

Sally rose up from the water with bubbles hanging on her. "Now that's a question the angels would have trouble answering."

"Be careful, Sister. Promise me you'll be careful?"

"No, ma'am. I promise I'll take full responsibility for my actions. I won't promise I'll be careful, not if it keeps me from having Alvie. I've never wanted anything worse in my life," Sally said.

Julie left Sally as she dried bubbles off her near-perfect body and searched in her makeup kit for an eyelash curler. She heard the kids giggling at the movie *The Land Before Time* in Chuck's room.

Julie watched her sister pad barefoot with only a towel around her to the bedroom. In a few minutes, she emerged, a butterfly in emerald green and spike heels where a cocoon had been minutes before. Her red hair swung around her shoulders and she wore happy even better than the green dress. Julie hoped it lasted the rest of her life. Every woman deserved that kind of happiness. Sally dropped a kiss on Julie's forehead and skipped down the stairs to answer the doorbell.

Julie slid down to the floor in the hallway and drew her knees up. She could hear Lizzy laugh at some antic of the dinosaur in the movie and Annie joined her. Chuck was telling them that dinosaurs were real animals a long, long time ago. Three kids. Different mothers and fathers. But brothers and sisters in every sense. Maybe fate did exist.

"So what's going on up here?" Griffin appeared at the top of the steps and sat down beside her before she even realized he was in the house. Everything was topsy-turvy in her world. Not a single thing was set according to the plumb line and everything confused her.

"Sally's off to Dallas for supper with Alvie. The kids are watching a movie. Elsie is cooking."

"No, she's gone home for the day. She made a casserole for us to eat for lunch and supper. It's tradition. After the sale, everyone helps clean up and then they get the rest of the weekend off. Talk to me."

"About what?" Julie asked. What she had in mind to do to him did not involve many words.

"The day. My folks. How you feel. Anything," he said. What he wanted to hear was her voice, mainly with a hint of a moan, but that wouldn't be happening anytime soon if she held to her I'm-wiser-than-you attitude.

"Do you believe in fate?" she asked.

"I believe that things happen for a reason," he said.

"My sister thinks the past six years are culminating right here this day on the Lucky Clover," she said.

"How's that?"

"Eli and Mamie. Alvie and Sally."

Griffin raised an eyebrow. "Eli and Mamie?"

He'd showered already and he smelled heavenly. She noticed that a few drops of water hung on the longer lengths of his black hair and one little dewdrop floated on his long, dark lashes. She reached up and brushed it away, a proprietary gesture that felt so right and made her want to do so much more. "That's what Sally tells me. Momma knew but thought I'd meddle so she didn't tell me. Likewise, I'm not telling Momma about Alvie because she might meddle."

"The world of women. I'll never understand it," Griffin said.

"That's all right, honey. Menfolk all get to start out as brand-new souls. Women are old souls. We understand life better than you do," she teased.

"Don't give me that Oprah shit. Tell me about Eli and Mamie."

"They've had a few dinner dates and Eli is happy again. His wife died ten years ago and he's never gotten over it. Blamed God for a couple of years and refused to preach. Now he's moving to Bowie, and he and Mamie are an item. Sally and Alvie are in lust or love or something in the middle. So therefore, my moving to Saint Jo must be fate, because my actions are giving Cupid lots of business," she said.

"Jealous?"

"Maybe."

"Reckon they're having hot, wild sex?" Griffin asked.

She blushed. "Griffin!"

"An honest question. Have they?"

"I doubt if Eli and Mamie have. Sally is glowing, so I don't know about her. Ask me again tomorrow and I'm sure I can give you a positive answer."

"Jealous of your sister? You give up your lifestyle in Jefferson, move to the boonies, and lose your house in a fire, move in here to keep the children happy. She walks into a barn and the richest man in Wyoming sweeps her off her feet. Eli walks into Mamie's store and she latches on to him. All you get is one night in the hayloft with a rusty, old cowboy."

"Damn straight I'm jealous. Why didn't you tell me he was the richest man in Wyoming? I could have already agreed to run away with him, and bein' as how he's one of those cowboys with honor, he would have been bound to keep his word. Now I've lost him to my sister."

"Seriously. Would you have gone with him?" Griffin asked.

"Seriously? No. He's handsome beyond words. He says the right things and I rather like the view from a pedestal. But no, I'm not jumping into another mess. I've had two. I'm not going to be a three-time loser."

"Want to join me in the den for a movie?" He had to get out of the close quarters of the stairway or he was going to start something right there that would get them both into trouble if three kids caught them.

"A real one that doesn't have animated characters?"

"You can even choose which one." He laced his fingers with hers and stood up, leading her to the den. The jolt rattled through her slim body like marbles in a Mason jar. When they reached the den, he opened a cabinet beside the built-in entertainment center and motioned for her to take her pick. She would rather have stayed standing there in the middle of the floor holding hands with him like they were sophomores than pick out a movie.

She ran her fingers down the plastic covers, amazed that the plastic didn't melt from the heat he'd left in her hand. A comedy. Drama. What did she want to sit on the sofa and watch with Griffin for two hours? What she'd rather watch was the sun setting and the moon rising from the loft doors of an old barn. They wouldn't have to share kisses or even touch each other, just sit there in silence and let nature surround them like a familiar, old, worn blanket.

The night before she'd crossed the line. Now things were going to be different and she had always hated change. It was what had sent her back to Derrick. Not wanting change had kept her glued to the apartment in Jefferson instead of finding her own way.

She found a season of *Saving Grace* and looked at it for a moment. "Let's watch a few episodes of this rather than a movie."

"You sure?"

"Of course I'm sure. I saw an episode one night after Annie went to bed. It's adult. It's funny. Grace is not afraid of anything."

"Whole lot like you. Give it here. I'll get it started," he said with a grin.

The first episode took off with Grace, Holly Hunter's character, making love with her partner. Julie fought back the crimson rash threatening to set her face on fire.

"Want me to fast forward?" he asked.

"Only if the kids come in," she said.

"I want to say something while she's busy and not solving a crime up in Oklahoma," Griffin said.

"Better hurry. I think she's going to have to go to the WSA meeting here real soon," Julie said.

"Your age doesn't mean jack shit to me. If I was twelve and you were eighteen, it might make a difference. It doesn't today. We both have kids the same age. So don't be throwing that at me anymore."

"I'll throw anything I please at you, Mr. Luckadeau."

"And one other thing. Just because of six years, you are not a hell of a bit wiser than me. I've lived. I've lost. I've survived. Just like you. So don't lord it over me. We are two people fate has thrown together for whatever reason. I'm attracted to you. Evidently you are to me, or you wouldn't have Annie."

"Graham didn't look like you," she said.

"We are identical twins."

"He had a shaven head and the dent in his chin wasn't as deep as yours. His eyes didn't glitter when he smiled. They were hauntingly lost, as if he didn't know where he was going and wasn't sure if he was going to like it when he got there. He had a rakish force that preceded him into a room. We were both drunk, and the next morning we were glad he was leaving the state and we wouldn't have to go through the formality of I'll-call-you or I-hope-to-hell-you-don't."

"If his head hadn't been shaved..."

"You'd still be different," she said.

Griffin smiled. She didn't see him as an extension of his brother but as a whole new entity. Well, hot damn!

The sex scene on the television was over and the

angel in the form of a man called Earl had arrived in Grace's life.

Julie wasn't surprised that he'd contradicted her on the age issue. It might not matter right then, but give it ten years. He'd be thirty-eight and she'd have crow's feet and a flabby stomach. He'd still look like a movie star with all that gorgeous black hair and sharp, blue eyes. Look at his father. At sixty plus, Jimmy Luckadeau was still good-looking, and Griffin's mother was gorgeous. All the young little tarts in Montague County would want a chunk of Griffin and he'd be saddled to an old woman.

Griffin reached across the sofa and laced his fingers through hers and they finished watching the episode together.

Three kids bounded into the room just as the credits were rolling. They wanted to know if they could have popcorn and hot chocolate for a snack. And could they watch a movie on the big-screen television in the den with Griffin and Julie?

"The life of a parent," Griffin said.

"Ain't it grand?" Julie said.

"Wish I had a dozen of the rug rats. Know a kid's shelter where we could go round up a few more? Maybe they'd play with each other and leave us alone," Griffin teased.

"You mean like a dog shelter? They've got kids in cages? Momma, we got to go get them out of the cages and bring them home and feed them," Annie said seriously.

Julie pointed at Griffin as she headed for the kitchen to make popcorn. "You explain. You caused it."

Chapter 16

THE CHILDREN WERE SO EXCITED THEY COULD BARELY SIT still for breakfast. Julie French-braided Lizzy's hair while Annie brushed her teeth. Then they swapped places and she did Annie's. Chuck was ready in his jeans and new boots, and he kept saying his verse under his breath over and over so he'd get it just right. Julie had already slicked his red hair back with mousse and made sure his glasses were washed. And afterward, since it was Christmas Eve, they'd have presents under the tree and Santa Claus would leave them something for the next morning.

Griffin looked like sin on a stick, or on the front of a condom wrapper, Julie thought with a deep blush. He opened the door for the ladies and he and Chuck stood back to let them out first.

"Chuck, we are riding with the most beautiful women in the state of Texas today, aren't we?" Griffin asked on the way to church.

Chuck fidgeted.

"Chuck has a girlfriend," Annie singsonged.

Griffin raised an eyebrow and looked at the little boy in the rearview mirror.

"And who is it?" Griffin asked.

"Marlee," he said shyly.

"Marlee who comes to church? That little girl who lives in Forestburg?" Julie asked.

He nodded.

"Well, she's a pretty little girl," Griffin said.

"She told me that she thinks Chuck is cute," Lizzy giggled.

"Chuck is cute. He's a very cute boy," Julie said. She dreaded the day when Annie said she had a boyfriend.

"Me and Annie, we don't like boys. They're yucky. The only boy we like is Chuck because he's our cousin," Lizzy announced.

Griffin winked at Julie.

"Daddy, drive faster. We're going to be late," Lizzy said.

"I'm afraid I'll forget my verse if we don't hurry," Annie said.

Julie winked back at Griffin. His world expanded with that one wink. He was definitely in love and for the first time. He'd only thought he loved Dian. That was infatuation compared to what he felt for Julie.

Annie and Lizzy gave each other that look that said grown-ups were so dumb.

When they reached the church and parked the truck, Julie carried in two casseroles for the Christmas social after services. Griffin picked up an enormous bag of wrapped toys to put under the tree for Santa to pass out to the good little boys and girls.

The children followed Griffin.

"Hummmph," Clarice snorted when Julie took her things to the fellowship hall. "I was hoping you'd be gone for the holidays."

"Nope, I'm right here," Julie said cheerfully.

"And fittin' right in," Alvera said from right behind her.

"This ain't your fight," Clarice said.

"Any fight is my fight, especially if you're in it," Alvera said.

"Go to hell," Clarice said and started down the hall toward the sanctuary.

"You first, darlin'," Alvera called after her.

"Why do you bait her like that?" Julie asked.

"Honey, Bette Davis once said that age ain't no place for sissies. If she don't like it, she can die and I'll drag out my black suit and go to her funeral. Don't expect me to cry, though," Alvera said as she followed Clarice to the sanctuary.

When it came time for the kids to say their verses, Julie held her breath. Griffin reached over and squeezed her hand, keeping it in his after they'd all three said their pieces loud and clear. For the first time, Julie realized that Annie was more like Griffin and Lizzy had Graham's outgoing personality. Something akin to cold water chilled her. Both of the girls could very well belong to Graham. There was absolutely no way to ever prove it, but Dian had opened the door to such a possibility.

The kids joined Griffin and Julie after their part of the program was over and Annie whispered, "Miss Temple said we did good."

After the Christmas program was finished, they all gathered in the fellowship hall for a potluck. The children played with their friends they hadn't seen since school had let out for the holidays. Little girls dashing off to giggle in the corners. Little boys posturing for each other and hoping the little girls noticed.

Julie hid in the hallway for a few minutes to keep from crying at the idea of them growing up.

Griffin stepped out of the men's room. "I can read your thoughts."

"And?"

"They can't stay little forever," he said.

She jerked her head around to find his eyes just inches from hers. "How did you know what I was thinking?"

"I was thinking the same thing. But don't worry. Santa will be here in a while and they'll be little again. He makes everyone young." Griffin planted a quick kiss on her lips.

"Then I'd better sit on his lap for a long time," she said.

He grimaced. "I told you that age didn't matter."

"And will it matter when I'm fifty and gravity takes hold of my fat cells?" she asked.

"I'm not too worried. I didn't see many fat cells up in the hayloft." He ran a finger down her upper arm and circled her waist with his arm. "Come on back to the dinner. The feeling will pass. If it doesn't, wait until they all three get into it about something that doesn't matter. Then you'll wish they'd hurry and grow up."

She let him lead her back into the fellowship hall, her hand entwined in his.

Clarice popped him on the shoulder when they got in line for dinner. "You are flirting with the devil," she quipped.

"Yep, I am." Griffin grinned.

"I'm serious. You can do better than that woman. Rachel broke up with the lawyer," she said.

Alvera looped her arm though Clarice's and dragged her to the dessert table. "Come on. Them kids don't need us old women interferin' in their lives."

Clarice pulled against Alvera's grip. "Let me go, you witch."

"Honey, you can talk plainer than that. Just forget it's Sunday and go ahead and call me a bitch," Alvera whispered.

"I wish you would have died at birth," Clarice said.

"And I wish I would have drowned you before you married my brother. He died to get away from you," Alvera said softly so only Clarice could hear it.

"Reverend Wilson, don't you dare eat up all that chocolate pie," Alvera said loudly. "Clarice here has had her eye on a piece all day. I made it especially for her."

"I hate chocolate pie and you know it," Clarice hissed.

"Explain that to Reverend Wilson." Alvera loosened her grip and left Clarice right beside the preacher.

Lunch was barely over when Santa Claus arrived with a big, "Ho! Ho! Ho!" and the children flocked around him. He passed out the presents under the tree. Lizzy and Annie both opened up a new Barbie in a princess gown. Chuck opened a ball glove, and the grin that covered his face brought tears to Julie's eyes.

She managed to keep them at bay until they got home. The children all raced inside to change their clothing and play with their Santa toys. Julie went straight to the kitchen and was leaning against the sink, staring out into the backyard, when Griffin found her. She spun around, leaned on his chest, and cried until there were no tears left.

"Why did you come in here?" she whispered when the dam dried up.

"You looked like you might need a shoulder," he said.

"It still hurts," she said.

Griffin kissed the top of her head, inhaling the coconut-scented shampoo and loving the way she fit into his arms. "I expect it will until we find out for sure where things stand with Chuck. I already feel like he's as much mine as Lizzy and Annie."

"You think they'll let us keep him?" The word *us* didn't escape Griffin, and his heart swelled up until it threatened to burst out of his chest.

"I hope so. I have a friend at the jail who is planning to talk to his mother and father tomorrow morning. I didn't want to get your hopes up, but there's a slim possibility they might relinquish rights to him. They are facing a ten-year sentence at the very least. I'm almost afraid to say the words out loud for fear I'll jinx it."

His words didn't take the pain away instantly, but they brought a measure of comfort.

"Want a cup of coffee?" she asked.

"I'd like more than that, but I suppose with three sugared-up kids, that's the best we can do," he answered.

"Did you see Chuck's face when he opened that glove?"

"I saw all their faces. And, honey, you are a damn sight stronger than I am. I went to the men's room and washed my eyes to keep everyone from seeing the tears. I'm supposed to be the big, strong daddy man, not the whimpering, slinging snot wimp," he said honestly.

"I'm making myself a homemade banana split with all three scoops of ice cream. I deserve it after that weeping fit. It's not long until dusk, and then they can unwrap our gifts from under the tree," she said.

Griffin raised an eyebrow when she got out the ice cream and an enormous bowl.

"You are going to share with me. I'm not getting fat

all alone. Tell me a story about fate working miracles. Anything to get my mind off the kids growing up and not even being interested in Santa. Or to take my mind off the fact that they might come and take Chuck from us." She split a banana and put three scoops of ice cream in the middle of it.

"Okay. Which one do you want? The one about Slade and Jane or the one about Milli and Beau?"

"Both. They were a little bit nicer to me at the party last week. I dreaded going, but Alvera is a sweetheart and she took my side."

"I don't see anyone or anything intimidating you."

Julie shook the spoon at him. "Those witches did. I thought they'd nail me to an altar and set me on fire. You Luckadeaus really do stick up for one another," she said. "So tell me about them both."

"Just one today. You can have one today and one tomorrow. By then you'll forget about the kids growing up. Hell, you might be prayin' for them to hurry up and finish high school and go off to college," he said.

"Bet me. I'll cry worse than they do when they graduate."

"I hope not. I don't have that many stories," he said.

"Okay then, one story," she said.

"Which one?"

"Milli and Beau. Katy Scarlett doesn't look like she should have Milli for a momma, does she?" Julie put the banana split on the table and handed him the extra spoon.

"Not with those blue eyes and blonde hair and Milli being Mexican. But there's an Englishwoman in the genetic woodpile. Milli's maternal grandmother is a blonde lady with English ancestors. One of the true blue bloods."

"You're kidding." Either the chocolate was working or the ice cream was freezing the lump in her throat.

"No, I'm not joking. Katy Scarlett looked like her grandmother, not her mother. They figured she was a throwback to that grandmother."

"Now my curiosity is really piqued."

"Well, the story goes like this. Milli was engaged to a man who was so rich he could buy a third-world country out of his back pocket. Met him when he came up to Hereford, Texas—that's out in the Panhandle, not too far from Amarillo—to buy cattle at her father's sale one year. He proposed a few weeks later and she accepted. But the sorry son of a bitch wasn't faithful and she caught him in a motel room with another woman."

"So then she met Beau and they lived happily ever after?"

"Not hardly. She broke it off with him and got an invitation to a wedding in Louisiana. Her high school friend had gone to college over in that area somewhere and met my cousin, Darrin Luckadeau. Milli went to the wedding, and there was Beau. His girlfriend had broken up with him. Threw him over for another Luckadeau cousin. Anyway, he was drunk as Cooter's owl and thought Milli was some kind of angel. They wound up in the back bedroom of a trailer that night. She was getting even with her ex-fiancé and poor old Beau was just trying to relieve a broken heart."

He stopped and ate several bites of banana split, then sipped coffee.

"Go on. We haven't got all day. The kids will interrupt us any minute," she said.

"Don't get your panties in a wad. I'm telling this

story. So anyway, Milli went home. Got a taxi the next morning and left before Beau woke up. The only thing she left behind was a memory and an earring. Poor old Beau. Whole family knew he was lucky in everything but love. He always had the worst luck with women. So here he came out of the bedroom hunting for an angel and the cousins staying in that trailer convinced him she was a figment of his drunken imagination. He went on the wagon that night and to my knowledge still doesn't drink."

"And?" she prompted impatiently.

"Milli came home from college at Christmas and she was pregnant. Her brothers were ready to go drag that ex back with a shotgun in their hands. But she swore it wasn't his baby and she wouldn't tell who the child belonged to. So Katy Scarlett was born into a Mexican household, but she's pure blonde Luckadeau. No one knew that, though, because Milli wouldn't tell. Then, when Katy was almost two, Milli's grandfather up in Oklahoma had to have his hip replaced. He asked Milli and Katy to help out that summer. Imagine Milli's surprise on her first day when she went to ride the fence row and found Beau on the other side."

Julie finished off the last bite of ice cream. "I know just how she felt."

"Yep, there they were on adjoining ranches. Beau's aunt had Alzheimer's and went to a nursing home after she gave her ranch to Beau, since he was her favorite nephew and she didn't have any children. Is that fate?"

"What happened?" Julie leaned forward and propped her elbows on the table and her chin in her hands.

"Beau was engaged to a schoolteacher named

Amanda, who was a real, honest-to-God bitch. Beau had been mooning after the angel who'd lost an earring, but he was about to marry this gold-digging schoolteacher, and that's the reason Milli was so cold toward you. Meanwhile, Milli had a child she was trying to hide."

"Didn't he recognize her?" Julie asked. "I mean if he was mooning after her, surely he had her picture engraved on his heart."

"He says something in the back of his mind kept telling him he'd met her somewhere. But Milli is not all sweet sugar candy. She's got a mouth and an attitude and they fought like cats and dogs from day one."

"When did they discover happily-ever-after?" Julie asked.

"Well, the night of his engagement party, his fiancée came around with intentions of breaking up with him but really got furious when she found out about the prenup all Luckadeau brides have to sign. He told me that there was the woman he'd proposed to wearing his ring and he looked out the window and saw Milli in the same dress she'd worn to that wedding, and by damn, he remembered it all. He was almighty glad the fiancée threw the ring at him and broke it off. He and Milli danced all night together and it became just a party instead of an engagement party."

"And Milli told him about Katy?" Julie asked.

"No, he found out at church when some little old man made the comment about how much his daughter looked like him. I guess there were really fireworks on the way home that day. It took a few more months and a lot more fights, but they finally admitted they were in love. I went to their wedding held up there on the ranch.

Beau's mother is elated to have a granddaughter. Milli's mother is happy to have a father for Katy Scarlett. So there's your miracle. What's the chances of Milli and Beau ever finding each other? What's the chances of them ever making Katy Scarlett on a one-night stand?"

"Graham and I did," she said.

"And you have your own miracle, don't you?" Griffin said shortly.

"Are you mad at me?"

"No, ma'am," he said curtly as picked up the ice cream dish and put it in the sink.

"Yes, you are. You got mad when I mentioned having a one-night stand with your brother," she said.

"Okay, yes, I did. Graham was my brother, the other half of me, and I loved him—but I don't want to hear about you sleeping with him. I don't want to hear about my ex-wife kissing him. I loved him, but I don't want to play second fiddle to him," Griffin said.

"It happened. And believe me, Griffin, you don't have to worry about playing second fiddle to your brother. You are much more intense and sensitive and all those things a woman looks for in a long-term relationship. Truth of the matter is that I don't like to hear about you and Dian being drunk when you made Lizzy, either," Julie said.

His blue eyes lit up. "Are you jealous?"

"I don't know. I'll think about it and get back to you," she said.

The children rushed in wanting cookies and milk and asking when it would be dark enough they could open presents.

"Saved by the kids," he said.

"They're always good for something or other," she

smarted off, and got up to help him pour three glasses of milk.

While they ate, Griffin made an excuse about going to the barn to check on a calf, put on his coat, and left. The children gobbled down their cookies and milk and ran back upstairs to play old maid cards for one more hour before presents could be opened. Julie poured another cup of coffee and leaned against the countertop, trying to make sense of Griffin's jealousy. She'd barely had time to think about it when Sally opened the front door and grinned sheepishly when Julie peeked around the corner. She wore plaid flannel pajama bottoms and a gray tank top and her straight, red hair hung limp.

"Hello. Mercy, is it really four o'clock?" she asked as she headed for the coffeepot.

"Looks like it was a good night," Julie said.

Sally sipped the hot liquid and tried to open her eyes wide enough to put Julie in focus. "What am I going to do?"

"You tell me." Julie joined her at the kitchen table.

"I wish I would have known Alvie a year, then Momma wouldn't throw such a fit," Sally said.

"Ever think of taking him over there one day this week to meet them?" Julie asked.

"I don't want to. They'll love him, but..."

"But you haven't told Momma you quit your job, have you?" Julie scolded.

"I'm going to marry him," Sally said.

"What are you going to do between now and then?"

"The wedding is Tuesday morning, and he'll be here in an hour to pick me up. We've got motel reservations in Nocona," Sally said.

"I'm not telling her, Sally," Julie declared.

"I've devised a way to do it. You just have to back me up, not tell a lie," Sally said.

Julie sighed.

"I'm going to call her after I marry him and say I decided to get married rather than teach this year. I'm not going to tell her I've only known him a few days. I've already had all my things shipped home. The truck will be there on Wednesday. I'd planned to stay in your old apartment until I found something else to do."

"So you've got two days to tell Momma. I'm glad I'm not wearing your shoes today," Julie said.

"She'll be so happy that I'm not an old maid anymore that she won't even ask how long I've known Alvie. Did you know his whole name is Alton Vernon Marlon? His mother called him Alton Vernon and his brother, who died in the Iraq War—that's why he owns the whole ranch—shortened it to Alvie."

"I don't care if his name is Santa Claus Scrooge. I'm not telling Momma," Julie said.

"I'll tell her when you and Griffin get married," Sally whined.

"That'll be a cold day in hell," Julie said.

Sally laughed.

"What's so funny?"

"You might as well quit fighting fate, Sister. Griffin is the man for you, the one you should have married in the beginning, but it wasn't the right time. Now it is. You will marry him."

Julie cleared the dishes from the table and put them in the dishwasher. "Don't hold your breath until that happens. You'll die of suffocation."

Sally giggled, then stopped so suddenly that Julie looked around to see if she'd fainted or died.

"Oh my gosh, today is Sunday. It was the church program! I'm a horrible sister. I should have set the alarm in the hotel room and gotten up in time to go see it." She rushed to Julie's side and hugged her. "Did they do good?"

"They did wonderful. I cried," Julie said. She didn't tell Sally that she'd done her weeping with Griffin's arms around her. Married, indeed! The woman had wedding cake for brains.

"Please forgive me. Ever since I walked into that barn, I've been so taken up with me and Alvie that I forget there's a world out there," Sally said.

"Forgiven and forgotten," Julie said.

"You always were the good daughter. I've been the bad child my whole life," Sally said.

"One time I wasn't the good one," Julie argued.

"And it got you a beautiful daughter. What do you think mine and Alvie's kids will look like?"

Julie spewed coffee across the table. "Holy shit, you are serious?"

"Did you think I was teasing? I'm packing my suitcases and we're leaving Texas Tuesday morning. Tomorrow we're going to Wichita Falls to look at rings. Alvie talked a jewelry store owner into opening up in the afternoon even though it's Christmas Day. I have no idea what he's paying the man to do that. Then Tuesday, we're going by the Montague County Courthouse to get married. We'd do it tomorrow, but the courthouse is closed on Christmas Day. You and Griffin want to go along and witness for us?"

"Sally, this is insane. You've only known him a few days."

"I love him and I'm going to marry him, so get used to it."

"So soon?"

"That's right."

"Can I say anything to talk you out of it? Wait six months. Live here six months, and if it's still real, you can marry him then. We'll have a huge wedding right here on the ranch. Caterers. Barn wedding. Or we can have it in Wyoming. Just wait, Sister, please," Julie begged.

"No. I've never been more sure of anything in my whole life. Be happy for me."

"You're just doing this to keep from telling Momma you quit your job, aren't you?" Julie said.

"I'm doing it because I love Alvie. Did the minute you dragged him over to the barn door. I never did believe in love at first sight or fate. I do now. And I'm not going to fight it like you're doing."

"I'm not fighting anything. It's just too sudden and too fast and—"

Sally put her finger over Julie's lips. "And it's my life. Alvie is everything I ever wanted. It's going to happen. Are you going with me?"

Tears streamed down Julie's face for the second time that day. "I wouldn't let you do that by yourself. You know I'm going with you. School doesn't start until Thursday, and Elsie can watch the children for us."

Sally hugged her again. "Don't cry. You'll make me cry. And bring the kids with you."

"If you are so sure, then call Momma and tell her the truth. Then I'll believe you," Julie said.

Sally picked up the phone from off the countertop and poked in the numbers. "Momma, are you sitting down?" she said when she heard her mother's voice.

"I am now. Are you all right? I've been trying to call you for a week. I even called the school and they said you'd quit your job. They're really mad at you because you didn't give them any kind of notice," Deborah said.

"I'm putting us on speakerphone so Julie can hear everything. This may take a while," Sally said.

"Why is Julie at your apartment? Is Annie all right? Why did she leave the ranch? I knew I should go up there and kick that Luckadeau woman's ass."

Sally got a case of giggles. "Momma said *ass*."

"Yes, I did. Does yours need kicking?" Deborah said.

"Hopefully not. I can't believe you said that word. But Julie is fine. I'm at the ranch with her, not at my apartment. Here's the deal," Sally said and went on to tell her mother everything truthfully from the time she started to have bad feelings about going back to school until that moment.

Julie listened.

Sally told it all and ended with, "All I could think was 'go home to your sister.' I did, and this is where I am, Momma. Julie made me call."

"Julie, you did the right thing. What do you think? Is this Alvie a good man?"

"Every report I've had is that he is, and he's so handsome it hurts your eyes to look at him, so they'll make you lots of pretty grandbabies," Julie said.

"As handsome as Griffin Luckadeau?" Deborah asked.

"I wouldn't go that far," Julie laughed. "But he's real pretty."

"Call me when you get to Wyoming, and I'll expect an invitation to the ranch real soon," Deborah said.

"Anytime you want to visit, there's a room waiting with your name on it." Sally all but breathed a sigh of relief.

"You're letting her off that easy? You'd have had me drawn and quartered for a stunt like this," Julie said.

"I've just got one word to that little temper fit and it's *Annie*," Deborah said.

"Yes, ma'am," Julie said.

Goodbyes were said, and Julie sank back down in the chair. "I can't believe she accepted it without a fight."

"Look at it from her standpoint. She doesn't have to pay for or plan a wedding, and she's getting a rich son-in-law and a new place to go visit. I'm going up to pack my things. Oh, I won't need my little truck anymore. You want it? It's paid for and I'll sign the title over to you if you want it," Sally said.

"Thank you and that answer would definitely be yes. You'll be taking Alvie's truck back to Wyoming?"

"Oh, no. Alvie sent it on back with the hired hands he brought with him. He came prepared to buy some cattle and they're already on the road back with them. We will fly from Dallas Wednesday morning. That big truck he's driving is a rental. We have reservations at a hotel on Tuesday night and Alvie will turn the truck in at the airport."

"So, a one-night honeymoon in Dallas. That doesn't seem so romantic. Is this the same girl who was going to Paris for her honeymoon or she'd never get married?" Julie asked.

"It is, but I'd rather live in a tent on the banks of the Red River with Alvie than go to Paris with anyone else in the world. Wyoming for the rest of my life will be a fairly nice little honeymoon," Sally said.

And that's when Julie believed her.

"Are you going with him again this evening or are you having Christmas Eve with us?" Julie asked.

"Please forgive me. I just came back to get a quick shower. I'm going with Alvie. I can't stand being away from him. Tell the kids I love them all and I'll see you Tuesday morning at nine o'clock at the courthouse. I've got to go upstairs and throw everything into a suitcase. Alvie is picking me up in another twenty minutes," Sally said.

"I understand. I really do." Julie hugged her.

Griffin barely made it back into the house when three kids hit the stairs in a dead run and grabbed him around the legs, begging to open presents. He'd spent a couple of hours in the barn putting bicycles together for the next morning—a red one for Chuck and two hot-pink ones for the girls—so he was already in the Christmas mood and it took very little persuasion.

Lizzy opened new clothes and a Barbie castle. Annie opened new clothing and two Barbie vehicles: the sports car and the minivan. Chuck opened his packages much more slowly than either of the girls, relishing each piece of paper and each gift as if they were gold. He had new jeans and shirts and a basketball hoop that Griffin would hang on the pecan tree in the backyard.

"And now it's Momma's turn." Annie handed her a present.

"For me?" Julie asked.

"From Griffin," Annie said.

Julie carefully opened the package, which contained

a small velvet box. It came from a jewelry store but was long and skinny. Inside was a charm bracelet with each charm representing something that had happened in her life since she'd moved to Saint Jo. A small house for the one she'd bought. An apple for her teacher job. A silhouette of each child's head with their first name engraved on it.

She could scarcely believe that Griffin had put so much thought and care into her present. "Thank you," she said softly.

"I'll add one for the sale night later on," he said.

"And what would that be?" she asked.

"A cow, because we sold cows," Annie said.

The *we* didn't escape Julie.

"I was thinking about a bolt of lightning or a flash of fire," he said with a grin.

Julie blushed. "How about a moon and some stars? Seems like I saw them."

"I think we both saw them," he said.

Lizzy pulled the last present out from under the tree. "And here's one for Daddy."

"For me?"

"It's a big 'prize and we had to be very nice and not tell," Chuck said.

He tore into the paper to find an eight-by-ten silver frame with a professional portrait of all three kids together.

The lump in his throat was as big as a watermelon, but he managed to get out a weak "thank you" before the kids hopped in his lap, telling him all about how they'd gone with Julie to Gainesville and had the picture made for him.

"It's the most beautiful thing I've ever had," he said.

"I knowed you would like it." Lizzy beamed. "Now would you please put my Barbie castle together so we can play before we have to go to bed?"

"Back to fatherhood." He grinned. "Seriously, thank you."

The only way it could have been better is if you'd been in it with them, he thought.

"Seriously, thank you," she held up her bracelet for him to fasten it around her wrist.

The only way it could be better is if it had a cowboy hat to represent you, she thought.

On Tuesday morning, Julie was up early and had the kids dressed by eight o'clock. She wore an emerald-green silk dress with a matching jacket. Griffin wore his standard Sunday outfit: black Wranglers, boots, a white shirt, and a sports coat.

They waited in the judge's chambers for ten minutes before Alvie and Sally came sauntering in. Sally looked ravishing in an ivory silk dress that hugged her body. Alvie wore the same outfit he'd worn to the sale party. The judge told them where to stand and the short civil ceremony began. Julie and Griffin didn't hear the vows Alvie and Sally exchanged because they were too busy stealing glances at each other. Alvie put a wide, gold band with a diamond half as big as an ice rink on Sally's finger. Julie and Griffin signed the marriage license as witnesses, and it was done. Sally was Mrs. Alton Vernon Marlon and on her way to Wyoming.

A cold north wind blasted across the courthouse lawn when they walked outside. Sally hugged Julie.

Griffin kissed the bride. Alvie hugged his new sister-in-law. Sally stooped down and gave all three kids a hug and told them they could come spend all the time they wanted with her during the summer.

"I almost made a mistake and took the wrong sister home with me. You made a mistake when you hooked up with Graham instead of Griffin. I corrected mine. Call me when you take care of yours," Alvie whispered in Julie's ear.

Julie was speechless.

Alvie started to drive away and then the truck stopped with a squeal of the tires. The driver's side window rolled down and Alvie yelled, "Julie!"

She looked up to see her sister's arm throwing a single red rose tied with a white ribbon at her. She caught it without even thinking.

"You're next!" Sally yelled as the truck sped away.

"How 'bout that?" Griffin said.

"It's bullshit," Julie said.

"No, it's a rose. It looks like a rose. It smells like a rose. It has thorns like a rose. I believe it's a rose," he said.

"This day has been too much," she said. "I thought I was moving into quiet country life and just look at what I've gotten myself into."

"It is normally pretty routine around these parts. You just got here during a busy time. Won't be long until summer is here and you'll be whining about being bored."

"I'll believe it when I see it. Let's go home." She carried the rose carefully. Tomorrow she'd hang it upside down and let it dry, then preserve the petals forever. Maybe when Annie or Lizzy got married, she'd incorporate them with the ones the flower girls would strew down the aisle at the church.

Good grief, she'd just realized that she planned on staying around to see Lizzy get married. It really was a crazy, mixed-up day.

Chapter 17

WITH THE BEGINNING OF SPRING AROUND THE corner, Griffin hired extra help. One day, he was coming home at a decent hour in the evening. The next, it was well past dark and he got there in time to tuck the children into bed, take a shower, and snore in front of the television for a while before he went to bed.

Mamie came to visit every few days. The romance between her and Eli was growing. They both came for Sunday dinner once, but after that, various members of the congregation invited them to dinner every Sunday. Sally and Alvie were still on an extended working honeymoon. Sally sounded happy when she talked about new baby calves, kittens in the barn, and the beauty of Wyoming. Julie hoped her sister kept those rose-colored glasses on forever.

And she was jealous as hell of both her brother and sister. Granted, she should love them enough to be happy for them, but it wasn't fair. They'd both found their happily-ever-afters, and she was beginning to want the same thing.

Winter months on the ranch were busy, but Julie found out quickly that all months were busy, some just more than others. Griffin had breakfast, gave the kids each a kiss, and went to work. Julie dressed them, took them to school, and came home after school to her normal routine. He'd said things could and would get boring. She'd begun to believe him and think more seriously about her own place. She'd almost decided on a double-wide trailer using the foundation and basement that were still on her property.

One day drifted into the next, and that one made its way through the pages of history until several weeks had escaped. Griffin hadn't kissed her again. He left early and came home late, and she wondered if the love they'd shared had been a figment of her imagination.

There was just barely the hint of a spring smell in the air one evening in the first week in February when she slipped out the front door to sit on the porch. It wasn't really warm yet, and there'd be lots of cold days still, but that evening she could smell the promise of what was to come. Crickets and frogs were singing, and a coyote lent its howl to the mixture.

"What are you doing out here?" Griffin asked from the doorway.

"Thinking."

"About what?"

"Life."

He yawned.

"Sleepy?" she asked.

"Tired to the bone."

"Good night, then."

He opened the door and stepped outside. The night air wasn't bad. Looked like maybe winter had done most of its damage, but he couldn't be sure. It would be a long time until it was really spring. He sat down beside her.

"Marita just called."

"And?"

"They'll be here on Friday to move their things out of the house. Paul will be moving in after that," he said.

"Tell me about Paul. I know Elsie pretty good and she's a sweetheart."

"Paul is fifty-five and Elsie is a little younger. Kids are already grown and gone. They are both hard workers, quiet and laid-back folks."

"It'll be good to see Marita again. I know Lizzy misses her," Julie said. "You know what I feel like right now?"

"I've got a feeling you are about to tell me," he said.

"Damn straight I am. I feel like I'm in a rut. I feel like I don't know where I stand in the grand scheme of things around here."

A broken record inside Julie's head said, "Run, run, run," and wouldn't be quieted.

"I told you there would come a time when you'd get bored," he said.

"Not bored. Oh hell, you don't understand a thing I'm saying," she said.

"You got that right."

Pickup lights turned down the lane. Julie watched them as if they were lights sent just to get her out of the doldrums. She was surprised to see Milli and Beau step out of the truck.

Beau called out as he crossed the yard. "Hey! It's late, but we were in the neighborhood. Got any coffee?"

"Sure. Come on in," Julie said.

"I'll just sit out here with Griff. Got a problem with a bull I want to talk to him about," Beau said.

Milli followed Julie into the house. "Date night. We went to Gainesville for dinner and a little shopping. Beau had ulterior motives. So here we are, making the big loop and going back home through the country."

"Elsie left brownies. The kids are in bed already," Julie said.

Julie arranged a tray with brownies and two cups of coffee and carried it out to the porch. When she returned, Milli had poured two cups of coffee and set the pan of brownies on the table.

"I've got a confession to make. I was determined not to like you. I got this idea that you were out to take Griffin for a ride, since Graham wasn't around for you to hoodwink. I was wrong. Nellie and Ellen got me and Jane told in a hurry when they heard that we'd been catty. I'm sorry," Milli said.

"Forgiven. Had I been in your shoes, I would have felt the same way," Julie said.

"So how are things goin' around here since the dance? Seemed like you and Griffin were getting along fairly well then," Milli asked.

"Tonight, honestly, all I want to do is run. Things were going pretty good and then *slam*, the brakes were put on the whole thing."

"Been there. Done it. Runnin' don't help."

"Griffin told me how you and Beau got together. I think of it as a fate miracle."

"A what?" Milli asked.

"I've doubted the existence of fate. You know my sister met and married Alvie Marlon in less than a week?"

"I heard about it. Cinderella story, ain't it?" Milli said.

"She had this theory that my moving to Saint Jo was all tangled up with fate and how because I moved here she had this uncontrollable urge to quit her job and come to see me. Then because she succumbed to the voices in her head, she met Alvie and it was all fate."

Milli sipped coffee and nodded.

"So," Julie continued, "I asked Griffin if he believed in fate and he told me about you and Beau and how you ran back to West Texas after you'd had the fling with Beau in the trailer."

"Oh, honey, I just went home that time. The time that I ran was another thing altogether," Milli said.

"Well, you know how men are. Bare bones only. When did you really run away?"

"After the afternoon in the hay barn. A storm was on the horizon and Poppy John left his tractor out. He wanted it put in the barn, so I rode my horse out to the pasture to take care of it. Fate has to be female—only a woman could plan something so intricate. Anyway, here comes fate again. Beau was out getting his prize bull away from a pecan tree in a lightning storm and we wound up in the same barn. One thing led to another and we damn near set the barn on fire ourselves."

"Milli!"

"Well, we did, and let me tell you, the sex was every bit as good as it was the night he was dog drunk in the trailer. It scared the liver out of me. The only thing I could hear was this booming voice inside my head that kept screaming at me to take Katy Scarlett and get the hell out of Dodge."

"What happened?" Julie asked.

"I got the hell out of Dodge. Made it all the way to the north side of Oklahoma when that old song by Trisha Yearwood came on the radio."

"Which one?"

"It's the one from the movie *Con Air*, 'How Do I Live.' Remember it?"

"Yes, I do. But what made that one so special?"

"It talks about getting through a night without him and asks how could she live without him. She says he's the world, her heart, her soul, and that everything good in her life is him."

The song began to play in Julie's head.

"So I called Beau and turned the truck around and came back home. Learned a hard lesson that day. I couldn't run from my problems or my heart. My mind might say that I had to run, but my heart refused to go. And I couldn't live without it. I stopped the truck and cried my eyes out. I was scared to death Beau wouldn't have me back and that he'd tell me to take my sorry ass back to Hereford and never come around him again."

"I think I'm a believer," Julie said.

"Just because I told you about my life?" Milli questioned.

"No, because of what you said about fate being female," Julie answered.

Milli picked up another brownie. "I love these. Be nice to Elsie or I'll steal her. Now tell me truthfully if you believe in fate."

Julie sipped coffee. "I do, and it's because of the timing. If I'd moved to Saint Jo before you went to Oklahoma, then you wouldn't be here to help me understand these feelings tonight. Only a woman could get lives organized in such a way that one woman could help another through a crisis. Besides, what were the chances that I'd have the feelings I had tonight, the same ones that told you to get the hell out of Dodge, on the very night that Beau needs to talk to Griffin about a bull?"

"You got a point there," Milli said.

"Hey, you women through gossipin' in there?" Beau called from the door.

Milli leaned across the counter and hugged Julie. "That's my cue. Hang in there. It'll work out. Maybe not as fast as your sister got hers solved, but Miss Fate will take care of it."

"I'll take your word for it."

"And make a trip to the barn. You'll be surprised how it helps every now and then." Milli winked.

"Griffin is six years younger than I am," Julie said.

"So what? You're both adults," Milli said.

The truck's taillights left Julie and Griffin sitting on the porch again. Her mood was only slightly better. At least the record inside her head had stopped. Now there was a very different song than what Milli had heard when she'd turned her truck around. It was by Trisha Yearwood, though. An older song called "Thinkin' About You." She began to hum it without thinking.

Griffin recognized the tune and the words ran through his head. It was the gospel truth set to music, for sure. He had been thinking about Julie, and he was ready to admit his life, his heart, and his soul weren't worth shit without her in them.

"Tell me a fate story. You promised me another one and we've never had the time for it," she said.

"It'll have to be short. I'm sleepy and it's getting late," he said.

"Give me the bare bones. I'll get Jane to fill in the details later," she said.

"Okay. I've got to go back to dirt, though."

"Why?" Julie said.

"Because that's where it starts. There were five little

girls who grew up together south of Bowie. I guess they were hellions. Granny Nellie says they were the very ones that they used for that Ya-Ya movie. She was one of them, and her sister, Ellen, was one, and there were three others. One of those five married and moved to Arkansas. The others stayed pretty close. The one who moved away came home once a year and they holed up in an old house and had a wonderful time. Then that one died, so they had their own personal little funeral. Put her picture on a raft made of Popsicle sticks or something like that and floated it out into the pond where they'd all five almost got caught skinny-dipping as teenagers. Set it on fire and gave her a private ceremony with a bottle of Jack Daniel's."

"What's that got to do with Jane and Slade?" Julie asked.

"I told you it would have to start at dirt. Anyway, the one that moved away, I can't ever remember all the names, had a daughter who had a daughter. Jane is the granddaughter, and she'd heard of the five little girls but had no idea who the others were. So remember that while I tell this part of the story. Jane is living in Greenville, Mississippi. She's pretty close to her twenty-fifth birthday, and when it arrives, she'll inherit her own oil company. She already owns a horse ranch. Her mother and father are both dead and her stepfather is the CEO of the oil company. But if she dies before she's twenty-five, he inherits everything. So he puts a contract out on her."

Julie clamped her hand over her mouth. "You are shittin' me."

"Nope, he really did, and it gets worse. He almost

carried it off. He hired a woman assassin to kill Jane. The woman had a boyfriend trying to break into the business, so she passed the job off to him, so he could make his bones." He stopped and yawned.

"Don't stop there," Julie said.

"Sure you don't want to save the rest until tomorrow night?"

She swatted his arm.

"So the man has to meet the mark, who is Jane, right? He goes to the oil company under the ruse of being some kind of art dealer and meets her. Decides to make a few bucks on the side. He courts her, takes out a million-dollar life insurance policy on her, proposes to her, and the wedding is about to come off. It's the night before and Jane can't sleep, so she goes out on the patio only to hear her groom and his girlfriend discussing the subject of her death in between bouts of lovemaking.

"Jane took only a few things and left some messages about having cold feet. She left her credit cards, took what cash she had, and ran. She left her car in the airport parking lot, took a taxi to the bus station, and bought a ticket to Dallas. When she got there, she had a tough time deciding on Houston or Wichita Falls. She chose the latter." Griffin yawned again.

"Keep going. It's not that late," Julie said.

"Meantime, Granny Nellie isn't supposed to be driving because she has macular degeneration and can't see. But Ellen has been visiting and wants to get home, so she rides the bus in and out of Wichita Falls. Slade said he'd take her to the bus station, but he's working late and the old girls panic. Granny Nellie drives to Wichita and has a wreck, which shakes her up, and even though she gets Ellen to the bus on time, she sits in the bus station awhile to settle her nerves."

"Why didn't Ellen drive? She's pretty spunky," Julie asked.

"That's the other story. Ellen is a piece of work. Married umpteen times and ornery as they made them back in the old days. Short version is that she likes speed and Jack Daniel's."

"I want to grow up and be just like her," Julie said.

"Well, you've got a head start with that red hair and sass."

"Tell me more," Julie begged.

"Granny Nellie is sitting there trying to calm her nerves when she thinks she sees this ghost, but it's really Jane, who looks so much like her grandmother it's uncanny. She sits down beside Nellie and before you know it, Nellie has talked her into working for her. Her jobs are to drive Granny Nellie and Ellen, when she's in Ringgold, anywhere they want to go, and to help with the kitchen duties. But she doesn't say a word about knowing who Jane has to be."

"So she met Slade and it was happily-ever-after?"

"God no! She met Slade, who thought she was a con artist of some kind and it was hell-ever-after. I was over there for Granny Nellie's party and he had this girlfriend who was the devil's spawn. That woman and her girls gave Jane and Lizzy hell all day long, and Slade was right there letting it happen. Lord, he hated Jane with a passion. And she didn't back down a step from him. I remember she said once that she was going to grow up and be like Ellen, too. Y'all are about two of a kind."

"I don't hate you, Griffin," Julie said softly.

"Well, stop the damn presses. There's a new front-page story."

"I wouldn't live with someone I hated," she said.

"So I'm just your roommate?"

"No, you are Annie's uncle by blood," she said.

"And what am I to you?"

"The jury is still out. You could be my little brother," she said.

He gritted his teeth. "Can't be. I'm not into incest."

"Go on with the story, please," she said.

"Where was I?"

"Slade hated her," Julie reminded him.

"Okay, he did that. Then, on the Fourth of July, they all went to see the fireworks in Terral, Oklahoma, which is just over the Red River from Ringgold. You'll see next week. We're going there for their sale."

"What?"

"We're going up there for their cattle sale. It's a lot like this one. We'll go the day of the sale because the Luckadeaus support each other that way. Besides, I've got my eye on a couple of heifers Slade is putting on the market. Then the next night, we'll go to the party. That red dress will do fine. They decided to do their sale this year at the Valentine season. Anyway, the kids will go because Hilda and Rosa will be there to babysit for us."

"Who are Hilda and Rosa?"

"Rosa would be the Marita of Beau's ranch. Milli can cook, but she's a rancher and would rather be out helping Beau than staying in the kitchen. Hilda is her grandmother's cook. They'll be there to watch the children in the ranch house for all of us. Don't worry. They are very trustworthy."

"And you are just now telling me all this?" Julie fumed.

"It's a whole week. You can't get ready in a week?"

She gritted her teeth. "Go on with the story."

"At the fireworks, two FBI people showed up with a poster that had Jane's picture on it. They claimed she'd run away from an institution. It was the two assassins, so Granny Nellie sent her and Slade off on a trip to outrun the killers. And in the end, the bad guys got their comeuppance."

"And Slade and Jane came back in love?" Julie asked.

"No, Slade came back and Jane cleaned house."

Julie frowned. "Cleaned house?"

"Yep, she called it cleaning house, anyway. She'd turned twenty-five while she and Slade were on the run, and when they came back, she sold the oil company and the ranch, then asked Granny Nellie for her old job back and five acres in the corner of Slade's property. She paid Granny an enormous sum for it—something like ten times what it was worth—and had a double-wide trailer set on it. It took a while longer, but finally Slade and Jane did admit that they loved each other and got married. It was quite a wedding. She was barefoot and everyone had a wonderful time that day. Lizzy was so happy. Slade didn't have a mean old girlfriend with two little daughters who called my daughter a skunk and made her cry."

Julie's eyes narrowed into slits. "Who did that?"

"I can't even remember her name. The woman Slade was dating when Jane came into the picture had these two little girls and they were just as mean as their mother," Griffin said.

"Point her out to me and I'll snatch enough hair from

her head that she won't be letting her kids make fun of others," Julie fired up angrily.

"The end."

"Okay, okay, so the story is over and yes, I can see that fate had a part in it, and I can also see that you are trying to calm me down because those mean little girls hurt Lizzy's feelings. It's the mother in me," she said.

"I know, darlin'. I see it every day. I live with it. I believe you'd fight a mountain lion for those kids. All three of them." He stood up and extended his hand.

She took it and hauled herself up from the porch only to find her body barely a foot from his. "You are right, I would." She stood on her tiptoes and kissed him.

He was about to pick her up and carry her upstairs to the bedroom when the damn telephone set up a howling ring in the foyer. He dashed off to answer it with her right behind him. Hopefully, Carl hadn't taken a turn for the worst.

He handed the phone off to her when she followed him inside. "It's Mamie for you."

"Hello," Julie said.

"I'm engaged!"

"Congratulations! Who's the lucky man?" Julie said.

"I'm going to be your sister," Mamie singsonged.

"I'm the lucky one. When?" Julie said, but inside, she was moaning that she was the most unlucky of all women. Damn it all, anyway. That was one dandy kiss and they'd been on the verge of even more. Someday she would repay Mamie. Just when she and Eli were making out, she'd call her and ruin the mood.

"Three weeks. Can we have it at the ranch?"

"Mamie and Eli want to get married right here in three weeks. You got a problem with that?"

"Not at all," Griffin said. "I'm going up to bed. You girls can plan weddings all night."

"Wedding. Not plural," Julie said.

He waved off the comment on his way up the stairs.

Julie listened for ten minutes and tried to put on her happy tone the whole time. But inside she felt like a seething, jealous bitch. She let Mamie gush on and on about what all they had to do with the wedding preparations. Then Mamie said Eli had to call his parents and Sally, so she had to go.

Julie put the phone back on the receiver and slid down the wall to sit on the hardwood floor. It had smelled like a rose. It had looked like a rose. It had thorns—but it was still bullshit because Mamie was getting married before Julie.

With a long sigh, she got back up and started up to bed. She opened her door just as Griffin opened his. "Decided I was hungry," he said.

"There's leftovers in the fridge and sandwich makings. Need me to go help with anything?"

"No, I'm smart enough to get a fork into my mouth," he snapped.

Why was he so angry? He and Julie bantered back and forth every day, but why did it upset him that night?

It was because he'd thought the kiss would lead to more. To feel her body next to his was what he wanted and, like a two-year-old, he was upset when he didn't get it.

"Have at it then." She shut the door in his face.

Before she made it to the closet across the room, he slung the door open, kicked it shut with his foot, and crossed the room in a few easy, long strides. He gathered her into his arms and kissed her so hard that her pulse galloped, her imagination ran wild, and every nerve ending in her body quivered in anticipation.

When they broke away, he started as if to leave.

"Good night, Julie," he said.

"Oh no, you don't." She grabbed him and ran her hands up under his T-shirt, pulling him close to her body again. "You're not kissing me like that and then leaving me to toss and turn all night. You started this, partner, and you're going to finish it."

"My room or yours?"

"Right here." She fell backward on the bed and pulled him down with her.

Sparks danced around the room in a bright array of colors. The headboard bumped the wall once and Julie reached up to hold it steady. It was more than sex, deeper than merely a lovemaking session. It was a blending of two hearts and two souls, the kind that transcended age, time, and space. When it was over, they were both panting but reluctant to let go of each other.

Breathlessly, she finally whispered, "What have you got for act two?"

He groaned. "You are insatiable."

"Yes, I am, and don't you forget it."

She rolled over to one side and pulled the edge of the sheet over her body. "Well?"

"Tonight, it's a one-act play, darlin'. If you want a three-act play, you're going to have to have a few more one-acts in between and not wait so long."

"We'll have to see about that." She smiled.

Sometime near dawn, he peeked out into the hallway and tiptoed back to his own room. Julie awoke five minutes before the alarm sounded and rolled out of bed feeling alive, awake, and alert. She hurriedly threw on a robe and rushed down to the kitchen. Coffee was perking and breakfast waiting by the time Griffin made it to the table.

And he acted like he did every single morning.

She could easily have strangled him until his blue eyes popped out on the table like two marbles. How could he behave like the night before had never happened? Easy. It was the same way he had acted after the night in the barn. For weeks now, she'd been waiting for him to make another move and nothing, nada, nil. He must have had the Dr. Jekyll and Mr. Hyde syndrome. One man in the kitchen, another in the bedroom. How on earth was she going to combine the two into one worth having?

The kids dragged themselves to the table, ordered pancakes and sausage, and sipped at orange juice until their blue eyes finally opened. By the time the plates were set before them, they were ready to eat and hurry back up to their rooms to get ready for school. It was Friday, and the weekend was right around the corner. According to Annie, school was fun and she loved to learn, but she missed playing in the backyard all day.

"You might want to call Jane today," Griffin said.

"Why's that?"

"I told you that red dress was all right, but it seems like last year, the ladies were wearing jeans and their fancy western things. I don't want to get in trouble," he said.

She threw a dish towel at him. "It's not what I wear or don't wear that's going to get you in trouble."

"Oh?" He raised an eyebrow. "Are we going to do that analyzing thing?"

"Go to work before I commit justifiable homicide and bury your carcass under the rosebushes," she said.

"A little psychology first. I tend to like to discuss what you're not wearing more than what you are wearing. But that makes you all mad and hot under the collar and you start this tirade about how you are so much older and wiser than the mere boy that I am at twenty-eight." His blue eyes twinkled.

"Out. Get out or I swear I'm throwing things that will hurt," she said.

"Yes, ma'am. My place or yours tonight?" He wiggled a black eyebrow.

"In your dreams, cowboy. Just go," she said.

"The barn, then? Reckon the kids will be all right in the house all alone?"

Her temper rose as well as her voice. "I said get out of here, Griffin, and I mean it."

You wanted him to act different and when he does you rile up in a rage. Make up your mind, woman, her conscience whispered softly.

"I'm gone. See you after school. I swear you are two different women. One when the sun goes down, another when the moon comes up. Are you part werewolf or something?"

She picked up the orange juice decanter and drew back with it. "I'm all bitch right now."

"We'll talk after the sun goes down. I like that Julie better anyway."

He disappeared out the back door, whistling all the way across the yard.

She set the decanter down and huffed. How dare he say that about her being two different people. That was her mantra, not his. Or was it? She tilted her chin up an inch higher. They were both acting like that, weren't they? Because what they had was a physical attraction that could possibly burn itself out in a few months. Their bodies screamed for it; their minds shied away. Hence Dr. Jekyll and Mr. Hyde.

She drove over to Mamie's for a peek at the engagement ring during her lunch break at school. Mamie was still floating around on the clouds way up above that number nine puff of white. She flashed her engagement ring at Julie the moment she walked through the door.

"Lookee, lookee. You're the first one to see it," Mamie said.

"What about your folks?" Julie asked.

"Guess we never did get around to that, did we? Granny raised me and left me this business and her house. I lived with her my whole life. Daddy was her son and he liked women—married eight times by the time he ran his car off the bridge between Terral and Ringgold when he was forty. Momma would have been fifty-one this year, but she OD'd when I was a year old. She was seventeen. Daddy got her pregnant when she was barely sixteen and they got married. He was a whomping eighteen that year. Nineteen when she died. Don't go feeling all sorry for me, though. I had Granny, and she loved me unconditionally. I've had a wonderful life. And now it just gets better. I've got Eli Donavan."

Julie couldn't keep the grin off her face. "You are something else, lady."

"So enough about me. What's goin' on with you and Griffin?"

Julie busied herself sniffing the various new candles. "Nothing much."

"Oh, come on. I can see the sparks between y'all," Mamie said.

"He's soooo..." Julie searched for the right word.

"So what? Handsome as hell? Sweet as honey?"

"Yes, there's that, but so infuriating. By night he's one person. By day another."

"That's life, Julie. At night when there's two people in love, they connect on a different level than they do in front of the rest of the world during the daytime."

"Who died and made you so damn smart?"

"My granny," Mamie said.

"I'm sorry. I didn't mean—"

"Hush. I mean it. She and I had these long, complicated talks from the time I was a little kid. She told me that about men. You ought to know it anyway, being a preacher's daughter. How did your parents act in public?"

"Okay, but—"

"No buts. Now they've been together...what? Thirty-something years, maybe forty? A long time. How do you figure they act in the bedroom?"

"Good God, I don't even want to think about that," Julie said.

"Aren't you glad for two personalities when you think about it? One to share with the world, one to share with just you? Now tell me about the one that's got its roots in the bedroom," Mamie said.

"You first, sister," Julie said.

"He's a stud," Mamie said.

Julie's eyes widened and crimson crept up her neck. "My brother?"

"Your turn," Mamie said.

"I wouldn't know," Julie lied.

"I smell a lie," Mamie said.

"Well, I wouldn't," Julie protested.

"You've got to stop lying or your ass is going to get burned," Mamie said.

"I'm going home. I've had all the sex talk I can stand for one day."

Mamie did something between a shiver and a wiggle. "Just wires me up thinking about it. I am going to call Eli and see if we can meet at a motel for dinner. I'll bring the dessert."

"Mamie!"

"Well, hell's bells, we can't meet in the parsonage until we're properly married. It wouldn't look right, now would it?"

Chapter 18

NELLIE LUCKADEAU AND HER SISTER, ELLEN, HELD COURT under the shade trees in the backyard of the Double L Ranch. Queen Nellie's short, gray hair had been cut in an easy-to-care-for, feathered-back style. She wore her trademark stretch jeans, a blue T-shirt covered with a denim overshirt, and cowboy boots. Queen Ellen's long red tresses were ratted up in a bouffant style. She wore red spandex capri pants, a yellow tank top, and a red sequined sweater.

Julie still had trouble believing two people so different could be sisters. Lizzy and Annie were more alike, and they didn't even share the same mother and father.

"Come on around and pull up a chair with us," Ellen shouted when she saw the Lucky Clover crew arriving. "Alvera has come to visit, too. She's in the kitchen right now getting a cup of coffee. I know she'll be glad to see y'all. We won't have many pretty days like this. Winter ain't through with us yet, but we're going to enjoy this day."

"Katy Scarlett is in the den playing, if you girls want to go in there. Tim and Richie are at the sale with their father, so you might want to go on with Griffin, Chuck," Nellie said.

"Can we go with you, Daddy?" Lizzy asked.

"You have to sit beside me and learn about cows," Griffin said.

"Does Tim and Richie have to learn about cows?"

"The sale barn isn't a place for kids to run and play. If you want to go with me, you have to be still and learn about cows. They'll be sitting with their daddy," Griffin said.

"Then we'll stay here."

"I want to go with you," Chuck said.

"Tell the boys when they get tired of cows to come play with us," Annie said.

"I'll do that," Griffin said.

Julie slapped Griffin's arm. "That was a cop-out."

"It is the absolute truth," Griffin said.

"Hate to agree with a man when us womenfolks are supposed to present a formidable front, but he's right. Kids shouldn't be in the sale barn unless they are there to learn. It's a place of serious business," Nellie said.

"See?" Griffin headed across the backyard.

"Don't you go getting all high-and-mighty with Julie," Ellen yelled. "She wasn't raised on a ranch but she's a fast learner, so watch out."

Julie pulled a green lawn chair across the yard and joined them. "Pretty day. Won't be long until it's so hot, we'll be whinin' for a day like this."

"It don't get too hot for me," Ellen laughed.

Nellie shook her finger at Ellen. "Don't you start about all your men and the hot times you've had. Just because you've got a fresh set of ears to entertain doesn't mean you have to."

Ellen winked. "We'll send her off to get us a beer or a glass of tea in a little while, and then I'll tell you stories that'll straighten that pretty red hair right out straight as a judge on Monday morning."

Alvera pulled up a chair and joined them. "She can do it. Ellen always had a wild streak. Took Nellie to keep her out of trouble most of the time. Don't know what would have happened if they'd both been wild as Ellen."

Ellen pointed at Alvera. "That is definitely the pot calling the kettle black."

"Don't pay any attention to her. I admit I was a hell-cat. Matter of fact, I still am. How are things over at the Lucky Clover?" Alvera said.

"Going well, from what little Griffin says. He doesn't tell me much, but then, I'm a city girl. I wouldn't know if it was making millions or if it was falling into bank-ruptcy," Julie said.

Ellen smiled. "We wasn't askin' about the price of hay or the vet bill."

"Now you shush up, Ellen. These kids don't need us old meddling women to get in their business," Alvera said.

Jane opened the back door and carried a cute little girl outside. The child was the absolute image of her father with just enough of Jane's mouth to make her beautiful. Jane wore jeans and sandals. Ellie was dressed in a pink knit romper with a matching hat and sweater.

Jane put the baby in Nellie's outstretched arms.

"They *might* need meddling old women to get in their business. I can remember two other stubborn folks who benefited from it," Jane said.

"Drag up a chair and entertain us before Ellen gets started telling Julie stories," Nellie said.

"So where's Milli?" Jane asked.

"She dropped off the two kids in the house with Hilda and Rosa and went straight to the barn. She says she's buying a particular heifer today," Ellen said.

"She knows cows as well as her husband. I could probably run Slade a close race when it comes to horses, but a heifer is a heifer to me. I let him take care of that part of the business," Jane explained to Julie.

"And where do you fit in?" Ellen asked Julie.

"I was raised in the city. Well, not really a city. A medium-sized town. Jefferson, Texas, over on the Louisiana border. We drove into Shreveport when we wanted something from the bigger city. I'm a schoolteacher and I understand that isn't such a good thing to be among the Luckadeaus. I reckon I could teach the cows to read or add two-digit numbers, but other than that, I'm out in the cold."

"Never know what you'll be next year at sale time," Jane said.

"In my own house again, I hope," Julie answered.

"Oh?" Nellie stopped baby talking and looked at Julie.

"I'm thinking about putting a double-wide trailer over on my five acres. Lizzy and Chuck can stay with me on the days they're not in school. The kids will have a fit when they don't get to spend every night in the same house, but they'll adjust. I'm just hoping Chuck gets to stay with Griffin," Julie said.

"Ten bucks." Ellen looked at Nellie.

"Pro or con?"

"Pro. She's sassy and she'll listen to reason instead of her heart. She'll do just what she said—put a trailer on her own land. That's pro," Ellen said.

"You got it. Double the ante? Twenty? I say it won't happen," Nellie said.

"Fifty. I live in Saint Jo and I'm better at meddling

than either one of you. Put me in for fifty on the con," Alvera said.

"What are they talking about?" Julie asked Jane.

"They bet on everything. I couldn't tell you how many times a twenty-dollar bill floated from Ellen's bra to Nellie's while Slade and I were figuring things out. Right now they're betting on whether you'll set a trailer on your acres or whether you and Griffin will stop fighting the inevitable and get married," Jane said. "Hey, put me in for twenty. Con."

"What's Ellen betting?" Julie asked.

"Pro. I'm betting you put that trailer over there on your own five acres and have a passionate affair with Griffin for a year and then marry him. You're smart enough to see if the sex is as good in a year as it is right here at first," Ellen said.

"I'll see your twenties and raise each of you five. I'm betting twenty-five that I put a trailer on my five acres and never marry Griffin," Julie said.

"Hey, hey," Jane said. "You're a strong woman but even the mighty fall, so Ellen and I will see your bet. You move out of the ranch house and into your own place, we owe you twenty-five."

"Not me, if you move out of the ranch house, you owe me fifty. I'm not playing with small potatoes," Alvera said.

"Fifty to you then," Julie said.

Milli climbed over the yard fence at the far corner. Two little blond-haired boys and one red-haired boy crawled between the rails and hurried off into the house.

"Who's betting with Ellen and what are we betting on?" she asked.

"Pro, Julie moves out of the ranch house and into a double-wide. Con, she marries Griffin by summertime," Jane said.

"How much?" Milli asked.

"Julie raised the stakes to twenty-five and says she's pro. She doesn't want to marry our cousin-in-law or even have a passionate affair with him. And to think we didn't like her because she was out to take Griffin to the cleaners," Jane said.

"Well, she is a schoolteacher and they can't be trusted. Put me in for twenty-five. Con. She's already been to bed with him. The fighting isn't over and the votes aren't in, but I'll say anyone who has wild, passionate sex with a Luckadeau isn't going to move out and leave it behind."

"Milli!" Julie gasped.

"Truth is truth. Pour chocolate or cow shit on it and it's still the truth when you get out the garden hose and wash it down. Griffin sent me to bring the boys in to play with Lizzy and Annie and to bring Julie back to the barn. He says you need to see what it's like to be on this end of a sale. I already bought my heifer. Griffin is spitting nails because I outbid his sorry ass," Milli said.

"Well, that's just great. I have to go contend with him after you make him mad," Julie said.

"Five. Pro." Ellen looked at Nellie.

Nellie shook her head. "I ain't losin' my money."

Julie followed Milli a few steps and looked back. "What were they betting on that time?"

"Whether you already know about that wild, passionate Luckadeau sex," Nellie said.

"Don't put me down on that one," Milli yelled as she went over the fence.

"You are all crazy women," Julie said.

"Probably, but ain't it fun? And only a Luckadeau man could put a glow on a woman's face like you got, so I'm not losing my money betting you haven't had sex. It's pretty evident that you have," Milli said.

Julie just smiled.

"See, you aren't even denying it," Milli said.

"I don't kiss and tell. It might have happened, but then it might not have," she said.

"Don't play coy with me, Julie Donavan. Is he any good?"

"Only a Luckadeau woman knows about the glow, so you tell me."

Milli laughed.

"I'm going to grow up and be like Ellen," Julie said.

"Then you'd better lose the bets and get on with life. That woman has had at least four husbands, and I wouldn't want to see the tally sheet on her affairs. It'd take the rest of your life to catch up to Ellen. She's forgotten more than you'd ever know even if you started right now."

"Ellen?" Julie couldn't believe Milli. Maybe the woman still didn't like her and was putting her in a precarious situation with the three older women.

"She grew up in the casual-sex, burn-the-bra-and-to-hell-with-it-all era. She can tell stories that would put an erotic romance writer to shame, and most of them begin with, 'Well, I bought a bottle of Jack Daniel's and guess where it led me.' She'll never grow up."

Julie smiled. "I hope not. She's a sweetheart."

"She's so much fun and she'd do anything for anyone, but honey, she's not a saint," Milli said. "There is Griffin up there. First row on the balcony. Stairs are that way." She pointed. "I'm going to the other side where Beau is looking at a few calves."

Julie climbed the steps up to the balcony overlooking the sale floor. Griffin motioned her over but kept a few inches of space between them when she sat down. Two elderly men in bibbed overalls were on his other side. Griffin wore jeans and a faded blue T-shirt. His straw hat rested on the seat between him and the older men. He couldn't think if Julie was touching him, not even shoulder to shoulder, and he really wanted to buy a particular heifer.

"This is Julie Donavan. Julie, this is Harvey Limens and Tom Miles." He made introductions when she sat down.

"Pleased to meet you," they said in unison.

"Likewise," she said.

"He says you're his lucky charm. His cousin's wife got a heifer he wanted and he says it's because you weren't here," Harvey said.

"I did not." Griffin raised his voice just slightly.

"Well, you damn sure should have," Tom said. "Honey, if he don't want you to be his lucky charm, you come on over here and sit by me. I'd even pay you to be my lucky charm."

"Man got a lucky streak in his hair shouldn't need a lucky charm," Harvey teased. "Wish I had all that black hair with a white streak in it. Maybe I'd get the pretty red-haired girls."

"Old man, you'd just like to have any color hair up there on that bald head of yours," Tom said.

"You're one to talk. All you got is a monk's rim left."

Old men or old women—seemed they delighted in pestering each other. Julie wondered if Harvey and Tom had already put down five- or ten-dollar bets on whether she'd bring Griffin good luck.

Slade and two of his hands herded a massive Angus bull into the center ring. Griffin leaned forward, placing his forearms on the rail in front of him, and studied the creature while they walked him around the pen.

Julie studied the man. He was the best thing since ice cream on a stick and she was in love. A quick pass through memory lane in a hayloft and her hands went clammy.

"Biddin' or passin'?" Harvey asked Griffin.

"Passin'. He's a fine old boy, but I'm not in need of new blood right now," Griffin answered.

"I'd buy him just to stand out there in the pasture and look pretty," Tom said.

"Not if I wanted him," Harvey said.

"We going to get into it?"

Harvey leaned forward and raised his hand when the auctioneer started the bidding. "I think we might."

"What are they doing?" Julie whispered.

Her warm breath was so close to his ear that passion stirred in his blood. He forced himself to think about something else. The heifer he wanted was coming up for bid soon, and if he started thinking about Julie, Milli would bid it right out from under him. After he bought the cow, Julie had better be careful or he'd have her naked in the hayloft so fast she'd wonder if she'd ever even dressed that morning.

He whispered back, "Bidding against each other.

They're both richer than Midas. Harvey is from West Texas. Milli grew up on the ranch next to his. Tom is from East Texas. They're old-time sale barn buddies."

Tom raised his hand to outbid Harvey and glanced over his shoulder at Griffin and Julie. "Y'all don't be talkin' about us. Pay attention to each other and not to us. I come up here next year, I expect to see a baby."

"Baby cow?" Julie asked.

"No, a baby Luckadeau."

"Stop your meddling, old man. They can take care of their own business without you," Harvey said.

"Will you save me a dance tomorrow night?" Tom asked Julie.

"Going once, going twice," the auctioneer said.

Tom raised his hand to up the bid. "You old fart. You nearly caught me off guard. Now that bull is going to cost you double."

"Why are they doing that?" Julie asked.

"It's a game from here on out and benefits Slade. Neither of them needs the bull. They both want it to win the game. It's kind of like the pile in the middle of a table at a poker game."

"But the money?" She gasped when she heard the bid go in excess of five thousand dollars.

"It'll get higher. That's one of Slade's registered bulls. He'll go for at least ten thousand and maybe higher if these two keep up a bidding war. Slade has raised him and about ten others for this day."

"Mercy. How much does a sale like this bring?" Julie asked.

"Ours brought almost three quarters of a million. Slade is hoping to top a million today."

Julie heard the big numbers but what stirred her heart was one little word...*ours*.

"How much do the cows go for?" she asked as the single little four-letter word rattled around in her head.

"Depends. A thousand bottom rate. Five probably, tops. Milli paid four for the one I wanted."

"Why'd you want that particular one?"

"She's a good breeder. She'd be an asset."

"I'll never learn all this stuff," she mumbled.

Ours. Yours. Pro. Con.

Harvey outbid Tom with a final bid of twelve thousand dollars. Tom swore that when the next bull came up for grabs, he was having it no matter how much Harvey dug out of his hip pocket. They headed toward the refreshment table set up in a tent outside the barn. Harvey said that he had a hankering for a barbecue sandwich, and Tom said he was crazy for eating that kind of food when there was chocolate cake.

Griffin looked over at Julie. "Don't let the old guys rile you. It's just their way. They've been teasing me every year since Dian left. At the sale parties, they've tried to fix me up with every woman from barely out of jailbait age to Ellen's buddies."

"Nellie and Ellen are just as bad," Julie whispered.

"Want to play along with them? Pretend you are truly with me the next couple of days. Don't slap me if I throw an arm around you like we're a couple. Let's give them something to talk about," Griffin said.

"I've got a bet going with the ladies," she admitted.

"What's the pro and the con?"

"Doesn't matter. It would help me win if we

snookered them into believing we were together. Make it a lot sweeter when I take their money," she said.

He extended his hand. "Deal, then?"

She shook it. "Darlin', if you ain't the most handsome thing here, I'll eat my hat," she drawled.

"Hey, make it believable. They can smell a lie a mile away."

"Deal," she said simply, but she didn't drop his hand.

Harvey and Tom were back in a few minutes, this time interested in buying a different bull. It took fifteen minutes, but Tom wound up with the high bid. When Slade led the next heifer into the ring, Tom looked over at Harvey, who shook his head.

Griffin put both his hands on the bar in front of him and began to bid, Milli working against him from across the barn. When the dust settled, Griffin owned the heifer for three thousand dollars and Milli waved good-naturedly, yelling above the din that the next one was hers. Beau pointed at his chest, telling Griffin that the next one was his.

"Why don't y'all just come over here any day of the week and buy what you want from Slade?" Julie asked.

"And ruin the fun, honey?" Tom leaned around Harvey and cocked his head to one side.

"For the whole next year, these cousins will gee-haw about who got the best deal. When that heifer Griffin just bought calves, he'll call Milli and swear it's the biggest, best calf ever born with the Lucky Clover brand and it's too bad she doesn't have such a big old bull calf to raise for her sale," Harvey explained.

"And when they get together for their family affairs, they'll all talk about how they're raising a calf that'll bring half of Fort Knox at the next sale. It's ranching, honey," Tom said.

"It's all Greek to me," Julie said.

"I'm not interested in anything now until late afternoon. You want a tour of the farm?" Griffin asked.

"If you don't want to tour it with him, I'll show you around. Matter of fact, you want to see something worthwhile, just crawl up in my pickup tomorrow night after the dance and I'll show you a real ranch," Tom said.

"Ah, don't make Griff jealous. He'd feel bad if we was to show her our spreads against his little ole chigger-and-tick operation," Harvey said.

She shook her head and smiled at them. "He is the jealous type. Gets mad every time I look at another man. Should've seen him when I danced more than once with Alvie Marlon at his sale."

"Now there's a man you shoulda gone home with. Owns half of Wyoming and could buy the other half if he wanted it," Tom said.

"And he's good-looking." Julie kept it going.

"Are you going with me or not?" Griffin's tone was short.

"Aha, we've made him mad. See, what'd I tell you? I look at you two handsome hunks and he gets all testy," Julie said.

Tom's blue eyes glittered. "Shame, ain't it?"

Griffin took her hand and led her toward the stairs. "I don't get mad when you look at another man. At least not if he's eighty years old."

"Is this conversation for real or is it part of the deal?"

"You decide." He kept her hand in his and they walked toward another barn closer to the house. They were in full view of the ladies, now several strong in the backyard. Kids ran in and out of the house. Lizzy and Annie, always together and easy to spot with that flash of white in their black hair. Chuck making friends and fitting in like he was a true Luckadeau.

"I don't care enough to decide," she lied.

"Okay, then you won't care if I start dating someone else?"

"You're a grown man. Do whatever you like," she said, but her tone had an edge.

"This is the barn where Jane took Lizzy to get her away from those mean kids," he said as he led her inside a hay barn. "Listen. Be very quiet."

Julie stood perfectly still, almost afraid to move. She'd been out to the barn a few times at the Lucky Clover, searching for the girls when they went looking for their kittens. Once she looked up to find a rat the size of King Kong staring down at her from a rafter. She had backed slowly out of the barn and hadn't been back.

"Are there rats in here?" she whispered.

"Probably. That's why we keep cats in barns—so the rats won't take over," he said.

"Then let's go." She shivered.

"You're afraid of a rat? Damn, woman! I didn't even think Lucifer could scare you."

She nodded slowly and deliberately. "The devil is nothing compared to a rat."

"Don't worry. Jane has kittens and momma cats in here. They'll take care of any rat that comes along. Let's go up in the loft, where you can see out across the lay of the land," he said.

"Why were we being quiet and whispering?" she asked.

"So we could hear kittens. There might be a new bunch hiding in the hay," he said.

Julie smiled as she followed him up the ladder. That Griffin even thought about finding kittens to show her endeared him even more to her heart. She sat down beside him on a bale of hay back in the shade. The loft doors were wide open and she could see for what seemed like miles. Gently rolling hills. Black cattle. Mesquite trees. A few horses grazing in the distance. Wide-open Texas spaces and lots of family.

"What are you thinking about so serious?" he asked.

"All this Luckadeau family," she said.

"When God said 'Go ye forth and multiply,' I think he was talking to the first Luckadeau from down in Louisiana. Then there were lots and lots of sons, as many as the grains of sand beside the sea, or something like that. You could quote it better than me since you're the preacher's daughter," he said.

"You've heard the stories about the preacher's kids, haven't you?"

"You tellin' me you were wild and woolly?"

"No, but I wasn't a saint, either," she said.

"Ever cheat on your husband?"

"Not one time. We were divorced, even though it wasn't final, when I met your brother," she said. "How 'bout you? Ever cheat on Dian?"

He shook his head and pursed his lips. "Didn't even kiss another woman. Guess she did more than I did."

He slid over a few inches until his thigh touched hers. "Kiss me."

"They can't see us. We don't have to play the game when we're in here," she said.

"I'm not playing a game right now, Julie," he said huskily.

She looked up and his eyes were all dreamy. She put one arm around his neck and the other on his chest and kissed him. She didn't know if she could endure fifty years of marriage to a man who rocked her world with his touch and whose kisses made her insides all soft and mushy, one who with a look made her wish she was in bed with him. Surely that kind of fire would burn itself out before their lifetimes were spent...or would it?

"Good practice for when I make those women think we are really a couple," she said when they broke away.

"I wasn't practicing for anything," he said. "I wanted to kiss you. I'd like to do even more, but there's too many people and we'd get caught for sure."

"You ready?" she asked.

"For what?"

"To go back to the sale. To go see about the children. To whatever. I'm not staying another minute in this hayloft with you, Griffin. It's too damn dangerous. I'd just die if someone caught us making love in the hay."

"Why?"

"Because...you know why. They already think I'm a hussy, and they're all just now beginning to treat me like I'm not out to take you to the cleaners," she said.

She headed for the ladder leading down and was in the doorway of the barn before he caught up to her. He grabbed her hand, and together they walked toward the yard fence, where he opened the gate for her.

Lizzy and Annie came at them in a dead run, both talking at once, telling how they'd got to hold Ellie and how cute she was and Jane said they could play with her some more.

"And when are y'all goin' to have one of them babies to play with? They're better than Barbie dolls," Annie said.

Julie blushed.

Griffin combed his hair back with his fingertips and stammered.

Granny Nellie burst out laughing.

Ellen threw up her hands defensively. "I didn't put them up to that, I promise."

Lizzy crossed her arms and tapped her foot on the grass. "Well, when?"

"That's a hard question. Can I think about it and get back to you with an answer?" Julie said seriously.

"That's what you always say. Jane says it takes nine months to make one of them babies, and that's a long time to wait. If you think about it, it will be even longer and I don't want to wait. I want one of them babies at our house," Annie said.

"You want a baby or a pony more?" Griffin asked.

Annie turned the tables. "That's a hard question and I'll have to think about it."

"Not me. I gots a pony and I want a baby," Lizzy declared.

"We'll see," Griffin said.

"That's what you always say when the answer is no. Well, then I want one for in my Easter basket," Lizzy kept on.

Griffin squatted down beside her and made her look in his eyes. "This is a subject that is embarrassing, Elizabeth. I want you to quit talking about it right now or Julie might decide to move," he whispered.

Lizzy's chin quivered, and she hugged Julie so tightly that she practically squeezed the air from her. "I won't never say nothing again, please don't move, Julie. And Ellen did too say something. She asked me and Annie if we didn't want one of them babies at our house."

"Aha," Julie exclaimed. "The plot thickens."

"Pro?" Griffin looked at her.

"She's trying to protect her twenty-five dollars," Julie whispered.

"Old vixen." Griffin grinned.

"Go play, girls. We'll be leaving in a little while, but we'll come back for the party tomorrow night," Griffin said. "I bet you'll get to play with Ellie so much you'll get tired of babies."

"Not me," Annie said.

"Not me," Lizzy echoed and ran back to the blanket under the shade tree where Ellie was propped up with pillows.

"Momma, I need to talk to you," Annie whispered.

Julie dropped down on her knees. "What is it?"

"We aren't moving, are we? I don't ever want to move. I'd be so sad if we didn't live with Lizzy and Chuck would cry, only boys aren't supposed to cry and he'd do it at night so you couldn't hear and we just can't move."

Griffin gathered Annie up in his arms and hugged her tightly to his chest. "Don't you worry, honey. We couldn't live without you at the ranch. You are part of it. So go play and don't think about it."

She kissed him on the cheek and joined Lizzy.

"Why'd you say that?" Julie asked.

"Because I don't want her to think she caused you to move out with her wanting a baby in the house. She's just a little girl. She shouldn't have to worry about adult things at the age of five."

"But we might move out and you just promised that we wouldn't," Julie said.

"No, I said we couldn't live without her at the ranch," Griffin said.

"You know how she took it," Julie said. "I don't ever lie to her."

"You accusing me of lying? Lizzy and I would have a hard time living without her now that we've had her. You telling me that you could separate them and live without Lizzy? If you are, then you've damned sure got me fooled."

"That's not what I'm saying." She bristled.

"How's my investment over there?" Milli yelled.

"Looking like a pro situation to me," Julie said.

"Ah, don't be calling the war won over one little fight," Ellen yelled.

"You want to tell me about this bet?" Griffin frowned.

"Darlin', your fragile little ego couldn't take it." She put her arms around his neck and hugged him tightly.

He frowned. "I'm going back to the sale barn. You coming with me?"

"Think I'll stay here for a while. Kiss me on the forehead so they'll think we've made up," she said.

"I can do a damn sight better than that," he said. He wrapped her up in his arms and laid one on her that made all the women swoon.

She joined the circle of women, pulling up a chair and sitting down not far from where Lizzy and Annie entertained Ellie. Her lips felt bee-stung and her face was crimson as she thought about other kisses and where they'd led. From there, her mind went to what happened when she'd let desire have its way before. She'd had a baby girl.

She realized she hadn't used birth control when she'd had sex with Griffin. Hadn't had any need for it in six years, so it'd slipped her mind completely. She felt all the blood leave her face. Now wasn't that the most immature act she'd ever pulled? She could blame the night with Graham on too much to drink. Both times with Griffin she'd been stone-cold sober.

In my defense, she thought, *I quit using anything years ago when Derrick and I decided to have a child. Or rather when I decided we were having one. Looking back, I don't think he cared one way or the other and probably was a good thing since it was his fault we didn't have one. I was all pumped up on fertility drugs when I got pregnant with Annie. It's a wonder she wasn't three or four or even six little dark-haired kids with white streaks in their hair. Now wouldn't it have been a royal hoot if I had had more than one and some were boys, blessed with the Luckadeau blond hair and blue eyes? In the same nursery with black-haired girls. That would have created a stir, now wouldn't it?*

"Whatever are you thinking about?" Milli asked.

"Nothing," Julie said.

"I bet it has something to do with whatever happened in those nine minutes they were in the barn," Ellen said.

"Actually it had to do with a very different nine minutes," Julie admitted.

"Want to tell us about it?" Ellen asked.

"No, I want you to tell me about why you don't drive anymore. Griffin said it's a good story," Julie said.

"Ahh, honey, that's a good tale. Sit back and let me

tell you about the time I bought a bottle of Jack Daniel's and met a man with a Corvette that had enough get-up-and-go to do a hundred miles an hour—the car, not the man. He was older than me and couldn't go but about seventy-five miles an hour."

Chapter 19

THE NIGHT AIR WAS PLEASANT. THE BAND HAD ALREADY geared up. Through the open barn doors, Julie could see people lined up at a buffet table. Slade's sale party was a lot more casual than the one they'd thrown at the Lucky Clover, and Julie liked it much better. From the way everyone in the barn was dressed, she was surely glad she'd visited with Jane before she got dressed for the evening, and she was already planning what their sale would be like the next year.

At least she was planning until she realized what she was doing and brought herself up short. By the next year, she'd be in her own place, and the Luckadeau women would take care of the sale. She might be invited, but then again, if Melinda had her way, maybe not.

Griffin wore a pale-blue western shirt, starched and creased Wranglers, a tooled belt with a big silver rodeo buckle, and his dress cowboy boots. His hair was a touch too long, but Julie loved it like that. The white streak flowed back and reminded her of Johnny Depp's in *Sweeney Todd*.

Julie had made a dash through Cavender's in Nocona and picked up a pair of boots, a western-cut blouse in lime green, and a new pair of Cruel Girl jeans. Her red curls framed her face and her mossy-green eyes sparkled. Griffin thought she was elegant in the red dress at their sale party, but that night he fairly well strutted into the barn with her on his arm.

Granny Nellie and Ellen were the first to greet them. Ellen wore her bright-red dyed hair up in a twist with lots of height and hair spray, and a swirling skirt in bright colors with a western ruffled blouse tucked into it. Nellie wore jeans and a bright-red blouse and boots.

While the Lucky Clover party had reminded her of a sheik's tent in the desert, this atmosphere felt like a real barn dance. Buffet tables were set up with fried chicken, steaks, baked potatoes, and so many side dishes and desserts Julie couldn't begin to count them.

"It's lookin' good. I changed my bet to con. You won't make it until summer," Ellen told Julie.

"Don't count your chickens before they're hatched and don't believe everything you see," Nellie said.

"What?" Griffin asked.

"It's a girl thing, but I'm thinkin' us old girls might have met our match," Nellie said.

"Are you talkin' about Julie?"

"Well, darlin', she ain't talkin' about you," Ellen said.

Nellie changed the subject. "The sale made even more than what Slade was hoping for, so we're all happy tonight."

"You two go get in line and eat. And, Julie, you better keep him real close tonight. There's lots of pretty women here who'd like to touch that white streak and see if it's as soft as it looks—or else touch something else on his body. He's a fine-lookin' cowboy," Ellen said.

"Yes, ma'am," Julie said with a wink.

"Want to tell me what that was all about?" Griffin asked.

They lined up behind Jane and Slade.

"Nope. I'm hungry."

"Me too, and I'm not even mad," Jane said.

"Thank God. We'd have to tell the caterers to put another steer on the spit if this girl was angry," Slade said.

Jane blew a kiss toward him. "He's telling the gospel according to Jane Luckadeau. When I get mad, I get hungry. First time he took me out to eat, he found out about that."

"Oh?" Julie asked.

"She'd just decked the lady I'd been dating," Slade said.

"Must be the curse of the Luckadeaus, whether we have blond or black hair," Griffin said.

"You hit his girlfriend?" Jane asked Julie.

"No, but I wanted to wipe up the highway with that bitch. She spanked Lizzy for not wanting to eat carrots. I still get mad when I think about it. What were you thinking, Griffin, dating a witch like that?" Julie asked.

Griffin threw both hands up, palm out. "Hey, I sent her packing when I found out, didn't I?"

"You should have done more than that. Call the caterers and tell them to bring out more fried chicken, Slade. Just thinking about someone hitting Lizzy makes me angry," Jane said.

Slade rolled his eyes toward the rafters. "She's got a special place in her heart for Lizzy. They made fast friends the first time Slade brought her to the ranch. She actually wanted Ellie to be born with black hair with a white streak. I told her she'd done latched on to the wrong Luckadeau for that."

Griffin's angular cheeks filled with color. At one time, he had thought maybe he'd talk to Slade about dating Jane since she'd been so good to Lizzy, but by the time he got up the nerve, it was too late. It was already evident by then that Slade would be the Luckadeau who wound up with Jane.

Slade and Jane piled their plates high and disappeared into the crowd, looking for a place to sit at one of the eight-foot tables covered with red-and-white-checkered oilcloth. When Griffin and Julie had filled their plates, Mamie motioned them over to the table she and Eli shared. When they sat down, Julie wasn't a bit surprised to see Milli and Beau and Jane and Slade at the same table.

"You should have gotten the T-bone," Jane told Julie.

"I thought you were having chicken," Julie said.

She cut a bite-sized piece of medium rare steak. She forked it and held it across the table toward Julie. "Here, taste this. Isn't it the best Angus you've ever eaten?"

Julie opened her mouth.

"Don't you dare say yes," Griffin said.

"The best Angus you ever put in your mouth better be from the Lucky Clover," Mamie whispered.

"Second best," Julie said after she'd swallowed.

"Almost had her, Griff," Jane laughed.

Among the men, talk went to the sale and Eli listened; among the women, to the upcoming wedding and Julie listened.

"So is the wedding dress a big ball gown with layers of fluff?" Jane asked.

"Hell no," Mamie said. "I'm not blind, girls. When I step in front of the mirror, I don't see a size five. I'm a healthy sixteen, and this little chubby girl would look a sight in that much fluff. I'm thinking a long brocade skirt with a matching jacket," she said.

"With red roses?" Jane asked.

"And hearts everywhere," Mamie said.

"What is Julie wearing?" Milli asked.

Julie hadn't even thought about her dress in the ceremony. "Me?"

"She's wearing the red dress she wore to the winter sale and she's carrying a bouquet of roses with white ribbons and pearls dangling from it. And while we're at it, would you two please serve the cakes?"

"Be glad to," Milli said.

Jane nodded and reached across the table to steal a chicken wing from Julie's plate.

"Be careful. We might've grown that chicken on the Lucky Clover," Julie teased.

"Best chicken I've had tonight," Jane said. "Am I going to win?"

Mamie's eyes lit up. "Win what? Are we bettin?"

Jane leaned forward and whispered in Mamie's ear.

"Put me in for twenty-five. Pro," Mamie said.

"You're going to be a preacher's wife and you are gambling?" Julie exclaimed.

"Which reminds me, I think it's time for us to carry on the tradition, since there's enough of us now," Jane said.

"What tradition?" Milli asked.

Mamie raised her hand like a grade-school girl. "I know. I know. Bridge night. And I'm all for it."

"Bridge night?" Milli asked.

"Once a month on a certain evening, we leave the kids with the husbands and meet somewhere for a girls' night out. Play a little bridge. Eat some chips and cookies. Drink a few…Dr. Peppers," Jane said.

"I'm the one with a store that has a back room, so I'm offering for the place. How about the third Thursday of each month? Julie and Jane bring the cookies the first time," Mamie said.

"Bridge?" Julie sighed. "I'm not good at bridge."

"Ellen's bridge. I think you and I both made the comment we were going to grow up to be just like her," Jane said.

Mamie cupped her hand over Julie's ear and whispered, "Poker night."

Julie's eyes sparkled. "For real?"

"Absolutely. Bring your purse, darlin'," Jane said.

Griffin caught the tail end of the women's conversation during a lull in the men's. "For what? Why would she bring her purse to something?"

"Don't ask. It's got something to do with a ladies' night out they are planning once a month," Eli said.

"And I think I heard something about chips and cookies," Beau said.

"And beer?" Slade said.

"I said Dr. Pepper," Jane protested.

"Yes, but it was after a hesitation," Eli said.

"You were supposed to be talking about cattle and ranchin'," Julie said.

"We are smarter than you think," Griffin told her.

"You ladies going to need a designated driver?" Eli asked.

Ellen leaned back from the next table. "If they do, I'll be glad to come around and bring them all home. Can I drive your truck, Slade?"

"Hey, we'll be able to drive ourselves. A preacher's wife wouldn't get sloshed playing bridge." Mamie grinned.

"And there ain't no way you are driving any of the Double L vehicles, Ellen," Slade said.

"Spoilsport." Ellen tilted her chin up and went back to the conversation between the four elderly ladies at her table.

The easy bantering went on until they'd finished their food and Slade wiped his mouth, stood up, and asked Jane to join him for a dance. As Julie watched them, the green-eyed monster attacked her again. They moved in graceful, fluid motion, not missing a single beat of the music and looking at each other as though they were still madly in love. That's what she wanted next time around: for a man to look at her like that on the dance floor and in the bedroom.

"Shall we show them up?" Beau asked.

Milli held up her hand, and the next two Luckadeaus took center stage. Milli melted into Beau's arms, and he looked down at his brown-eyed angel.

Julie sighed.

Eli held out his hand to Mamie. "May I have this dance, my lady?"

"You two-step?" she asked.

"Yes, ma'am, with the best of them," he said.

"I'm getting more than I bargained for." She grinned.

Julie was very proud of her brother in that moment. He might not wear boots and a western-cut shirt, but he executed a fine two-step in his pleated black slacks, pale-green, button-down, collared shirt, and loafers. Mamie fit well with Eli and they looked happy. For the first time since his wife died, Eli had life back in his eyes.

"Shall we?" Griffin asked.

"Is this part of the deal?"

"It's anything you want it to be. I just want to hold

you in my arms and dance with you. I want to be the one with you like they're with each other," he said.

"I'd love to dance," she said.

He led her to the floor, and in minutes everyone else stood on the sides, keeping time to the music as Griffin's white streak and Julie's bright-red hair were a blur to the beat of a fast song. Her heart thumped in her chest like a bass drum by the time the song ended, and everyone clapped for them.

"You are really good," Julie said breathlessly. "And now I need something to drink."

"And a bit of fresh air?" Griffin said.

"Part of the deal?" she asked.

"Like I said, Julie, tonight can be anything you want it to be. It's your call."

"Then I want a Coors in a bottle and a few minutes outside the barn and to hell with the deal," she said.

She noticed Nellie and Ellen both smiling as they carried their bottles out of the lights and into the shadows. So they thought they were on the winning side of the bet, did they? Well, they were dead wrong. She'd have all their money and Mamie's, too. One hundred dollars free money to buy hot-pink towels for her brand-new trailer house.

Griffin hopped up on the tailgate of a black pickup truck and patted the place to his side. "Come on up and rest your feet."

She hitched a hip up and wiggled her way into a seated position. She tipped the beer bottle back and took a heavy slug. The burp that followed was not ladylike.

"Excuse me," she said.

"Not bad manners, just good beer," he chuckled.

"Thank you."

"Okay, this has been a lot of fun, yesterday and today, Julie. But where are we really?" he asked.

"Backward," she said.

"Want to explain?"

"Not really but I will. We live together already, only it's for the children, and we've been to bed with each other, so there's that relationship, but we both fight it," she said.

"Two times doesn't constitute a relationship, and I quit fighting it a long time ago. Future now, please," he said.

"I could love you so easy," she said.

His heart refused to beat for two seconds. She'd actually said the words out loud. He leaned over and kissed her passionately.

She pulled back and went on. "But."

"Does there have to be a but?" he asked.

"Yes, definitely. Milli and I were talking at the sale yesterday. She and Beau got everything turned around backward, too. Baby first. You know that. Just before their wedding, her mother sent them on a three-day honeymoon."

"I never heard about this," Griffin said.

"She sent them to a remote cabin on the beach in Mexico for a few days. Know why?"

"Have no idea, but I like the idea."

"It was for them to see if they liked each other."

"But they were in love. From the minute he realized who she was and who Katy was, they were in love," Griffin said.

"Yes, they were. Like I said, I could love you. I already like you," Julie said.

"But are we fighting each other or fighting against love?" he asked.

"Who knows?"

"We're both passionate. It's the way we are. We fight with passion. We make love with passion," he said.

"People don't live in the same house every day and always agree. I argue with Mamie, and you know what happened when I first met Milli and Jane. It took a while for us to even be civil. We're just now forming a friendship. Let's work on the friendship thing awhile and see where it leads."

"Okay." He nodded.

"You're willing to do that?"

"I am. Friends don't sleep together, do they?" he asked.

"I'm afraid they don't."

"It ain't going to be easy. Frustration can make for some damn big fights. During this friends-only time, do we each get to date other people?" Griffin said.

Julie's eyes narrowed into slits and she set her mouth in a firm line. Thinking about Griffin in the arms of another woman turned her pea green with jealousy. However, the thought of falling in love and promising to love him until death parted them scared the crap out of her. How could they ever separate after they'd said the vows in front of Lizzy, Annie, and hopefully Chuck? All three kids had faced enough in their five years without going through divorce.

"Do you want to date other people?" Julie asked.

"Do you?"

"I don't know. There are a lot of unattached, blond cowboys in that barn."

It was Griffin's turn to have jealousy rear its head. "I don't want you to date, so I won't either."

"Okay, then that's rule one," Julie agreed.

"Any others I should know about?"

"Yes. You've got to start talking to me. Tell me when your mother and sister are visiting the ranch or when there's going to be a big sale or when we're going to a party, and give me some warning. If nothing else, write it on the calendar," she said.

"I guess I can do that," he said.

"And"—she looked at him and his smoldering, blue eyes locked with hers—"you can't look at me like that. Friends don't undress each other with their eyes."

He ran a hand down her backbone. "How about with something more?"

Shivers sent goose bumps all the way to her scalp.

"I think it's time we went back inside," she said.

"Chicken?"

"You bet I am. Scared shitless," she said breathlessly.

"I won't hurt you, Julie. I promise."

"I'm not afraid of you, Griffin. I'm afraid of me."

"I've got a confession. You are a fantastic mother to the children. You are strong, and you never back down when you are right. I've liked you for a long time," he said.

"Then I suppose we have to see if love and like will bond and hold well enough we can trust it to keep us through tough times as well as good ones," she said.

"Let me know when you figure it out. Ready to go back inside and show 'em how to dance?" he asked.

She was amazed. He didn't pressure for more. He admitted he liked her. Had she truly met her knight in shining armor? Was there such a thing as fate for her?

"I am," she said simply.

They danced until midnight, then woke the children up from a pallet on the floor in the den and listened to them prattle all the way home about their cousins, from Ellie to Tim and Richie and a dozen others Julie had yet to sort out in her mind. The Luckadeaus had indeed gone forth and multiplied, and most of them were ranchers. She'd met Slade's uncle and his two sons who weren't into the ranching business, but even they knew how to enjoy a barn dance.

The kids were already dressed in their pajamas and went right to bed without a fuss, leaving Julie and Griffin in the foyer.

"I really did have a good time the past two days," Julie said.

"So did I, and we did it without too much fighting," Griffin said.

"Guess we did. Does that mean after a while, we'll get passive and—"

"Julie, there's enough heat between us to last two lifetimes. I've never felt like this about another woman," he said.

That sucked every ounce of breath out of her lungs. It came damn near to straightening her hair. Derrick had never said something like that and certainly not with so much passion in his eyes. Graham had certainly not said anything like that. And the two young men that she'd had flings with in college wouldn't have had the maturity even to know such language.

"And while we're on the subject, I'm a thinker, even if I sometimes forget to tell you about events and things. I've talked to my lawyer and he's drawing up papers. Should we ever fall in like and love and are willing to admit it, I want to adopt Annie. She's a Luckadeau and, as Graham's biological child and my adopted one, she will have equal rights to the Lucky Clover with Lizzy. They'll inherit together when we are ready to step down."

More air left Julie's lungs and she gasped. "Annie is a Donavan."

"Annie has the Donavan name. But look at her. She's a Luckadeau."

"I think I'm going up to bed on that note before we end the good days with a big fight," she said.

"Think about it. I'm in no hurry. You can have until next summer or two years."

He waited until she was on the second step and touched her arm. When she turned, he planted a kiss on her lips that almost caused her to throw caution to the wind and propose to him on the spot.

"Think about that, too." He whistled all the way to the kitchen.

Sunday afternoon found the children in the den playing games and Griffin in the library working on finances. After church and lunch, he had put on pajama bottoms and a comfortable shirt and disappeared behind closed doors.

His normal duties every two weeks included bringing up the ranch spreadsheet and authorizing payment of a dozen bills, including household utilities, feed bills, and vet charges. Then he printed checks to pay his hired help for the past two weeks. He would rather pay them once a month simply because he hated the bookwork, but that was too long to ask a man to go without a paycheck.

At two o'clock, Julie slipped inside and set a glass of iced tea and a plate of cookies beside him. She was almost to the door when she heard him swear. When she turned back around, he'd laced his fingers behind his head and was glaring at the computer screen.

"Damn. Damn. Damn. I *hate* bookwork. I may hire an extra person just to do this," he said.

"What?"

"Write paychecks. Keep track of insurance payments. Run the business end of the ranch. Days like this are when I miss Graham. He loved this part. I hate it."

She went back to his side. "How often do you take care of this?"

"Every two weeks, and that's too damned often."

"Every other day would make the job a lot easier."

"Then you do it every other day and I'll pay you."

"Show me," she said.

He did, and she had another job.

She'd done basically the same job in college working part-time for an auto dealership. Not quite as big as running the books for the ranch, but pretty much the same. Put what came into the ranch in the bank, pay bills, write paychecks, make sure the Social Security payments got sent on time, fill out the forms, and write a check for insurance payments.

"I really, really like you today," he said from the other side of the desk as he watched her work.

The printer spit out the paychecks. Then she went to work on the payments that needed authorization codes. He unlocked a safe behind a desk door and handed her a leather-bound book. "There's everything you need in there. Codes. Safe combination. All of it."

"You are trusting me with this?" She was amazed.

"I trust you with my daughter. She's far more important than this," he said.

"I bet you did miss Dian," she murmured.

He shook his head slowly. "Dian never knew one thing about this office. She would have wiped me out if she'd had access to the checkbook and those codes. She was young, immature, and very self-centered."

"I'm sorry," Julie said.

"Never thought I'd hear those words escape from your mouth," he said through gritted teeth.

"Hey, when I goof, which is seldom, I apologize. Let's get it out and get it over with."

"Just pay the bills and write your own paycheck," he said. He went to stand at the glass wall and stare out into the courtyard.

"How much?"

"You decide. Whatever it's worth," he said.

She eased out of the chair and crossed the room, plowing through the heavy tension and silence all the way. She slipped her arms around his waist and laid her cheek on his back. "Are you over the pain and hurt she inflicted on you, Griff?"

"I am, but I'd never get over you doing the same," he said.

"Why?"

He turned and gathered her into his embrace, hugging her for the longest time before he planted a kiss on her forehead. "Because I've fallen in love with you. I've fallen in like with you. I've just plain fallen for you. I want you in my life. I can't give you my kingdom like Alvie offered because it's tied up on paper, but I would if I could."

She reached up and touched his face. "Griffin Luckadeau, is that a proposal?"

"It is."

"Then my answer is yes. I like you too. I like the comfort we have between us, but I also like the passion. I like looking out the kitchen window and seeing you hop over the fence as you come home for dinner, but I also like sitting beside you in church. I like the way you smell after your shower in the evening, but I also like the way you tuck your hands inside the bib of your overalls. Most of all I like the way I can trust you. I've thought about it for two whole nights—actually can't sleep for thinking about it. I love you. I like you. I want to spend my life with you."

"Are you serious? I figured you'd fight me on this."

"I did, and I don't want half or all of the Lucky Clover. I just want its owner's heart," she said.

"Honey, you've had that for a long time. When?"

"Eli and Mamie deserve their time right now. Maybe after their wedding?"

He moaned.

"We're engaged. We're not just friends. We are two adults, like you said when I told you I was six years older than you. Since we are not just friends anymore, let's go upstairs and celebrate," she said with a twinkle in her eyes.

"Right now? What about the kids?" He grinned.

"Right now. The kids are playing and my room has a lock. We only have to have a one-act play to celebrate. But, honey, on our wedding night, I fully well expect the whole three-act Broadway production," she said.

He swept her up into his arms and carried her up the stairs to her room, where they undressed each other in a flurry of clothing—socks and undergarments landing all over the room. What they shared was wild, passionate, and left them both panting. Julie couldn't imagine what a lifetime of fast, wild sex, slow lovemaking, or anything in between would be like, but it sure looked fascinating from where she was right then—staring at the most handsome cowboy in the world with his naked leg slung over her body.

"Sleep," he moaned.

"Forget it. If we've got time for a nap, we can use it for something a hell of a lot more fun," she said.

And they did.

Chapter 20

A NORTH WIND RATTLED THE BARE TREE LIMBS outside the ranch house, but inside, a glowing blaze in the fireplace kept the place warm as women hustled and bustled in every room. Furniture had been moved out of the living room and chairs set in every available space for guests. Twinkle lights and garland were wrapped around the stair banisters and red roses graced the dining room table and the metal arch in the den.

Mamie and her court had been given a bedroom to get ready in. The Luckadeau ladies were crowded around a vanity helping dress her. Milli set a circlet of fresh white roses around a pile of soft curls on top of Mamie's head. Jane applied makeup and Julie helped fasten her skirt and jacket.

"I know now why they have flowers at weddings," Mamie said nervously.

"Because hundreds of years ago, when folks only took a bath once a year, they did it in the spring, and by June the bride was getting pretty ripe already, so they gave her a bouquet of flowers to take the smell away," Jane said.

"Maybe so, but the reason we still carry them even now when we take baths every day is to have something to hold on to. My hands are shaking worse than the night Eli proposed to me," Mamie said.

"If you are that nervous, we can all be in Cancún by breakfast. I know how to run out on a wedding even at this late date. We can sneak out the back door, get in my truck, and let Ellen drive us to the Dallas airport. Bet we can be there in under an hour with her driving, even if we stop for a bottle of Jack Daniel's at the first liquor store," Jane teased.

Mamie giggled. "It's not nerves that I don't want to get married. It's nerves that I'm not good enough for him or that I'll be a horrible preacher's wife."

"We'll have no more of that kind of talk. You are talking about my friend, and I don't let people talk about her like that. Besides, is this the same woman who encouraged me to move to Saint Jo?" Julie asked.

"I guess it is," Mamie said.

"And that move changed a bunch of lives, didn't it?" Julie asked.

Sally poked her head in the door. "I heard that, Julie. It damn sure changed my life, and I'm grateful to you for it. Is the party in here?"

Julie hugged her. "Well, look what the cats have drug up."

"Speaking of what the cats have drug up, I'm going to be a momma cat. I got pregnant the first week we were married. When are you getting one, Mamie?" Sally asked.

"ASAP," Mamie answered. "Where's Alvie?"

"Down there sitting with the men. Eli is so nervous he's chewing his lip," Sally said.

"Then he's more nervous than you are, Mamie, so stop fretting," Julie said.

Jane patted Mamie on the shoulder. "You'll forget all about that nervous stuff the first time you have a big old fight, anyway. Congratulations, Sally. I guess by the way Julie didn't squeal that she already knew about the baby."

"She did. I saw you the night of the sale, but I was so thunderstruck by Alvie I'm not sure I remember names. Tell me if I'm wrong. Jane, who looks like Ashley Judd with that brown hair. Milli who looks like Jennifer Lopez, only with a darker tan and a hell of a lot prettier."

"She's a charmer," Jane said.

"Is the hen party in here?" Melinda cracked the door.

"It is. We weren't expecting you," Julie said.

"It was a spur-of-the-moment thing according to Momma. She said Mamie was getting married, and she was bored, so she made Daddy and Matt bring us down here. We've got rooms at a hotel in Dallas when it's over," Melinda said with a wink at Julie.

"So tell us, Sally. Is the honeymoon still going strong even though you're pregnant?" Julie asked.

"Had a rocky day about two weeks ago, but it's back on course. Here, let me fasten your skirt. I've got a feeling there could be a baby bump under this skirt before long. I picked hay out of her hair after the sale," Sally said.

"Hey, hey, tell us more," Jane said.

"This is Mamie's day, so hush," Julie said.

"Okay, it's my day and I'm nervous as hell, so I want a story. Tell me about the speed bump in the honeymoon that was going to last forever," Mamie urged.

"You sure? I don't want to intrude," Sally said.

"I'm very sure. The ceremony starts in fifteen minutes, and I'm about to hyperventilate. Tell me something to get my mind off walking down the stairs without falling and saying my vows without crying," Mamie said.

Sally smiled. "Lord, I'm glad I went to the courthouse and didn't have time to think about anything other than buying a rose to throw at my sister."

"Which is bullshit anyway because Mamie is getting married before me, so I wasn't the next bride," Julie argued.

"Stop arguing with her, or I won't hear about the first fight," Mamie said.

Sally sat down on the end of the bed. "Okay, here it is. I came home from the grocery store to find a tall blonde in a black teddy laid up on my bed with rose petals strewn all around her, two glasses of wine already poured on the bedside table, and a gleam in her eye."

"Damn. What did you do?" Jane asked.

Sally smiled and her eyes widened.

"You didn't…" Julie started.

Sally nodded. "I did. Grabbed her by the arm with one hand and twisted it up between her shoulder blades. Damn thing wouldn't pop off like a Barbie doll when I played karate, but I got to admit, I tried real hard to make it. Then I got a fistful of hair and hauled her to the front door, where I threw her flat on her ass in a foot of snow. She didn't stay there very long. Jumped up like a windup toy and tried to run to her truck without touching the snow in her bare feet."

"And?" Julie asked.

"Alvie came home and had the audacity to laugh when I marched him to the bedroom and asked for an explanation."

Julie raised an eyebrow. "I suppose he landed in the snow too?"

"No, but he talked real fast and he didn't stutter. She's a lady who used to come around every so often. They had this agreement. On a certain day of the month, she'd make him very happy. She had no idea he had gotten married. He had no idea she didn't know. He promised she'd know in the length of time it took him to make a phone call. He put it on speakerphone so I'd know for damn sure. The next day, the furniture store in Jackson Hole brought out a brand-spanking-new bedroom suite, because Alvie was sleeping on the couch and I was sleeping in a spare room until he got rid of that damned mattress. The audacity of him, expecting me to sleep on a mattress where he'd had another woman."

"Don't make me laugh anymore. I'm going to bust the stays in this damn long-line bra," Mamie said.

"Not to mention our makeup." Jane dabbed her eyes with a tissue.

"You want to fly in once a month for our poker night?" Milli asked.

"Sounds like fun. Maybe once every three months? But this is about Mamie. It's her day. God, I'm so glad you see something in my dorky brother that appeals to you. He's been a damned old zombie for ten years. It's good to see him biting his lip and in love," Sally said.

A light knock turned their attention to the door. Julie opened it to find Lizzy and Annie in their pretty red velvet Christmas dresses.

"Can we come inside, Momma? Just for a minute so we can give Aunt Mamie a hug before the wedding?" Annie asked.

Julie nodded. "Come right in."

Mamie squatted as far as possible and opened her arms. "You two are beautiful. You need to wear red every day. It's gorgeous on you."

"But, Aunt Mamie, you are the pretty one. Momma, can you find us a Barbie outfit like this?" Annie fingered the brocade on Mamie's suit.

"That's a tall order. For now, go on downstairs and sit

with Grandma Deborah or Grandma Laura. Whichever one has room beside her. I hear the music. It's nearly time to get this show on the road."

Sally, Milli, and Jane all followed the girls down to the den and found their husbands. Julie picked up her bouquet and handed Mamie hers. The room that had seemed so small a few minutes before was suddenly huge and silent.

"Thank you," Mamie said.

"For what?"

"For not fighting God or fate or whatever brought you here. You've brought more happiness into more lives than you'll ever know," Mamie said.

"Hush, you'll make me cry."

"When are you and Griffin going to do this?"

"We don't want to steal you and Eli's thunder. And I was supposed to ask you before now, but everyone was in here and we wanted it to be a little bit of a surprise. And besides, I didn't want to put you on the spot, so you can say no and it won't hurt my feelings. Since the families are all here, would you mind terribly if we made this one a double?"

Mamie squealed and reached out to hug Julie. "It would be the most perfect thing in the world. Did you already get your license and everything?"

"We got it last weekend. If you want to have the day all to yourself, Daddy will marry us tomorrow morning before my parents go back to Jefferson."

"Hell no! Let's do it up right," Mamie said.

"Thank you so much. Okay, that's my cue. I'm on my way. Pray real hard I don't fall on my face down the stairs."

Mamie blew her a kiss. "You do the same."

Griffin stood beside Eli in front of the arch, and the minute he saw Julie, there was no one else in the room. She was beautiful in jeans and T-shirts, gorgeous in red satin, but in the dark-green dress, she was breathtaking. He'd never thought the day he'd gone searching for Lizzy that he'd fall in love with the red-haired banshee with dirty feet who came around the end of the house. But he had, and she'd promised to marry him. His hair really was a lucky streak.

Mamie followed, and Eli stepped up to the bottom of the stairs to lead her to the arch. Once her hand touched his, he stopped biting at his lower lip.

"Dearly beloved, we are gathered here this day." Luke Donavan began the ceremony.

Julie scarcely heard the words. Her heart had set up a banging in her ears that took all thoughts from the vows her brother and Mamie were exchanging. She had a sudden bout of straight-up fear that lasted about three seconds until she looked up into Griffin's blue eyes. Doubts might come, but Griffin looking at her like that would erase anything that threatened their relationship.

"And now I pronounce you man and wife," Luke said. "You may kiss your bride, Eli."

Mamie threw her arms around Eli's neck and didn't wait for him to do the kissing. She rolled up on her toes and planted one on him that said Eli Donavan was hers for all eternity and no one had better ever get in the way.

The kiss ended and Julie handed Mamie her bouquet. Strange, she couldn't even remember Mamie giving it to her, she'd been so busy chasing her fears.

"And now it gives me great pleasure to present for the first time, Mr. and Mrs. Eli Donavan," Luke said.

Everyone clapped as Mamie and Eli wound their way through the people toward the back of the room where the wedding cakes waited on a table draped in white satin.

Luke looked at Julie.

She nodded, reached out for Griffin's hand, and whispered, "Mamie said it would be fine. You absolutely sure?"

"Never more sure about anything in my whole life," he said.

Luke cleared his throat. "Before you all jump up and run, I have an announcement. Since the room is decorated and both the families are already here, Julie and Griffin have expressed a desire to make this a double wedding. So if everyone will sit still for another few minutes, we'll just have their wedding right now."

In the buzz that filled the room, Mamie and Eli turned around and walked right back up the aisle. "We want to be the witnesses," Mamie said.

"I think that's fair enough," Luke said.

Griffin took Julie's hands in his and the room went quiet. "On the night I proposed, you only asked me for one thing, and that was my heart. I give it to you tonight along with my name and my love."

Julie swallowed the lump threatening to send tears down her face. "I never believed in fate or luck, but I've got to admit, something brought me to Montague County, and I'm glad for it. You and our daughters aren't the only ones who have lucky streaks, Griffin Luckadeau. I have one too, and it brought me straight to you. I give you my heart and my love."

"And now, dearly beloved, we are still gathered

here in the presence of God, family, and friends to join Griffin Luckadeau and Julie Donavan in holy matrimony," Luke said.

When the ceremony ended, Luke said, "And now you may kiss your bride."

Griffin picked her up and kissed her passionately. "I love you," he whispered when the kiss ended.

"And I love you," she whispered back.

"Does that mean we are sisters?" Annie asked Lizzy.

"I think it does," Lizzy whispered.

"Well, hot damn," Annie said.

Sally and Alvie snickered.

"I give you Mr. and Mrs. Griffin Luckadeau for the first time. And, Griffin, you've got your work cut out for you," Luke teased.

"Don't I know it." Griffin grinned.

Hands were held out as Julie made her way to the back of the room. She reached into the bouquet she'd carried for Mamie's wedding and brought out folded bills. She put a twenty and a five in Nellie's hand, and the same amount in Ellen's, Milli's, and Jane's. Alvera got fifty. Mamie held out her hand at the wedding cake table and Julie put a twenty-dollar bill in it.

"What's that all about?" Griffin asked.

"I always pay my bets, and it's the best money I ever spent," Julie answered.

When everyone had gone home after the reception, Griffin pulled Julie down to sit on his lap in one of the folding guest chairs. "I really do love you, Mrs. Luckadeau."

"I can't believe I'm really one of those obnoxious Luckadeau women." She kissed the end of his nose.

"What's a noxous Luckadeau?" Lizzy asked.

"It's what you'll grow up to be," Julie told her.

"Come here, all three of you," Griffin said.

Annie and Chuck came from the den where they'd been playing with wedding decorations and joined Lizzy, the three of them in a line with Chuck in the middle.

"Do you understand what happened here tonight? Julie and I got married," Griffin said.

"Does that mean Griffin is my daddy like he is Julie's and I can call him Daddy?" Annie asked.

"Yes, it does. I have adopted you, Annie. From now on, even at school, you will be Annie Luckadeau."

"I'm 'dopted! That means you really are my daddy, don't it?" Annie said.

"It does but—" Griffin started to tell her that she didn't have to call him that until she wanted to do so, but that on paper she was now his daughter as much as Lizzy was.

"Yippeee. I've got a daddy," Annie said with a wiggle of her head. "Lizzy, your daddy is my daddy and I get to call him that all the time. Ain't that right, Daddy?"

Lizzy's eyes filled with tears. "But now Annie has got both and I want a momma like Julie 'cause I want to grow up to be just like her."

"I'll be your momma." Julie smiled.

The girls high-fived.

Chuck walked to the door, and his chin began to quiver.

"We have something else to share with you kids tonight. Chuck, can you come here and sit on my other knee?" Griffin asked.

Chuck did but he didn't look up.

"Are you happy living here with me and the girls?" Griffin asked.

Chuck nodded.

"I'm glad to hear that. A man needs a boy around to help him when there's so many women in the house. You reckon you'd be happy living here the rest of your life?"

Chuck nodded again.

"I know you miss your real momma and daddy a lot sometimes, but they are going to be away until you are almost a grown man. They have agreed to let me adopt you and the papers are being fixed up for that. Would you mind changing your last name and being a Luckadeau?"

Chuck looked up with love and amazement in his eyes. "I'm like Annie and Lizzy now—I'm a real Luckadeau?"

"You are a real Luckadeau if you want to be. If you want to still be a Chester, I can leave it like that on the papers," Griffin said.

The girls waited with big smiles on their faces until he put up both hands. They high-fived him and Chuck threw himself into Griffin's arms.

"I want to be a Luckadeau like Annie and Lizzy. Does that mean I can call you Daddy, too?"

"It does, Son," Griffin said.

He looked at Julie. "And can I call you Momma like Annie does?"

She nodded.

"Today is the best day of my life," he said.

Giggles could be heard all the way into the den.

"Let's get those rug rats to bed and go make another one," Griffin asked.

"Which room is going to be ours?" she asked.

"I was thinking maybe we'd move over to the first

one on the left when you go up the steps. It was my parents' room and my grandparents' before them. I think that would be fitting."

"I like that." Julie snuggled down into his arms. "I like you, Griffin."

"I'm very glad. I was afraid the jury might stay out a lot longer."

"It's in. I'm guilty."

He toyed with her hair. "Then I sentence you to a lifetime of carrying my name and being my wife."

"I'll serve my time, but that doesn't mean I'll be one of those little walk-behind-you-three-steps-and-agree-with-everything-you-say women," she said.

"Any day you do that, I'll start getting my affairs in order."

"Why?"

He gathered her tightly into his arms and hugged her. "Because if you act like that, it'll be because you are about dead. I can't live without you. So I'll get my affairs in order and get ready to die of a broken heart."

"That is the sweetest thing you've ever said." She wiped at a tear.

"Well, I'll be hanged. If I'd known you just needed some sweet-talkin', I could've gotten you to the altar months ago," he teased.

"And maybe I'll even get a little dark-haired son with a lucky streak out of the deal."

"Honey, you might get a dark-haired daughter but any sons will have blond hair."

"Then I'll wait until Lizzy and Annie grow up and get dark-haired grandsons. Or maybe there's a dark-haired gene hiding somewhere in Chuck."

He swept her up into his arms and carried her up the stairs to the bedroom. He laid her gently on the bed and kissed her until she forgot that they had three kids to put to bed.

"I love you, Julie Luckadeau. The day you walked into my life was my lucky day," he said.

"I think everyone in this house got lucky the day I moved to Saint Jo. Let's get those kids to bed and I'll show you just how lucky you are," she whispered.

THE END

Keep reading for a sneak peek of the first book in the Holiday, Texas series by Dylann Crush!

All-American Cowboy

Chapter 1

No three-hundred-pound piece of prime pork was going to get the best of her. Charlie Walker adjusted the tilt of her cowboy hat against the glare of the Texas sun and leaned down, putting herself eye to eye with the enormous pig. "Someone's not feeling very photogenic today, huh?"

Baby Back grunted in response and made a break for the right. Charlie dove after her, trying to grab the pig's blinged-out collar. She missed by a country mile and went down, sending a cloud of dust flying as her hip hit the gravel with a crunch.

"Ouch!" Charlie scrambled to her feet with a scowl. If that's the way the hellacious hog wanted to handle things, then so be it. She could play dirty too.

Charlie brushed the dirt off her jeans and sighed. On second thought, no. She was going to play this smart. Her mama always said the best way to get someone to cooperate was to kill them with kindness. Forcing something close to a smile, Charlie took the giant marshmallow she'd been saving as a special treat out of her back pocket. Baby Back obviously wasn't going to earn the reward with good behavior. May as well use it as a bribe. "*Sooey!* Here, piggy, piggy."

Baby Back's ears perked.

"You want an ooey, gooey marshmallow?" Charlie tore off a tiny bit and tossed it in Baby Back's direction.

The pig snuffled it out of the dirt, squealing in appreciation.

"Come on, piggy. Want some more?" Charlie lobbed another chunk, waiting until Baby Back was snout-deep in her search before taking a tentative step toward her. If she could just grab the collar… She leaned in, her fingers almost grasping the hot-pink band of leather.

Baby Back rushed her, snagging the marshmallow out of her hand, knocking her flat on her rear end, and dashing toward the damaged stretch of fence before Charlie could so much as blink. With a thud and a crack, the rail split. Baby Back bolted through the break in the fence and disappeared.

Again.

Add another exclamation point to the day from hell.

"Almost had her that time," Darby, Charlie's best friend since birth, called from her safe perch. "I swear, if you'd just lunged a little bit farther..." She raised a bottle of Coke in Charlie's direction and took a swig.

Charlie took her time getting to her feet. "*Almost* doesn't count—"

"Except in horseshoes and hand grenades, right?" Darby served up a wink alongside the smart-ass comment.

"Yeah. That's what Sully used to say, anyway." Sully: her boss, mentor, and the last living Holiday in Holiday, Texas. Well, the last living Holiday until he'd passed away, leaving her struggling to keep everything together.

Darby's amusement faded, her eyes crinkling with concern. "How you holdin' up, sweetie?"

"Okay, I guess. I just wish I knew what was going to happen to the Rambling Rose."

Sully's lawyer had surprised everyone by keeping

his mouth shut for a change. The only tidbit of gossip anyone had been able to extract from Buddy Hill, Esquire, was that he'd been trying to contact Sully's grandson—some hoity-toity real estate tycoon from New York City—about the will. The Rambling Rose was the oldest honky-tonk in Texas and had been in the Holiday family for more than 125 years. Charlie couldn't imagine working anywhere else.

Hopefully she wouldn't have to.

"I know Buddy's trying to figure that out," Darby said. "Hard to believe this will be the first time in history we don't have a Holiday on the Rose's float for the Founder's Day Parade."

A deep ache pulsed in Charlie's chest. She rubbed the spot over her heart with her palm. Sully had always loved being the grand master of the annual parade. But she couldn't think about that now—she had bigger issues. Like the fact that her maintenance man had walked out on her this morning, her bartender had forgotten to put in an order for the favorite local brew, and she hadn't crossed off a single item on her to-do list for the biggest concert of the year.

Or—she huffed out a sigh—the fact that a tour bus full of senior citizens had pulled up not ten minutes ago, wanting some of The Rambling Rose's famous ribs and a picture with the most celebrated pig in Conroe County.

One problem at a time.

"Damn pig. I'd better get the truck and chase her down. Last time she got out, she plowed through Mrs. Martinez's garden and ate all of her green peppers." Charlie secured the gate behind her—not that it would do much good unless she found someone to fix the fence rail. "I'm still getting blamed for her salsa coming in second place at the county fair."

"Remind me why y'all insist on having a pet pig as a mascot?" Darby climbed off the rail of the broken pigpen and fell into step with Charlie.

"Tradition. You know Sully. The Rambling Rose has had a pig on staff ever since it opened. They sure as heck aren't going to lose one on my watch." Not even if her watch might be coming to an abrupt end. She ducked through the back door of the honky-tonk and grabbed her keys off a hook. "You coming?"

Darby shook her head, sending her dark curls bouncing. "I'll leave the pig wrangling to you. I gotta get home and get dinner going. Waylon will skin me alive if he finds out I spent all afternoon hanging out with his baby sister."

"Now I know that's a lie." Charlie yanked open the door of the late model dually pickup. "He's got you on such a high pedestal, I'm surprised you don't get a nosebleed from the lack of oxygen."

"He does love me, doesn't he?" Darby slung her arm around Charlie's neck and pulled her in for a hug. "We'll try to stop by later if your mama's up for watching the kids."

Darby and Waylon had been married for nine years, but it could still get weird, thinking about her BFF swapping spit with her brother. So she tried not to think about it at all. As in, ever. "Has she ever not been up for watching them?"

"True. Okay then, save us some seats up front tonight, okay? That band is supposed to be real good." With a squeeze and a quick kiss on the cheek, Darby stepped away. "And don't worry about Sully's grandson. He'll probably fly down, take a look at the place, tell you what a great job you're doing, and be on a plane back to New York City before you even have a chance to pour him a draft of Lone Star."

Charlie snorted. "Oh yeah? With my luck he'll realize he's always wanted to manage the oldest honky-tonk in Texas, and he'll toss me out on my backside."

"He might just like your backside." Darby waggled her perfectly plucked eyebrows.

"My backside isn't up for review. Besides, if he ever does have the nerve to show up around here, he'll be the one getting tossed on his ass. Would it have killed him to pick up the phone and give Sully a call sometime? Maybe even come down for a visit?"

"Honey, I know you loved Sully like family. But not everyone loves as fierce as you. Give the guy a chance."

A chance? In the eight years she'd worked for Sully, there'd been no word from either his son or his grandson. It had broken her heart to watch the cancer eat away at him, knowing she was just about the only family he had left.

But Darby was right about one thing—she did love fierce. Fierce enough to know that the most important thing to Sully was keeping The Rambling Rose in the family. So even if it killed her, she'd do whatever she could to ensure his dying wish came true. She'd try to give his grandson a chance, assuming he had the decency to show up sometime in the near future.

"Hey, will you let Angelo know I'm hog hunting? Maybe he can stall lunch so I have a chance to bring back the prodigal pig to pose for pictures."

"You bet. Good luck."

With a final nod to Darby, she climbed onto the bench seat and cranked over the engine, refocusing on her task. How many times had Baby Back broken out over the last month? Two? Three? She'd have to find someone to patch up the pen again. She'd lost count of how many mascots they'd had over the years, but none of them had ever been as ornery as Baby Back. That pig had a devilish streak as long and wide as the Rio Grande.

She shifted the truck into Drive and wondered if anyone would believe her if she said the pig got taken out by a combine. Sully was the only one beyond the tourists who gave a hot damn about the pig. She gripped the steering wheel tight, fighting back a fresh surge of emotion.

For Sully.

Then she put the pedal to the metal and fishtailed out onto the main two-lane road that would take her through the center of Holiday in pursuit of the runaway porker.

Beckett Sullivan Holiday III scrolled through the slides of his presentation one final time. He'd been working his butt off for the past four months. This would be the project his father would finally trust him to handle on his own from concept to completion.

He'd done the legwork. He'd done the research. He'd done the whole damn thing short of signing the papers. There was no reason he shouldn't be allowed to take the lead. No reason except his dad's uncompromising need to maintain a viselike grip on all things under the Holiday Enterprises umbrella. Which, fortunately or unfortunately, depending on how he looked at it, also included Beck.

The way Beck saw it, the project up in Morris Park should be a slam dunk. Holiday Enterprises would garner some positive press for a change, and he'd be able to come through on a long overdue promise to an old friend. He was ready.

His phone beeped and he silenced the alarm. Showtime.

He tucked his laptop under one arm and headed toward the conference room. No matter how much time he spent in the room his dad considered his pride and joy, the view managed to steal his breath every time he entered. Two walls of glass provided a 180-degree view. Situated in a corner of the fifty-fifth floor, standing up against the windows always made him feel like he was floating above midtown Manhattan.

"Ready, Son?" The elder Holiday stood at the head of the table.

Beck nodded and took the seat next to him as the rest of the management team filtered in. As head of one of the most successful real estate development firms in Manhattan, his father—or just Holiday as he preferred to be called, even by his son—usually had his pick of opportunities. It was up to his team to come up with the ideas, do the grunt work, and make recommendations at their weekly management meetings.

This time Beck would get the go-ahead. He could feel it. It would finally be his turn to take the lead on a project that would mean something.

Beck sat through the six presentations ahead of his. He listened, took notes, and tried to swallow the lump of apprehension that had taken up residence in his throat. He'd been through the drill hundreds of times over the years. But he'd never pitched a project like this before.

He wiped a clammy palm over his suit pants. No need to be nervous. He'd worked with these people his entire career. Besides, how could his dad refuse the chance to spread some goodwill when the neighborhood—and their company—so obviously needed it?

Holiday shot down the executive golf course one of his minions had spent the past nine months putting together, then turned an appraising eye on his son. Beck swallowed and stood. His turn.

"Most of you know about the affordable housing apartments we're building in the Bronx. What you probably don't know is that by building on those Morris Park lots, we're displacing the kids who have been using that property as a safe place to play." Beck scanned the faces of his coworkers. No one offered a smile of encouragement. No one gave him a sly thumbs-up. No one knew what to make of this departure from the *money makes more money* mentality. But they'd catch on.

He continued, playing to their heartstrings. "There's another lot two blocks over with a condemned apartment building sitting on it. The city is willing to sell it way below market value. I'm going to show you why it makes sense for Holiday Enterprises to use that space to build its first community park."

By the time he wrapped up with a detailed analysis of the tangible and intangible benefits of the park, the smile on his dad's face pretty much guaranteed approval.

But then Holiday steepled his fingers under his chin and shook his head.

"So you want me to buy a crumbling building and knock it down so a handful of kids have a safe place to hang out and sell drugs."

Beck almost didn't know what to say to that. "No, sir. I want us to buy a property for pennies on the dollar and create goodwill by donating it back to the community as a place where the residents can gather." Beck pointed to the screen where the last slide still appeared. "Imagine the ribbon cutting. The press would go nuts. This kind of project is unprecedented."

"It's unprecedented because it's a dumb-ass idea. I appreciate all the work you put into this, Beck. But I've decided to have you manage the details on the boutique hotel in the Village instead."

Beck's heart went into free fall. "The Village?" He cleared his throat, trying to prevent his voice from cracking. "But the P&L shows we won't break even on that project for at least ten years."

"What can I say?" Holiday shrugged. "I like the Village."

"But you're wrong. We need the good publicity, and Bronx needs—" Shit. He'd violated Rule Number One: never criticize the boss. Especially in front of the entire management team.

"Sorry, Son. It's a pass. Try again next time." The smile spread over his father's lips but didn't reach his eyes. Beck felt like he was looking into the face of a great white shark. Predatory. Cunning. Lethal.

He'd already shot himself in the foot. May as well bury himself while he was at it. But somehow, before he could finish the job and tell his dad exactly what he thought of his new plan, the intercom buzzed.

"What is it, Joyce?" Holiday asked.

"Sir, I'm sorry to interrupt. You have an urgent call on line two."

"We're in a meeting." His tone was clipped, flat, unemotional.

Joyce's voice faltered. "I know, sir. But it's, well, it's your father."

Holiday's chest puffed up and he leaned over the speakerphone. "You tell that sonofabitch that I don't care what kind of emergency he has down there. He needs something from me, he can go through my lawyer."

An awkward silence fell over everyone present. Eyes sought out interesting patterns in the marble floor, fingers toyed with expensive fountain pens, and legs shifted under the table.

"Um, sir. He's not actually on the phone. It seems he's passed. His attorney would like to speak to you."

His dad hissed out a breath and an unreadable flicker of emotion flashed across his face, so fast that Beck thought maybe he'd just imagined it. He'd never seen his dad react that way to anything and wasn't sure how to respond. Holiday had made it clear on numerous occasions that the family he'd left behind in Texas was not up for discussion.

"Sir?" the voice came through the speaker.

"Dad?" he murmured. "You okay?" Beck put his hand on his father's shoulder.

With a quick shake of the head, he swatted Beck's hand away and regained his bearings. "Meeting's over. Can I have a few minutes?" The team stood and filed out of the conference room. "Beck, stay."

Once the room cleared, his dad shifted the speaker to the end of the table. "Go ahead and patch him through."

The phone line clicked. Beck cleared his throat while he studied his old man. How would he feel if his father died? A fleeting twinge passed through his gut. They saw each other every day. They worked together, wined and dined connections as a team, and both appreciated a day spent out on the golf course.

But they'd never been close. Emotional distance ran deep in his family, at least based on how Holiday seemed to be handling the news of his own father's death.

"Beckett Holiday here. Who am I speaking to?"

"Hi there, Mr. Holiday. This is Buddy Hill calling from Holiday, Texas. Your father, well, he passed. I'm so sorry for your loss."

Based on his father's reaction, they could have been discussing the weather. No flicker of pain, no momentary hint of grief, no sign of emotion crossed his face.

"What can I do for you, Mr. Hill?"

"He asked me to, well…upon his death, he wanted me to contact you. We need to know what kind of arrangements y'all would like to make. And then there's the matter of the will."

Holiday reached for a pile of papers and tapped them into a uniform stack. "I trust you to make any necessary arrangements."

"Certainly, sir."

"And you can send a copy of the will to my attorney. I'll have Joyce get the contact information for you. Now if that's all—"

"Wait." Mr. Hill must have sensed the conversation was coming to an abrupt end. "About the will. One of the stipulations is that it must be read in person."

"Figures that old bastard would find a way to pull me back there one way or another. Couldn't do it while he was alive, so—"

"It's not for you, sir. Your son, Beckett Sullivan Holiday the Third, is the only beneficiary named in the will. We'll need to know how to reach him."

Beck shifted in his seat as his dad's blank gaze settled on him. He'd never met his grandfather. Never even held a conversation with the old man. What could he possibly have left him in Texas?

"Sir?" Mr. Hill's voice floated through the phone.

"Beck's right here, Mr. Hill. Just give us a moment." His dad pressed the mute button, then pushed back from the table and stood. "Good timing, Son. Since you won't be wasting your efforts on that park anymore, you'll have time to scoot on down south and find out what kind of games the old geezer left for you before you get started on that new hotel."

Beck grappled for a response. He didn't have time to take off for Texas. Not with everything else going on. But the lawyer with the Southern twang had piqued his curiosity. Why would his grandfather, a virtual stranger, name him in his will? There was only one way to find out.

He unmuted the phone. "Hi, Mr. Hill. What can I do for you?"

"Beckett Sullivan Holiday the Third?"

"Yes, sir. But please, call me Beck. How long do you need me down there?" he asked.

"Well, ideally a few days. At least on this initial trip."

"What do you mean initial trip?" Visiting his dad's hometown might be fun for a day or two. Maybe he'd get a chance to learn about the mysterious family Holiday had left behind. But more than one trip? He didn't like the sound of that.

"I can explain everything when I see you in person. How soon can you be here?"

Beck swiped through the calendar on his phone. His schedule was jam-packed for the next week and a half. But it would be best if he got down there and took care of things as quickly as possible. He didn't have much time if he wanted to secure that lot in Morris Park.

He wanted to ask about his grandfather—how did he die, did he suffer at all, was he alone at the end—but a quick glance at his dad's frigid profile made him bite down before he uttered a word.

"Are you there, Beck?" Mr. Hill asked.

"Yes. The earliest I can make it would be next week. I can fly down on Friday morning and spend the weekend."

"Per your grandfather's instructions, we'll have to have the service before that."

Beck glanced up as the door clicked shut behind his dad. "That's fine. I understand."

"I'll have my secretary contact you with the details."

Beck gave the man his cell number and ended the call. He stepped to the window to study the controlled chaos of the city streets far below. What would he find in Texas? His father rarely mentioned the small town where he'd been born and raised. Beck knew his grandmother had died before he was born and that his grandfather once owned some tiny little hole-in-the-wall bar. But he'd never heard from the man, and his dad had always been a stone-cold wall of silence on the subject.

His gut twinged with a pang of regret. He should have pushed harder. Now he'd never have the chance to learn more about his roots. Maybe there would be someone in Holiday he could ask about his family. There had to be records, photos, something left over from his dad's younger days.

He glanced at the larger-than-life picture of his dad decorating the conference room wall. Holiday had come a long way from that tiny town in Texas. If he'd wanted Beck to know about his childhood, he would have shared. His dad was right. The old man probably left him a hound dog or a pickup truck. Beck would get in and out of there as fast as possible. It would be a pain to rearrange his schedule to make the trip, but he'd be back before the Manhattan society page even knew he'd been gone.

He blew out a breath, then turned his attention back to his laptop to pore over the details of his rejected proposal. He was many things, but not a quitter. There must be an angle he hadn't explored.

With the sun beginning its descent over the Manhattan skyline, he settled in for another long night of work, his mind already back on business, his thoughts thousands of miles away from whatever waited for him in the Lone Star State.

About the Author

Carolyn Brown is a *New York Times*, *USA Today*, *Wall Street Journal*, and *Publishers Weekly* bestselling author who has published more than ninety books. She credits her eclectic family for her humor and writing ideas. She was born in Texas but grew up in southern Oklahoma, where she and her husband, Charles, a retired English teacher, make their home. They have three grown children and enough grandchildren to keep them young.

TEXAS RODEO

A groundbreaking contemporary Western romance series with real-life Texas rodeo action

By bestselling author Kari Lynn Dell

Reckless in Texas

Bullfighter Joe Cassidy is a hotshot in the ring…but falling in love with fierce single mom Violet Jacobs? That's a whole new rodeo.

Tangled in Texas

Injured bronc rider Delon Sanchez thinks things can't get worse…until he learns his physical therapist is his oh-so-perfect ex, Tori Patterson.

Tougher in Texas

When rodeo producer Cole Jacobs loses one of his cowboys and his cousin sends along a replacement, he expects a Texas good ol' boy. He gets longtime rival Shawnee Pickett.

Fearless in Texas

Rodeo bullfighter Wyatt Darrington can never let Melanie Brookman know the truth: that he's been crazy in love with her for years.

Mistletoe in Texas

Hank Brookman is ready to return home for the holidays and make amends. Most of all, he hopes Grace McKenna will give him a second chance at love so they can celebrate Christmas—Texas Rodeo style.

"A fun, wild ride!
You need to pick up a Kari Lynn Dell."

—B.J. Daniels, *New York Times* bestselling author

For more Kari Lynn Dell, visit:

sourcebooks.com

Also by Carolyn Brown

LUCKY COWBOYS
Lucky in Love
One Lucky Cowboy
Getting Lucky
Talk Cowboy to Me

HONKY TONK
I Love This Bar
Hell, Yeah
My Give a Damn's Busted
Honky Tonk Christmas

SPIKES & SPURS
Love Drunk Cowboy
Red's Hot Cowboy
Darn Good Cowboy Christmas
One Hot Cowboy Wedding
Mistletoe Cowboy
Just a Cowboy and His Baby
Cowboy Seeks Bride

COWBOYS & BRIDES
Billion Dollar Cowboy
The Cowboy's Christmas Baby
The Cowboy's Mail Order Bride
How to Marry a Cowboy

BURNT BOOT, TEXAS
Cowboy Boots for Christmas
The Trouble with Texas Cowboys
One Texas Cowboy Too Many
A Cowboy Christmas Miracle

What Happens in Texas

A Heap of Texas Trouble